Give Me Again All T"   ıere

Also by Rosemary Sturge

Death of a Daughter of Venice

A Storm in Summer

Black Nazareth

Give Me Again All That Was There

Rosemary Sturge

Copyright ©2019 Rosemary Sturge
Rosemary Sturge has asserted her right under the Copyright, Designs and Patents Act 1988 to be identified as the author of this work

This book is available as an
e-book and in print from Amazon

If you would like to contact the author please see her website
www.historical-novels.co.uk

Cover photograph
Loch Druidibeag, South Uist, Outer Hebrides
Photograph: Mike McFarlane/ iStock

To all my readers, wherever you are

Historical Note

This is a work of fiction, and by no means to be relied upon as historically accurate. I don't know whether Betty Burke was a real person. Tradition has it that Flora Macdonald disguised Bonnie Prince Charlie as her 'Irish spinning maid' of that name, and dressed him in women's clothing, in order to help him escape to the Isle of Skye from the long Island, the three adjoining Hebridean islands of North and South Uist and Benbecula. I've given myself multiple headaches reading as many contemporary and more recent accounts as I could discover, but they are all somewhat contradictory, (and in some cases strongly disagree with one another!) about who did what, when, and where, but none of them deal specifically with this point. The best case I can make for Betty's existence is that thirty years later, when the 1745 Jacobite rebellion was forgiven if not forgotten, Dr Samuel Johnson and James Boswell visited Flora and her husband at their home on Skye, and she told them exactly the same story she had told those who interrogated her at the time, and since there was no longer any need to pretend Betty existed if she didn't, I've chosen to believe that she did, and this is her story!

The Title

'Give Me Again, All That Was There', is a line from a poem entitled *'Sing Me A Song Of A Lad That Is Gone'* by Robert Louis Stevenson (1850-1894). He wrote it as an alternative wording for the Skye Boat Song. Unlike the folk songs in the story, it isn't, of course, contemporaneous but I felt it had the right wistful tone for Betty's reminiscences.

Characters in the Story

(*denotes a real person)

In Edinburgh:

Elizabeth (Betty) Burke	An Irish 'spinster', out of luck
Flora Macdonald*	A young lady of character
Mistress Effie Dalgliesh	Flora's Aunt
Mistress Afton	A cook with a painful hip
Agnes Morrison	An ill-natured lady's maid
Thomas Gowrie	An unpleasant steward
Wee Jessie	A young maid, overworked
Colonel James Dalgliesh	Of the Regiment of Highland Militia
Sergeant John Begg	A Militiaman, but whose?
Allan Ramsay*	Painter of portraits
Lady Elliott	A Lady of fashion
Miss Ann Elliott	her daughter
Nessa Jordan	A fishwife
Jonty Nichol	A baker's boy

In Uist:

Angus Macdonald*	Flora's brother, gentleman farmer
Penelope*	His betrothed
Bridie Mor	Cook/housekeeper to the family
Lechie	Her man
Archie, and several others	Her bairns
Alasdair Mor	Her father, a fiddler
Elsbet	A tiresome teenaged maid
Màiri	Her sister, with a hare lip
Rhuri Macdonald	A fisherman with his own boat
Dougie	His son
Lord Clanranald*	The Clan Chieftain
Lady 'Clan'*	His wife
Isobel, Marianne, Margaret*	His children
Colin	An elderly postman
Shona	Lady Clan's maid

Ailsa	Her niece, 'just'
Bruce	A Sailor
Peg Macdonald	Grandmother to Elsbet and Màiri
Charles Edward Stuart*	A Prince
Con O'Neill*	
Felix O'Sullivan*	Friends and Supporters
Neil MacEachen*	of Bonnie Prince Charlie

At Dunstaffnage Castle

Mistress MacKie	Housekeeper and gaoler
Duncan	An interrogator
The nameless one	Another interrogator
Davie	A nervous youth

Vienna, 1747

A fine, sunny spring morning, and the bells of St Stephen's ringing out for some service or another. I pause on the step, my broom in my hand, wee Flora wrapped tight in my shawl. To be sure, haven't I maids to sweep for me? But today I've set Clara and Constanza to change the bed linen. 'Tis a fine reputation Burke's Hotel has, here in the heart of Vienna. Diplomats from all the countries in the world are staying here, and English travellers too, wanting the comforts of home, even in these troubled times when it's no an easy task to find all the things they're wanting. We're striving, always, to give them satisfaction. John, my husband, is gone out already to seek for fat capons in the market, and gather on the Empress's behalf what people are saying of the latest conflict in Silesia. Just now, as I paused at my sweeping, a man passed by wheeling a handcart piled high wi' flowers. Ach, the spring blooms! He tipped his feathered hat to me, and I bowed to him over my broom, thinking, *but ye niver saw the machair! Ye niver were in Scotland, in the Hebrides, in the Long Island in spring, when the machair bursts into its carpet of flowers!* In my dreams I oft times find myself walking barefoot on the white sands there, my spindle in my hand and the seabirds wheeling and crying overhead. Sure, 'tis a grand life I have here, and a better one than a poor spinster lassie from Belfast could ever have hoped for, but still I miss the Long Island – oh, give me agin, all that was there!

Chapter 1

Edinburgh 1745

Till A Sad Misfortune Me O'er Came

I stumbled and righted myself, my booted feet sliding on the wet cobblestones, the broken sole of the one catching and tripping me. Barely seeing my way in my panic, I fear I was mumbling aloud, trying to order in my head what I would say, not caring at the other mutterings all around me as I pushed through the press of bodies in the street. Dirty bodies they were in most cases, hanging about by the market stalls in the Grassmarket, hoping for free pickings, stinking o' the drink. A filthy old fella with no teeth in his head made a lunge at me, grabbing at my breasts and making a rent in the bodice of my gown. I flung away from him, and he swore, but made no move to follow me. This was how he spent his days, no doubt, pawing at the bodies of any females as went by.

'Elizabeth Burke's my name, Ma'am,' I'd made up my mind to say. 'I'm a spinster, from Belfast.'

Sure, I could say that here in Edinburgh? Would I need to be explaining?

'As can spin flax for linen, wool, cotton. Wheel or drop spindle. I can nurse the sick, lifting, turning, washing. Sure,' I'd say, ' 'tis no bother to me.'

The letter Mistress Buchanan had given me, I clutched it in my hand like 'twas a tinker's tuft of white heather. I'd no notion what was in it. 'Twas folded and sealed with wax, and I was afraid to break the seal. I can read well enough if I take it slow to spell out the words, but I was afeared 'twas terrible things she'd written of me. I'd broken that blue china bowl. They said 'twas valuable.

All I knew, this damp grey Edinburgh morning, smoke from chimneys making dirty finger marks on the clouds hanging low above the wet rooftops, was that Miss Evangeline was dead, and I'd been turned off. She'd no more need of a stout young Irish woman to lift and turn her in the bed.

'Go to the registry office, girl,' Miss Evangeline's cold-eyed sister, Mistress Augusta Buchanan, had told me, before turning me out the door. 'Here, I've written that you're honest. They'll find you a place soon enough if you're not too choosy.'

She'd twitched her nostrils, the way these Edinburgh ladies do when the night slop buckets are left stinking in the passage way, or they've a rough Irish servant girl about the house as they'd not want to be keeping feeding.

Edinburgh was a foreign place to me, a girl from Belfast. I'd no notion how to find this office they'd told me of. One of the maids whispered behind her hand 'twas just beyond the Grassmarket, on the east side, the door painted green. I shoved, desperate I was now, through the press of rough, reeking, beggar-bodies that hung about that place, seemingly idle as the day was long, and found my way to the green door. Green for the luck of the Irish?

It didn't seem so, not straightway. There was a note pinned on it. My heart sank down to my crack-soled boots.

'Closed, due to a bereavement till Friday next. Och, *there's* a disappointment,' a voice said.

I turned and found a young woman at my elbow. She was short of stature, neatly but not smartly dressed in a cloak of brown broadcloth, with a matched bonnet trimmed with dull grosgrain. Dark curls peeped out from under the brim. Her complexion had a fresh tinge, her cheeks stained with rose, as though she was used to go about in the open air. Might she be a governess, I wondered? Could it be that she too had been turned off?

'Can *I* offer you any assistance?' this young woman then said, her eyes taking in my own shabby cloak. She spoke with an assurance I wouldn't have expected from her humble looks. I supposed she must have seen the fearfulness in my face. Perhaps, despite her old fashioned clothes, she was looking for a maid, and not seeking employment for herself? 'A Minister's daughter, would she be?' as the Edinburgh ladies might say.

'Are you looking for work?' she asked.

'Oh Miss, to be sure!' I said, my hopes rising just a little. 'Would you be knowing anyone that'd take me? My poor mistress died, and I'm out of a place. I'll take rough work, scrub work, *onything*, Mistress... for I've nowhere to go this night!'

To my shame, I burst into noisy, slobbering sobs. I held out my scrap of paper.

'She, my poor mistress's sister, Mistress Buchanan, she said she'd given me a good character,' I managed to blurt out. The rain was beginning.

The little lady in brown glanced up at the sky, and sighed.

'They all told me 'twould be drier here, not so wet as we have it out in the isles. An untruth, like so many they told, and the rain falls dirtier here in Edinburgh. Let us go...'

She paused, lips pursed up, wondering mebbe where we *could* go, me with my boot sole flapping.

'Over there. I mind the church will be open,' she said.

I'd never been inside a Protestant church before. It smelled different to St Brigid's at the end of our street at home, where Ma used to take us childer, away from Da's fists when he'd drink taken. Sure, they wouldn't have the incense here, I knew that. No statues, not even of Our Lady. No, not even the Lord Jesus. Just a plain wooden cross above the altar, and a cream linen cloth. Fine woven, the best quality. Still, 'twas dry in there, out the rain, and nobody came near. The little lady sat in one of the pews and gestured I might sit too. She laid her gloves on the seat between us, and prized open Mistress Buchanan's note. Wrinkled and damp 'twas now, from the rain.

'Your name is Betty Burke, and you're originally from Belfast?'

'That I am, Ma'am.'

She carried on reading the note, her brow creased in a frown.

'Beautiful flowing handwriting she has,' she remarked, 'but not easy to read.'

The reading of this note seemed to take longer than the writing of it had taken Mistress Buchanan. I began to despair again, thinking Miss Evangeline's sister had numbered every one of my faults. I looked around at the Church. A strange bare place 'twas, but I thought, if this young Miss turns agin me, mebbe I could slip back in and sleep the night in one of these pews? 'Twould be better than to roam the streets amongst the beggars till dawn. My Da always *said* he was a Protestant, though I doubted he'd ever attended ony church.

'She writes that you're willing, but a slattern. Now what would *that* be?'

I stared. Why was she asking? Did she not know what a slattern was?

'I don't… Miss, I think she's saying 'tis untidy I am. My clothes…'

I ran my hands down my patched and faded gown (now wi' a rent at the seam).

'I'd niver ony good clothes, do ye see? And 'twas board wages only, so I'd niver enough monies to buy new. I'm that tall and broad at the shoulder. It's not easy to clothe one of my stature.'

Ah, forgive me, it's not a word I've met before. I'm more used to the Gaelic. *Slattern*, that's untidy?'

'It is, Miss.'

She spoke the Gaelic? There was a surprise. She wasn't an Edinburgh lady at all. She'd mentioned the isles. Which isles would those be?

'I see. I cannot say it of a room? This room is slattern-*ly*?'

'I'm thinking not, at least I niver heard it.'

'Clothes. We could find you better ones,' she said. 'I know I've passed a wee shop that sells them. On one of those wynds that leads down from the castle. Not new, but in good order, from what I could make out. You came from Belfast to nurse a sick woman?'

'That I did, Ma'am. Miss Evangeline Boyd. She'd some cruel sickness, and she'd heavy bones and no one could lift her without doing her hurt, saving myself. I was working as a spinster. Flax for the linen. I had to give up my place there when I'd to nurse my mother till she died, but my master there was sorry for it. He was a friend to the Buchanan's and Miss Boyd, and he askt me, would I travel to Edinburgh with Miss Evangeline, and take care of her, since he knew I'd nursed my poor Ma well.

'Mistress Buchanan brought her sister here to Edinburgh to seek a clever doctor,' I added, 'that could mebbe help her, but 'twas no good.'

'And now this sister, this Mistress Augusta Buchanan,' she tapped the paper with her finger, 'turns you out of doors without paying your fare back to Ireland? That's very ungrateful, surely?'

My eyes filled up with tears again, and I could not speak. Poor Miss Evangeline would never have treated me so, *never*. Sure, I didn't especially want to go back to Ireland, now that my mother was gone. I'd no home there but with my brother, and his sharp-tongued wife was not the kind to make me welcome in their cramped quarters above the shop… but I didn't say this to the little lady in brown. I tried to wipe my eyes on my sleeve without she'd notice.

'As it happens,' she said, glancing up from the letter once more, 'I find I'm needing a maid for just a wee while. My name is Flora MacDonald, and I'm biding awhile here in Edinburgh, with a relative. My home is in the West, in Uist, the Long Island. Did you ever hear of it?'

'Never, Miss.'

'The isle of Skye then?'

'Mebbe, Miss.' Truly, I had not, but I didn't want her to know how ignorant I was.

'Is it far?'

Miss Macdonald sighed. 'Too far. If it was close I'd be away home on the morrow. I was persuaded to come here to Edinburgh with my cousins from Kintyre, but then they were prevailed upon to join a party of friends near Dunbar. I don't know these people, and the invitation didn't include me, so I stayed on here with an elderly relative, thinking I'd go about and see all the sights of Edinburgh. But then what do I find?'

She threw up her hands.

'Och, 'tis nae decent for a young lady to walk about the streets here on her own. Tsk, tsk!'

The way she could mimic those Edinburgh ladies was just grand.

'A lady should *always* be accompanied by her maid whenever she steps oot the door! I should have guessed it maybe, for I was here once before, a few years back. I'd a short time here studying at a seminary for young ladies. But then when we went out it was always with one of our instructresses, never on our own.'

She sighed and shrugged her shoulders.

'My aunt – I call her my aunt, but it's more that she's a cousin in my grandmother's generation – is in poor health and cannot spare her own maid, and when I took Jessie, the kitchen lassie, what did the Cook do but threaten Aunt Effie with her notice! It's difficult, do you see? I was thinking, through yon registry office, maybe I'd find someone who only wanted a position for a week or two whilst she waited to take another post? My cousins didn't know when they left how long they'll bide at Dunbar. It could be another week, or more. So maybe I can offer you just a week or so's work? Or it could be, if we suit one another, you'd care to accompany me back to the Isles and teach two of the young lassies of our household to spin?'

'I'd be glad to, Miss,' I said, from the bottom of my heart. Indeed, if she'd said 'just for this day, this night', I'd have gone with her. I hadn't even a penny in my pocket for a place in a lean-to amongst the crazy and the drunk. If she'd invited me to follow her to distant China come the morning, I'd likely have gone.

'Good, then let us step briskly through this rain and find that clothes shop I mentioned,' said Miss Macdonald.

Evidently her sharp eyes had had time to take full account of my shabby appearance.

'I've passed that wee shop many a time and I'm curious to see what they sell! My aunt would suffer a seizure if she thought *I* was wearing a hand-me-down gown,' she said.

Then she softened it by adding, 'although if I were at home and busy about the farm I wouldn't think twice about wearing someone's good cast-off. Indeed I often have done so! It seems to me these Edinburgh folk cast away garments that still have years of wear in them.'

I judged the woman who had the clothes shop was cut from the same cloth as Miss Flora's aunt. She wrinkled her nose at the sight of me.

'I take it this is a charity case, Miss?' she said to Miss Macdonald in a thick whisper, her face turned away as though she supposed I might not hear her. 'Your kindness does you credit, Miss, but beware! Many of these women who declare themselves destitute are nothing but cheats. You'll likely fit her out and off she'll go and sell every stitch on her back for drink before the day's out.'

At these words I'd say we both saw a sharp change in Miss Flora Macdonald. She was a small woman as I've said, soft voiced, a little dumpy, not more than passable in her looks, her nose too long, her brow too prominent for beauty. You could walk by a dozen like her in the streets of ony town without taking a second peek. However, at the shop woman's words her spine stiffened, her nose lifted and her lip curled.

'That is my business not yours!' she snapped. 'I have chosen to "fit her out" as you put it, and I believe my money is as good as anyone's. I want Betty to have three gowns – and mind they're long enough – two work gowns, and a better one for church and walking out. Then she'll need a nightshift, two under-shifts, aprons, a good cloak. Och, and boots. A stout pair, since we may be travelling out to the Isles shortly, and a lighter pair for every day.'

'Very well, Miss,' said the shop woman, her lips tight, 'but dinae say I didnae warn ye.'

Miss Flora did not deign to reply. 'A cloak bag,' she said to me, spying one in the corner of the crowded room and stepping across the piles of boots and shoes scattered across the floor. 'You'll need a bag, Betty. Oh, and this shawl will be just the thing!' She pulled it down from a shelf.

'Green and white plaid, for MacDonald of the Isles. This was woven in the West surely, perhaps even in my Mother's household!'

Did she not live in her mother's household? Yet she was unmarried. Why was that, I wondered? If I managed to stay in her employ for more than a day or two, I'd mebbe find out, but I wasn't for setting my hopes too high. I was in no case to be imagining myself set up. The relatives might return from Dunbar, wherever that was. The aged aunt and her cranky cook might take agin me and order her to turn me off straightway.

Still and all, I thought, as I laced up a pair of boots (which the shop woman insisted were a man's) and cast my broken ones aside, I'm getting a passel of good clothes out of it. They'd be hard put to turn me out naked. Then straightway wasn't I ashamed o' myself? I was thinking just as the shop woman supposed, that if came to it I could sell these things, one by one, not for the drink, but to keep myself from starving in a gutter.

Although Miss Flora Macdonald had complained that Edinburgh rain was dirty (she said the smoke from the coal fires made it so), she seemed untroubled to be walking in it. She'd parted with quite a sum to the clothes woman to make me decent, but although it was some distance to her aunt's house, it seemed she'd no thought of taking a carriage. On and on we tramped through the drizzling wet, down the tail of the Royal Mile (though I did not then know its name) until we reached a neighbourhood of tall houses she told me was called Canongate.

'Those grand gates you can glimpse below, at the bottom of the street,' she said, 'lead to the old Palace of Holyrood, where the Kings of Scotland used to bide.'

'Perhaps they will agin, Miss,' I said.

'I don't know about that,' said Miss Flora Macdonald, 'there's talk enough out amongst the islanders that the French King will send young Charles Stuart over any day now, with an army at his back to challenge King George in London, but 'tis probably just talk. My brother thinks King Louis will never do it.'

She stood still despite the rain, and turned to face me, her eyes, brown with a touch of blue-grey like the morning light through the hazel woods, fixed on mine, verra serious.

'Best you never speak of any of *that* in my Aunt Effie's house, Betty. Talk of wars and such things frighten her into spasms, and besides you never know who might be listening. Some people here fear the Jacobites, others think they have a just cause. Opinions are divided in this town, *very* divided, I'm finding.'

No need to warn me, I already knew of these opinions. Once, when Miss Evangeline still had the strength to rise, and had me help her down to spend the afternoon on the sofa in the drawing room at Ballymore, as the Boyd's big house in Antrim was named, she'd spoken of this Charles Stuart.

'They say he's very good looking, Bonnie Prince Charlie,' she'd sighed. It seemed she was reading about him in some magazine she had. 'Nobody could say that of *any* of the house of Hanover!'

'Don't be silly, Evangeline!' snapped her sister. 'He'll turn out a wastrel and a drinker like his father and grandfather before him. *And* a Catholic!' Mistress Buchanan shuddered at the thought.

'Oh, but who can resist a handsome prince?' yearned Miss Evangeline.

'Nonsense! Handsome is as handsome does! And what did his father ever achieve but fighting and destruction? Disruption to trade? Henry told me his family lost a fortune in the Fifteen when Leith was blockaded.'

I'd learned from the other servant's talk, that Mistress Buchanan's late husband had been an Edinburgh wine merchant in a good way of business (although she liked to give the impression that no one in her family had *any* connection with trade) and the

Old Pretender, as they called him, the Prince's father, with his luckless invasion back in 1715, had left the Buchanans with holes in their pockets. ('Tsk! Tsk!' as the Edinburgh ladies say).

So there was no need to warn me. I found trouble straightway in Aunt Effie's house, though it seemed at the time to have little to do with princes or politics.

Chapter 2

No Light in the Window, No Welcome at the Door

'Twas a tall narrow house, the number eighteen on the door, and all was narrow within, rooms, stairways, and minds. Miss Flora, as I'd already begun to call her in my thoughts, did not apply the knocker, she'd a key, and let us into the high dark hallway.

' 'Tis the steward's day off. The others will be taking their midday broth in the kitchen,' she said, 'so leave your bag and cloak here, and it's there I'll take you first and introduce you. Then I'll go up to my aunt and let her know you're come.'

I followed her down a dark passageway, my new boots aclump on the flagstones. Miss Flora, reaching the door at the end, paused, and looked back at me over her shoulder.

'I'll warn you, they're no very friendly, my aunt's servants,' she said, 'they dislike me for my uncouth island ways. Pay them no mind.'

Then she pushed open the door and we entered the kitchen. It was better lit than the hallway or the passage, with some daylight streaming in from high windows set near the ceiling. All that could be seen through them were the yellowish rain-soaked walls of another house, or mebbe an addition to this one.

Two women and a young girl sat around a bare scrubbed table. The older women's faces registered surprise and disapproval at our appearance. The young girl barely lifted her eyes from a bowl of grand smelling broth.

'Good day to you!' said Miss Flora brightly, nodding to each in turn. '*This*, Mistress Afton, Miss Morrison and Jessie, is Betty Burke, who is to be my maid whilst I'm biding here. I trust you'll treat her kindly and find her a bowl of that broth? I'm away up to my aunt just now. Will I take a tray for us both up with me?'

Mistress Afton, who I guessed would be the cook, since she was named for a married woman (whether she'd ever been wed or no) lumbered slowly to her feet. She walked awkwardly, favouring one leg. She was a heavy-set woman, not fat, but broad, with thick beetling eyebrows which mebbe made her appear angry when she was merely cranky with her painful hip.

'You'll *no*, Miss Macdonald,' she said, 'Jessie'll take your tray. She *already* took one up to your aunt, but 'tis nae bother.'

She turned to the brick hearth where a heavy black pot was keeping warm, and began to ladle broth into a bowl. She might *say* 'nae bother' but it was clear to me she meant the opposite. Miss Flora was breaking the rules. In a polite household the young ladies do not go bustling into the servants' quarters and offer to carry trays. This must be my first taste of Miss Flora's wild island ways!

Jessie, who couldn't be more than eleven or twelve years old, hopped up from her stool and started placing plate, knife, spoon and napkin on a tray, together with a floured bap and a pat of butter. As she passed me to collect the bowl of broth from Mistress Afton, she gave me a wee sideways smile. Quick as a wink! The first sign of spring in this frost-bitten place, the first nod to admit that I existed. She followed Miss Flora out the door.

The woman Miss Flora had named as Miss Morrison, and (I'd been with Mistress Buchanan's household long enough to fathom these matters) was surely lady's maid to Aunt Effie, sat still as a tombstone. She chomped on her bread which she dipped in her broth from time to time. She was a thin, stringy woman, her sparse hair scraped back into a meagre knot beneath her starched cap. Her eyelids remained lowered as though she was either shutting out the sight of me or praying. Mebbe both. Mrs Afton now thumped down a bowl of broth before me and told me to 'pull up a creepie'.

When I looked doubtful she said, 'You're no Scots? Burke's a good Scots' name, indeed I mind there are plenty o' Burkes in Glasgow – in Edinburgh even. Pull up a *stool*.'

'Thank you, Ma'am,' I murmured low. They'd catch the Irish in my speech soon enough. The broth was full of vegetables and set my mouth watering, or mebbe it seemed so good because I'd had nothing but the scrapings of the porridge pot at Mistress Buchanan's that morn.

'So Miss Macdonald has engaged you as her maid?' Miss Morrison had a deep voice, deep as a man's.

'Yes, Ma'am.'

She sniffed. 'You'll make a strange pair, out walking. She a wee clootie dumpling, and you as tall as the castle flagpole! Was it that the registry had no one more suited?'

'Yes, Ma'am.'

I tried to leave it at that, but now both women had their spoons hung suspended above their bowls, their eyes fixed on my face.

'I'm more used to being with an invalid,' I added, 'but the poor sick lady I've lately been with… passed away. So I'm between places. Miss Macdonald was after seeking someone just for a week or so.'

'She's *said* to you she's leaving in a week or so?' Mistress Afton demanded.

'I doubt she knows, exactly, Ma'am.'

The cook snorted. 'Would that she'd make up her mind and go! First it was her and those cousins of hers. Here, they said, for "the season", dances, musical evenings, card parties and the like. Then those two are off to Dunbar without so much as "by your leave", and no word of when, or *if,* they'll return. And we're left with *her*, stravaigin all over the town, without a thought for how folks would see sich behaviour in a young woman that's supposed to be respectable. Or how poor Mistress Dalgleish would feel when she heard of it!'

'And herself, Mistress Dalgleish, not well enough, poor soul, to be gadding about *or* hosting card parties!' declared the lady's maid.

I found myself longing to hear more from them about Miss Flora. After all, what did I know of her but what little she'd confided in me? Whatever could she have done to earn all this ill-will?

'She's from the islands?' I ventured.

Two pairs of eyes were raised to heaven.

'Islands inhabited by savages!' hissed Miss Morrison. 'Folk say they've nothing but dirt floors to their houses there. Even the so-called gentry!'

'And rag manners to match!' added Mistress Afton. 'But maybe that'll no bother you, if that's Irish I hear coming out of your mouth?'

I sat straight, determined they should not put this Irish girl down.

'I've worked in very good houses,' I said. (I spoke true, to stretch the cloth. I'd been first at Ballymore, and then at Mistress Buchanan's Edinburgh house. Dirt floors in neither of 'em!) But then the door opened and wee Jessie stepped back into the kitchen.

'Miss says you've no need tae go up,' she said, addressing me. 'Mistress Dalgleish is resting the noo. Miss says will it be all right wi' you tae sleep wi' me, seein' as you'll no be here sae lang? Mistress Dalgleish said 'twas good enough for Morag,' she added, looking at me doubtfully.

At the child's words there was a great hissing of indrawn breath in that kitchen. Miss Flora should not, I could hazard, have entrusted a message like this to Jessie who was no more than a *wean*, as the Scots say.

'Surely, I'll be glad to sleep along wi' you, Jessie. That's hoping you don't snore!' I spoke in haste, to ward off what the other two might find in words to express in their indignation. None of them were to know that only two hours since I'd believed I would be tramping the streets with no place at all to lay my head this night.

Jessie gazed at me, with round grey eyes. 'I dinae snore, leastways Morag niver said I did!'

'Then that's settled between us,' I said. 'Did Miss Macdonald say when she wants me to wait on her?'

'Aye,' replied Jessie, raising her eyes to the ceiling to aid her recalling of the second half of the message, 'Aye, she said tae take yer ease and finish yer broth, and then tae come tae the hallway when half an hour's passed, for the rain's gone awa, and she's minded tae go oot and view the pichures.'

The air in that kitchen you could have rent in twain. Mistress Afton let out a gusty lung full. Her ample bosom rose and fell.

'She wastes no time, that young woman. Out to see the pictures indeed! Why can she no bide here and sit wi' Mistress Dalgleish? You'd think, having forced herself upon the Mistress —and I'll only half believe she's true kin – you'd *think* she'd stay by her, instead of stravaigin all over like she does!'

I thought it best to keep a close mouth, although I believe my mind was made up in that instant. If the battle lines were being drawn, 'twas to Miss Flora's flag I'd be rallying!

Jessie, mebbe aware of the strains in the room, sat herself down and began to spoon in every last mouthful of her broth, although 'twas surely cold by then. She mebbe knew what was coming next.

'Jessie! Leave that and get ye to the sink! I want those pots washed and dried, and then ye can go and dust the dining room!'

'Yes, Mistress,' the child jumped up, collected a bucket of hot water from the range and scurried over to the stone sink.

'I'll give Jessie a hand with the drying, will I? Since Miss Flora doesn't want me the while,' I said, thinking to keep the peace. The cook scowled at me under her beetle brows, but said nothing.

'I suppose Mistress Dalgleish's never mentioned replacing Morag?'

I'd my back to her as I reached for a drying cloth, so I knew she must be addressing Miss Morrison. The lady's maid gave no reply, but the silence behind me seemed freighted. I imagined heads were being shaken. Jessie, up to her elbows in suds glanced sideways at me, and I thought she looked troubled.

'I'll away and sit by the Mistress,' Miss Morrison now announced. 'Forbye, when she wakes she'll want me to read to her.'

She stood and straightened, her knee joints cracking like gun shots.

'Miss Macdonald could do that,' grumbled the cook.

'She could, but Mistress Dalgleish is used to *me*,' replied Miss Morrison, and I knew then that the maid was jealous. Miss Flora had probably offered, would most likely be happy to serve her aunt in such a way, but this dried up old stick of a lady's maid would never let her, not while she could find ways to prevent.

'She's nae but a flibberty gibbet, *that* one,' Miss Morrison said, confirming my suspicions. 'I couldnae trust the mistress wi' *her* wild notions! Why, I've seen the books she brings back from yon circulating library! Scarcely a decent improving text among them! I even heard her asking her aunt if there was a bookseller in the town. Verra like, she's after that shameful book some terrible man in London has written. *Pamela*, or some sich!'

'No!' Mistress Afton sounded less horrified than curious. I thought to myself that if Miss Flora *had* a copy of this book she, Mistress Afton, would be eager to see it. As indeed, I confess, would I, having heard Mistress Buchanan rail against it when poor Miss Evangeline had wondered if she might send for it.

I turned back to my task, suddenly aware that Jessie was murmuring something at my elbow.

'I'm reet glad you're come,' she whispered, 'I'm that afeared, sleeping lonesome! Afeared he'll come fer me…'

Her large grey eyes held mine, beseechingly. I gave her a quick wee smile in return, meaning 'I hear you, lassie'.

What was this? Who was *he*? Just a child's fear of the dark? Of a bogle? Or something more than that? I leaned closer, that she might say more, but Mistress Afton had hobbled near, intending I guessed to inspect the quality of the washing (and the drying, since finding fault with Miss Flora's new maid would, I thought, be pleasing to her). Jessie bent her head over the bowl and was silent.

Chapter 3

There's Many A Horse That's Slipt An' Fell

Once I judged half an hour was passed, I donned the green and white chequered shawl Miss Flora had bought for me, and waited for her at the foot of the stairs in the shadowy entrance hall. She did not appear immediately, but I knew well that a maid must wait upon her mistress's pleasure.

Whilst I did so, I'd time to examine the shawl. If the rain was gone, I thought 'twould serve outdoors in place of a cloak. 'Twas of woven sheep's wool, a plain deep green criss-crossed with a fine white stripe. A simple "tartan" this, nothing like the more elaborate clan tartans I'd seen on the packet boat as we crossed over from Donaghadee, or glimpsed in Edinburgh as we journeyed the streets to Mistress Buchanan's house. It felt soft and warm against my neck and arms. Woollen yarn was not something I'd worked with too often, but I knew enough to recognise its quality. This was delicate work, using wool from a superior clip. Most probably, as Miss Flora had proposed, woven in a careful household like her own mother's, where they took a grand pride in their labour and used the finest materials.

Settling it around my shoulders in that dank hallway, I found myself singing softly under my breath.

'I'll put on my gown of green, as a forsaken token...that will let the young lads know that the bonds of love are broken. There's many a horse that's slipt an' fell, and risen agin right early...many a lass that lost her lad, and found another right fairly.'

I hadn't had a lad to lose, but I'd lost my place. Now, for a while at least, I'd found another.

'You are not forsaken, Betty, here I am!'

I hadn't heard Miss Flora's feet on the stair. She'd a light step surely, and sharp ears! She was smiling, so I'd not offended her with my singing. Evidently the words of the song were familiar to her.

'No, Miss, 'tis just a song, a Scottish song, mebbe? I heard one time from one of the fiddlers in Belfast. This fine shawl you've given me made me think on't!'

'I know that song well! We've travelling fiddlers and their lassies who come roving through the islands every year. Do you like to sing? You've a tuneful voice,' she said.

'I like it fine. Times I sang for Miss Evangeline when she couldnae sleep for the pain,' I dared to inform her.

'If you come with me to the Long Island you'll hear some grand singing… *and,* Betty, did you ever hear a chamber orchestra?'

'No, Miss.' A chamber orchestra, whatever would that be, I wondered? 'No, I never did.'

'Neither did I!' she replied laughing as she settled her own shawl about her shoulders, 'but someone has sent Aunt Effie two tickets. Wednesday at four in the Assembly Rooms here in Bow Lane. Music composed by a Herr Handel. A German gentleman, she tells me. My aunt doesn't feel well enough, but I'm most curious to go. Assuredly it's not a thing you'd ever see or hear out in the isles. I fear they'll make the maids wait in the lobby, but you should be able to hear something.'

'To be sure, Miss, thank you,' I said, not having an inkling whether this was a treat or an endurance I was being offered.

'Then we'll go,' she decided, 'but *that's* for the day after tomorrow. This afternoon, while the rain holds off, I've promised to change my aunt's books at Ramsey's library. Then we should have time to take a wee peek at the pictures at Mr King's gallery. Will that suit you?'

I blinked at her, and mebbe my mouth gaped. Wild island ways indeed! A mistress asking her maid did something suit her? I'd niver heard of such a thing!

I bobbed her a clumsy curtsey, and fell over my tongue with 'to be sure, Miss, surely, and whatever your honour is wishful to do.'

'Then let's be off while the weather holds!' she said, and tripped lightly down the front steps and away, the basket of books on her arm, myself scrambling after her with my boot laces unravelling.

'Miss Flora,' I whispered as I caught her up, ' 'tis myself should carry the basket, surely?'

'Och!' she said, startled, 'I do believe you're right, Betty!' and she handed it to me, laughing. 'It's no wonder these Edinburgh folk give me strange looks. I'm not used to having a lady's maid. We've maids aplenty at home in my mother's house, and my brother's too, but that's because we need them for the dairying, and the weaving. I've always dressed myself, and if I want to take up something that's heavy or awkward, one of the lads about the farm will always come and aid me.'

'Well, Miss,' I replied, doubtfully, 'I'm not used to this kind of work either. I hope I can give satisfaction.'

'We mun learn taegether!' she said, putting on a broad accent and chuckling. People passing as we walked along gave us many a sideways glance, wondering, I'd doubt not, who these two strange women were, walking the damp pavements side by side and laughing and talking together, mistress and maid? 'Twas not at all what the world expects, nor what it approves. Even a raw Irish girl knew it, but Miss Flora seemed to care little what the polite world of Edinburgh thought.

'Here we are,' she said as we approached a handsome building with a steep stair before it, curving up to the upper floor. 'Mr Ramsay's shop is below and the library above. Mr Allan Ramsay the elder, or so they tell me, was, and for all I know still is, a wig maker, but he sells books and periodicals below and has his lending library above, so we'll climb the stairs.'

We did so. As we approached the top, I was wondering should I enter? Should a maid wait for her mistress outside, or go in with her? How little I was realising I knew of the work of a lady's maid.

As we reached the top of the staircase, a fashionably dressed lady was just on her way out the door, so both Miss Flora and I pressed ourselves against the guardrail to let her pass. I noticed she gave my mistress a pained glance, pulling her skirts aside and calling over her shoulder in a low voice to her daughter (their manner of dressing seemed to show they were kin) who followed at her heels, 'Come, Ann dearest, we're holding these good people up!'

Though the words were polite, her face told me that she considered Miss Flora (not to mention myself) quite beneath her notice. Miss Flora, who evidently recognised her, attempted a polite bow, although the top step was narrow and disallowed anything elegant. She certainly got nothing elegant in return, although Miss Ann favoured her with a puzzled frown and a wisp of a smile.

'Lady Elliot and her daughter,' Miss Flora whispered, as the two ladies made their way down the steps, their silken overskirts billowing up around them in the breeze 'She's an acquaintance of my aunt. I've met her but twice when she made morning calls on Aunt Effie. Evidently I made no favourable impression!'

She stepped inside the library, and since she hadn't told me to wait, and I was still carrying the basket of books, I followed at her heels.

Ach, niver have I seen so many books as they had in that place! They'd a library at Ballymore sure enough, though half the shelves there were home to nought but spiders' nests. Oft times Miss Evangeline had sent me thither for this one or that, chiefly poems, since she said the volumes that contained them were slim and light to hold, and the lines shorter. After one or two of my faltering attempts she niver asked me to read them aloud to her.

Sure, I can read. Ma paid, when she could, when there was some wandering scholar set up a school for a year or so in our Townlands district. A hedge school, they called it, though we gathered in the barn as belonged to an old Quaker man. If I take my time, and some great long word does not rear up in my face to make a fool of me, I can read well enough, but the thought that someone might set out to read all the volumes this Mr Ramsay had collected, well! It fairly took my breath!

'It's impressive, is it not?' murmured Miss Flora, seeing me standing like a wooden post and with my eyes stretched wide. 'I'm permitted, at home in Uist, to borrow any book I care to from the stock our Clan chief and his lady have in their home at Nunton, but they've nothing to compare with this. But then Mr Ramsay is a scholar himself and has written many poems and treatises. I'll just choose what I think my aunt will like, and then we'll away to view the paintings. This same Mr Ramsay's son, I should explain, Mr Allan Ramsay the younger, is a fine painter of likenesses and I'm told Mr King has some of them on display in his gallery.'

A silent fella in white gloves took the basket from me and removed the books we'd brought, flicking through the pages of each one to see they were unspoiled. There were no other people there, but he said nothing, either to Miss Flora or to me, though he bowed to her from time to time. It was as though we were in a church and he the presiding clergyman!

It didn't take Miss Flora long to pick out the books. Evidently she knew well what her aunt would like. When the basket was handed back to me, I saw that there were two books of what I supposed to be sermons and another volume, bound in red morocco with written on the spine of it two names, *Joseph Andrews* and *Henry Fielding*. I couldn't tell what this meant, whether one was the name of the book and the other the man that wrote it, but I thought it more likely to be poems than sermons. Or if not poems, for I could see 'twas lengthy, then what?

'I shall read that one myself,' said Miss Flora when she saw me peering at it, 'before offering it to Aunt Effie.' She chuckled as we descended the steps, 'I'm sure 'twill prove most interesting. The attendant had not had time to replace it on the shelf. Lady Elliot had just returned it!'

After descending the steep stairway we hurried through crowded streets quite unfamiliar to me. Unable to leave my charge in the sick room for so many days, I'd hardly had ony sight o' this town. Today I kept close at my new mistress's heels as I'd no notion how to find my way back to Canongate should I lose her amongst this press of folk. Miss Flora walked quickly and, despite the difference in our heights, I'd to make good use of my longer stride to keep up.

When we reached the place she sought, a lofty building that might once have been a warehouse, she at once entered without giving me the word to wait, and so I followed her inside.

Beyond an outer lobby was a large high room, lit by small casements up near the ceiling. In the centre of the floor were a number of chairs upholstered in brocade in the French style (Mistress Buchanan owned a set, as she liked her neighbours in Antrim to know) on which some fashionably dressed ladies were seated. Other ladies, and a few gentlemen, were engaged in walking around the walls, gazing intently at the paintings displayed there. They were all pictures of grandly dressed people who seemed to stare back at those who were staring at them. Very lifelike and convincing to my way of thinking. They'd portraits on the walls at Ballymore of the people who had lived there in former times. *These*, even such an ignorant one as myself could see, were extremely fine. Almost I could have taken them for living men and women, peering in at us through panes cut into the walls. Two of the gentlemen present had quizzing glasses which they flourished before each one and spent some time examining every detail of their painted clothes and ornaments.

A sturdy fella of about thirty years, dressed in a suit of fawn superfine (I've an eye for fabrics from my former occupation) rose from where he had been seated, conversing with two ladies, and strolled across to greet my mistress with a bow.

'Miss Macdonald! Your servant! Allan Ramsay at your command. Welcome! Are you a connoisseur of the arts?'

For the first time in our short acquaintance, my new mistress seemed flustered (he was a fine looking young fella to be sure).

'You know my name!' she exclaimed.

'Why yes, you were pointed out to me, strolling with your cousins I believe, in the precincts of St Giles, last Sabbath gone.

You're related to Colonel Dalgleish and his mother I understand? You're on your own today. Your cousins did not care to accompany you?'

Miss Flora began to explain why her cousins were not with her, and the artist, for this must be he, took her arm, led her gently towards the pictures and began to name the sitters.

Since I knew I must stand out like a crane amongst this assembly of peacocks, and the women seated in the centre of the room were giving me affronted glances, I melted back as well I could against the nearest wall. My only neighbour there was a sad-eyed beauty in a gown of ivory sateen. Being rendered in paint only, she couldn't say if my company was an offence to her. She'd a label affixed, stating her name, *Anne Bayne*. Later Miss Flora told me she was Mr Ramsay's wife, only lately dead in childbed, poor sweet young creature.

The artist appeared quite taken with Flora, though I wondered at it since she'd not that air about her that betokens wealth. And wealth was surely required to purchase one of his portraits?

Nevertheless, he seemed delighted to have her company and led her about the room, stopping before each of the persons peeping down from the walls.

The two women of fashion he'd left abandoned were less pleased. They soon rose from their seats in a flurry of silks and satins and fine India stoles and made for the door to the street, one murmuring to the other, as they paused to shake out their skirts and arrange their stoles about them,

'She's the by-blow of a Macdonald Chieftain – or maybe a niece – adopted perhaps,' one of them said, 'Of no account in the general way. Certainly there's no *money* there – but if the Prince *does* come, and the Macdonalds rally behind him as they did for his father in '15…'

At which I saw her companion shudder, saying, '*Surely* his Highness will not set those wild clansmen on Edinburgh as the old Pretender did? I remember my poor mother telling me they were all terrified to leave the house! They barricaded themselves indoors for a fortnight!'

'We may have to do the same,' replied the other woman, casting a frown at me over her shoulder, '*if* Charles Stuart comes.' She lowered her voice, but my ears are sharp, 'If that big strapping young woman is a Macdonald *maid*, Lavvy, can you picture what their *men*servants might be like?'

'But Lettie, we have the Government's own Highland Militia stationed here in the castle now? *Surely* they'll be able to repulse…' their voices dwindled and died as they crossed the outer lobby.

I looked down at my flannel petticoats, my stout boots. A Macdonald maid, I thought, you should have seen me earlier today, dressed in a gown so thin you could see the light through it. Miss Flora treats her servants a sight better than ever proud Mistress Buchanan did!

Young Mr Ramsay was guiding Flora back to me, paying her pretty compliments.

'One day, Miss Macdonald, I hope to have the honour of painting *your* portrait!' he was saying.

She smiled and bowed her thanks. '*My* portrait? No indeed, Sir! I'm sure I shall never merit such an honour.'

But of course she *did* merit it, and he did paint it. 'Tis one of several likenesses of her, but much the best, or so I've been told. I've niver had the good fortune to see it. But that was for the future, and a long way off on that damp, cloudy Edinburgh afternoon.

Chapter 4

Blow The Candle Out

After the household had supped the evening's meat and tatties, Miss Flora took me upstairs to the withdrawing room to be presented to her Aunt. As I'd feared, my looks did not find favour with that lady. Mistress Dalgleish was a tiny woman with a fretful air to her, much swathed in shawls, and hedged about with footstools, small tables, and painted leather screens to keep away the draughts. Miss Morrison hovered behind her chair, ill-wishing me and Miss Flora both, as I could plainly see.

'Well, dear,' quavered this Aunt (or had Miss Flora said she was a cousin only?) allowing herself a glance in my direction, 'I suppose this lassie will *do* for you for the while, though I could wish they'd have found you a less gawky creature. Still, better you should have *someone* by you, these troubled times, than to be gadding about the toon by your lone self.' She turned to Morrison, saying, 'When does Gowrie come in? I feel so much safer, as you know, when he is by.'

' 'Tis his day oot, Ma'am,' opined the maid. 'He's away tae Leith so he may come late.'

I gathered from this exchange that Gowrie was the steward. Mistress Buchanan had always referred to her steward as her "butler" in the English style. This Gowrie's existence had been mentioned over supper amongst the kitchen folk, but with, I'd sensed, less than liking. Seemingly he was a favourite with Mistress Dalgleish, which I'd supposed at the time explained that.

'I'll be to my bed early, I'm sae weary,' sighed Aunt Effie, 'but I'd be grateful, Morrison, if you'd put your head around the door and tell me when he comes in. Even if 'tis late. I'll rest easier with a man within the house. *Now*, Flora, you promised you would play for me.' She waved a hand in my direction, ' Send your girl off to help them in the kitchen.'

'Certainly, Aunt Effie! Betty, go and see if Mistress Afton has need of you, and then you may go to your bed. I'll send for you in the morning.'

As I withdrew, she was opening the lid of the spinet that stood in the corner of the room, and setting a sheet of music up before her. It seemed my new employer had some talent for the making of music, as well as a liking for hearing it. Myself, I think the spinet a poor brangle-jangle thing, preferring the giddy scrape of the fiddle or the rowdy swirl of pipe and fife, but in my mind I was applauding Miss Flora. *That*, I thought, hearing the first tinkling notes as I descended the stairs, is something sour-faced Morrison cannot rival!

Later I lay in bed, the candle snuffed, weary to my bones but not yet sleeping; piecing through the patchwork of the day. A half-blown moon shone through a hole in the meagre window blind. Beside me wee Jessie, though 'twas true she did not snore, snuffled like a young piglet, sound asleep as soon as she'd laid down her head.

Whilst I, who had spent so many recent nights between drowsing and waking in a chair beside Miss Evangeline's bed, my ears and my mind alert for her cries of pain and distress, found that I could not straightway sink down into slumber and forgetfulness. Even now when there was nought to prevent it. I heard, perhaps crossing the end of the street, the night-watchman calling the hour. Eleven of the clock. In these fourteen hours gone, where had my life wandered?

I saw, in my mind's eye, myself in threadbare gown and broken boots, pushing my way through the uncaring throng. Standing dismayed at the barred door of the employment registry office. Sitting in the cold church with the hard edge of a bench pressing the tender flesh behind my knees. Then crouched on the floor of the old clothes shop pulling on second-hand boots, under the unfriendly eye of the shop woman. *Then*, striding through the drizzle beside Miss Flora down to the house in Canongate...

meeting those cold glances from the women in the kitchen… laughing with Miss Flora over a basket of books…

I was adrift at last, sliding down into slumber, when the door of the room was flung open, and I was back home in Townlands. A wee girl agin, sharing a straw filled mattress with my two younger brothers.

Whiskey. 'Twas the smell I suppose that roused me, taking me back through the years to those times. Even before the rough hand seized my shoulder I was awake and fighting him off. 'Twas my father, come to flay us all, my poor brothers especially, for some imagined naughtiness of ours that he'd discovered in the bottom of a whiskey jar.

Yet while my body flinched from the expected sting of the leather belt, my conscious mind rose like a fish leaping the falls at Crumlin. 'You're not my Da! I'm a child no longer! Whoever you are, leave me be!' A great boney hand clamped my mouth and I bit him. Bit him hard. My teeth are strong.

I'd think it must have been his roar of pain that roused the household, although I hardly marked it as I fought my way from the tangled bedclothes and reared upright. The door was open and I saw him pitch away from the bed, a vague silhouette against the light from a lamp left burning dimly in the passageway. A big man, and the whisky fumes hung in the air like a fog.

Beside me Jessie reared up screaming, ' 'Tis him! 'Tis Gowrie! Dinae let him, Betty! Dinae let him!' She clung to me, sobbing, hindering my attempts to get out of bed and seize the room's one stool, so that I might fend him off should he turn and attack me again.

Then there were women's voices calling out. The creak of boards in the passageway and the scuffle of hurried feet. Faces at the open door. Mistress Afton, hotching her bad leg, her hair in papers. Miss Flora holding up a branch of candles. Morrison, grim-faced, with her hair flattened to her skull under a net.

Gowrie turned and saw them, and with a roar barged between

them. We heard his boots pounding the boards of the passage way, the stairs, and then the great front door was wrenched open and slammed hard behind him. The whisky-breath seemed to follow him out.

'He's gone,' said Miss Morrison in her deep voice, as the sound died away. 'He'll no come back agin tonight.'

The fat cook said nothing but stood panting, her bosom heaving as if she'd been running hard.

Miss Flora stepped over to the foot of the bed, the candle branch held high to examine our faces. 'Betty! Jessie! Are you hurt?'

I was too dumb-struck and breathless to answer her with anything but a shake of the head, but Jessie burst out wildly, ' 'Twas him did that to Morag! He said he'd kill her if she told!'

'Aah! Morag. So *that* was the true story,' said Miss Flora softly, and I could sense from the set of her shoulders that she was verra angry. She turned back to the two women in the doorway. ' 'Twas never the butcher's laddie that got her with a babe as you told me. 'Did you know about this? Did you *know it and say nothing*?'

They shook their heads, 'No, Miss Flora.'

'I think you guessed it though! Mistress Afton, go at once to the kitchen and heat a pan of milk. Put in some leaves of valerian for the shock these lassies have had. Morrison, hie you to my Aunt, for I'm certain the noise that fiend made will have wakened her. I'll come along and speak to her myself… and I'll fetch a cup of hot milk for her too.'

'She's…your Aunt is sleeping sound!' said Morrison, her voice the bleat of a sheep, 'I…I gave her a dose of laudanum in her chocolate.'

'And why was that?'

'I knew…I knew Gowrie would most likely be the worse for drink, Miss. If she saw him like that, if she heard him shouting and kicking at the furniture… she'd dismiss him.'

'And *why* did you not want her to know he's a vicious drunkard, Morrison? Miss Flora's soft voice had suddenly acquired an edge sharper than a paring knife. 'So that he could attack these lasses with impunity?'

'No, Miss! I never thought he'd do such a thing!'

'So why?'

'He… he's family,' Morrison winced, her mouth a puckered seam, 'My mother's brother's son. Uncle was good to me and my mother after my father died. I wanted Tam Gowrie tae have a chance! He's good enough fella… when he's sober.' She raised her head, and there was a spark of angry defiance in her eye, 'Anyways, I dinae believe he did that tae Morag. No, I dinae, whatever young Jessie says! And how do we know this… this young woman of yours didn't lead him on?'

'I niver set eyes on yon fella in my life!' I sprang up, gasping at the injustice of her words.

'Put your shawls about you, lasses,' said Miss Flora, giving her shoulder to Morrison, 'and we'll go down to the kitchen where there's fire to warm you. Cook must have the milk on the range by now.'

Then, turning again to her aunt's maid she said, patting the pocket in her gown, 'I've a letter here from Betty's previous employer, stating that's she's honest. She says she never saw that man before, and I believe her. Don't try to shift the blame, Morrison! Go now, and check that Aunt Effie is sleeping undisturbed, and if so, go to your own bed. And don't try to blether out lies to her in the morning either. I shall be up betimes and speak with her myself. I'll have my aunt call the locksmith. That man must never come to this house again, do you hear?'

'If the Mistress says so, Miss.'

'She will say so, when I tell her what occurred tonight! And mind, I shall go up to the castle if needs be, and tell what happened to Colonel Dalgleish himself!'

Chapter 5

For I Might in the Battle Fall

'Clean linen aprons, the pair o' ye!' Mistress Afton handed them to us as we stood in the cold kitchen on the next morn. 'Ye'll no go up to Mistress Dalgleish looking like tinkers' hoors! We're no used to disturbances in this hoose!'

Seemingly that was to be her line. All very regrettable 'nae doot', as she might say, that the steward should attack the young women of the household, but she had decided that it was as much our fault as his, simply for living and breathing and being of the female sex.

Jessie, already woebegone from the after effects of fright and lack of sleep, burst into tears. 'Och!' she wailed, 'we'll be turned off, and then what'll me Mammie do? There's five bairns after me at hame!'

'Hush, Jessie!' I begged, moving to brush back her tangled hair and straighten her cap, ' 'twas no fault of yours, child. Miss Flora will speak up for us. Hush!'

'Hmmp! I would nae rely on that!' said the cook, intent on stretching her own apron strings around her thickened middle. ' 'Twill depend on the Mistress's mood. She liked Gowrie fine, a big strong fella, and always verra polite to her – and Miss Flora has outstayed her welcome if you ask me.'

I feared, when we three servants stood lined up before Mistress Dalgleish, that Mistress Afton might have the right of it. Morrison hovered with smelling salts at the lady's elbow, but Miss Flora was not in the room. My heart misgave me. Was my new mistress gone? Had she been banished away from Canongate?

'Whisht,' quavered Mistress Effie Dalgleish, 'this is a terrible thing I've been hearing, terrible! I *cannot* believe it of Thomas Gowrie, indeed I cannot!' She fixed me with watering blue eyes. 'Morrison tells me you deny you ever saw the man before times?'

'That I niver did, Ma'am,' I said, bobbing a curtsey, and trying to hold my voice quiet but steady.

'But 'twas dark, Morrison says. 'How can you be sure, lassie? You've been in Edinburgh a number of weeks now, by what my niece Flora tells me. How do we know you didn't meet with Gowrie in the streets while you went out to do the messages for your former mistress?'

'Niver to my knowledge, Ma'am,' I replied. ' 'Twas not myself was sent to do the messages from Mistress Buchanan's house. I seldom went out the door. 'Twas employed to care for a sick woman I was,' I ventured to add.

Mistress Dalgleish pressed her lips into a stubborn line. She was the kind that doesn't want to hear ony thing contrary to her own notions. 'Twas clear to me she'd made up her mind that I was somehow at fault, that I had 'tempted' this man, Gowrie. To my dismay I could feel tears begin to prickle in the corners of my eyes. I must not weep, I thought. I must stand up for myself. Jessie slyly tucked trembling fingers into mine.

'*Although*,' Mistress Dalgleish went on accusingly, as though this was another fault she'd found in me, 'you're no beauty, a lanky ill-favoured creature at best. I'd have thought any man would want something better looking. Is she any good at her work?' she suddenly asked of the cook.

Mistress Afton, dumbfounded by this sudden demand, allowed her mouth to fall open like a frog about to croak and no words came, but then to my relief I saw that Miss Flora had come into the room, a letter in her hand.

'Mistress Afton can hardly tell you *that*, Aunt Effie. Betty is *my* servant and I've found her willing enough so far. You've questioned Betty? Are you satisfied she never saw Gowrie before?'

'That's what she says.'

'Mistress Buchanan found her honest.'

'I don't know this Mistress Buchanan, but I suppose it must be so. But what am I to do, Flora? Soon you'll be leaving us, and I'm afraid to be all alone in this great house with only a sad parcel of womenfolk. Suppose the French King *does* send this Stuart laddie over at the head of a great army?'

'Dear Aunt, your own son, the Colonel, will be the first to know if danger threatens! He'll send men of his regiment to defend you. Why don't you write to him? Tell him just that Gowrie has proved unsatisfactory, and what can he suggest? I'll willingly walk up to castle and make sure he receives it. I'm *convinced*, Aunt Effie,' she said, laying a soothing hand on the old woman's shoulder, 'that my Cousin James would not wish you to suffer a *moment's* disquiet.'

'I suppose I'd best do that,' Mistress Dalgleish said, grudgingly. She sat a while, mumbling her mouth and fidgeting with her shawls. 'I'd be a deal easier, I'll admit, if my son *were* here. Indeed, I don't understand why he can't live here with me anyway. That draughty old castle must be so drear. Cold and damp, even in the summer as it is now. It cannot be good for him. He was so delicate as a boy. Isn't that so, Morrison? Night after night I sat up with my child, applying hot compresses to ease his poor little chest.'

'And thanks to your good care, dear Aunt, he is now a Colonel of his regiment!' said Miss Flora, briskly. 'Do let me find your quill and a sheet of paper,' she added, suiting the action to the words.

'Excuse me, Ma'am,' the cook spoke for the first time, 'are you wishful we should be getting back tae our work now?'

'Yes, yes! Go to your work,' the old woman waved us away as though she had forgotten why she'd sent for us. Beside me Jessie let out a long sigh of relief. We'd not been turned off this day! Her Mammie and those wee brothers and sisters were safe enough the while.

'Nothing was said of Morag this morning,' I ventured to remark to her, once we were away from the drawing room, and I'd been set to help her make the beds. It seemed Mistress Afton had decided that whatever Miss Flora might believe, I was to be a maid of all work. Left to our own devices, Jessie had given me a quick tour of the main apartments. Most of the house was closed up, the blinds drawn, the rooms dingy and neglected. From the windows of

Mistress Dalgleish's bedroom little could be seen but moss-choked gutters and a lone herring gull preening his feathers on the roof ridge across the street.

'No, and it willnae be. They dinae want to hear it,' the child replied, her expression closed and sad. 'He was a'ways pawing at her in the corridors and on the stairs, and then one day he pulled her into his room and… did that. She tried tae tell Mistress Afton, but 'twas no use. *That one* does nae hear anything she does nae want tae!'

'Poor Morag. Do you know, did her family take her back?'

'She'd no one. She was frae the orphans' place. Where could she go but the poorhoose?' Jessie punched the pillows as though she was punching Gowrie's face. 'An' I heard she's deid.'

'Dead? Ach, poor girl! Is that certain, Jessie?'

'Certain enough. Old Nessa, the Wifie that calls here wi' the fish tellt me. Morag had monies saved, a wee small amount frae her wages, and she went tae one of those wimmin that can get rid o' the bairn fer ye, but 'twas nae good an' she's gone tae heaven and the poor bairn too,' Jessie's pinched wee face crumpled and she gulped back a sob.

'Jessie, that's terrible, so it is, I'm right sorry! But at least this Gowrie's gone now. You needn't be afeared.'

'Until the next one comes,' said Jessie, thumping another pillow. At barely twelve years old, what reason had that child to have faith in the people around her to keep her safe? It made me sad and angry to think on't. At her age I'd been in the flax paring sheds amongst the women, safe enough, if not always happy. It entered my head to say I'd stay, *I'd* make sure no one harmed her, but I held my tongue. 'Twas a promise I knew I'd no way to keep.

Just then Miss Flora appeared at the door. 'Ah, there you are, Betty. Come, get your shawl, we're away up to the castle. My aunt wants her son to come and advise her. She won't rest easy until he tells her what to do.' She smiled at Jessie. 'I'm sure he'll get her to engage more servants to help *you*, Jessie. I'll let him know how it is that you've too much to do. Mistress Afton is suffering mightily with that painful hip of hers. She can't help you as she might. A couple of extra maids to help with the work, that'd be a fine thing, wouldn't it, Jessie?'

'Yes, Miss,' said Jessie, tugging the counterpane into place, her face a blank.

'Miss Flora,' I risked, once we were away from the house and striding up the Royal Mile once more, 'I feel I must tell you. That man, Gowrie, 'twas *Jessie* he came for last night… at least, so she believes, and he cannot have expected to find *me* sharing her bed.'

Miss Flora stopped, and turned to me. 'I think so too,' she said, grimacing as though she was chewing on something sour, 'and those women knew it, although I *could* never, *can* never make Aunt Effie understand such a terrible thing! The shock would send her into palpitations. Neither her heart nor her understanding are strong, and 'twould be all be my fault if the shock killed her. I will do what I can with the son, Colonel James Dalgleish. He's fair man I believe, and I think he'll listen to me. I'll do my best to make that house a safer and happier place before I leave. As I think I must.'

She patted her pocket. 'The post boy came early with a letter from my cousins at Dunbar. It seems my cousin Ewan was riding with his friends when his horse shied and crushed his leg against a stone gatepost. His leg is broken in two places. Jane, his wife, tells me they won't be returning by Edinburgh now until he's fit to travel which may be several weeks. I can't impose on Aunt Effie any longer. I must find a way to travel home to the Long Island. Would you be willing to come with me, Betty?'

'Why, surely,' I told her, without a thought more, 'I'll come a roving with you, Miss Flora!'

Chapter 6

Build Me A Castle

He had his mother's face, Colonel James Dalgleish of the King's Highland Militia. I'm not sure if they'd named them the 42nd then, or I only heard that in later times. He was a slightly built fella of perhaps thirty-five years, with a fair complexion, and large light blue, slightly bulging eyes. Smart in his regimentals with a tartan sash across his chest, but not what they call a dandy. He wore a neat wig close to his head with a curlicue behind, tied neatly with a narrow black ribbon.

'Cousin Flora,' he said, laying the letter down on his rosewood desk with what I saw were unsteady fingers, 'this has come at a very bad moment. That my mother should in *any way* be connected to… what I fear may be a scandal… and at this very time when Miss Ann Elliot has just consented to be my wife. This man Gowrie…' he pressed his lips together and breathed through his nose, in and out, 'he was my man. I sent him to my mother, but I had no idea he might… I cannot say how sorry I am that anyone in that household should suffer such a terrible insult. However, as it is, there is no need to fear any recurrence.

'Flora,' he went on, 'you are not a young woman of a nervous disposition? I've been told how bold and brave you are, going about the town to see the sights on your own. Not at all *missish*, I understand?'

'I think I'm reasonably courageous,' said Flora, sounding puzzled, as well she might be at this talk of a "bad time" and "scandal," and his suddenly revealing that he was to marry the young lady we'd encountered so fleetingly on the staircase of Mr Ramsay's library. 'Pray, for what do I need my courage, Cousin?'

'Would you… could you bring yourself to view a corpse?'

Whatever my mistress had expected from this visit, it was not, surely, this? Her eyes widened for a moment in shock, but then she said, quite calmly, 'Certainly, Cousin. Whose corpse am I to view?'

'And your maid…' he'd managed to notice me, standing in the shadows. This stone-lined room, deep inside the fortress, was lit in the main by a branch of candles on his desk. 'She'd better accompany us,' he said. 'I imagine she has smelling salts and so forth about her, should you need them?'

Her question about whose corpse we were to view went unanswered. I was briefly flustered. I'd no smelling salts, should I have thought of such things? I couldn't imagine Miss Flora, after dealing so staunchly with us all after Gowrie's attack, ever being in need of them.

We followed her cousin down mony a cold dark passageway. One of the soldiers walked ahead having produced and lit a lantern. 'Twas a dank, cold place this castle, built on a great mound high above the town, as my own eyes could testify. Within however, it felt as though we were miles below the earth. I did not wonder that Mistress Dalgleish thought it unhealthful.

We entered a small room, deep, surely, within the fortress. No windows here, not so much as an arrow squint in the stone work. At a signal from the Colonel the soldier lofted the lantern. Before us was a rough bier set on trestles, and on it lay a man.

He was a big heavy-set fella, his face unshaven, his hair wild and dirty. He'd britches on that had once been good black sateen, though they were mired now and rent at the knee. If he'd worn a coat 'twas gone, and his white cambric shirt was torn and stained. He'd bled a good deal from a wound to the left side of his chest.

Miss Flora gasped softly at the sight. 'Oh, 'tis Gowrie!' she said.

'Thomas Gowrie,' repeated Colonel Dalgleish. 'The Watch found him in one of the Wynds just before midnight. Killed by a knife wound to his heart. The knife we have, it was left in the wound.'

The soldier who had accompanied us, lifted it from the bier and held it up for our inspection. Miss Flora shook her head. The Colonel's eyes flicked quickly to me, and I shook mine too. The only knife I'd seen in the house at Canongate was the one Mistress Afton used for paring vegetables, and that I'd only seen when Jessie had washed it and handed to me to be dried.

'I have to ask you, Flora – this attack upon the maidservants – at what hour did it occur?' the Colonel continued.

'About eleven of the clock, Cousin,' she stated. 'Betty, you will bear me out?'

I nodded and bobbed another curtsey when his eyes turned back to me. 'Sure 'twas then, Sir. Maybe a little later. I'd heard the Watch call the hour just before, Sir.'

'You'd never seen this man before?'

'That I niver did, Sir.'

I could not even have said for certain this was Gowrie. The corpse could have been onyone, but I thought it best to be silent. What could I have said, except that 'twas dark, he was a big strong fella, and the stench of drink was on him? The corpse had been a big strong fella too, and the faint whiff of stale whisky still hung about him, even in death.

'Having roused the household he ran off? No one left the house to follow him?' the Colonel asked Flora.

'A crew of womenfolk such as we were, Cousin? No. He was very drunk, and roused us all except your mother, who'd taken a sleeping draught. Once he was gone I took Betty and Jessie down to the kitchen, and had the cook make them a calming drink. Then Mistress Afton and I fastened the inner bolts on the doors back and front, in case he should return. I sleep in the room above the front door. There's only that high gate in the yard behind, and that's padlocked at night. Not one of us went out till morning, Cousin, if that's what you are wondering? I slept but lightly, and I'm sure I'd have heard if anyone drew those bolts.'

The Colonel took one of those deep breaths that fill the cheeks and flare the nostrils, and blew it out through his nose. 'This, alas, is more difficult than you know, Cousin Flora. There are things I must tell you, but in confidence. Shall we go up to the ramparts?

Then you and I can speak privily. Your maid can accompany us, but she can wait at a distance whilst we walk about together and seem to admire the views?'

Miss Flora gave me an anxious glance. Would a rough Irish girl like myself understand my place in this? I suppose she was thinking we'd only been together so short a spell, and she'd had no time to instruct me in my duties.

Propriety. I'd first heard that word at Ballymore. I'd never known of it afore, though I've a liking for words and I store up new ones whenever I hear them. Propriety. A girl at the spinning wheel, a servant, a young woman in my station of life, has no need of such a thing. It means, or so I think, that everything must *appear* correct, proper. An unmarried woman who has any claim to be of the gentry class should niver be alone with a man, save her father or her brother. Even though Miss Flora was in some way related to the Colonel and they called each other "cousin", they could not be seen alone together in a secluded place for fear of scandal. "Tsk! Tsk!" I could hear Mistress Buchanan's voice in my head.

When the doctor called to examine Miss Evangeline she'd made me understand that I must stay by her sister at all times, "for propriety" even though Miss Evangeline was over forty years of age and too sick to know or care what was done to her. And the eminent Doctor Borthwick himself, wasn't he an old fella, bent and crabbed with age? And with no thought but of what physic he might proscribe to ease her pain?

So I understood that I must accompany Miss Flora and the Colonel out onto the castle ramparts, and remain where they could see me, and I they. Yet far enough off that I might not hear what was not for a servant's ears.

I caught my breath as we emerged onto these ramparts, and not just from the climb. *Edinburgh.* For the first time, seeing it laid out below, I saw the town for a place of beauty. In the early morn it had lain under a coverlet of cloud, its tall sandstone buildings yellowish grey and forbidding. By the time we'd scrambled up those several stone stairways into the open air, the sun had shredded the clouds into rags tossed by the wind across a ground of blue. Now it lit the rooftops of the town below and glinted on distant hills. Green hills all around, to the north, the east, the south. (if there were any to the west I could not see them for the great bulk of the fortress itself.) Edinburgh lay below me like a jumbled necklace of agates lying on a crumpled emerald cloth. What a wonder to me were all those trees! In all my time here I'd seen nothing but streets, buildings; nought of green beyond the weeds between the cobblestones. I'd had no notion until now that Edinburgh was a city surrounded by woods and parkland. In the distance I could see the shimmer of water, of a loch perhaps, or even the sea itself.

Since I supposed a maid must remain standing as well as out of earshot, while her mistress received her cousin's confidences, I moved to the battlements the better to admire this view. The soldier who had guided us up here stood at the foot of a flight of stairs to some higher look-out, having snuffed out the lantern and placed it on the ground.

'Dinae go too close, lassie,' he suddenly spoke, making me jump, 'Yon height can mak yer heid reel.'

Startled, I turned to look at him. Now in the daylight I saw him to be an older fella than I'd thought when he'd sprung up the stairs ahead of us, his hair iron grey and roughly tied back with a loop of red braid, his complexion dark and seamed by service out of doors. His tartan plaid was not the neat body sash I had seen on the Colonel. *His* plaid was full, several ells of fabric by my reckoning, and hung heavy from his shoulder. I could well believe this man might unroll it on some night manoeuvre and sleep in the heather, as I'd been told the Highlanders do.

'I thank you, Sir,' I said, to be polite, 'Would you be knowing the names of these hills beyond the town?'

Her cleared his throat, a harsh sound. 'Irish, huh?' he said. 'Have we no Scots lassies then, to suit Miss Macdonald's requirements?' Without waiting for me to answer he said, 'Yon hill straight ahead o' ye, wi' the sharp drop frae the summit, that's the one they call Arthur's Seat. Once, they tell me, 'twas a volcano, but 'tis deid noo. Wad a lassie frae Ireland know what a volcano is?'

'To be sure,' I replied, annoyed by his supposing me an eejit, ' 'tis a mountain that spews out fire.' Then my eyes filled with tears, thinking of Miss Evangeline and those magazines she'd always had about her. Once she'd read a piece out to me, telling of these exploding mountains in Italy and way to the north of us, in Iceland she said, and she'd shown me drawings of how that could be. Today, as I now sorrowfully recalled, even at this moment, 'twas likely they were laying her poor dead body in the ground.

'If *ye* didnae murder Tam Gowrie, ye wee Irish giantess, and the Colonel believes Miss Macdonald didnae,' the soldier interrupted my sad thoughts, 'who did, do ye suppose?'

I decided to ignore him, keeping my back turned and my eyes fixed on the scene below. I've met with mony a one who scorns the Irish. 'Tis of no use to argue with them.

'For *someone* did,' he went on, 'The Colonel placed that man in his mother's hoose, fae a good reason. That he might come and go between the castle and the toon, and tell what he heard and saw in the streets. And the ale hooses too, o'course.'

So, I thought, this man Thomas Gowrie had been a spy? And Colonel Dalgleish had placed him in his own mother's house? Hadn't I heard him say so, just now? To discover what? *Jacobites.* Was someone in that house a Jacobite sympathiser? Surely not Mistress Dalgleish herself, speaking so fearfully as she had, of the rumoured invasion? Miss Flora? I'd discovered from the talk of the women at the picture gallery that she'd some connection with one of the clan chieftains – those fierce men it seemed everyone in Edinburgh feared so greatly. What she'd said to me about "divided opinions", and her doubts that this Prince and his army would ever come, had given me a different view. But what did I really know of her?

I turned slowly and faced the soldier. Staring straight at him now, I changed my idea of him once again. He was not so old after all, despite his grey locks. His face was nut brown and lined from the sun. *The sun?* He must have served long in warmer climes than this one. 'What is your name, Sir?' I asked, 'I have a right to know it, since you seem to think ill of me.'

'John Begg,' he replied, 'though I doubt ye do have sich a right!' He laughed, 'and your name, lassie?'

'Elizabeth Burke.'

'Och, I'd 'a thought 'twould be Margaret, since you're sich a long Meg,' he replied, grinning.

'And you are John *small*,' I hurled back at him. I'd heard enough of the Erse, the Gaelic tongue some speak in Ireland, to know the meaning of Begg!

I've niver had a sweetheart, but hadn't I lived a long year amongst the men servants of Ballymore? Hadn't I learned to dodge the pinching fingers, the grappling hands, and to parley the stable lads' sly insults? I've learned, and learned well, that no man likes to think ony part o' him is small!

'Touché!' replied my tormentor, chuckling. Now there was a word I didn't know at all, although as I've said, I've a grand fancy for words. This *touché* he must surely have learned in foreign parts where the sun shone stronger than the weak beams that lit these battlements this morn.

'A lass o' spirit! I like that fine!' he said, chuckling, 'Now I think on't, I believe I've used the name, *Burke* myself, now and then. John Burke, aye, that has an honest ring to it. I'll remember that!' He grinned and gave me an insolent salute.

Chapter 7

Farewell, Edinburgh

'Miss Flora?' As I followed at her heels in thought-filled silence down the length of the Royal Mile once more, I'd decided I must speak agin. 'You must pardon me for asking, but what'll I be saying to Mistress Afton and Miss Morrison? They'll be wanting to hear what befell Mr Gowrie. Will I tell them he's dead?'

She stopped then, and turned to face me, chewing on her lower lip.

'I suppose you must,' she said. 'As soon as you appear around that kitchen door, the eyes of those two will demand your budget of news! You may tell them he's dead, Betty, and that we're none of us suspected of causing it. My cousin the Colonel assured me of that.'

(Ha! I thought, so he may have said, but that fella, John Begg, still thinks otherwise!)

'But say no more than *that* if you please, Betty,' she continued, 'Colonel Dalgleish is coming to Canongate himself this evening to tell his mother that he has offered for, and been accepted by, Miss Ann Elliot. 'Tis only right that Aunt Effie should hear it first from his own lips and not glean it from the servants' prittle-prattle.'

'Will she be pleased, Miss?' The words were off my tongue before I could clamp my teeth on it.

However, my mistress was not offended by my boldness, but took time to consider this awhile before she replied. 'Perhaps. Perhaps not,' she finally said. 'She'll be glad he's to marry and bring his bride to Canongate, for that must mean he'll be very much more at home, and the house will be opened up and new servants employed. I've seen Miss Elliot on only two or three occasions, and she appears to me to be a sweet and gentle girl. There can be no objection to *her*. However…' she paused, choosing her words, '*Lady* Elliot is far from being a favourite with my aunt! Aunt Effie thinks her a vulgar, overbearing woman, who has already shown she's one who'll push her way into the household if given half a chance. *Now we see why she was so eager to pay morning calls!* Cousin James will have to be firm with her from the first I'd say, or the sparks will fly!

'That said,' she added, 'as I understand it, Miss Ann's portion is her own from her late father, Sir Archibald. 'Twill be hers outright on her marriage, my cousin tells me, so her mother (she is actually her step-mother) will have little to say to it if he bars his doors to her once they're wed.'

I'd seen enough of the house in Canongate to know that it was in sore need of refettling. Many of the rooms, as wee Jessie had shown me, were shut up, blinds drawn at the windows, the furniture fast asleep beneath Holland covers. Perchance Colonel Dalgleish had little more but his soldier's pay? Miss Ann Elliot was to bring him a handsome dowry.

I said no more, since 'tis not a maidservant's place to offer her thoughts or ask questions, but I glanced sideways at Miss Flora. Had she, I couldn't help but wonder, had some hopes of the Colonel herself? Could it be that the cousins she'd spoken of, who had brought her from Kintyre (which I knew to be in the west somewhere) and then left her here alone, had hoped she'd make a match with James Dalgleish? If so, they'd be disappointed that their scheme had failed. Although I searched her face whilst she was speaking, if Miss Flora had suffered a disappointment I couldn't see ony sign of it.

'Cousin James agrees with me that I should wait no longer in delaying my return to the Long Island,' she went on, quite calm and tranquil to my eye. 'To have a young unmarried woman living in what is after all *his* household, when he is betrothed to another, *must* present an odd appearance! When I told him how things have fallen out with Jane and Ewan, he saw at once how difficult that has made my position, and he offered to find me a military escort as far as Glasgow.' She paused, gazing around, seemingly trying to mark the street and the buildings about us, the stunted rowan tree in the close, as though she needed to recall where she was, and where she might be, mebbe, on the morrow.

'Betty, we must make ready to leave, almost immediately,' she now said, 'within the next few days. Cousin James tells me there are regimental couriers travelling back and forth by fast post-chaise to the garrison there. Since these rumours of invasion by Charles Stuart and his supporters have become so rife, it appears they go almost daily. I must pack my trunk and be ready. Do you still come with me, Betty?'

'To be sure I will, Miss Flora!' I replied right heartily, but I'll admit 'twas not the notion of these far flung islands to which we were to travel that excited me at that moment, but the thought of the post-chaise. A post-chaise! Mistress Buchanan's people had met us at the Port of Glasgow in a lumbering old coach she'd hired, but I'd never travelled, never hoped to travel in one of these fast, light equipages! Now wouldn't that be a grand thing to be boasting of to my brother, Danny? Whenever I should see him agin.

Miss Flora's thoughts were on other matters. 'I am sorry for it, but we shall have to forgo hearing Herr Handel's music tomorrow afternoon, Betty. The Colonel may send this carriage at any moment. I cannot risk being away from the house when it comes.'

'Verra well, Miss,' I replied, for I still had no notion what the music of this "hair" man could be or whether I should have liked it.

Jessie's face crumpled when I told her we were most likely leaving within a few days, and to my great surprise Mistress Afton, too, declared herself "put about" at my going.

'Just when we're getting used tae having another pair of hands!' she scolded. (Jessie and I, having eaten our broth, were seated at the kitchen table cleaning the silver with wine lees and soft rags). 'Morag gone, Gowrie gone! How am I expected tae run this great barn o' a hoose wi' nae able bodies left tae lend a hand?'

I had given my word to Miss Flora, so I could not relieve her mind. ' 'Twill be better, I promise you,' I whispered across the table to Jessie. 'You'll see.'

Jessie's sullen expression told me she didn't believe it, and I nearly fell into a fit of mirth when a grey barred gull alighted on the high window ledge above her head with the same mistrustful look in his round yellow eye.

'I could *ask*, Betty?' Mistress Afton spoke to me over her shoulder as she stirred a stew at the kitchen range, 'Ye're nae *bound* to Miss Flora, are ye? I could ask if we could keep ye on? If Mistress Dalgleish cannae find a body tae replace Thomas Gowrie straightway, we'll be needing someone tae bring in the coals and draw up water frae the well. Ye're a big strong lassie, ye'd be able tae tackle that work?'

I shook my head, smiling. 'I'm promised to go wi' Miss Flora and teach some of the young island lassies to spin,' I said. A small satisfaction, this, I thought, and I wished that Mistress Buchanan might know of it! Two days since she'd turned me out, penniless, onto the street, and here was someone less clutch-fisted than she, eager to offer me employment. Two days ago, pushing my way, wet, cold and fearful, through that crush of bodies in the Grassmarket, I'd have jumped like a salmon at a fly, at carrying coals and drawing water. *Ony* work *then* I would have taken, believing myself like to starve to death, that I might have a roof over my head and food in my belly.

'Spinning is my trade,' I told her, rubbing carefully on the bowl of a spoon and catching sight of my own slab of a face in it, ' 'tis what I've been bred up to.'

Colonel James Dalgleish came to the house in Canongate that night, and told his mother, in the presence of Miss Flora and within the hearing of his mother's ever watchful maid, Agnes Morrison, that he was to marry Miss Ann Elliot, daughter of the late Sir Archibald Elliot of Carnguissie.

Mistress Effie Dalgleish had wept, 'half happy, half sorrowful,' Morrison reported when she came down to the kitchen 'tae warm some milk and brandy for a composer,' as she put it.

We three, Mistress Afton, Jessie and myself, paused in our tasks (kneading bread dough for the cook, washing and drying the dinner plates for Jessie and myself), all ears. Even I, who'd known the secret, was curious to hear how the news had been received.

'Och weel,' said Mistress Afton, *'that's* put paid to what we all supposed was Miss Flora's wee game!'

'Did she faint away at the news, Miss Morrison?' Jessie demanded.

'Miss Flora? Not she. Quite unconcerned to all appearances! No thought of marrying the Colonel ever entered her head! A cold-hearted creature, to my thinking. Not that…' the lady's maid paused in thought, 'not that, in some ways the *Mistress* might have preferred Miss Flora. Ye all ken the Mistress! Anything new, it worrits her. This Miss Ann may be an amiable young woman and the Colonel's choice, but she's bound to make changes. Big changes, nae doubt. Mistress Dalgleish will find that awfu' hard.'

'Is she rich?' hissed Jessie to me. I think she'd suspicioned that I'd known this news all along.

I whispered back. 'A dowry from her father, Miss Flora told me,'

'So *that's* why Miss Flora talked of new maids tae help me! She knew he was going tae wed this other one!'

I nodded. 'Colonel Dalgleish told her this morn, before he took us to see… the body… Gowrie's body.'

'An' she was nae bothered tae see a corpse?'

'Forbye,' the cook interrupted, having evidently thought things over, 'she'd know all along she'd nae hope. The Colonel mun marry well, whatever his inclinations! Miss Flora has nae a bawbee tae bless herself. And her family's nane o' the best they say.'

Morrison, pausing in the doorway with the cup of "composer" on a tray, nodded in a meaningful fashion at these words, and addressed me, ' 'Tis best ye be aware o' that, Betty. 'Tis a wild place you're going tae. Miss Flora may seem to *you* to be a respectable young woman, for all she's inclined to be a mite free in her ways…

but her mother was nae better than she ought tae be. Allowed herself to be carried off across the water by some brigand before Flora was out of leading strings! 'Tis no wonder she's nigh on twenty-four years of age, and cannae find herself a husband!'

After she left there was silence for a spell in the kitchen, no sound but the coals settling in the grate and the thump of heavy saucepans being laid to drain on wooden boards. All our heads were busy wi' thinking on't.

'So Tam Gowrie's deid,' the cook suddenly remarked, 'and nae loss there, and we mun get used tae new ways. Verra like the Colonel's bride will do the choosing o' a new steward, new maidservants. I only hope we three will give satisfaction and be kept on. I couldnae face ganging tae a new household at my time o' life. And Aggie Morrison's reet. Mistress Dalgleish will tak changes awfu' hard – but there's no denying this hoose needs plenty o' siller spent on't!'

Chapter 8

A Gentleman On Horseback, He Came Riding By

'They say this is the best way,' Miss Flora told me as we bowled along through the outer edges of Edinburgh town. 'This road between Edinburgh and Glasgow is a reasonably good one. I'd have liked to go by Loch Lomond and up through the glens, which is the *true* Road to the Isles, but 'twould mean horseback, and Cousin James shuddered at the thought of the wild country and the clan lands we'd have to pass through. And I don't suppose you're a rider, Betty?'

'No, Miss,' I replied, alarmed, 'I niver yet rode on a horse's back.'

I didn't tell her that I already knew the road we were following. Hadn't I journeyed it coming from Glasgow with Mistress Buchanan and her sister, when we came from the boat from Ireland? In a great lumbering brute of a travelling coach that seemed to tumble its wheels into every pothole and ditch. With poor Miss Evangeline crying out in pain every yard of the way? I'd had no chance then to mark these fields and hedges, the green o' the trees, the wayside flowers that I saw now as we left the soot-smirched sandstone town behind.

'We must be grateful to James for this fine post-chaise and our escort, I suppose,' Flora added, not sounding too grateful at all.

'Yes, Miss,' I was watching the bobbing head of the outrider as we moved over the ground as though the divil himself was after us. He'd a "heeland bonnet" I saw, pulled low over his brow, his hair and face concealed. Could he be John Begg, I wondered? Or was it just my fancy? I'd understood well enough that Colonel Dalgleish wanted us out of Edinburgh, and I didn't suppose it was entirely to do with his forthcoming marriage. His "connection" with a Clan family wouldn't be something he'd care to have folks dwell upon just now. This was his way of getting rid of a suddenly embarrassing relative. A fast military transport to the Highland Militia's garrison in Glasgow, 'carrying urgent letters to a Major Henderson.' He'd seemingly told Flora this the night he came to the house in Canongate to acquaint his mother with his plans to wed, and to settle her domestic troubles.

'I know you'll deliver them faithfully, Flora,' he'd added that morning, four days later as it turned out, as he saw us both to the carriage, 'your journey will provide cover for my dispatches. At the same time it will appear only right and reasonable that I should send my cousin forth in comfort and with adequate protection. The country you'll be travelling through is that of a Chieftain who is said to be loyal to the House of Hanover, so there should be no risk of attack, but these are difficult times, and one never knows. A Chieftain may swear his allegiance to the Crown, but his sons may act otherwise.'

Now, with a small sigh, Miss Flora settled herself against the squab of the corner seat in the carriage, removed her bonnet, unlaced her boots, and placed her stockinged feet on the seat opposite. I noticed she'd a hole in one toe. When we got to journey's end and I could find some wool, I'd offer to darn it. I may lack the smart appearance a lady's maid should have, but I can darn as neatly as the best o' them!

' 'Tis forty miles to Glasgow,' Flora said, 'so we may as well rest easy, Betty. 'Tis hard work being a lady I find, and not much to my liking! I'm sorry, mind, not to have seen more of the Season.' Seeing, perhaps, a puzzled frown upon my face at this she went on, 'You'll have heard of the Season, Betty? When all the great families, and those that like think themselves of high degree, come to Edinburgh to meet and take part in all kinds of revelry? It's nothing, I understand, to what they have in London, but still, balls and card parties, picnics and such? Even some of the Highland Chieftains and their wives and daughters will generally be there, although my Aunt heard many stayed away this year. It's when young women are "launched into society" by their mothers, each of them hoping to meet a fine young man to marry.'

'Was yourself hoping so, Miss?' I found myself saying, the words tumbling across my tongue once agin before I could stop them. I'd no business to ask any sich a thing, but Miss Flora only laughed.

'*I* didn't have such hopes, Betty, but my cousin Jane will be disappointed! She promised me that if I came with her and her husband, she'd seek out the very man for me. If they hadn't gone off to visit with Ewan's old school fellow near Dunbar, and if he hadn't met with an accident there… she'd have been seeking invitations for us to every card party, every ball, every kind of select entertainment Edinburgh society has to offer. But 'twas not to be! Lady Clanranald will be disappointed too,' she added. 'She lent me a ball dress of blue silk, trimmed with Russian needlepoint lace — which I've never yet had on my back — *and her pearls*. The Dear Lord save us, Betty! I hope we remembered to pack those?'

'The dress is in your travelling trunk, Miss, and the pearls too, rolled inside your woollen stockings,' I said, proudly. I might be new to my duties, but hadn't I watched Mistress Buchanan's own maid, Gladwell, at her work before we left Antrim? And hadn't she warned me always to wrap ony thing of value, rings and jewels and sich, inside my lady's stockings?

'Miss Flora?' I could not stop myself from asking now, 'are we sent away because that man, Thomas Gowrie, died? Does your cousin the Colonel still have a suspicion, for all he said, 'twas someone in your Aunt's house – myself even – might have killed him?'

'Good Lord, no!' said Miss Flora, 'James is no fool. Gowrie was a big hefty fellow. If you, or I, had done so, how could we have carried him to that Wynd near the castle where they found him? 'Twas a good quarter of a mile above Canongate, and even so late in the night there were folk abroad, and the watchman was about his rounds. He thinks it most likely Gowrie was involved in a drunken quarrel. And we know well enough he was drunk, do we not?'

She was silent for a moment, and then said, 'James is only anxious to avoid folk knowing how Gowrie behaved to you and Jessie… and that poor lass, Morag. He feared if *that* tale got abroad Lady Elliot might make her daughter withdraw from the engagement. If my Aunt and her servants keep close mouths, the Colonel believes no one will know Gowrie ever came near the house that night. You may be sure he'll explain to Mistress Afton and Miss Morrison how important it is to avoid a scandal. No doubt he'll hand them vails to hold their tongues. Wee Jessie too, although I'd doubt *she* ever has cause to speak to anyone outside of the house?'

'The fishwife,' I answered, frowning over what she was telling me, 'Jessie likes to talk with the fishwife that comes to the kitchen door. She's a woman named Nessa Jordan, and it seems she was friendly with Morag. They enjoyed a gossip together, I'm thinking. Jessie said to me that this was the woman who told her that Morag had tried to get rid of the baby, and both of them were dead.'

'Dear God, that's so sad,' sighed Miss Flora. 'I never thought of the trades people. I doubt Cousin James has thought of them either. The fishwife. And the coal merchant and the grocer's laddie, I suppose? All the tradespeople who serve Aunt Effie and call at the kitchen. Mistress Afton is slow to get to the door with that bad hip of hers, and she sends Jessie to attend to it?'

'Yes, Miss. She sends Jessie a good deal on every occasion. That child has too much put upon her. But I daresay things will be easier for them all if the Colonel is to employ extra servants?'

I did not mention that Jessie seemed to guard jealously these times she talked to the tradespeople at the kitchen door. I'd offered to go, but Jessie insisted she must do it, and on the few occasions I *had* been the one to answer the door, whoever had called had seemed more than a little disappointed not to find wee Jessie there.

'I hope things will be easier for them all,' Flora replied. 'As you'll have guessed, Betty, this betrothal of my cousin's will be the cause of a number of changes to that household. All the rooms are to be opened up. New decorative schemes are to be put in hand. Several more servants employed. I believe you could have stayed on if you'd wanted to, Betty. Mistress Afton spoke highly of you! "A willing hand," she called you, and that's high praise from her, I'd imagine.'

'I didn't want to, Miss Flora,' I said, and meant it. 'I said I'd come to the islands wi' you, and that I will.'

'Good. I feel sure we'll deal well together,' she replied, settling herself with her head supported by the chaise's plump upholstered cushions, and closing her eyes.

There were a hundred questions I'd have liked to put to her. What would we do when we reached Glasgow? Would we be going straightway to the harbour? Or if not, where would we bide the night? How would we be finding a suitable ship to carry us to these islands of hers? Did she have money enough in her purse to pay our way? And this man riding hard at my shoulder, a sword at his side? John Begg? Was he there to protect us from brigands? Or to see that we truly left? Seeing us off, not from Edinburgh alone, but the mainland of Scotland itself? *Brigands*. I recalled Morrison's tale of Miss Flora's mother being carried off by such a one. Was there ony truth in it? Or was it merely a piece of Morrison's jealous spite? Flora herself had spoken of her "mother's household" as though her mother had survived this "carrying off" and now lived a settled life where she and her maids worked at their looms.

I'd risen early that day, as servants must. Jessie and I had heated cans of water and carried them up to Mistress Dalgleish and Miss Flora. Whilst Jessie was upstairs, a baker's laddie had called at the kitchen door with fresh bread and baps. When I answered his knock he'd seemed quite put about, and demanded to know where Jessie was? Laughing, I told her later she'd a follower, but Jessie was angry with me now she knew I was leaving, and wouldn't crack a smile. Then we'd laid breakfast trays and taken those upstairs. 'Twas hard on a body's knees, I can tell you, traipsing up and down those steep narrow stairways.

So, with the steady rattle and jolt of the chaise, my own eyes now began to droop, but I jerked myself into wakefulness. John Begg, if 'twas he that rode – now before, now beside and now behind the chaise – should not see me napping! The heavy-set coachman sat up before us, unmoving except to flick at the reins, never glancing back. We, his passengers, might have been so many parcels or bundles of letters. I noted, however, that he'd a pistol laid easy to his hand, on the box beside him.

'Twas July now, and in the south facing meadows lines of men were raking the last of the cut hay. Sheep cropped on the rolling hills. Herds of fat kine followed one another slowly down to a broad, free flowing river. This district, Mistress Buchanan, had informed me on that inward journey so many weeks ago, was Lothian, a fine fertile county. More pleasing to *her* sight, seemingly, than green Antrim. Tending to Miss Evangeline as I then was, I'd barely caught more than a glimpse of it. Now I tried to note everything that came to my eye, comparing it with what I was used to seeing in Ireland. More slated roofs amongst the thatched here. The wayside inns looked cleaner, more prosperous, with many chimneys which told of fires in all the rooms. The cottage children, round-eyed, fingers in their mouths as they watched our swift progress, did they appear to me plumper, rosier of cheek?

'My brother breeds cattle,' Miss Flora suddenly roused herself and spoke. 'You'll see his herd, when we get to South Uist. 'Tis not easy to raise cattle on the machair, and with the gales that blow two thirds of the year!'

'Miss Flora, forgive me? Do we go to your mother's house or your brother's? Are they close by?'

Miss Flora laughed aloud. 'Close by? No, not at all. Angus farms at Milton on the southern-most isle of Uist, close by the village of Askernish. 'Tis my family home, the place where I was born. After my father died my mother re-married and lives on the isle of Skye with her second brood of chicks. I spread my time between both houses! Angus is courting a girl from North Uist, but they'll not be wed for a wee awhile yet, so I keep house for him when he needs me, and help with the weaving and the dairying. When we've settled weather I get some of the fishermen to take me over to Skye to help my mother – when she'd a new babe in former years – but nowadays if she wants a hand with the weaving, or laying down preserves against the winter.'

'So, which one do we now go to, Miss?' said I, bemused.

'Why, that will all depend on the weather! And what boat passage we can hire, and where the boat is bound. The Minch, the body of water twixt the mainland and the outer isles, can be rough at any season of the year. If we can find a sea captain who's willing to sail down the Clyde, around the Mull of Kintyre, and on up the coast as far as Skye, we might go there. Or he might leave us on Kintyre – where we can beg a bed for a night or two on the farm at Largie, where my cousins bide – Jane and Ewan, who are fixed just now at Dunbar while his leg heals. I don't doubt his mother will be glad to have news of them. Then 'tis two day's sailing, or maybe three, in a fishing boat o're the waters to Uist. We'll find shelter, and a welcome, Betty, from some of my kinsfolk, wherever we make landfall!' she added, smiling at my bemusement.

I couldn't say I'd not been warned. Almost the first thing I'd been told of, in the kitchen of the house in Canongate, was Miss Flora's "wild island ways." Now, as it seemed, they were to be my ways, too.

Chapter 9

Blow the Wind Southerly

I can tell you little of Glasgow, for I hardly saw that town. Our chaise (will you mark how I'm saying *our* chaise, as though 'twas a lady I'd become?) took us straightway to the militia barracks where Miss Flora handed over the packet of letters that the Colonel had given her, and then we were away agin to a tall house, not unlike Mistress Dalgleish's. This, Miss Flora told me, was where Major Henderson and his wife resided, and here we were to spend the night. Mistress Henderson was a young woman with a brood of childer, and another about to burst forth into the world at any minute, by the looks o' things. Poor woman, she was distracted enough by her bairns, and could barely walk about for the latest one bowing' her back, but she had her servant – she'd only the one, a lame old woman – give us bread and cheese and thin beer, and set up a truckle bed for me to sleep on at the foot of one provided for Miss Flora. The Major, it seemed, remained at the barracks, "on guard", for fear this Stuart Prince should come sailing up the Clyde at the dead of night whilst the whole town was snoring.

'Poor soul!' whispered Miss Flora, 'we're the last thing Mistress Henderson needs. I suppose my cousin gave the order that the Major should house us, and he in turn passed on the order to his wife. I think we should retire early to get out from under her feet and save her candles. I doubt she'll think it odd, as very likely we'll be departing at first light. Sergeant Begg has gone down to the harbour to find us a passage.'

Begg. So *'twas* he who had escorted us thus far. And verra like, I thought, he'll be choosing a boat that will sink once 'tis out of sight o' the land!

However, he did not, and for the simple reason that he came with us. 'I've ma orders frae the Colonel,' he informed Miss Flora as we stood on the deck of a trim sloop, 'tae see ye safe tae yer brother's door at Milton.'

'Twas a cloudy day and a brisk breeze bellied the sails and pushed us speedily out of the river's mouth into the wide firth.

'The captain is willing to sail the Minch?' Miss Flora enquired of him. She sounded surprised.

'Nae, that he is not! He'll tak us tae Campbeltoon on Kintyre, and frae there I'll hire a cart tae take ye tae to this hoose o' Largie. This is where yer kinfolks are biding?' he replied.

Miss Flora agreed that it was. 'Cousins. It was my grandmother's home,' she said, 'although she lived and died on Uist, having married my grandfather, the Reverend Ranald Macdonald. He was a Presbyterian Minister, who'd a grand mission to convert the Catholic heathen in South Uist.'

'And did he so, Miss?' the soldier enquired, interested.

'He did not, though 'twas not for the want of trying!' she answered, laughing. 'I barely remember him, I was only a wee girl when he died. He was a giant of a fellow with a great loud voice like unto the wrath of God, so that folk said his Sabbath day sermons could likely be heard in *North* Uist. But there he would be preaching to the converted, for they were all Presbyterians already!

'And are ye no nervous, Miss, tae live amang these folk, with all this talk of the Catholic Prince coming tae raise the clans agin?'

I felt 'twas discourteous of John Begg to be quizzing my mistress so. Who was he but a common soldier? It angered me and I let him see it, but she seemed untroubled by it.

'No, I shall be amongst my *ain* folk as they say, my kinfolk,' she said. 'Protestant and Catholic, both. We live and let live on the Long Island, and there are Scots of all persuasions, are there not, who think a Stuart King might do more for Scotland than the House of Hanover?'

John Begg said nought to this, though I fancied her reply did not please him. He excused himself and went and stood in the prow of the ship, watching the spray begin to drench the deck as the wind increased and the waves rose and fell beneath our vessel. I'll not deny that my stomach began to rise and fall with them.

'Are you a good sailor, Betty?' Miss Flora asked, as the deck began to heave beneath our feet.

'I *had* thought so, Miss!' I replied.

Coming from Ireland on the packet boat, as I now realised, the sea had been almost flat calm. Never having been to sea before I'd not realised that to be a mite unusual. 'I'm more afraid to be blown overboard, Miss, in this hurly-burly wind!'

We went and sat on two empty whisky barrels in the lea of the deckhouse, and although my stomach roiled and my head felt tight and heavy, 'twas no more than discomfort. Miss Flora, however, was an excellent sailor, and soon tired of this, and went and leaned on the rail looking out to see the land on either side of us. From time to time she called out to me the names of the islands that were situated in this great sea inlet. These, however, were not *her* islands. The Firth of Clyde, she called it. 'Bute, Cumbrae, Arran, Holy Island!' she'd call out above the rising wind, and then she'd stroll back to me to ask how I did.

'The Minch can be a deal worse than this,' she said, a deal too full of cheer for my liking, 'but we're to take a fishing boat from the shore by Largie, so we'll hold out for fine weather for your stomach's sake! My brother will be pleased to have me home, but since he's no reason to expect me so soon, he'll not be worrying. Either he's had some fine days, and all the hay crop's dried and carried, or it's been wet and it's all spoiled.'

By the time our ship hove into Campbeltown loch, the clouds had thickened and the rain had set in. 'Twas a small wee place, so far as I could tell, to be calling itself a town, but John Begg found a carter on the quay waiting on custom, and had my mistress, myself and our luggage aboard and away before I'd any time to look about me. The carter produced a piece of tarpaulin as a shield from the rain, and Miss Flora and I took turns to hold it over our heads against the downpour.

By the time we reached the house at Largie, our arms ached

from holding them above us and the hems of our skirts were soaked to our knees. How right Miss Flora had been to coax a pair of thick boots out of that woman in the clothes shop. My feet within them were as dry as the inside of a hayloft! 'Twas a luxury for me, a girl who'd gone barefoot until I was twelve years of age, and earned myself enough at the flax scraping to buy me a pair wi' only a few thin places in the soles. My eyes filled up for a moment at the thought of Miss Flora's kindness, but I swiped the water away with the back o' my hand before she'd ask me what the matter was.

Old Mistress Macdonald in her neat white farmhouse on the estate of Largie, that was the mother of this Ewan, was more put about to discover how he and his bride had left Flora alone in Edinburgh, than she was to hear of his broken leg. We were seven days in that place until the rain and wind died down. I mended a flounce on one of Miss Flora's gowns, and darned some sheets for Mistress Macdonald, whose old eyes were troubling her.

Miss Flora finished knotting a fringe, and showed the young maidservant there how to make griddlecakes, all the while listening to Mistress Macdonald whilst she told tales of Flora's grandmother and a parcel of other relatives whose names, as was natural, were unknown to me. Then, when at last the rain lifted, Miss Flora walked down the track to the shore, and spoke coaxingly to one of the fishermen, that he and his sons should take us north o'er the water to the island of Uist.

I was with her, but I cannot say how she did it, for they spoke Gaelic – 'twas the first time I'd heard her do so – and to begin with it seemed to me he was verra disinclined. Later she told me the reason.

' 'Tis not the journey over,' she said, 'he believes tomorrow will be fine and calm, but he says 'twill not last, and the next day strong easterly winds will be against him We'll need to make harbour in one of the smaller islands of the Inner Hebrides. Once we've arrived on Uist, he could be stuck there a week or more before he could return to Kintyre. I told him he could catch as many fish off the outer isles as he can from here, but he said what use was that to him? They would all be rotten and stinking before he got home!'

I was wondering the while, where now was John Begg? Since we left the harbour at Campbeltown we'd seen neither hide nor hair o' him. Had he reneged on his intention, on what he'd said were his orders, to deliver Miss Flora to her brother's door? I didn't ask Miss Flora about him. I was sure he didn't trust either of us, myself in particular, and he made me verra uneasy. If he was gone, back to Edinburgh, then I was glad of it. Or so I told myself.

We set forth before first light the next day. All the talk, such as there was, was in Gaelic as we made the crossing, so I know little or nought of what was said. Though the sea was calm and blue under a pale clear sky once the sun rose, 'twas a small boat, and rode low in the water. Thus the waves slopped over onto our feet, and the hems of our gowns were wet through once agin. There was nought on which passengers could be seated except to squat in the bow on a pile of coiled ropes – which was better than the pile of stinking fishing nets in the stern. Miss Flora seemed quite at her ease, and I strove to appear so too. For most of that long day there was no wind to make it worthwhile to hoist a sail, so the fisherman's four sons and a nephew took turns at the oars and rowed. And whilst they rowed, they sang. And Miss Flora sang with them!

They were Gaelic songs, rowing songs to help the sailors keep their strokes in time. Some of the tunes were familiar to me however, and whilst I'd little idea o' the meaning, my ear soon learned the choruses. So I sang too, and oh, how finely our voices blended. How sweet and silvery was the sound as we skimmed across the waves, whilst the white seabirds rose and fell, seeming to hang suspended on the air currents above our heads. When the sailors tired in the late afternoon, the wind obligingly rose, the sail was hoisted, and for the latter part of that day we made good speed.

Only, it seemed, as far as the island of Mull. No matter how hard the sturdy fishermen rowed, or the sail carried us skimming across the wave tops, Flora told me, the distance to South Uist was too much to achieve in one day. Or even two, as it turned out. Flora and I slept on straw mattresses at an inn on the tip of Mull, and then the next night in box beds with an old woman Flora said was a distant kinswomen of hers, on the isle of Coll. Where the fishermen slept I niver heard, but they made no complaint. They'd caught a number of fish that day just by casting a line from the boat. We ate them at the old woman's croft, and the weather stayed fair.

'Twas a journey of happiness and good fortune, only one small cloud marred it. As we approached the islands – for Uist is like a kite with a tail of smaller islands trailing below it. Miss Flora named some of them for me, Vatersay, Mingulay, Barra, Eriskay. The fisher laddies paused their singing to shade their eyes and stare after a tall ship on the southern horizon. She was moving away from us, slow and steady, her sails half-furled.

'French? Can you be sure?' Miss Flora asked them. They told her they believed so.

'A French brigantine,' she explained to me. 'I wonder what *she* may be doing in these waters?'

It seemed she was not the first French ship they'd noted. In these last few months they told her they'd seen several.

'Are they smugglers? Traders of some kind?'

'Nae, lass, spying, seeking out good places to make a landing,' she discovered from the old fisherman. 'Looking where yon Stuart laddie might bring his army ashore!'

'I suppose it could be so,' she said later. This news had made her uneasy. 'The old Stuart Prince, this Prince Charles' father, landed at Peterhead in Aberdeenshire in 1715, but now all the East coast ports, my cousin James told me, are heavily patrolled. Blockades are ready to be put in place if they're needed. The Prince may believe his most loyal friends are here in the West, making ready for him. Though…I don't know… I believe he may suffer a mighty disappointment.'

Chapter 10

Now Haying Is Over...

The old farmhouse at Milton, how shall I tell of it? 'Twas a low, squat, stone building agin a low rise, hunkered down against the storms. 'Twas thatched with heather, so that the windows peered out like eyes set beneath heavy brows. These gave it a disapproving air that reminded me of Mistress Afton! All the rooms had floors of packed dirt, just as Agnes Morrison had predicted, save the kitchen and the parlour which were flagged with stone. But you must not be thinking 'twas a poor place, not at all. They'd tall chimneys that drew the smoke from the rooms, and on the parlour floor they'd rich rugs made, Miss Flora told me, in far off Persia. They'd grand furniture too, of polished oak, carved and worked, and every bit as fine, and better cared for than ony I'd seen in Canongate, or even Ballymore. One of the sideboards, agin Miss Flora informed me, was inlaid with mother-of-pearl, and came from Paris! In the parlour, too, was her own beloved spinet, together with her sheet music, and her spinning wheel, and from the beams above hung a beautiful six-branched silver candelabra.

And the beds! Oak testers with the coat of arms of the Macdonalds of Clanranald carved on the headboards for Flora and her brother and any guests they might have, and goose feather mattresses to lie upon, even on the box beds for the maids! Oh, but I niver had a more comfortable sleep than I did at Milton, even when the Atlantic storms came battering at the doors and windows.

Miss Flora's brother, Angus, was away from home when we arrived. 'Twas evening, but in July the days there were still long. The maids told us there'd been a grand spell of fine weather. The hay was all in, the cattle were away grazing the summer grass up in the eastern hills. Angus had taken the chance to go courting his betrothed, Miss Penelope Macdonald, who lived in the North of the Long Island. It seemed everyone here in the islands was a

Macdonald, or even if their name was something other, then they were still cousins in some greater or lesser degree. 'Twas mightily confusing. So many were known by some "nickname", usually a Gaelic one. I niver did fathom them all.

I should tell about this island of Uist, how 'twas, so you can picture it in your mind's eye. 'Twas a bare place, the hills rising only in the east, and hardly a tree to be seen except in the sheltered glens to the east, though there were wild flowers of every colour. Above all arched the sky, and the clouds, ever changing with each breeze. Uist came in three parts, almost three separate islands, except when the water was low you could walk across the fine white sands from one to another easy, if you judged the tides aright. Walking north through South Uist, where we were situated, close to the wee village of Askernish, then came Benbecula, on which lived the Clan Chieftain, Lord Clanranald and his wife, whom everyone called Lady Clan, at a place called Nunton. Miss Flora told me the Clanranalds had once owned a castle, the name of which was Ormiclate, but it had burned down, and so they were fixed at Nunton. (I'll be telling more of the Clanranalds later.) Then came North Uist, where it was said they were all Presbyterians, and amongst whom lived Miss Penelope and her family. I cannot tell you any more about North Uist, for I niver went there.

When we stepped in the door, Miss Flora calling out, thinking Angus would be there, we found only the two young maids, Màiri and Elsbet, seated at the kitchen table cleaning silver candlesticks with rags, just as Jessie and I had cleaned the knives and spoons back in Edinburgh, except Jessie and I made a much better job of it, I can tell you!

Up they jumped, with cries of surprise and greeting I suppose, as it seemed they spoke little but the Gaelic, and Miss Flora greeted them in return, and explained who I was.

'Now, you two will need to be practising your English,' she told them, for Betty here is from Belfast in Ireland, and has only a few words of Erse. And you're to pay good mind to what she tells you.

Betty is my personal maid and has worked in fine houses in Edinburgh and County Antrim in Ulster. She's a rare hand at the spinning, both the distaff and the wheel, and I want you to learn from her.' She picked up one of the candlesticks and shook her head over it. 'She'll show you a better way to clean these too. These would never pass muster with Mistress Afton, my Aunt Effie's cook-housekeeper in Edinburgh, now would they, Betty?'

'That they would not,' I replied, attempting to smile in a friendly fashion, 'but I'll show you how to do it.'

I cannot say Elsbet and Màiri looked delighted at this news. I was soon to learn they were a pair of lazy creatures, good natured most times, and biddable sometimes, but nowhere near as sharp and quick as young Jessie, though they were fourteen and fifteen years old to her twelve.

Straightway then, since we'd eaten very little since we left Kintyre, and Miss Flora had also promised victuals to the old fisherman and his relatives, she sent Elsbet to fetch Bridie. Bridie was an older woman who came and cooked and kept house for Angus when Flora was away, though she'd a house and bairns of her own close by. Angus having gone away to the North island she, naturally enough, had taken the chance to spend some time in her own home about her own affairs. The two young maids she'd left to do the milking of the house cow, the feeding of the hens and the goats, and between times, to be sure and clean the silver.

On hearing from Elsbet that Miss Flora was come of a sudden, with her new maid from Edinburgh and a parcel of fishermen expecting to be fed, this Bridie came running as though the Devil was after her. We saw her from afar, stumbling over the tussocky grass with her apron flapping loose and her coil of hair coming unpinned and tumbling down her back. By the time she reached us she was too breathless to speak, but Miss Flora spoke soothingly to her in Gaelic, and she calmed herself, re-tied her apron, and began to order the young maids to bring out bread and butter and a cured ham from the larder, and draw some porter from the barrel for the fishermen.

In the end, we'd a fine meal set out at the long table in the kitchen, and we called the men in to it. We all sat down together to eat, Miss Flora too, although Bridie tried to persuade her to take hers in the parlour.

So, we were merry together, men and maids and the lady of the house, which was Miss Flora Macdonald, when her brother came riding into the yard on a tall bay horse.

He wasn't a big fella, Angus Macdonald of Milton, taller than his sister, but not by many inches, and at my first sight of him, I thought he looked worrited – and perhaps not a little annoyed to find his kitchen full of strange folk eating up his provisions.

Flora jumped up straightway to greet him, happy to be seeing her brother once agin, and began to tell him how it came about that these fishermen had brought us o'er the water from Kintyre, but 'twas clear he wasn't of a mind to listen, and he drew her aside and spoke quietly. What he said caused the bright smile to fade from her face.

Bridie must have known the signs – a man hungry and troubled, and like to be vexed – and she rose from her place and loaded a plate and took it through to the parlour, where Miss Flora followed him, and straightway closed the door on our interested faces.

At the table the talk between the fishermen and the maidservants flowed on, hazarding, I don't doubt, on what Flora's brother might be saying to her, what news he'd brought. But now the talk 'twas all in Gaelic, and there was no Miss Flora to insist on English so that I might be part of it. I knew from Màiri and Elsbet's sly glances that they spoke of me too, and probably not in a kindly fashion. I was a foreigner, a stranger, and they didn't want me there. 'Twas a lonesome feeling. At Ballymore too, I'd been made to feel a lesser creature, inferior to those who had been trained up in "service". The servants in that house looked down their noses at me, the rough girl with the strong arms and an ugly Belfast twang to her speech. Miss Evangeline, however, had never minded how I spoke, and had always dealt kindly with me, even when she was half crazed with the pain she was in.

These people of South Uist had a beautiful soft way of speaking, pleasant on the ear, even though I couldn't understand them. We didn't speak the Erse in Belfast, or a few words only. Would I be able to learn it? I hadn't realised when I said so blithely to Miss Flora that I would come with her to the islands, how lost and lonesome I might feel amongst these strangers.

What Angus and Flora said together that evening, brother and sister, only I was to know straightway, because afterwards Miss Flora told me.

'You're to be my confidante, Betty!' she said, much later, when the fisher folk were gone to bed down in the barn (the old man having decided, against all the gloomy pronouncements he'd made when we left Kintyre, that the wind had veered just enough to see them safe at least as far as the isle of Coll next day, if they left before it grew light). Bridie was gone to her man and her bairns, and the two young maids had been set to wash the dishes. Angus left us to see to his horse and attend to the livestock. We settled ourselves in the parlour. Miss Flora seemed to find it only natural that I should sit there along with her.

'Angus will not have me share the news with the maids and the farmhands unless we must, for 'twill stir them up prodigiously, and there'll be no dealing with them.' She spoke in low voice. 'They're excitable folk. My brother and I always speak English together so that we can be private, but you're bound to overhear our talk, so I might as well tell you.'

'I'll keep a still tongue, Miss Flora,' I assured her, taking up the stocking I had vowed to mend for her nearly two weeks ago. Miss Flora bent her head over her shawl and the fringe she had begun attaching whilst we were staying on Kintyre. She seemed to be seeking for her words.

'It appears the Prince is come,' she said, dropping her voice and gazing around to be sure one of the young maids had not crept into the room. 'My brother called at Nunton on his way back from the North Isle, and Lord Clanranald and Lady Clan were up in the boughs with the news. It seems he came ashore on the isle of Eriskay yesterday, and plans to ride across the causeways at low tide to call on them tomorrow evening.'

'That French ship we saw, Miss?' the words slipped from my mouth.

'Almost certainly, Betty. The *Du Teillay*, she's called. Prince Charles Edward and his henchmen came ashore from her on Eriskay. What we saw must have been her making way in case the Militia men that patrol the sea lanes caught sight of her. The sea bed there on Eriskay drops steeply and the bay is sheltered, so the ship managed to get close enough for them to wade to land. They're staying there with Angus Macdonald – not my brother! A kinsman who's tacksman there – I mean who farms there – but the poor wee man is terrified the Militia will hear of it, and his house is not to the Prince's liking, being apt to fill up with smoke from the cooking fire. It's is a black house and has no chimney. So tomorrow night, when 'tis dark, they plan to ride across the causeway here and on up to Benbecula and Nunton.'

I found my breath suddenly tight in my chest, 'With… *with an army*?' I managed to ask.

'No, only a handful of men who have come across with him from France. I don't know how many, perhaps six or seven my brother has heard. It seems *he*, Prince Charles Edward, set out with two ships, but one, the *Elizabeth*, was struck by cannon from a British naval vessel and badly damaged, so she had to turn back for Brittany.'

'But what will he do *here,* Miss Flora?' I was dazed, not sure how much of what I felt was fear and how much bewilderment. I'd not been here a day yet, but already I was realising this was a wild place, and as far as I could see lonely of much human kind. How could this Prince raise an army in such a place?

'Is the French king sending his army following after?'

'So the Prince seems to be hoping. Don't look so worried, Betty! *They'll* not come to Uist. That would make no sense. We islanders couldn't feed and house an army even if we were willing. No, the plan, the *Prince's* plan, is that the Clan Chiefs, here in the Isles and on Skye, will raise an army of clansmen and go over to the mainland to raise more. He hopes to take Edinburgh and then march south, gathering support along the way. He believes the French king will *then* send his troops up through the English counties in the south east and they'll meet together and march on London. The Prince insists that if Scotland supports him, the French King has sworn he will give him men and money.'

'Do you believe that will happen, Miss Flora?'

'It seems most unlikely,' she said, pausing to bite off a thread. 'Angus is furious, "An ill-thought-out plan", he says. My brother has some sympathy for the Prince's claim to the throne, and even believes he might favour Scotland and set laws in train to ease her poverty, but he believes *this* is a wild scheme and doomed to failure. Lord Clanranald is beside himself and has taken to his bed. He's an old man now, and much troubled with gout. 'Tis certain he's in no case to lead the Clan in the field of battle. If his kinsmen want to go with the Prince, so Angus says, he'd probably not forbid it. I'd doubt if he *could*. He supported the Prince's father's campaign, thirty years ago, but he was a young man then, and in good health. He's no stomach for it now. But… 'tis difficult. Can he say "no" to Prince Charles Edward when he supported his father so ardently? And it seems the son is counting on him? Is he to deny the Prince, and turn traitor to the Jacobite cause in his old age? Angus says he thinks to send his brother, Alasdair of Boisdale, tomorrow early, to reason with the Prince. To urge him to abandon the plan, at any rate for the present.'

We sat silent for some minutes, our needlework idle in our laps, absorbing the shock of this news. I found my fingers were trembling a little. You're a fool of a girl, Betty Burke, I was thinking! You need not have come here. You could have stayed in

Edinburgh. But would that have been any safer?

'So what must *we* do, Miss Flora? Are we in danger?' I was remembering of the women at Mr King's gallery, talking of barricading themselves inside their houses. I shuddered at the memory of Gowrie, attacking me as I slept. A band of soldiers might do much worse. I recalled – all unbidden – John Begg, and wondered where he was. Why had he deserted us without a word? Had he heard talk in Campbeltown perhaps, of an invasion coming from the West, and turned back for Edinburgh? These tidings suddenly more important than seeing Miss Flora safe to her home? I thought it must be so, and wished I had not answered him so saucily. The fella had done nothing but poke fun at me, but I'd have felt much safer now, if we had him by.

'Danger? No, I think not, Betty,' Miss Flora was saying. 'No, but Angus wants us to stay at home, close to the farm, and on the morrow invite all our near neighbours to a ceilidh in the evening, so we'll be singing and dancing and making a fine noise… and no one will hear the troop of horsemen ride by on their way to Nunton! Lord Clanranald will see the Prince. He must at least hear him out. That is, if his brother cannot persuade him to abandon the plan altogether.'

'A ceilidh? That's a hooley, as we'd say in Ireland?' I asked her.

Miss Flora burst out laughing, 'A hooley! Is it so? Really? I like that word! Yes, we'll have a ceilidh or a hooley if you prefer, and I'll send word for Alasdair Mor, Bridie's father, to come with his fiddle. We'll have some fine singing. You too, Betty! You have a delightful voice. You shall sing for us, as many Irish songs as you like!'

'But will they come, your neighbours? At such short notice?' I was puzzled where these neighbours must be. So far, I'd seen few dwellings near at hand.

'Fear not, they'll come!' said Miss Flora. ' 'Twill not even strike them as strange. Here am I newly returned from Edinburgh, and longing to tell of what I've seen and done there. And haven't I brought home with me my new maid? They'll be curious to see you,

Betty. A new face! A new voice!'

'I hope they will not be disappointed when they hear my singing,' I said, knowing full well that my face would hardly excite anyone.

'I'm sure they won't,' said Miss Flora Macdonald. 'It is the Prince, I fear, who'll be disappointed when he hears from Alasdair of Boisdale that the Lord Clanranald is not minded to give him money or men.'

Chapter 11

I Met With Captain Farrell

Next morning found me wishing heartily for wee Jessie. I'd slept uneasy, despite the comfort of a feather mattress and a goose down quilt, but on rising I found Miss Flora tying an apron over a plain round gown, already full of plans for the day. The evening's ceilidh was, she'd decided, to be a grand event to celebrate her homecoming. One of the farm laddies was already dispatched on the pony to issue invitations far and wide. She and Bridie would do the cooking, and she was counting on me, she said, to supervise the two young maids, Màiri and Elsbet, in clearing the parlour and rearranging the furniture to make space for the music and dancing.

Bridie, coming in then, heard these orders, and gave me a quick smile and a shake of the head, mebbe for pity that this task should fall to me. It was the first sign I'd had of her that she might have some kindly feelings towards me. Seemingly, dealing with the two young maids had oft times fallen to *her* lot, and now she was more than happy to be relieved of that burden!

I'd never been set in charge of such a thing in my life, but even so I'd a deal more idea than those two giddy colleens! Mistress Buchanan had once, and only the once, during my time at Ballymore, held what she called a *"soirée musicale"*, with a little dancing after supper for the younger guests. My only duty then had been to deliver Miss Evangeline safely to the sofa, bolster her about with rugs and cushions, and take her away in her Bath chair when, as I always expected, she grew weary and pined for her bed. For sure, I'd taken little notice that evening, of how the room was set out. However, it seemed to me obvious that here we must move the table aside, set the chairs around the walls (bringing more chairs from about the house) leaving space in the centre of the room for dancing, and placing Miss Flora's spinet at the end furthest from the door.

Jaysus! I set those two daft lasses to move the table and chairs, and what must they do but raise the chairs up without the slightest care, clashing the legs of them together, and scraping the feet of them down the parlour's fine wooden panelling! Elsbet swung one of them aside as though 'twas a bundle of peat, and came near to causing a graze along the side of Miss Flora's precious spinet! And myself shouting at them to take care! If they understood *ony* English I began to doubt, for the little amount of notice they took. Mebbe it was my Irish way of speech, or mebbe, I decided, they weren't *wishful* to understand me and do better.

How well I then understood Bridie's relief that this charge had passed to me, and how I craved for wee Jessie! I thought of her, working like a little slave in that tall house in Canongate, neat, willing, and particular in all she did. Would that I had her here to show these foolish creatures how to go on. When I set them to roll up the carpet, the one Miss Flora had told me was from far off Persia, that had been a wedding gift and her mother's pride and joy, what must they do but go at it like two giggling eejits in their hurry to be done with it, so that it was rolled all uneven like to nothing but a corkscrew!

Fortunately for them, Bridie came and called them to go outdoors and seek for eggs in the ditches and the tussocky grass (the hens being in the habit of laying away) for the feast, otherwise I might have taken up the broom and used it on their backs!

So I was crouched on the stone-flagged floor, re-rolling the carpet to make all neat, and place it beneath the table lest the dancers trip on it, when I heard a masculine tread, and a shadow fell across the floor. Thinking it must be brother Angus come to survey my work, I took no notice, until I received a sharp nip to my behind.

Startled by the pain and suddenness of it, I let out a screech, and scrambled angrily to my feet. To find myself face to face with a tall, untidy man in sea boots and a dirty military coat. He'd wild straggling hair beneath a drooping woollen bonnet, a crumpled neck cloth and a limp length of tartan wound about his broad shoulders. I'd never seen him before, but I think I half guessed straightway who he must be. The brigand! He'd only the one eye. The place for the other was just a puckered scar.

'A thousand pardons, lassie!' he said, grinning and sweeping off his bonnet in a deep bow, 'I thought you were Bridie Mor. She's used to my funning. I see I must introduce myself. I'm Hugh Macdonald of Armadale, and you must be my daughter Flora's new maid? Betty? Is that right? From Belfast by way of Edinburgh, the folk out there about the crofts are telling me? No hard feelings, eh?' He chuckled, his one eye twinkling, in no way disconcerted by my angry expression. 'Flora must be about somewhere?'

'I believe she's in the kitchen, Sir,' I said, speaking through clenched teeth. 'She plans to hold a ceilidh this evening. Being just back from Edinburgh,' I added, suddenly aware that I might be revealing too much. Although he *looked* as I'd imagine a brigand or a pirate to appear, his clothes disreputable, his hair a tangled mane, 'twas a poor excuse for a Highland Militia jacket he was wearing, and the dim and faded tartan wound about his shoulders completed the tale. This man was, or claimed to be, a loyal servant of King George the Second, he who was seated on the throne in London. He was a Captain of the Highland Militia, set to patrol the Western Isles! Could it be that he'd heard of the Prince's arrival on this neighbouring island of Eriskay? I felt the skitter of mouse feet run down my spine.

He must have realised that I was staring at his clothes, for he looked down at his coat and breeches, and chuckled. 'Shockingly untidy, ain't I? M'wife despairs o' me, and I've nae doubt I'll be hearing the rough side o' young Flora's tongue! I'm trying to blend in hereabouts, d'yer see? If I go about dressed like those smart military fellas in Edinburgh, not a soul on this island would ever speak tae me, and very likely some fella lying up in the heather would be pleased to take a pot shot at me. Still, I've a decent pair o' breeks and a sound pair o' sea boots, and that's good enough for me!'

My thoughts he must have been able to read as they passed across my face, (I was picturing Colonel Dalgleish and John Begg, the one almost dandified, the other neat and serviceable), for he now said, 'And remember, will ye, that I'm forced tae scramble in and out of dirty fishing boats the day long! Patrolling these islands for His Royal Majesty King George of Hanover is no easy task, lassie! And I'm no sailor! Why else did I serve long years as a mercenary in the armies of the King of France with my feet on dry land, when I could have built myself a neat little craft and gone fishing?'

'To be sure, I wouldn't know, Sir,' I said, since he seemed to expect a reply.

He nodded, perhaps thinking as so many do, what indeed would an ignorant Irish lass like myself know about anything? He sketched a bow and tramped towards the door. Then, turning to look back and seeing me bending to try and lift the rolled carpet, he said, 'Here, lassie, let me give ye a hand wi' that!'

Together we heaved the roll aloft, and deposited it under the table against the wall.

'A fine touch on the keys, Flora has,' he commented, nodding towards the spinet as he dusted off his hands. 'The Clans have been good to her. I'm meaning Lord Clanranald and his lady, ye ken? Very likely ye'll not have had chance to meet them yet? My wife and I, *we* couldn't have given Flora the education she's had, as she fully deserved to have. A bright and clever wee thing always, our Flora.' He sighed. 'Some of my expectations didn't work out as I'd hoped when I left off campaigning in the Low Countries and came home. Marion, that's my wife, always wanted her girl to have the proper education for a young lady, but we could never have managed it, what with the ill-luck I had with an inheritance that should have come to me, *and* our own parcel o' bairns coming along. Lord and Lady Clanranald next to nigh adopted her. Treated her as a daughter! I'm sure 'twas decent of them, and she's made good use of her chances. But how will she find a husband that's a match for her, with all her book learning and her music? You tell me that!'

I held my tongue at this. I was hearing Agnes Morrison's sour words echoing in my head, 'Her family's nae of the best, ye ken?' This Hugh Macdonald must surely be the man, the very same "brigand" who'd carried off Flora's mother, "whilst she was still in leading strings!" Not much of a wonder then, surely, that Colonel James Dalgleish, and the many other likely young bucks Flora might have encountered in Edinburgh would be thinking to look higher for a bride? Whoever would be wanting this wild buccaneer as father-in-law?

'Miss Flora is a fine person, Sir,' I said, after a pause, 'a good person. She was so kind to me when I found myself benighted in Edinburgh after my mistress died, and I was needing to find work. Some young fella will come along, and recognise her worth, surely?'

'You think so, lassie?' he said, watching me with his head on one side, his one bird-bright eye fixed on my face, 'Do you indeed? After an acquaintance lasting how long? Less than three weeks? I hope you may be right. 'Twould greatly relieve my dear wife if that proves so. I'd better go and find my paragon of a daughter now, and not hold up your work.' He paused to look around, 'This all has the air of a grand party Flora has put in train for this evening. Good food and some fine music I'm thinking. I'm only sorry I can't stay and trip the measure with you all. *Au Revoir, Mademoiselle* Betty!'

On that, he departed, leaving me mighty puzzled over his final remark. *Au Revoir?* This could hardly be Gaelic? Then I remembered Mistress Buchanan's *soirée musicale*. French! Mistress Buchanan, and Miss Evangeline had taken lessons in the French tongue – Italian too – as girls at their Edinburgh seminary for young ladies, and they liked to let their Irish friends know how well educated they were, speaking a phrase in the French tongue now and agin. '*English* girls don't learn French,' Miss Evangeline had told me, 'because the English and the French have been forever at daggers drawn, but *Scotland* has always thought well of the French.

The *auld alliance*, we call it, ever since the days of Mary Queen of Scots, she that was Queen of France before ever she came to be Queen of Scotland.'

So Flora's disreputable step-father knew French? For sure, so he would. Hadn't he said he'd lived and fought many years in the French army? He must know that country and the language well. How did he marry that up with his service as an officer in the army of King George? How did he keep himself supposedly loyal to the King's Parliament in London, and the Provost in Edinburgh? And that led my mind to further questions. Why had he come here today? Had he heard a rumour of the arrival of Prince Charles Edward Stuart? And if he had, what was he intending to do about it?

Chapter 12

'Twas At The Ceilidh

By eight of the clock that evening the dining parlour at Milton was crammed with folk. I wouldn't have believed there could be so many living on that island, but Miss Flora seemed to be expecting them all. They were old and young, poor… and not so poor.

'There are crofts all about, up and down the island,' she'd said airily, 'and we're well known to be hospitable. Young Calum didn't need to speak to everyone. Once he'd spoken with a few they'd be passing the word on. Indeed, there would have been a party here from Benbecula, but the Chieftain is sick, and later the tide will be wrong for them to cross back over the causeway. Come, Betty, the company are all waiting to meet you!'

Waiting to meet me? 'Twas the first time in my whole life onyone had ever said that. I'd have preferred to slip in quietly and hide myself in the shadowy corner by the grandfather clock, which, unlike most of the human folk present, was a deal taller than I was. They were a small race in the main, these people of Uist.

I was wearing my best gown, the one Miss Flora had bought in the old clothes shop, and had said was suited for "church attendance and walking out," neither of which I'd yet had the occasion to do. I'd a lace cap over my hair which Miss Evangeline had given me. (In the latter days she'd said the band was too tight and it hurt her head even to have such a light thing laid upon her.) Her gift had been a discomfit to me after she died, lest Mistress Buchanan should think I'd stolen it. But I'd sneaked it away inside my sleeve onyway, to remember Miss Evangeline by. My indoor boots I'd scrubbed free of dust with a bunch of heather, much to the amusement of Màiri and Elsbet, who seemed certain that their own bare peat-stained toes were all that was needed for "the dancing."

Seeing as there was no help for it, I tried to still my trembling limbs, took a deep breath and followed Miss Flora into the crowded room and across to the spinet.

She turned to the assembled company and addressed them in Gaelic, bidding them all welcome and thanking them for coming. So I understood, and indeed I was beginning to catch a word of the Gaelic here and there. Belfast folk didn't use the Erse, and for certain 'twas niver encouraged by the ladies at Ballymore, but my mother had known it, and her mother before her, and so perhaps I'd more of it tucked away inside my head than I'd thought. And surely many of the words must be similar? If I could just tune my ear to the way the people here spoke them?

As Flora sat down and began to play, I cast a glance over to Màiri and Elsbet, seated on the floor by one of the windows, cramming their mouths with oatcakes and slices of beef, Angus having brought home a side of it (a gift from his betrothed's family). I was thinking to myself, *You two may sit there smirking, but I've a good ear, and soon I shall have the better of you!*

Flora played two pieces and then sang in a sweet high voice. 'Twas clear to me they all loved her and her singing. Glasses were raised and they called loudly for more, but Flora gestured that my turn was come, and the busy room grew quiet, voices stilled. I took in several deep draughts of air and laced my fingers together before me so that they should not see them trembling. Miss Flora nodded to me, and I nodded back. I was as ready to begin as I ever would be.

I sang 'Gown of Green', I sang, 'The Shady Woods of Truagh', and then Flora called Bridie over to join us, and together we sang 'There Are Three lovely Lasses from Banyon', which we'd half practised together in the kitchen whilst we sliced the cold meats and arranged them on the silver platters. I was easier now, for they were all listening with flattering attention, and my voice was loosened and soaring up, sweet and true. Indeed, wasn't I almost laughing when I sang out the chorus, 'There are three lovely lasses from Banyon, and I am the best of them all!' I knew as well as onyone, *that* could never be true. Miss Flora Macdonald was the best of us all, both in her looks and her person, and everyone there could see it!

'So, *that's* why my sister brought you here,' said Angus Macdonald, speaking close at my shoulder as, singing over for the while, I helped myself to the oatcakes and beef. 'I should have guessed it. Music is what Flora loves above all things. I wondered that she should suddenly decide to employ her own maid. She never felt the need for one before, but to have someone to sing duets with, to teach her new songs, that I understand!'

'Still,' he went on, sounding, I thought, a warning, 'I hope you'll make yourself useful about the place and earn your keep.'

I was wondering how I could answer him, but was saved from the need by Alasdair Mor, Bridie's father, who struck up his fiddle for a jaunty reel. At the first notes and with many a yell, the crofters abandoned their plates and glasses and whirled wives and sweethearts into the dance.

Bridie and her man went spinning by beneath the silver chandelier, and as they passed me she thrust her baby into my arms. The great roar the wee man set up at this rough abandonment was only partly drowned by the fiddle!

'It's sorry I am, wee fella,' I told him, and set him on the table's edge to watch. I'd been surprised to begin with at how many of the crofters had brought their bairns and babes in arms, but it seemed this was the custom. I'd been too long away from my own people, and now I thought back to my grandmother's house, I recalled it had been the custom there too.

Now that he could see his mother and father laughing and dancing together, wee Archie stopped his noise, and all I'd to do was make sure he didn't fall, and try to keep his baby fists out of the platters of food. Of this I was not too successful! Watching the dancers, I'd time to ponder on what Angus Macdonald had said to me. I could see him on the far side of the room, standing watching his sister dancing with a tall, older man in sea boots. Later, when she claimed her little boy again, Bridie told me this was Rhuri Macdonald of Boisdale, 'a man o' substance that owned his own boat,' and so I learned that in this place, surrounded by the ocean on the edge of the world, a girl brought up amongst the gentry class may stand up with a fisherman. Tsk! Tsk! No wonder the Edinburgh ladies had cherished their doubts about Flora!

Her brother, Angus, was a grave looking young fella, perhaps thirty years of age or more, and not above the middle height. He was smartly dressed tonight in a coat of dark superfine and with a snowy linen neck cloth at his throat. I felt he disapproved of me, and had done since the day he came home and found all those visitors eating their heads off in the kitchen, myself perched amongst them. To be sure, he'd the look of a man with many cares on his shoulders. What he'd said to me hinted that money must be one of them. He wasn't pleased that his sister had brought home an extra mouth to be fed, no matter how sweetly she might sing for her supper. Flora had told me he bred cattle on the island's thin sandy soil, and perhaps all was not well with them at this season? Agin, I thought it possible – and anxieties about money might be part of it – that his wooing of Miss Penelope Macdonald in North Uist was proceeding too slowly for his liking? Or perhaps he was just a very serious minded fella? Wasn't he, after all was said and done, the grandson of the "strong minister" the late Reverend Angus Macdonald, who had laboured long and hard, and with small reward, to bring the people of this island to his own notions of the Lord God? A streak of sombre thoughtfulness could be part of the younger Angus's character. Thinking on't, I realised that although Flora had a light-hearted way with her, no one could say (barring mebbe the jealous tongue of Agnes Morrison) that she was frolicsome.

Ach, how could I be forgetting? The Prince! Angus himself had brought word of his arrival on this chain of small islands. He and his followers could be riding by this house at this moment, even as the scrape of the fiddle and the yells of the dancers hid the sound of hoof beats. When Alasdair Mor paused in his playing just then to take a dram, I found myself straining to hear them. No such sound reached me, though the July night was as warm as perhaps the nights ever were in these northern islands. The doors and casements were all thrown open to the breeze from the sea, but beyond the lighted rooms of Milton, all was silent except the gentle wash of the waves upon the nearby shore.

'Don't look so anxious, Betty!' Flora, her cheeks flushed from the dance, now appeared at my side, 'You're a stranger here, and folk will look warily on you until they get to know you, but now they've heard you sing they'll soon be taking you to their hearts. Come, why don't you dance with Rhuri here? He's a fine dancer and good patient teacher. He'll be happy to show a newcomer our steps, won't you Rhuri?'

'That I will, Miss Flora.'

Whether he was happy or no, the tall fisherman was patient and polite. Of course I knew he'd no wish to dance with me, but I suspected that for Flora Macdonald he would do anything she asked. A year on, I was to discover what this loyalty would cost him, but on that warm summer night at Milton he undertook to teach a clumsy maidservant the steps of a reel.

'Tis certain *I* shall never be praised for my dancing! Even when my head has learned the steps, my feet are slow to follow its commands. But when the dance ended he thanked me gravely, and said only, 'That's a fine voice you have, mistress, will you be entertaining us once more this night?'

I answered then that I didn't know but would do so if Miss Flora wished it.

'That I'm right certain she will,' he replied, and sure enough, when the dancers tired and old Alasdair Mor laid down his fiddle, complaining that his arm ached with bowing and his throat was parched, Flora called me again to the spinet.

She sang two Gaelic airs, and I sang 'My Lagan Love' and 'The Green Hills of Antrim', and they applauded me warmly. But not so warmly as they did Miss Flora. She was the first lady of this place, and they loved her. Loud were the cheers when one of the young farmhands, Calum, he who'd been sent out to issue the invitations to the ceilidh, stepped forward face aflame, to present her with a white rose. Miss Flora smiled and thanked him, and pinned it to the bodice of her gown.

That rose, the white rose, was the emblem of the Jacobites. I didn't know it then. Calum must have plucked it in the small flower patch before Milton's front door. Perhaps he knew what it meant. Perhaps she did too, but she chose to take it as an innocent gift of thanks from the assembled company, and accepted it with a grave curtsey and a smile.

Chapter 13

The Water is Wide

In times past, I recall an old fella (a neighbour of my grandmother's he must have been) speaking of his days at sea. This old man had sailed many voyages to foreign lands and had as many tales as voyages to tell, as he sat in Gran's cabin with a jug of her home-brewed liquor at his elbow. I'd not thought of Michael Jury for many a long year, but I brought him to mind next day as I walked amongst the dunes and along the clean white sands below Milton. In the far southern oceans, so he'd told us, amongst the islands of Greece, the sea is not grey, nor even the blue of the sky above, but takes on the hues of emeralds and sapphires. 'Emeralds and sapphires, changing, ever changing, the one to the other!' he'd declare, 'and mebbe even a hint of rubies in there, as the water curls amongst the rocks.'

What perhaps he never knew, never saw on his voyages, was the sea on a fine summer day around the Outer Hebrides? Since our arrival on South Uist, we'd hit a spell of fine sunny weather. (Flora joked it was to welcome me, but warned I must not count on its lasting), and today as I paced slowly back and forth along the shore, those emeralds and sapphires washed over my bare feet, each wavelet as cold and glittering as a jewel.

I'd hitched my skirt hem and petticoat up through my apron strings so that they were clear of the water. My boots and stockings were perched above the tideline, amongst the limpets and cockleshells left there by the winter storms. With the shaft of my distaff tucked beneath my left arm, the thumb and forefinger of my right hand teasing out the wool fibres, and my spindle slowly revolving from my little finger below, I was walking back and forth in the shallows, spinning.

Màiri and Elsbet, seated atop one of the dunes, their skirts up to their thighs and their bare legs coated in sand, watched me bemused.

'But why would ye be walking in the water when ye could sit you down upon a chair and use the wheel like Miss Flora does?' Elsbet demanded. (I had begun to suspect she knew English well enough when she needed it.)

'Because I cannot drag a spinning wheel down to the shore,' I told her. 'The wheel is a quicker way to make your yarn, true enough, and on a cold wet day 'tis only sensible to sit indoors and use it. Today, *as she told you*, Miss Flora is minded to turn out the parlour top to bottom after last night's ceilidh, and wash the curtains and the bed hangings while she's about it. So she wanted us out of the house. 'Tis a fine day for drying, and she's Bridie to help her.'

'Bridie must help her, but not you, Betty? Are ye too grand to be doing washing and scrubbing?' Elsbet challenged me. 'They're saying Miss Flora's maid will have proud Edinburgh ways.' At this I nearly burst out laughing. Proud Edinburgh ways! Is it myself?

Flora had told me the history of these two sisters whilst we ate our oatmeal, first thing that morn. They were orphans, she'd explained, and lived with their grandmother in one of the black houses along the shore, close by, but hidden from view just now, in a dip in the land.

'Angus and I felt we should do something for them,' she'd told me. 'The grandmother is old, too old to have charge of them, her mind grows cloudy. Since their mother died with her last child, and their father was lost at sea, they've no one. No one wanted them, for they're too weakly and slow witted to be useful on a croft. There's an uncle or a cousin at Frobost, another settlement on South Uist, you'll soon understand that here it's quite possible he is both, the clan is so inter-married! *He* would take the girls, but his reputation is not savoury. I'm afraid he would make them the object of his lechery, and they're too foolish to resist. Elsbet is perhaps brighter than her sister, but Màiri… poor child, you'll notice she's a deformity of her lip? She was born with a split to the roof of her mouth, so it's almost impossible to understand what she says.'

She sighed and shrugged. 'I *try* to be patient with them, Betty. Believe me, I know how maddening they can be! Poor Bridie has been mithered to death with them all the while I've been away, and she and I really *long* to bottom out the parlour and wash all the curtains whilst this rare fine spell of weather lasts! So *please* will you take them away from the house and teach them to spin... or gather seaweed to spread on the machair, or *anything* at all you care to do with them!'

I'd brought them down to the sandy edges of the machair above the shore, away from the house, and set them to "card" by which, for those of you that niver worked with wool, is meant "comb out a fleece with wire-toothed carding paddles." This they were to do whilst I demonstrated the use of distaff and spindle. 'Twas a mistake, as I soon discovered, for those two lasses could never take hold of more than one idea at a time. If they took their eyes away from drawing the spiked paddles through the wool to watch what I was doing, they soon jabbed their fingers on the barbs and then I'd to scream at them to stop before they dripped blood on the clean fleece!

So now they sat idle, as I was sure they much preferred to be, skirts rucked up and bare legs dangling, on the edge of the low sandy bluff. And here was Elsbet demanding to know if I was too "Edinburgh proud" to wash and scrub!

'I'm neither Edinburgh proud or Edinburgh humble,' I told her. I waved my distaff hand out over the glittering ocean. 'I was born in Belfast, just down across the water there, over in Ireland. I can wash and scrub wi' onybody! I can wash fleeces, tease flax, card and spin. I can do the dishes, clean silver, tidy a room, and make up beds. I can take good care of a sick person, keep them clean and comfortable, and find ways to ease their pain...'

'Why would ye do all that rather than earn siller frae the singing?' Elsbet demanded, cutting short this recitation of my talents. 'Folks is always coming here from Ireland by the fishing boats, tinker girls and such like. They go singing and dancing at the inn by the Change House on the shore at Loch Boisdale, and the men that's waiting for the ferry there gives them money. Mebbe they have to give a deal of it to the man is with them,' she added thoughtfully, 'he that plays the fiddle or the bodhrun. Ye've naebody to do that. Ye should find yerself a man!'

'Rhh M'tholth,' mouthed Màiri.'

'She means Rhuri Macdonald!' translated her sister, '*he'd* mebbe take ye, since his wife is deid. He that danced wi' ye last neet at the ceilidh?'

I stood below on the shore looking up at these two minxes, not knowing whether to be angry, or to laugh at their impudence. 'I can see you want to be rid of me! But I'm no dancer and neither am I looking for a man. So you'd best get used to me. Miss Flora wants me to teach you to spin, but that's for another day now. We'll finish the carding.'

They stared at me, round-eyed with puzzlement. Why ever would I not be wanting a husband? Their faces told me that they couldn't imagine anyone making such a choice. How right Miss Flora was to fear these two could be easily led into the clutches of loose living men. I didn't wonder for a moment that she found them so vexing. How often she must regret her kindly impulse in taking them in! What simple tasks *could* they be put to? Even marrying them off to local lads was hardly a likelihood. Elsbet was not a bad looking lassie, were she cleaner in her person and not so idle, but as my poor mother would have said, 'Looks will nae wash the clothes nor cook the dinner!'

I stuffed spindle and distaff into my apron pocket, and scrambled up the place where the bank had crumbled to join them. 'So, first we'll finish the combing of this fleece,' I decided, 'and then, if there is time, you shall both try your hand with the distaff.'

'There'll be no time,' said Elsbet, confidently, 'Look, the sun's high already? Miss Flora and Bridie will be calling us tae eat.'

Màiri mumbled something in happy agreement.

'Two kinds o' meat!' Elsbet evidently understood everything her sister said, 'and Miss Flora will let us hae butter tae our bread! 'Twas a great feast the night, and plenty left over!'

So we sat working at the knots and tangles of the wool, the teeth of one paddle opposing the other, until the combings resembled a downy cloud of palest brown, the pile of fleece from a little Hebridean sheep lifting now and then in the slight summer breeze. I'd to place one leg across the mound, lest it float out over the water and away. Although the girls worked at the pace of a snail, they were silent for once, Elsbet having given over for the while her attempts to rile me.

I'd a moment, now, to gaze out across the emerald and sapphire sea, with its gentle lacelike wave crests, and wonder. To wonder whether the rim of Ireland itself was hidden in the haze just below the horizon? To wonder where the Prince and his companions might be amongst these nearer isles stretching away below us? If they were still there at all? Miss Flora had started to tell me something, how yesterday the man she called Alasdair of Boisdale had taken his boat to meet with them. But what the outcome had been, whether they *had* ridden up to the Chieftain's house on Benbecula last evening, I didn't learn, because Bridie had come into the kitchen at that moment, calling out that she was here, and ready to begin the wash.

Still, I could find no help for it but to wonder, as I tugged my cards through the snags and tangles of the fleece – those little black and brown coated sheep must spend their days ramming themselves through thorn bushes! 'Twas a mighty secret Miss Flora Macdonald had entrusted to me. It made me verra uneasy.

I looked sideways at the two girls, as their combs ceased to move through the wool. And then I heard Bridie calling. They'd sharper ears than mine, those two! Up they jumped, leaving everything where it was, eager to be first at the kitchen table.

Slowly I gathered up the fleece and the combs. It would be a shame if the fleece were to float away on the breeze and be snagged agin on the wind-scoured hawthorns. Thinking to put on my shoes and stockings before I returned to the house, (Trying, mebbe to show myself as a 'lady's maid frae Edinburgh,' as Elsbet supposed?), I weighted the soft cloud of fleece with pebbles and slid down the dune to where I'd left my boots. I was seated on the backshore, ready to stretch one of my stockings over my toes, when a movement in the water caught my eye.

In the sea before me, something was struggling to reach the shore. A seal? The girls had pointed out two of them basking on rocks some distance away when first we came down onto the bluff. I watched, thinking surely a seal would swim smoother, gliding through the water, not straining, rising and sinking, as this one seemed to be?

Then I understood what 'twas I was seeing. A man, swimming, or trying to. Seemingly he'd the use of only one arm, so that he rolled in the water and despite his kicking legs, was making slow progress. I dropped my boots and stockings and picked my way across the shingle. Then I ran across the wet sand to the sea's edge.

'Will ye be holding on there? I'm coming!' I called, cupping my hands to my mouth as I began to wade into the water. 'You're close in to the shallows! Try will your feet touch the bottom, and I'll help ye!'

He must have heard me for he tried to stand, and his feet must have brushed the seabed, but the next wave threw him forward and he disappeared below the surface. Heedless of the growing weight of my wet skirts I waded forward and seized him by the back of his sodden coat.

'Come on, Mister!' I said. 'Try to stand agin, will ye? 'Tis shallow over the sands from here on in. If you can stand, I can get a hold of you around your middle and get you out! You're nearly there. Don't be giving up on me now!'

He attempted to stand, but his legs gave way, and now he was kneeling on the sandy bottom with only one good arm to support him, ready to sink and slide down beneath the waves agin. It's as well I'm strong in the arm! Holding onto the collar of his coat and the belt to his britches, I dragged him upright and forwards onto the beach, where he collapsed and lay gasping on the white sand, like 'twas some great fish I'd caught.

Awhile he lay there panting, and spewing up sea water. Then he rolled onto his good side, opened his eyes, and tried to speak. 'My arm. Fell…over… board. Thought I was…done for…trying tae swim…wi' a broken arm.'

'So I'm after seeing, John Begg,' I said. 'And now what'll we do with ye?'

Chapter 14

Soldier, Soldier

He struggled to sit up, but fell back again. More sea water dribbled from his mouth and he lay there, panting and gasping. I was casting my eyes over his damaged arm.

'If ye'll let me, I could try to push your arm back into its socket?' I said. 'Now I've looked at ye close, I'd say 'tis not broken but only dragged from where it should be. Once before I did it for my brother, Pat. 'Tis painful for the moment, but then it will be good as new. Pat did it falling from a peat cart,' I added, 'he said what I did was torture like the Devil himself devised it, but 'twas fine after, and he swore no doctor could have done it better.'

'She's right, you know,' said a man's voice, and I looked behind me to find Miss Flora's Papa approaching, the soles of his tall sea boots swishing softly through the fine white sand. 'Dislocation, man. Your shoulder's dislocated. You must be the fella they sent from Edinburgh?'

Without waiting on ony reply, he stepped behind John Begg and hauled him into a sitting position. The soldier yelled aloud at this treatment, but I darted forward, seized his shoulder with my one hand, raised his arm in the air with the other, and gave it a mighty shove, so that the head of the bone clicked back into its place. Captain Macdonald laid John Begg down again and stood brushing off the grains of sand on the seat of his britches.

'Splendid work, lassie! He'll come to in a minute and be fine,' he said. 'I haven't seen that done so neatly for many a long year! We'd an old woman, a camp follower, when I was serving with the French army in the Low Countries, could do what you did, and did it for many a casualty. Falling from a horse was the regular cause. I'm pleased to see my daughter knows how to choose a maidservant with a wealth o' talents!'

'You know this man, Sir?' I demanded.

Hugh Macdonald grinned at me, his one eye twinkling, 'I came here to meet him. I suppose you did the same?'

'No, Sir,' I replied, ' 'Twas just now I saw him struggling in the water.'

Why I was reluctant to declare to Miss Flora's step-father that I knew John Begg, I can't tell. Although 'twas true enough I'd had no thought of *meeting* him, on this shore or any other. So it wasn't a lie I was telling. Since he'd arranged our transportation from Campbeltown to the MacDonald farm on Kintyre, I'd seen neither hide nor hair o' John Begg, nor ever expected to. I'd supposed he'd been recalled, having set us on our way, to the garrison in Glasgow, or to Edinburgh itself. But now here he was, soaked to his skin and half drowned into the bargain, on the white sands of South Uist. Hearing my voice, he opened his eyes and sought mine. He said nothing, though he grimaced, but I caught his meaning well enough. He wasn't wishful I should tell Hugh Macdonald that we were old acquaintances.

'I'd best get back to the house,' I said, wringing the seawater out of my sodden skirts, 'Bridie Mor bade us come and eat. The girls ran ahead, but then I saw this fella…'

'That was a fine deed you did here, lass,' said Hugh Macdonald, drawing close to me, and patting my shoulder.

I stepped away from him, quick, thinking next he'd be pinching my behind again.

'I'll take care of him now, being as he's the Highland Militia's responsibility, and I'm their main man in these parts. You run to your bread and meat, lassie. There's a fine spread left over from Flora's ceilidh. She was good enough to grant me a pocketful!'

From his disgraceful military jacket he dragged a hunk of bread and beef and began to tear at it. 'Enough so I can share it with this fellow, and I'll see his clothes are dried out… you run along now, lass!'

I climbed back over the dune, boots in hand, pausing now and then to lay them down and wring at my wet skirts. I glanced back whenever I did so, not entirely easy in my mind. I'd no real reason to distrust Captain Macdonald, save that he was the kind is free with his pinches. I'd no cause to suppose he might do John Begg harm. For that matter, what cause had I to appoint myself John Begg's defender? To be sure, that man could take care of himself! 'Twas none of my business that he'd abandoned Miss Flora and myself, and instead come secretly to this place. Was he come to find where the Prince was hiding? Had he found where he was, and in the finding been attacked by those henchmen that had come with the Prince from France? And been thrown over the rocks or from a boat into the sea?

It was of no use to tease my mind over it. I gave my damp skirts a last squeeze and hurried over the flower-strewn machair up the gentle mound before the house. There was a Gaelic word I knew! 'Tis the same word in Erse, I'd heard my grandmother and her friends use it. This machair, the grazing land, round about the farmhouse of Milton was starred with wild flowers. Daisies, yellow hawksbit, pink clover, lady's smock, and many others I couldn't name, grew here amongst low rocks that poked up through the earth's crust. These outcrops now were covered with bedsheets, table cloths, caps and petticoats, their white folds stirring gently in the soft breeze as they dried. Nearer the house Flora and Bridie had stretched out the heavy scarlet brocade curtains over some larger rocks, and weighed the hems down with sea-washed pebbles. Wash day at Milton, and a grand day for drying!

I glanced back once more before I reached the house. The two men on the shore were hidden from my eyes now by the shelf of land above the shore line. What they might be doing and saying I couldn't guess. The sea was the deep blue-green of peacock's feathers. Seen from this height the waves were rolling gently in over the pale ridged sand to the tide line. Each one broke crisply on the shore with a flourish of white like the starched lace trimming on a fine lady's petticoat.

'Sure, 'tis beautiful!' I said aloud, and puzzled over my own words. It hadn't been given to me in life to be considering was a place or a thing beautiful, or was it not? A working girl such as myself must keep her eyes on her spinning wheel, the bobbin slowly filling as the thread spooled. When the working day was over most times I was too weary, trudging back to the lodging room I'd shared with my mother, to raise my eyes and admire a grand sunset lighting the West, or the stars coming out above. And when, after Ma's death, I took to sick nursing with poor Miss Evangeline, I'd hardly had the time to glance out the window.

I stepped through the kitchen door into the gloom of Milton's kitchen, and when my eyes began to be used to it, saw Flora and her brother, and Màiri and Elsbet seated around the table, well filled plates of food before them. Bridie was seemingly gone to her own place.

'There you are, Betty!' exclaimed Flora, 'I was just about to send Angus to look had you fallen in the sea and drowned!'

I gave the company a grin and grimace. 'Close enough, Miss,' I said, fashioning a tale, as I'd known I would need to. 'I went to fetch my shoes and stockings from below on the shingle and slipped on a piece of bladder wrack into a pool. My skirts are wet and clinging to me. I'd best go and change before I sit down with ye!'

I saw the puzzled frown on Elsbet's face as I passed her by. Mebbe she didn't remember there being any ribbon of seaweed on the shore just below where we'd been sitting? Or mebbe she didn't see why I'd be bothering myself to change a damp gown? 'Tis sure I am *she'd* niver bother, but sit the rest of the day with the wet cloth stretched over her grubby knees. Chances were she'd no other garments onyway. But I had. Miss Flora had set me up just grand in that old clothes shop in Edinburgh.

When I joined them at the table, Flora was speaking to her brother. 'Can you spare the pony tomorrow? I need to go up to Nunton to return the things Lady Clan lent me, and see how she does. She'll want to hear an account of how everything was in

Edinburgh. I'll just bide with her the day, I won't stay over. The tides will be right, going and coming. I'll take Betty with me. Lady Clan will have heard about her, and she'll want to meet her. Bridie says she'll set the girls ironing.'

Angus chewed thoughtfully on a crust, before he spoke, 'Ironing?'

'Yes, Bridie says Màiri does well enough. Elsbet's too hasty and scorches things, but she can fold and help hoist up the curtains.' Màiri wriggled in her seat with pleasure at this lukewarm praise, whilst her sister pulled a sullen face.

'No bother,' Angus agreed. 'I'm thinking of riding Ossian up to the shieling tomorrow, he needs a good gallop. And I'd like to see how Finn and Gilbert are managing with the beasts, so you can take Tibby. Will you want the trap?'

'Yes, please,' said Flora to my great relief. 'Betty doesn't ride.'

'Very well. I'm thinking it may be the last day of fine weather for the while,' he said, helping himself to another slice of beef. 'No doubt the Clanranalds will have news of their own to share.' He raised his eyebrows to her in a meaning fashion as he said this, and I understood he meant news of the Prince. Was he still on the island of Eriskay? Or had he been persuaded that his presence in the islands was not so welcome as he'd hoped?

This set me wondering as I ate, should I now be telling Flora and Angus of my encounter on the sands? That the High Command of the Highland Militia in Edinburgh were looking for the Prince, and had doubtless sent John Begg here to find news of him?

What then of Captain Hugh MacDonald? He'd told me he has the Militia's "main man" in these parts, and he'd spoken as though he had fully expected to meet with John Begg. Yet, somehow I felt he was not entirely to be trusted, that he might be a man who "rode two horses" as they say. What did Angus feel about his step-father? I'd the notion that although Flora seemed to tolerate the older man with easy affection, her brother's feelings about him might be less warm. I chose to keep a hold on my tongue. At least until I could speak to her alone.

Later in the evening of that day, the sun still riding in the Hebridean summer sky, we gathered in the washing and rough folded it in baskets, ready for the ironing Bridie and Màiri were to tackle next day. Elsbet had made herself scarce, offended it seemed, that she wasn't to be trusted with the smoothing irons, but Màiri, encouraged by Bridie's scant praise, came and helped. I wondered then, if Màiri was perhaps more capable than she at first seemed. If she could be coaxed and praised to do more? Unable to speak clearly, and always relying on Elsbet to speak for her, 'twas natural enough that she followed her sister's contrary ways.

As we gathered up the baskets, she made a sudden long, low warbling sound in her throat, strange and beautiful to the ear in the quiet evening air, under a sky soft with pearly pinks and blues like inside of a shell. I stared at her in astonishment, but Flora, who had been doing her share alongside we maids, laughed aloud.

'*Mouth Music*, Màiri? Are you looking forward to the waulking? There won't be any for a good while yet.'

I had no notion what they were talking about, but afterwards Flora explained that there was a special kind of singing that the islanders used to accompany the finishing of the woollen fabric they wove, the tweed.

'Once it's taken down from the loom it's washed to remove rough fibres and the surplus dye. Then it has to be squeezed and stretched to create the felting which makes it waterproof and durable. We call that process waulking,' she said. 'The tweed is laid on a flat surface, and then a team of people take hold the edges of the cloth and pull together – and so that we all *do* pull at the same time, just as a crew of fishermen must when they're rowing, we have a singer to lead us. The words of the song are sung by the leader, and a chorus is repeated again and again by the work team. The words are not especially important, it's the rhythm which keeps everyone working together, pulling on the cloth at the same time.

Mouth Music, *puirt à beul*, we call it.'

'And Màiri can do this? Even if the words she sings are not clear?'

Flora looked doubtful. 'Perhaps. She's never done so before, to my knowledge.'

But perhaps she *could*, I thought. The cleft in the roof of her mouth meant she'd never speak clearly. There had been a child in our Belfast street similarly afflicted. But probably there was nothing wrong with Màiri's throat. I vowed I'd find out. If nought else, she might teach me this mysterious Mouth Music.

Chapter 15

I Thank Thee, Lady Fair

Bouncing along over rough ways in a pony trap is not something I've a taste for, although I'd done it many times with my brother, Pat. Ach, poor Pat! I'm still wondering each day what became of him? From a boy of twelve, Pat worked as a carter, at first for another man, until he saved enough to buy a nag and a rough-made cart of his own. Most days, he drove his cart to the loading dock at Carrickfergus. He'd work for onyone that wanted to send stuff down to the ships, and he'd bring back loads and packages on the same terms. Old Molly, his horse, would trudge the road to Carrickfergus harbour, with Pat at ease with the reins in his hand, and oft times myself seated up beside him. I'm built strong for a woman, as I've mentioned before, and I was a good help to Pat if we'd a load of heavy sacks to shift. Then when Ma first began to be sick, we needed the money I got from regular work at the spinning, so I couldn't be spared.

Pat went on his own, he didn't mind. He said speed wasn't important. His customers knew he would deliver their load, sooner or later. And so it went on, until one day Pat didn't come back.

They found Molly with the empty cart, her bridle tied to a ring in the harbour wall, but there was no sign of Pat. Folk said mebbe he was inveigled into the tavern for a drink, had one too many and was somewhere sleeping it off. That wasn't like Pat, and the landlord of the tavern swore he'd niver set eyes on him that day. Pat wasn't one fer the strong drink. He'd liked to sit on the harbour wall and name the types of ships that were there, the big heavy-loaded merchantmen, the frigates, the sloops and the brigantines.

It seemed he was vanished away, nor have any of us who knew him set eyes on him from that day on. The fella he was delivering packages of fine linens for, kicked up a great hullabaloo, saying someone must have cut Pat's throat in order to steal the goods, but this didn't prove to be so. A week later when the packet boat returned from Liverpool, the purser confirmed that Pat had handed over the packages, and they'd been delivered safely to the warehouse on the Liverpool shore.

I think, and will always believe, that Pat was pressed. I make myself go on believing it, because I want to fancy it possible that one day I'll see my favourite brother again. Press-ganged men have been known to come home they say. On occasion. All those we asked were agreed there'd been a British Navy Man O' War in the bay around that time, although we never found onyone who could say they'd seen the crew ashore the day Pat disappeared. But that's what Danny and I agree must have happened. It broke Ma' heart, so it did.

I always think of Pat whenever I'm asked to ride in a cart, and as we jogged on our way to Nunton next day, Miss Flora MacDonald at the reins, he was very much in my mind. I just hoped they hadn't treated him too harshly, beaten him with the cat o' nine tails. Pat was such a gentle, easy going boy. I couldn't imagine him firing a cannon or plunging a sword into an enemy that was attacking the ship. However, they have to do what the captain tells them. Or be thrown overboard to drown.

So, to begin with, as we rode along that day, my eyes were turned inward upon my memories, but gradually I became aware of our surroundings; of the soft beauty of the day, of the neat crofts, huddled together oft times so that they might be sheltered from the winds of winter. Of the small lakes or lochans, like puddles of blue sky, each one edged with russet reeds, yellow flag irises, pink campion, and the fluffy white balls of bog cotton. To the east, the land rose up in a line of hills, their slopes patched with rough blanket squares of bracken and purple ling.

'Do you see that croft, Betty? Flora said, pointing. 'That's where Elsbet and Màiri live with their grandmother. You see what a poor place it is?'

It was what the islanders call a black house, since it had no chimney, only a hole in the thatch for the smoke from the cooking fire to escape. You can mebbe picture how the smoke swirls about inside the one room on blustery days? It blackens the walls, the furniture, and even the hands and faces of those that live there. This did not shock me, why would it? Many of the other crofts round about lacked chimneys, and indeed we've plenty like them in Ireland. This one however, was badly neglected compared to others on the edge of the settlement of Askernish. At some time the thatch had caught fire, the wind being contrary, blowing back sparks which set it alight. This had been doused, no doubt by helpful neighbours, but the smoke and water had dribbled down walls that had once been whitewashed. This had flaked away leaving them now grey and streaked with soot. There were no windows. A piece of tarred canvas had been fixed over the large hole in the roof the fire had created, but it was flapping even in this day's gentlest of breezes. In wet weather it would be of little use. A few broken sticks of furniture lay discarded against the side of the house, weeds growing through them. Bedraggled fowls pecked about before the door.

Beside me, Flora sighed. 'Angus says the weather's on the change. Tomorrow or the next day will bring rain. I'll try to speak to the Lord today. Something more must be done for them, poor souls.'

For a moment I thought when she spoke of "the Lord" she meant the Lord God, but then she went on, 'Lord Clanranald is a good man, but he grows old, his health is not robust, and he can be indolent if no one draws his attention to matters. In any case, Old Peg MacDonald, the girls' Grandmother, is a difficult old wifie. Angus has been to her croft any number of times, but although he knocks and shouts through the door that he hasn't come for rent, she'll not let him in!'

I wasn't sure what to say to this, or even if Miss Flora expected me to say anything, so I held my peace. I'd bad memories myself of the knock and the shout at the door. Why else would anyone come knocking, save they wanted money from you? If they came in friendship, wouldn't they just sing out their name and come in? We didn't lock our doors by day, and I couldn't imagine it would be different here.

'It's our Clan system,' Flora went on. 'Angus holds Milton, which he inherited from our father, at the will of the Chieftain. In return he keeps an eye on all the small croft holders round about, collects the land rents, and reports to the Chief if anyone is in difficulties. The Clan demands loyalty, but it also cares for those who've fallen on hard times.'

Because I'd been thinking of Pat, mebbe dragged off to fight wars in lands and on oceans he'd niver heard of, I found myself saying, 'Miss Flora, if the Clan Chieftain orders the menfolk to war, do they have to go?'

'In days gone by, I suppose, yes,' she replied. 'If a rival Clan attacked the Macdonalds, all the men would be expected to defend our traditional lands, but there's much less of that kind of thing nowadays. We are not so uncivilised as to be forever quarrelling over trifles and taking up the claymore and the *sgian dhub* against our neighbours!'

'But this Prince, Miss?' I went on, 'If your Clan Chief decides to support him, will your brother have to join this army he hopes to raise?'

My words startled Flora, and she must have jerked the reins, for the pony shied and the cart jolted wildly in the rutted track.

'No, no! I'm certain Angus wouldn't! He has the farm to run, and anyway, he would stand fast. He says the Prince's notions are foolish, ill-considered. He doubts there is any real appetite for dislodging the Hanoverians from the throne. It's true, he says, that they dealt harshly with Scotland after 1715, but on the other hand some of what they did has turned out to have good uses. The creation of a Highland regiment, as well as quelling outright rebellion, helps keep the peace between what were once warring clans. MacDonald and Campbell are no longer at each other's throats all the time. The roads the English built were intended for the speedy deployment of troops, but anyone may use them, and the movement of goods and travellers through the Great Glen from east to west is much easier. And would a Stuart king do more? Once he had his throne in London, Angus fears he'd forget all about us. It seems Lord Clanranald agrees with him. Angus told me he was quite horrified when he heard the Prince was on Eriskay. I'm hoping we shall hear today that Charles Stuart has thought better of it, and set sail back to France!'

I supposed I must have said more than a maid should, to provoke this outburst, and I fell silent. Flora was silent too, as the pony jogged on over peaty heathland, and then we bowled more smoothly across the sandy causeway that separated South Uist from its sister isle, Benbecula.

It was around noontide when we drove into the stable yard at Nunton. I'd been expecting something grand, a Chieftain's great dwelling, a castle, a fortress set about with a moat and a drawbridge mebbe, but it was just a larger house than Milton, stone built with many chimneys, neat and prosperous, set against the distant bens, and with fields before it, and gardens and dovecots and barns all about. There was a walled garden to one side, sheltered from the winds, and it was there we found Lady Clanranald seated under a cleverly wrought bower adorned with sweet-scented climbing roses. Her daughters were with her and one elderly maid. She'd been working at her embroidery frame whilst one of the girls read aloud from a primer in the jerky tones that children employ for such tasks. Flora had explained to me that she was the Chieftain's fourth wife, so I wasn't surprised to find her not a great deal above thirty years of age, and her daughters young girls of nine and ten.

Lady Clan dropped her needlework, leapt to her feet at Flora's approach, and surged forward, laughing, to embrace her.

'Flora! Dearest Flora, we heard you were back! How delightful! How are you? How was Edinburgh?' She looked at me rather doubtfully 'Is this your new maid? They tell me she sings?' (who could have told her?)

Flora laughed at this outpouring, 'Too many questions all at once, dear Lady Clan! Which should I answer first? Yes, I am well, never better! Yes, this is Betty. *Yes*, she sings beautifully. I found I had need of a maid in Edinburgh, and when it was time for me to return home she kindly agreed to accompany me. Presently I'll explain why that was. Just let me catch my breath!'

'My dear, sit down! I'll send for a dish of tea! Shona, go and bring some, please. Children, take this plate of crumbs and feed them to the doves whilst Flora tells me all her budget of news!'

The children ran off happily to the stone dovecot and the fluttering white doves in the far corner of the garden. The maid, Shona, trudged away with the tray on which a china teapot and a delicate china cup had been placed, and with the bundle which contained the borrowed gown and the pearls tucked beneath her arm. Nobody said what I should do, so I sat myself on the edge of the wooden step which led up to the bower, as much out of the way as I could make myself.

So much out of the way indeed, I could barely hear what Flora and the Chieftain's wife were saying. That was as it should be. I knew a maid should retire modestly and not be seen to be eavesdropping, although naturally I was disappointed! Their voices rose and fell, sometimes I caught a few words, sometimes a sudden great buzzing of the bees, busy amongst the sweet scented roses, meant I heard nothing at all. I soon realised however, that it wasn't a great deal I was missing. Lady Clanranald was an "Edinburgh Lady." Not, I hasten to tell, one of the proud, disagreeable ones, but a lady none-the-less. I could tell from her way of speaking, the way she dressed her hair, the fashionable gauzy dress she wore, her elegant kid slippers, her light tinkling laugh. And of course she wanted to hear all the latest gossip, the "on dits" from the Edinburgh Season. What was everyone wearing this summer? Had Flora met this person or that? Which balls had she attended, which parties? Each of Flora's answers was met with little cries of sympathy or disappointment. *No balls?* Only *one* card party? Only two dinners, and she'd met no one very remarkable at either of them? Fie, for shame! Flora explained about Aunt Effie's infirmities and Ewan's accident. More cries of astonishment and sympathy. Then Shona came with the tea tray, the children came running back to see if there might be more cake, and Flora's recital was interrupted.

We maids were not offered tea or cake, not that I'd expected that we would be. It seemed to me now that Miss Flora MacDonald inhabited two very different worlds. In one she was a close confidante to the Clan Chieftain's wife, modest and ladylike, behaving just as fashionable young women are wont to do. In her other existence she was the sister and housekeeper to a farmer, ready to roll up her sleeves and tackle heavy work, happy to sit at the kitchen table amidst the maids and the farm hands and eat with them when the day's work was done.

Shona, having delivered the refreshments, now came and planted herself down beside me. 'I suppose if *you* may sit, *I* may take the weight off my puir feet,' she announced. She had a look of Agnes Morrison about her, a thin stringy woman with sparse grey locks beneath her starched cap. I thought her expression seemed angry, but it was difficult to tell for her face was much lined, and her soft Highland voice sounded merely plaintive.

Eavesdropping, without making it obvious to everyone that I was doing so, was no longer possible, so I thought I might as well apply butter to this woman. 'Have you worked long for Lady Clanranald?' I asked her.

'Five year. Five year straight, and my feets is killing me,' said Shona.

'But it's a good place you have here? She's pleasant lady to work for?'

'Och, fine enough. They're too soft though! The old fella's past it, grown soft with all her cosseting! Won't stir himself. Should be taking up his claymore and his musket, now this Stuart Prince is come! Call on the clan to rise up! But will he? He will not!'

Now here was a shock for me! Angus Macdonald of Milton had forbidden Flora and myself to say anything to the other servants about the Prince. Yet it seemed the Clanranald retainers knew all about him, and this one at least wanted to rally to his cause.

'And the other servants? Clanranald's men? Do they follow the Prince?'

'Most, they do! So they should! I lost my father and two brothers in the Fifteen. So much good Scots' blood spilled, and we've had nae vengeance!'

Shona, an elderly Jacobite rebel, and a bitter one. Who, I thought, would have thought it?

'You're Irish, I'm hearing? Can we count on the Irish? No, I suppose we cannae. Fickle folk, the Irish!'

Now she had me thoroughly flustered! 'I...I wouldn't know,' I stammered. 'My mistress there read out a piece about the Prince in a magazine she had, but when I left Ireland there was no word that he was thinking of leaving France.'

Of course I knew that many Irish people did hate the English, and I imagined cared nothing for this German princeling that sat on the throne in London. 'I'd think he would find supporters in Ireland,' I said doubtfully, 'I don't really know much of such things.'

I did *not* say, and many also hate the Scots, whom they see as having stolen the province of Ulster from them. I've heard say, too, 'twas James, the Sixth King of Scotland and First of England who settled all those Scots families there, but I'd the notion that Shona wouldn't want to be reminded of that.

'If only I were a man, I'd go to him myself, despite my puir feet!' she mourned. 'Och, 'tis Bonnie Prince Charlie for me, the Young Chevalier!'

Chapter 16

The Belle of Belfast City

When the tea drinking was o'er and the afternoon sun was gone from the rose bower, I offered to accompany Shona back to the house and help wash and dry the china, but evidently my lukewarm response on behalf of the Irish had spoiled my chances. Shona made it clear she didn't want me or my help. I had been judged and found to be beneath her consideration. Then Lady Clan whisked us all indoors to her elegantly furnished salon, so that I might demonstrate my virtues as a singer accompanied at her spinet, a finer instrument even than Flora's. The little girls came running in with us, demanding that they too should sing, so while their fond Mama seated herself at a distance with her embroidery, Flora played, picking up the tunes as I sang them. I taught the children the skipping song, 'I'll Tell My Ma,' which made them giggle and clap their hands.

'I'll tell my Ma, when I get home, the boys won't leave the girls alone,' I sang, to squeals of mirth, 'they pulled my hair, they stole my comb, but that's all right till I get home.'

'Did they? *Did* the boys tease you, Betty?' the elder one, Isobel, demanded.

'Ach, no. You see how tall I am? I was always the tallest, even set against the boys in our neighbourhood. Any lad that thought of teasing *me* knew he'd be sure to get a slap around the head for his pains! And if that didn't give him the right notions, I'd two brothers to fight for my cause.'

'You aren't handsome or pretty, like the song says,' said young Marianne, weighing me up, 'so the song can't be about you.'

'Sure 'tis not!' I agreed, ' 'tis a song the little girls at home sing when they're skipping in the street.'

They stared at me, puzzled, and it took me a moment to understand why. There were no streets here on the island. These two children had never seen one.

'One day, I'll take you to Edinburgh,' their Mama responded from her sofa, 'then you'll see what a street is. It's just a road lined with shops and houses, and paved places at either side for the people to walk upon whilst the carriages and carts go by. Here on the Long Isle we've just roads and tracks.'

Then, before we had chance to say or sing more, we were interrupted by male voices at the door. In came two men, brothers by their looks, but one frail and leaning on the arm of the other, who, by his nut brown visage and sturdy stance, was the younger and in more robust health.

Lady Clan surged to her feet to greet them, and I understood that the older, frailer, man must be her husband, Lord Ranald Macdonald, and the other his brother, Alasdair of Boisdale.

A whirlwind of activity immediately began so that the old fella was seated, cosseted with cushions and given a footstool for his gouty foot; whilst more tea was ordered and the children sent off to find their nurse. Flora was greeted, summonsed from the spinet to his side, and her cheek kissed. 'Twas clear to me she was a prime favourite with the old man, as dear perhaps as his own daughters. Or it could be even dearer I decided? Lady Clan had lost no time in sending the noisy little creatures away!

I wondered what I should do. Should I have gone with the children? But no one said anything, so I retreated into the window bay, and kept a still tongue. In place of Shona, this time a young lad came with the tea, and with it a bottle, from which a splash of brandy was added to the old laird's cup. He stood a while at the old man's shoulder, seeming to think a second splash might be called for, until her ladyship waved him away.

'So, my dear,' began old Lord Ranald, addressing Flora, 'how did Edinburgh strike you? Apart from dancing with all the dashing young blades, what did you see and hear? What of our relative, young James Dalgleish? How does he find himself?'

Flora settled herself on a second stool so that she was close the old man's ear, and began to recount the news that James Dalgleish had now risen to the rank of Colonel in the Highland Militia, and that he was betrothed to a Miss Ann Elliot, whom he hoped soon to marry.

'Archibald Elliot of Carnguissie? Never heard of him! Some jumped up Lowland fellow who has made his money in coal or candlewax, I make no doubt! You say the daughter's a pretty lass and has a good dowry? Ach, well, James wouldn't have done for you, Flora. No spirit to him, none at all!'

'Pockets to let, more like, Sir!' said Flora, laughing. 'He's good man, Cousin James, but not for me, nor I for him! I don't believe his father can have left him well provided for. He seems only to have his pay from the Militia. He needs to strike a good bargain in his marriage, and by all I hear, Miss Elliot is well dowered as well as charming.'

'Hmmp! Mayhap, mayhap!' grumbled the old man, 'forbye, whatever his father left him, his mother will have wasted. Euphemia never had any idea of household management, and she must have thrown away hundreds in her younger days, playing at loo. Effie was the worst card player I ever set eyes on!'

'Still, *enough of the Dalgleish's*,' he lowered his voice, perhaps recalling that there was a servant in the room. Or perhaps he never even noticed me, silently winding up some of his wife's embroidery silks which the children had scattered, whilst striving to remain invisible in the window seat. Perhaps his caution was for whomever amongst his own servants might be passing the open door or the youth who had brought the tea, lurking, ready to be called, in the room beyond?

'How did the *mood* in Edinburgh strike you, Flora?' the old man went on in a confiding tone. 'What do they think there of Charles Stuart?'

Flora took in a deep sighing breath, and spread her hands, 'I don't know, Sir. It seemed to me that things there are much as they are here in the islands. Some are vehemently for him. Some equally against, believing that no benefit, only trouble, can come of an ill-timed offensive. Some, like poor Aunt Effie, are merely bewildered and frightened, afraid their comfortable settled lives will be destroyed. No one knows if an invasion is really likely, although the Highland Militia seem well prepared to repel one. And I believe, no, I *know,* that Cousin James has informers who report back to him, as I would suppose they must also to men more senior than he. They say all the ports on the North Sea coast are watched and guarded, and can be blockaded at a moment's notice. I fear that's all that I can tell you, dear Sir!'

'Yet he is here, in the West, in the islands, the Young Pretender,' growled brother Alasdair, speaking for the first time. 'Leastways, he *was.* They planned to sail the Minch on this morning's tide, making for Loch Moydart to meet up with a bunch of young hotheads there who claim they can raise an army.

'As I've said, I did my best,' he said, turning to his brother, 'I warned him not to expect anything of us. Thirty years have gone by. You and I were young, eager, lads then. We gave his father our loyalty, our men, and what monies we could. We fought like fiends at Sherriff Muir, and what did it gain us? Nought. Good men killed, and it beggared us for the next thirty years! Of course the present generation think they can do better, but there was no Highland Militia to oppose us in those days, and still we couldn't make sufficient headway. *Now,* as Flora here says, the government in London have a regiment well trained, well disciplined, and well armed. True, some may be willing to turn their coats for Bonnie Charlie, but by no means all! No, it's a foolish undertaking, and I fear nothing good will come of it.'

'James Dalgleish? Would he be one of those who might turn his coat? If the thing looked at all possible?' the old Chieftain asked wistfully.

Flora gave a tiny shake of her head, 'I doubt it, Sir. He's made a career for himself as an army officer serving the Government in London, and his position in life suits him well. He's about to marry and settle down to found a family. The thing would have to be completely failsafe, and it isn't, is it? Angus says there is no guarantee the French king will send an army to help take London, and if he did it would be for his own benefit, not Charles Stuart's. We could find ourselves vassals of France, and how would that profit us?'

The two old gentlemen sighed. To be sure, they wished it could be otherwise, but life had disappointed them.

'Two of my sons are over there on the mainland just now,' said Lord Clanranald, 'and I suspect they are amongst those planning to meet with him. I can't stop them if they choose to involve themselves in his affairs.'

The company sat silent for some minutes, musing, I suppose, on what that might mean.

'I saw Neil MacEachen was with the Prince,' said gruff Alasdair suddenly, seemingly addressing Flora. 'It appears he's abandoned his plan to enter the priesthood. You and he were playmates as children, were you not? And for a while he was here, of course, as tutor to my brother's sons.'

Flora did not answer immediately, and then she said, lightly, 'So, Neil's with the Prince now, is he? A brand new Cause for him. I wonder how long *that* will last? He was always a laddie for sudden passions, even as a wee boy. One summer he and I spent long days building reed huts by the lochan. Then one morning he didn't come. Reed huts were for babies! For girls! Suddenly it was boats. He found an old dinghy washed up on the shore and spent every waking hour trying to make it seaworthy. Then it was something else... religion it might have been, and he couldn't speak to Presbyterians like me anymore! I haven't set eyes on him in a long while. Anyway... it's time I was leaving you all, or we shall miss the tide!'

She sprang to her feet and signalled to me gather up our shawls. We would be leaving immediately, she insisted, to be well ahead of the tide. There was no hurrying Tibby, she said, and the old pony didn't care to get her fetlocks wet.

Lord and Lady Clanranald tried to persuade Flora to stay the night, but no, she'd promised her brother she would return that day to rescue him from those two terrible girls! Bridie would have left food, she told them all, but Elsbet and Màiri, if Angus came late from the shieling – where he'd planned to ride out that day – would probably have eaten his portion as well as their own! There was laughter and further protestations. The ill-behaviour of the two young maids was plainly a well-worn topic. Lady Clan continued to beg Flora to stay, saying she could send one of the stable lads to Angus with a message. If he rode quickly he could remind the girls to behave themselves, and be back before the tide turned. Flora would have none of it however, and still laughing and chattering about the sins of Elsbet and Màiri, she swept us out into the stable yard.

I was disappointed to be leaving, for the talk had been enlightening to an eavesdropper. I was sorry, too, that the Prince seemed to have departed the islands already. I found I was curious enough about him to wish to take a peek at him myself. And curious too, about this Neil MacEachen, the mention of whose name had flustered Miss Flora MacDonald.

As we crossed the yard, I glimpsed Shona, sour-faced at the kitchen door, watching our departure with a scowl on her face. I'd a horrid inkling that if we'd stayed I might have been asked to share a bed with her, and hear a further sermon on the fickleness of the Irish.

As soon as I took my seat in the trap, and before Flora could take up the reins, I was startled to notice a piece of white paper, folded many times, the outer fold marked, as I could just make out, squinting sideways as the pony caused the trap to lurch forward, with the letter B. It was tucked between my seat and the side of the cart. The B must surely be for Betty? Someone had left me a message. I hoped it wasn't Shona, leaving me a curse.

Chapter 17

I Sent a Letter to My Love

We drove home through the beautiful light of evening, the sky filled with thin, feathery clouds glowing pink and a pale orange from the sinking sun. The crests of the distant waves, too, were tinged with silver and carmen against a swell of what looked to my eyes like rippling silk of the deepest blue. I pondered what dyes might create so pleasing an effect, and doubted any could. The great black-backed gulls floated in slow, graceful arcs above our heads, rising and falling on invisible breezes, their white bellies and the edges of their powerful wings now and then gilded by the sun's late rays.

'Our sunsets here are highly praised by those who've ventured from the mainland to see them,' said Flora, breaking the silence between us. 'Tonight is beauteous, but you see these cloud formations above us that resemble the scales on a mackerel's sides? And those great clusters of cloud crouching on the horizon? Together they warn me it will almost certainly rain tomorrow. Our spell of fine weather is over, just as Angus predicted. How glad I am that the wash is completed, and that we managed to visit with the Clanranalds before the weather broke!'

' 'Tis most likely raining in Ireland already, Miss,' I agreed, staring at those massing clouds out at the edge of the Atlantic ocean, and suddenly feeling homesick for Belfast. Although what had I there to be missing? Only Danny, working late amongst the coffin boards in his workshop, and his sharp-tongued wife, Maeve, in their cramped room upstairs, counting every penny and finding none to spare for housing Danny's sister.

'It rains a good deal in Ireland does it not?' Flora asked.

I'd the feeling she was trying to distract me, lest I asked her awkward questions about what I had overheard from the old chieftain and his brother at Nunton, or about this Neil MacEachen, the mention of whose name had set her in a flurry.

'To be sure, I'm well used to the rain,' I agreed. Silence fell between us once more. I'd the mysterious folded paper clutched tightly in the damp palm of my hand. I was impatient to see what it was, but it wouldn't be right to be peering at it when whoever had placed it in the cart had put it there in secret, where only I would see it.

'Miss Flora?' I suddenly decided that things must be made clearer between us. ' 'Tis unused I am, to a maid's duties. I never was a *lady's* maid before, and I'm unsure, times, of what I should be doing? Did I do wrong to stay in the room when the Lord Clanranald and his brother came in? I thought mebbe… mebbe I should have gone when her Ladyship sent the children away, but I was on the wrong side of the room, and… it would have been awkward to pass them by.'

'You're afraid you heard matters discussed that you shouldn't have? I'd forgotten we were speaking in English,' said Flora thoughtfully, 'I'd have told you if I thought you should leave. There's no harm done. I believe the Clanranalds' servants must know all about the Prince and his companions. That laddie who brought tea for Lord Clanranald, he didn't hurry away, did he? He must have heard a deal of what was said.'

'Shona knows, for certain, Miss Flora, her Ladyship's maid. She told me she's strong for Prince Charles and the Jacobites! The Young Chevalier, she called him! She said if she were a man, she'd go to join him.'

'Would she indeed?' Flora snorted with amusement, her discomforted mood vanished away. 'I wonder what the Prince would think to find *that* crabbed face at his elbow! She's been with the family for years, muttering and grumbling, and Lady Clan is too soft hearted to turn her off.'

'She took against *me*,' I said. 'She decided I was a poor creature, because I couldn't reassure her that the Irish would support his Highness. To be honest with you, I've no idea whether they would or no. I'm certain there would be those who would, but when I left

Ireland there was no talk amongst the ordinary folk of any rising. Not that *I* ever heard, but he hadn't then left France.'

'You've family in Belfast, Betty?'

'Just my one brother now, Miss, and his wife.'

'They've no interest in politics?'

'No, Danny has some joinery work and the burying of the dead. Maeve goes into the houses and lays out, corpses that is, in the neighbourhood, and takes in washing. 'Tis hard to make a living in a district like theirs where folk have so little themselves. They've no time or inclination for politics.'

'I would have said the same was true, hereabouts,' said Flora, 'but it's beginning to seem as if I was wrong. Prince Charles Edward must have a winning way with him!'

Just before we reached the causeway between Benbecula and South Uist, we met a smart chaise going in the opposite direction. In it was a plump faced fella wrapped in a good many rugs. Signalling to his servant to rein in, he seemed inclined for speech. Flora greeted him politely enough and said how pleased she was to see him looking better and able to drive out, but added that she could not stop or we would miss the tide. He called after us that he hoped to be well enough to call at Milton soon. Flora waved her hand in acknowledgement and drove on. The tide waits for no one.

'That was our Minister, the Reverend John MacAulay,' she said. 'He's been sick these past weeks with the shingles, poor man. It would seem he is now on the road to recovery and means to take up his duties again.'

She said no more, and Tibby picked up her hooves as the cart began to roll more smoothly over the hard-packed sand. Soon, all too soon for me, she had us on the other side and onto the boggy moorland amongst South Uist's lochans, where a great cloud of midges swooped down on us, and we could hardly speak for the wretches flying into our faces, our mouths, and biting at our arms and necks.

'Oh, this won't do!' cried Flora, 'they're flying straight into my eyes, I can't see where I'm going!'

She reined in the pony and jumped down to pull at a bush of yellow flowering bog myrtle, tearing off branches to bat the creatures away. That was Miss Flora Macdonald. Anyone else would have asked her maid to do it. Whilst she was about it, I took the chance to remove the crumpled note with the letter B upon it from my palm, and stow it in my bodice. (I'd no particular reason to hide this letter whatever it might be, from my mistress, except that I supposed that whoever had written it *wished* me to keep it secret.)

Once back in the cart, she gave me my own switch of bog myrtle and we rode along, both of us whisking and slapping at the midges in a vain attempt to have them leave off plaguing us. I recalled my grandmother saying that the scented flowers of the yellow bog myrtle drove away 'the wee beasts', but mebbe the Irish midges are more faint-hearted than the Scots? I was certain Shona would think so!

'Once we're home and closer to the breeze from the sea it will be better,' spluttered Flora, as she spat some of the pests out of her mouth. 'I wonder how the Prince likes their onslaughts? First they say he was half choked by the smoke from the fire in old Angus's black house – though smoke does keep the midges away! Now, he'll have to learn to parry these terrible creatures. I'm hearing they're just as bad in the mainland glens. He's a brave laddie indeed if they don't make him turn tail and hie him back to France!'

I made no reply to this, being unwilling to unclamp my jaw for speech and let those imps of the devil fly in.

During the night the weather changed just as Flora had warned me it would. In the hours after midnight, the wind rose, at first whistling soft insistent tunes around the window shutters, and under the doors. Then it grew stronger, and shrieked wildly like a mad creature demanding to be let in. The shutters began to clatter and bang, the window frames creaked and strained. Rain drops first drummed on the window ledges and then attacked the window glass, like pellets sprayed from a musket. One of the barnyard doors must have worked loose and each gust of wind clouted it back against the wall, so that it echoed as if it were the oft repeated thud of a distant cannon. The day was already showing half-light around the shutters, although it must be still early by the clock. In these Hebridean isles on the edge of the world, the sun sinks below the horizon for only a few hours during the months of summer.

I slid from my bed and askt myself, should I light a candle? Last evening there'd been no private moment to read my note. I'd removed it from my bodice and hidden it under my pillow before I slept. Elsbet was asleep in one of the other box beds, but my rising did not immediately disturb her animal snufflings. Asleep, she recalled wee Jessie to my mind. Oft times both Elsbet and her sister slept in the house at Milton, sometimes one or both went home to their grandmother's black house. I understood that they might think one of them should be with the old lady, but I niver worked out why she should sometimes need both, and at other times neither. I'd a notion I'd not yet had a chance to test, that it depended on what was for supper at Milton.

As I drew my work gown over my nightdress and draped my shawl about my shoulders, Elsbet stirred and muttered in her sleep. No candle then, the scrape of the tinder box and the sudden flame would be sure to rouse her. Elsbet was the one body within this house I would least wish to share any secrets with. *If* there was anything secret about it? It could, even as I'd half jested to myself, simply be an "ill-wishing" spell from Shona. "Irish woman, go back where you came from!" It might even be in Gaelic. How then would I know what it said?

I wrapped myself about in my green plaid shawl, thinking to slip outside into the dawn where there would soon be enough light to read by. If Elsbet woke she'd think me gone out to the privy, though we'd a bucket supplied for night soil to save us that bother.

The wind had died away to a few sharp gusts now. I tried to be sure the lifting of the door latch was hidden by the rattle it made. If Elsbet heard it, it didn't break into her dreams.

Out of doors the rain had ceased, although the wind was still driving in off the sea, the grey waves hurling themselves at any rocks that thrust up from the seabed close in to the shore, breaking in a tumult of white foam and spray. A lone rowing boat, moored by a rope to an iron ring in the rock, had been dragged out by the retreating tide during the night and then thrown back onto the shingle on its side. Gone, as though they had never been, were the lovely colours of sky and ocean from the night before. Now the island was crouched down in a colourless world of close matched heaven, earth and sea. Impossible to see where the horizon ended and the sky began. The Eastern bens were lost in a thick-woven blanket of cloud. A single gull rode on the air currents but he fought hard to steady himself, and gave up the struggle as I watched, wheeling away to find shelter. Even the grass beneath my feet was grey with tiny spider's webs, each seemingly carrying a thousand thousand drops of dew, waiting for the sun to bejewel the flowery machair below.

I stepped gingerly across the grazing land to the sea, the dew like ice to my bare feet. The wind tugged roughly at my hair and shawl, and I shivered in the dawn cold.

I don't know why it came to me that the shore was the place most suited to the reading of my note. Or no, perhaps I'd already guessed who had written it, and this was the place where I had seen him last.

I half slid, half clambered, down the rough path made by people and animals, onto the sands, and padded along the water's edge until I reached the beached rowing boat. Then I settled my behind against its cracked staves, and unfolded the paper. A flock of oyster catchers further along the beach flew off in alarm, crying like a chime of silver bells.

It had been written in a bad light with a bad pen. There was no salutation.

Written in haste, lass. My horse is gone from the stable, stolen away. I know who the thieves are, but they were too many for me to stop them, and my *pistol arm is still weak. I shall follow after them, even though 'tis across the wide channel. Since ye seemed inclined to do me one favour (which was the repair of my arm) perhaps ye will do me another and pay attention to what you can discover hereabouts. I do not trust even the Militiamen here to tell a straight tale. Store up in your mind any incidents, any incidents <u>at all</u> until I return, and then recount them to me.*

Signed: JB

'It was *two* favours I did you *if you please*, John Begg!' I muttered under my breath, although the white sands were deserted of humankind at this hour, '*first* I dragged you from the deep when you were like to drown, *then* I put your arm back into its socket – no, wait, it was *three* favours I did!'

The third favour? I had refrained from telling Hugh Macdonald of Armadale that I'd met John Begg in Edinburgh, and of the happenings that had led to that meeting. Or that he'd had been tasked by a Colonel of the Militia there to escort Miss Flora Macdonald to her home, although I'd suspicioned all along that his real task was something else.

When he disappeared, and then was washed up on this beach, I felt certain I'd guessed aright. I spelled out his note once more. What did it mean?

Ach, don't be supposing me an eejit. I understood straightway that "the horse" was Prince Charles Edward Stuart, "stolen away" by his friends and supporters to the mainland, to this place called Loch Moydart, (I'd even learned the name of one of these friends, Neil MacEachen). I understood that John Begg had discovered their flight and gone after them, but what did he mean by "incidents"? What did he expect to happen here that I could tell him of when he returned? Surely now the Prince was gone, not having received the welcome, and more particularly the fighting men and monies he'd hoped for, there was nothing more that could touch this island on the very edge of the world?

What should I do with the note, I wondered? It had been written in haste as he said. What might be the outcome if it were found in my possession? The first matter, the stolen "horse." I thought nothing could be proved by that, if someone should find it and read it. Horses are stolen every day, as surely here in the outer isles as in any place else? Horses are valuable creatures, and their rightful owners, if they guess who are the thieves, will try to get them back. But the second part, where he was asking me to spy on the people here? Surely, wasn't that risky? Risky that he should write it, in case another saw it and knew his initials, JB? *More* than risky for me however, if someone saw it in my possession! It could place me in peril – if that someone was of the Prince's party – and would get me turned off as a disloyal servant if my mistress or her brother read it.

John Begg, I thought, growing verra uneasy now, you would have done better to have left that second part unsaid. I must rid myself of this. But how? 'Twas written on thick rag paper, and even folded small it had not been easy to hide it in my clothing. Probably no one would ever look beneath my bed-pillow, unless Elsbet should decide to poke her nose into my belongings. Or Miss Flora should take a fancy for another grand washday.

'Twould be best 'twas not found at all, but how could I hide it or better yet, destroy it? To tear it into strips would still leave the problem of getting rid of the pieces. At Milton, the peat fire was kept alight in the kitchen at all hours for the cooking, but would I ever find myself alone there long enough to burn it without someone asking what I was doing? I could bury it? Here on the shore? No, the great spring tides were long past, but last night's storm had shown me what a boisterous tide can do even in high summer. My hiding place could easily be washed clear. Rag fibres are durable, and mebbe it wouldn't melt away entirely in the water?

I said to myself, 'John Begg, I may have done you a favour, or two or three, but just now I'm wishing I had not!'

And wasn't I doubling the power of that wish when I saw who now came walking along the edge of the waves? 'Twas still early, surely not much more than four or five of the clock, and I couldn't see anyone stirring yet at Milton or the nearby crofts, but here came Captain Macdonald, Flora's step-father, tramping along the tide line in his great sea boots! He was still a distance off, but I was taking no chances. I turned away and stuffed John Begg's letter back into my bodice.

Chapter 18

Early One Morning, Just As The Sun Was Rising

' 'Tis the wild Irish Rose! Good morning, lassie,' Hugh Macdonald hailed me as he approached. 'What brings *you* to the shore so early? Can it be *an assignation*? Aye, I ken you're hoping to meet someone, and I suppose I am not he?' he chuckled, showing a good few missing teeth, and his one eye twinkled enough for two in ony other man.

I could see that in his prime, Flora's step-father must indeed have been a fine looking fella, and I was thinking he was still a handsome rogue for his time of life. I judged he was perhaps nearer fifty than forty years of age.

I'd learned the word "assignation" first at Ballymore. One of the parlour maids, who thought herself superior to the rest of us servants, had boasted how she'd made an "assignation" with a young man who worked as a clerk in the nearby town. Nothing came of it, because Mistress Buchanan found out and forbade her to meet him.

'No, Sir, I have no assignation! I didn't think to meet *onybody* so early in the morn. I was thrust awake early by the noise of the wind. In Belfast, amongst so many buildings, we don't have the force of it you have here. I'm hoping I'll get used to it in a while and be able to sleep on. I didn't want to be waking Elsbet, so I came out here. Do you know what's o'clock, Sir?' I was speaking too quickly and too much, to cover my uneasiness at his sudden appearance.

Hugh Macdonald delved into the inner pocket of his unkempt military jacket and produced a handsome pocket watch. A costly time piece it was. He'd told me the first time we met that he dressed carelessly for a purpose. If he dressed finely, or so he said, the island people would have none of him.

'Just on five-thirty, exact to the minute!' he said, snapping the case closed and returning it to his pocket. 'Why, what time did your lover appoint?' he added with a knowing chuckle.

'As I told you, I have no lover!' I replied, trying to keep my voice as light and jesting as his own. 'I've been here little more than a week. How would I be catching a lover so soon?'

'How indeed! Though yon laddie you hauled from the waves the other day must surely feel grateful to you?'

'So I should hope!' I retorted, 'since I saved him from drowning.'

I was wondering while I was bandying words with Flora's Step-Papa, ought I to ask how John Begg was? Would he expect me to do that? I'd left him with this man, feeling a little uneasy about it at the time, but the letter I had scratching against my breast bone told me he was well enough, and perhaps already off the island, chasing after the Prince and his companions.

'He was a Militia man like yourself?' I tried. 'Twould seem unnatural, I thought, to show no interest at all in a man whose life I'd saved.

'So it appeared,' said Hugh Macdonald, and his mouth twisted sourly, 'came to check up on *me*, I fancy. I'd had word to expect him, to meet him on this shore, as you saw. I left him with Alasdair and Katy Mor to recover, but they say he went off again by early evening. I hoped he might come back to this spot and tell me more of what he wanted, but I imagine he's gone with the tide,' he sighed. 'Nae doubt reporting back to Edinburgh! Someone here on Uist has complained about how we patrol these islands, was the impression he gave me, so he was sent to put me right! I'm ground between the rocks here. No one likes a Government Militia man whoever he is, and the Chieftain here is not mine, my allegiance is to the MacDonald of Slèat on Skye, so I can expect little support from folk here.' He looked at me, hangdog, as though he hoped for some sympathy, but I felt disinclined to give him any. It was, after all, John Begg who'd been attacked and thrown into the sea, not he.

'What do you suppose happened, Sir? To this man I saved from the deep? Did he tell you how it came about, that his arm was wrenched from its socket? A strange accident, surely?' I was curious to know, and I'd decided it wouldn't seem too odd in me to ask.

We were stepping warily, Hugh Macdonald and I, *feinting* like swordsmen, my brothers would have said. He suspected me of knowing more than I'd told, but he couldn't be sure, couldn't prove that I hadn't set eyes on John Begg for the first time only when I dragged him out of the sea.

'There are always things going on in these islands, lassie,' he said, shrugging his broad shoulders. 'Smuggling mainly. The whisky goes out, and the brandy comes in! Tariffs? What tariffs?' he grinned. ' 'Tis bound to happen. I keep my one eye wide open, but I cannot be everywhere. Some of them, we catch at it, and they don't like me for it! Some we *don't* catch, and then their neighbours don't like me for that either! I tell you, I'm a vessel ground upon the rocks! I only know what yon man, Begg, told me; that he'd been set upon by a gang of men who threw him from a low cliff from whence he was swept into the sea. What *he* was doing on Eriskay, or over here on South Uist, *or* what they were doing, I don't know. Although I have heard talk of a French ship in the offing, so nae doubt 'twas brandy!'

'Eriskay? Which one is that?' I asked. I had nearly said, *but aren't the Prince and his followers gone from Eriskay?* However, thanks be, I stopped my tongue in time.

' 'Tis the isle immediately to the south of this one, lass, with Barra a little to the west. Below them, is – he counted them out on his fingers – Fuday, Vatersay, Sandray, Roisnish, Mingulay, and Bernesay, and below that nothing but the sea until you come to Ireland! It's a pity the tide doesn't go out far enough to let you walk home to your kinfolk in Belfast! You can walk or ride from one to the other of these islands when the tide is low, just as you can from this one to Benbecula.

'I hear you and my daughter were visiting with the Chieftain and his lady wife yesterday?' he said, suddenly changing the matter of our talk. 'Now there's man enjoys a drop of good brandy! Did you enjoy your visit?'

'Why yes, Sir. Your daughter is a great favourite with them I think?'

'Indeed, as I believe I told you when we met before. They've done a great deal for Flora, treated her like their own daughter.'

'They were delighted to see her, safe back from Edinburgh, Sir. The old gentleman isn't too hale and hearty, but seeing Flora seemed to cheer him.'

I wasn't sure why I was telling this to Hugh Macdonald. To distract him, mebbe, from the badinage about my having a lover? Which I doubted he believed. I'm sure he hoped to trick some piece of information from me – some word I might drop that showed that I knew what John Begg was truly about. Or if I knew who the men on Eriskay had been? Or that I might understand that he'd prefer it if I'd remove myself back to Ireland? If that was what he was hinting?

He was a difficult fella to fence with, and I wondered, having gone without my full allowance of sleep, how long I could keep it up without some slip of my tongue. All the time I was thinking of that piece of paper, riding up just below the neck of my gown, that could give me away. I didn't know what powers a Captain of Militia might have. They were charged, I knew, with keeping the peace. According to Flora's Papa they also went after smugglers. Could he arrest the Prince and his followers? I rather thought he could, although I wondered if he would? Could he even arrest me, if he could prove I'd told him a pack of lies?

He was a strange, wily character for all his twinkling eye and smiling mouth. A man who very likely "drove two horses". What would he do if they bolted in opposite directions? Which way would he jump?

So 'twas a relief to see that we were no longer the only two awake and walking on the sands. Angus Macdonald came clambering down to the beach, neat as always, even in his shirt and britches, his feet bare, and with a bucket in his hand.

'Good morning, Angus!' his step-father greeted him. ' 'Tis no use coming here for milk, the milch cow is above on the machair!'

'I know where the cow is!' snapped his son, 'I've arranged to meet Tam Mor here for a pail of his herring.' He nodded out across the bay, where a boat had lowered its sail, and oars were being slipped into the water. 'Flora is up and stirring the porridge already,' he said, addressing this to me, 'and you could put more peat on the fire and make ready to help her cook the fish. Lady's maid, or no lady's maid, as I've said before, we expect you to make yourself useful, lassie!'

I would have liked to excuse myself, make him understand that I hadn't intended to idle here. Nor, as I feared he might suspect, had I come down to the sands for an *assignation* with his step-father. Hugh Macdonald was, as I'd already discovered, the kind to make free with the maid servants if given the slightest encouragement. He'd call it *funning*.

However, the news that I was to make preparations for the frying of the herring solved one of my problems. I was to build up the fire, and I might never have a better chance to dispose of John Begg's letter!

Thus I made no excuses at all. Let Angus think what he would. I hurried back to the farm kitchen. By the back door I tarried long enough to retrieve the letter and tear it into pieces. Indoors, I found Flora, as her brother had said, stirring the meal on one of the hobs.

'Good morning, Betty!' she greeted me, 'have you been outdoors already?'

'I woke early, Miss,' I said, 'and didn't want to disturb Elsbet. I met your brother who told me he's bringing a pail of herring up to the house shortly and bade me build up the fire. Can I do that now, is the porridge ready?'

'Ready enough! I'll leave it on the hearth to simmer. There's a basket of peat in the corner. You know how to build a fire?'

'Ony Irish girl can build a peat fire, Miss!' I said.

And thus I disposed of John Begg's letter, placing the pieces carefully beneath the layers of peat as I added them to the range. Flora had gone to rouse Elsbet, and presently Bridie came in with a basket full of wool that she'd combed at home, and made ready to be spun. Then Angus arrived with the bucket of herring, and the kitchen became a busy hive as the fish were gutted and the frying pan prepared. By the time we'd the first fish cooked and ready to eat, Màiri appeared, closely followed by Hugh Macdonald. Angus must have invited him to eat with us, although I sensed those two were often at odds. Their relationship seemed tight as stretched twine. Perhaps 'twas no wonder. Angus, being older by some years than Flora, must have resented this man carrying off his mother, and having rule over him, as I imagined he would have done, whilst the boy was growing up. Mebbe the older man would have liked to take possession of the farm? Perhaps he was inclined to give his capable step-son unwanted advice, and this vexed Angus?

'It seems you're always feasting in this house!' Hugh declared, as we gathered around the table, our bowls of porridge soon disposed of to make way for the fish. 'I hope you're salting down some of these for winter,' he added, confirming my suspicion that he didn't always deal delicately with his children.

Angus scowled, but Flora said cheerfully that she would be sure and do so. Tam Mor had promised them a whole creel, and she was certain he would keep his word.

'So, what has been happening hereabouts?' the step-father demanded once he'd eaten his fill, and slouched back in his chair. 'What's this I'm hearing of wild men on Eriskay throwing one of my Militia colleagues over the cliff into the sea?' His one eye caught mine as he said this, seemingly commanding me to say nothing. There was no need, I had no intention of uttering a word. I was just afraid of what *he* was going to say. It also struck me for the first time that whatever John Begg might have told him, it could not have happened on Eriskay. With his painfully damaged shoulder he could never have swum so far.

The others looked startled or bewildered in their turn. 'I've heard nothing,' said Angus. 'Which Militia man was this?'

'Not one you'd know, an Edinburgh man. John Begg his name is.'

At this Flora exclaimed aloud. 'John Begg! Sergeant Begg? He was the man our Cousin James sent to escort me home, Papa. Once we reached the farm at Largie, he disappeared. I imagined he'd returned to his other duties. We were safe enough there, and he must have seen he'd be delayed a long while, waiting for the Minch to be passable. Did he come out to the islands after all?'

'It seems he did,' said her step-father, his voice full of meaning, or so it appeared to me, quivering in my seat at the thought of what he'd say next, 'and met up with some ruffians on Eriskay, or so he said. Smugglers, maybe? What think ye? Has anyone offered you a barrel of brandy?'

Angus shrugged, 'Not to me. I've heard nothing.' He sounded bored and unconcerned, yet he must guess, surely, who those "ruffians" were?

'Poor man,' said Flora.' Is he…?'

'Dead, no. He survived. However, he's now disappeared again. I'm concerned for his welfare.'

I'll wager you are – *not*, I thought, and was mightily relieved to have burned the letter. I said nothing and neither did anyone else around the kitchen table, although, knowing what I did, I thought Angus, Flora, and even Bridie, looked a mite uncomfortable. The two young maids carried on eating, their minds seemingly quite empty of guilty knowledge, or indeed of any knowledge at all.

I was sure Hugh Macdonald would now betray my part in John Begg's rescue, but apart from a quick glance in my direction he said nothing about it.

'These ruffians,' he went on, 'there have been rumours of a French brigantine, the *Du Tuilly*. Has anyone mentioned it to any of you?'

'Yes, when Flora came over from Coll. You saw it, didn't you, Flory? The fishermen pointed it out,' said Angus. 'It was heading south even as Flora arrived. I thought you knew of it, Father? You were here a few days ago. I supposed you were checking on it then.'

'You never mentioned it, son.'

'We always *assume*, Father,' Angus said, his voice grating impatiently, 'that you are better informed than we are in such matters. You know I would never accept contraband, and I haven't heard of anyone else being offered any.'

There was a long silence. I realised that although Hugh Macdonald knew perfectly well who had been on Eriskay, he wished for some reason to establish that he did not, and that he would prefer that no one else would admit to it either. We were to say nothing, to know nothing.

'Perhaps, Father,' Angus eventually said, 'you'd care to come down and have a word with Tam Mor? He's brought the boat close in, close enough to hail him. If anyone knows anything about contraband being brought ashore, he will.'

The two men rose from the table and went out. We womenfolk looked at one another and breathed out gusty breaths. 'Does he think we don't know?' Bridie asked.

' 'Tis more complicated than that, Bridie,' said Flora, '*he* knows, he knows *we* know, but he wants us all to pretend we don't know anything at all.'

'You mean about the Prince?' demanded Elsbet, suddenly. 'Did the Prince fight the Militia man and throw him over the cliff? Oh, how I wish he may have done so!'

Chapter 19

The Larks They Sang Melodious

It was impossible to keep the secret. Everyone on the Long Island now knew it. The Prince had been here, alighted like a rare bird of rich plumage, and then flown off before you could be sure of his markings. Although the weather over the next weeks turned swiftly from days of sunshine to days and nights of rain and storm, it seemed the hardy fisher folk were still able to pass back and forth across the wild Minch. Such real news as there was, the brother and sister at Milton heard, though for a long while it amounted to very little. Then things began to happen more speedily, as when you make a ball of snow and roll it down a hill. It grows bigger and travels faster, and so it was with the Prince Charles Edward's campaign.

'Summer snow! It will all melt away unless the King of France, or the money men in Edinburgh or Glasgow, can be persuaded to lend him money to buy arms! Or if the Chieftains open those iron-bound chests and give up their ancestral hoards to be melted down. I don't see that happening!' scoffed Angus, but for once it seemed he might be wrong.

In the evenings, Flora and Angus sat late in the parlour, talking it over. Oft times I was present. My foot on the treadle kept the spinning wheel humming, but my ears are sharp and neither of them sent me away. The Chieftains and their men were gathering, coming together to meet on the mainland in this place they named as Glenfinnan. One after another, these ancient Clans were declaring allegiance to the young man they called Bonnie Prince Charlie, and moreover, digging deep into those iron-bound chests for silver and gold! Flora told me their names though they meant little to me. 'Twas like a chant, MacDonnell, McPhee, Fraser… Cameron, MacLaren, MacNeil… MacDonald of Glengarry… but not Macdonald of the Isles.

Lord Ranald MacDonald himself did not stir from his home at Nunton, nor did he unlock any iron-bound chest, sending only messages about his fragile health. However, his sons, it was whispered, children by one of his previous marriages, had now joined with the Prince on the mainland, and when his kinsmen and his servants began, first one and then another, to vanish across the water, he issued no decree forbidding it.

Angus Macdonald of Milton however, tacksman, gentleman farmer, made complaints aplenty when his own farmhands began to disappear without a word. First Calum slipped away, then Finn, then Gilbert.

'I'm right sorry, Betty,' Angus said to me, finding me one morning with Elsbet and Màiri in the byre. 'I know you came here as Flora's maid, and never expected to be asked to do farm work, but I'm afraid all of us must now take our turn.'

'I niver milked a cow before, Sir,' I said, 'but to be sure, I'm willing to learn,' which was true. My loyalty was to my mistress, Miss Flora Macdonald, who had rescued me from starvation on the streets of Edinburgh. I never allowed myself to forget that. The Prince and the anxieties he'd brought to these island folk did not greatly concern me. He was flown away to the mainland of Scotland, far off. I'd food to eat, clothes to my back, and a bed to sleep in. I was quite at my ease here, learning the country skills my grandmother had known, and taking pleasure in them. Whilst the soft days of summer lasted, I could ask for no more.

Elsbet and Màiri struggled at the spinning (though both were improving at my constant badgering) and had jumped up, eager to show me, when I'd told them I should be glad to learn to milk the cow. Milking was something they could both do, though I fear the poor beast got rather a rough time of it at those impatient young fingers.

Another time, mourning the loss of the third of their farm lads, Flora confided in me, ' 'Tis foolish, and I fear for them, but I find it hard to blame them. They've seen nothing outside these islands, and suddenly they've been offered this great adventure!'

'And will suffer a vast disappointment, if not a great deal worse,' grumbled her brother, spreading some butter that we'd churned afresh that morning on his piece. 'Untried lads, and old fools like Gilbert, armed with rusty swords and pitchforks against the mighty artillery of the British Army! They say the Government is to send the crack regiments. Cannons, artillery! They'll be cut down like the wheat of the field!'

Angus, at this time, became more and more inclined to come out with speeches that sounded as though he'd found them in the Bible. I supposed he'd learned them from his grandfather, the Strong Minister, whilst scarcely out of the cradle. Indeed, now I thought of it, it was a puzzle to me that although Angus said a grace before each meal, and in Edinburgh Flora had bought me a good pair of boots "for church attendance", there was still no suggestion of our going to church. Three more Sabbaths passed, but apparently the Presbyterian minister, the Reverend John MacAulay, must have suffered a setback, and was still laid up with his indisposition. I wondered why, if he was well enough for evening drives, he still forsook his preaching duties? However, since I had never attended a protestant church and was wary of making a fool of myself there, not knowing how I should act, I did not ask.

Almost daily, at this time, Angus wrote to his betrothed, Penelope, urging her to take care, and to plan some place of safety in case she and her family should ever need it.

I thought, now and then, of Mistress Dalgleish and the household in Edinburgh. Had news reached them of that standard raised at Glenfinnan on the nineteenth day of August? Surely it must have done so? When September dawned and they heard (as we did) that the Prince's army was marching on Edinburgh, how fearful they must have been!

Flora had heard no word of Cousin James. No doubt he was fully occupied planning the defence of the castle, whilst sending urgent despatches to London for reinforcements. I wondered if his wedding had taken place, and what he might do to provide a safe haven for his bride, together with his mother and her household, in the face of a siege of the town? There had been no letters at all from the mainland for Flora, so 'twas no use for me to ask her. I'd never had another note from John Begg, and no longer expected one. If he had indeed caught up with the Prince, his "stolen horse," he'd evidently had no luck in parting him from the "thieves."

Away from the farm however, I suppose the news and the rumours of news were constantly being exchanged amongst the islanders. I guessed at this, just from people's wary speech and sly glances, although most times they spoke Gaelic. No one spoke unkindly to me, but as an Irish girl I was an outsider, a foreigner, and they plainly felt uneasy about sharing what they considered to be no affair of mine.

Late in September, Captain Hugh Macdonald, calling at Milton with a small detachment of Militia men, as he often did when supposedly patrolling the islands to keep us all in check, told us of a battle won near Dunbar, at a place called Preston Pans. (What had become of Flora's cousins? Had they ever made it home to Kintyre?) I'd imagine only Flora, Angus, and myself had any but the vaguest notion where these places might be. Old Hugh, describing this battle, could not keep a note of pride from his voice as he told of the mighty charge by the Prince's Highlanders that had scattered the Redcoats before them.

'Aye, I know, I know!' he said, seeing the surprised looks of his step-children. He sighed, ' 'Tis strange to me, to be on the contrary side!'

Meanwhile, between visits from Flora's step-papa, much of this "news" or lack of it was spread by an old fella named Colin Macdonald, who was kept busy riding to and fro on a knock-kneed nag, acting as courier and postman to the islanders. Before this time, so Bridie told me, he'd apparently been close to bed-ridden and his daughters ready to call in the priest, but news of the Prince's invasion had given him a grand new lease of life. On his way to and from the Macdonalds of the North island, he would call at Nunton and bring messages to Milton from both Lord and Lady Clan. Of what Lord Clanranald said to Angus I heard only what he shared with his sister, and she in turn thought it right to pass on to me.

Lady Clan's messages, Flora often read aloud to me. (She longed, she said, to see Flora, and as soon as the tides were more favourable, she was minded to ride over to Milton, but just now her Lord needed her, his health was so poor, and she must not be trapped away from home, even for a night.)

There was little of substance to be learned from her letters but what we knew already. Lady Clanranald was discreet, and ever loyal to her elderly husband, but mebbe there was more than a touch of wistfulness behind the words she penned? A wish, hid between the words, that she might at least have set eyes on the Prince? That he had been so close to Nunton, practically on her doorstep, and yet she hadn't seen him? Whatever the present danger, I guessed Lady Clanranald would – and, as Flora said, who could blame her? – have liked to entertain a *Royal Prince* at her table. If only the once.

After all, as Flora explained to me, whatever the rights and wrongs of his claim to the British throne, he *was* a Prince. A Prince of the royal blood, *nobody*, not even King George himself or his tribe of sons, denied this. All were bound by ties of marriage to half the royal houses of Europe. Cousins in some degree even, Flora thought, through their mothers, daughters of the Polish Royal House of Sobieski. She tried to explain these links to me, but royal houses and dynastic marriages mean little to a flax spinner from Belfast, and I wouldn't be certain they meant much more to her.

Flora wrote, in reply to Lady Clan, that she in her turn longed to see her good friend, but with the farm lads gone, she could not, at this time, desert her brother. There was much to do. Tibby, the pony, had cast a shoe, and with summer on the wane, Angus would be bringing the cattle down from the shieling in the Eastern hills. Bridie and Lechie, her man, were to help with this.

In the end, on a fair October day when summer seemed to

linger in the isles, we all went, and made a festival of it, loading creels of picnic food into the pony cart (Tibby having been shod once more.) Angus "outrode" the herd on his tall horse, Ossian, with his sheepdog, Tara, guarding the other flank, and the rest of us followed on foot. Elsbet complained a good deal, and Màiri whimpered, walking "sae far" over the pricks of dry heather and rough stony ground in their bare feet, but Flora had us singing to distract them.

How we sang, Flora, Bridie, Lechie, myself, and even Angus, all the way home to Milton, with the hairy, long-horned cattle plodding slow and steady before us, down from Ben Sheaval to the east of the island towards the farm close by the western shore. Elsbet sulked, but Màiri tried to join in with her own strange warbling *puirt à beul* from deep in her throat.

Flora and Bridie taught me a new Gaelic air, Mo Bhean Chomin, a sad tale of love rejected, and I taught them 'Twas Pleasant and delightful one midsummer morn, with its choruses that can never fail to move the heart as the company's voices rise up in harmony. That day though, with midsummer well past, and with words telling of a young man going off to war, it left me with a melancholy feeling. When we sang, 'Our ship she is waiting for the next flowing tide,' I thought of that warship in Carrickfergus bay and my eyes were bleared with tears for my brother. Poor Pat, mebbe bound, against his will, for 'the East Indies where the loud cannons roar,' and I daresay the others thought of their neighbours and kin folk who had slipped away to the mainland of Scotland to join Charles Edward Stuart. Certain 'tis that when the song was over we all walked on apace in silence the while, even as above our heads the last of summer's skylarks "sang melodious" as the sun sank down into the Atlantic Ocean.

'Aye,' sighed Lechie, who seldom spoke in company, although he was a fine singer, 'Summer's awa, and winter will soon be crying at the door. In a month we'll be setting up the weaving frames.'

'Most of the wool is spun ready, Lechie!' said Flora, laughing,

'Bridie, Betty, and I have been busy, but there's a deal else to do before winter sets in. Herring to salt down, fruit to preserve, bacon to cure.'

'Aye, and plenty of tasks about the farm,' warned Angus, looking down on us from his high perch astride Ossian, 'walls and fences to mend, the dried peat to carry and stack by the house. Tomorrow, I'd like those of you that can be spared from the kitchen (he meant myself and the two young maids) to go down to the shore and gather kelp to spread over the northern slope of the machair. The sheep have cropped away the goodness during the summer and we must needs give it heart.'

'Ach, why must *we* do it?' wailed Elsbet, 'I hate that work, wi' my back bent like an auld woman!' She turned to her sister, muttering, 'We should hae gone wi' Calum, 'twould hae been a fine jaunt.'

'No 'twould not!' I snapped, tired of her sulking, 'you'd have had to walk a great many more miles than you have today, and no grand picnic to refresh you whilst you took your ease in the midst of the day!'

'And no comfortable box bed to sleep in come the nightfall,' added Flora, 'Fetch some Carrageen Moss from the shore tomorrow, Elsbet, and Bridie'll make you a sweet junket for your supper!'

'Ah, Carrageen!' I breathed, 'That minds me of my grandmother. I haven't had it for many a long year.' Thinking to encourage Elsbet, I said, 'Let us lay a wager! I'll wager you that I find it first, but whoever finds it eats the first spoonful!'

Later, thinking it over before I slept, I wondered, not for the first time, at how my life had turned out. It was as well, I thought, that I never truly was a lady's maid! How would Mistress Buchanan's Gladwell or Mistress Dalgleish's Morrison have felt if they had been told they were to go down to the beach next day and gather up the seaweed?

Chapter 20

A Comb to Buckle My Hair

I was untangling myself from a clump of oarweed whose leathery tendrils had wrapped themselves about my ankles, when I saw it. A glint of silver in a mesh of bladder wrack, kelp, and a length of tarred rope. My boots and stockings were beneath an overhanging bank jutting out above the tide line, for today the wind-harried clouds were spitting drops of rain. My skirts were kilted up above my knees to keep them clear of the incoming tide. A foam of grey seawater was already hissing over my bare toes. I didn't call out. Elsbet and Màiri were some way off along the shore. Màiri was bundling kelp into a standing creel. Elsbet, seated on a rock with her back to me, was studying a tide pool at her feet, or mebbe sulking, or just being idle. She'd a couple of wooden spars and a small bundle of kelp laid beside her, the sum total of her beachcombing over this last couple of hours. If she'd found any Carrageen for sure she'd have come running across the sands to triumph over me.

Watched by a pair of bright-eyed corbies perched on a nearby rock, I bent and poked my fingers cautiously into the seaweed bundle, mindful that there might be a hermit crab or a starfish waiting in there to nip at me. I pulled the glinting thing out. 'Twas a comb. Not such a comb as a lass like myself might pull through her hair to make herself tidy or keep the lice at bay. No, I knew what 'twas. When I held it in my palm I was back once more at Ballymore, with Miss Evangeline seated in her great bed, propped up on many pillows, and with her beloved magazines spread about her on the quilt. She'd one open at a page that showed engravings of the latest fashionable ways for a lady to dress her hair. One of the drawings was supposed to represent a Spanish lady, a *donna*, and she'd a comb like this one to hold a piece of fine black lace hanging down behind her, and mebbe a rose fixed on the crown of her head. Miss Evangeline had told me this lace veil she had on was called a *mantilla*.

The teeth of the comb I now held in my hand were made of horn. Two were chipped and broken off short. The head of the comb, however, was of silver, and across its width was inscribed (or stamped, or carved? I wouldn't know how 'twas done) a man on a horse with a hound at his side, chasing a running deer. The silver was beaten thin, but it felt heavy in my hand. Some lady's treasure this. A precious thing lost. Perhaps 'twas even worth a few coins? How had it come here, thrown up on the shore by the tide? I pulled away the last tendril of seaweed and slipped it into the pocket of my apron.

I was thinking, what would I do with it? Then I heard Bridie calling, and saw her standing above us on the dune, holding down her skirts, her hair and her shawl tossed this way and that by the wind. Màiri and Elsbet went running, eager for their dinners. Elsbet did take up the spars, but Màiri left the creel of seaweed behind, heedless that the tide would carry it off long before she returned. I took my time, collecting my boots, shouldering the straps of my creel and then carrying Màiri's in my arms before me. I could feel the comb lying in the bottom of my apron pocket, jouncing against my knee as I walked. By the time I'd laid the creels by the kitchen door, I'd settled a dispute with myself. I must show them the comb. I couldn't keep it secretly, any more than I could have kept John Begg's letter.

So 'twas that I stepped into the kitchen, my hand in my pocket ready to fetch it forth and astonish them all. Only to discover that the household were not at the table ready to eat as I'd expected, but standing about, their mouths agape in shock, at the sight and sound of the Reverend MacAulay, raising his voice in anger at Angus.

'It's a disgrace, I tell you!' the Minister squawked. He'd a voice like a cart's axle as needs the oil. 'Did you do *nothing*, Sir, *nothing*, to prevent these men from going?'

Angus shrugged and spread his hands, 'What could I do? I had no notion they meant to go, for they did not tell me.'

'Yet, you must have known these… these *popish* fellows might go running after this Stuart upstart!'

'No, why should I? Many men of all persuasions seem to favour him,' said Angus, his face white and his mouth tight with anger, 'It's not a matter of religion alone. Gilbert, as you must know, is one of your own congregation.'

'While I have been indisposed, I had hoped *you* were setting an example to these ignorant men! Making clear to them where their duty and their loyalty should lie! George of Hanover sits on the throne by the decree of Parliament, and by *the will of God!* It is not for his subjects to question what God has ordained! If this *pretender* gains a foothold we shall all be under the thumb of Rome! Do you forget, Sir, all that your grandfather strived for here in South Uist?'

'I do not,' Angus replied, 'but many feel that this is a matter of politics rather than religion. Men say that Scotland has no voice. Everything is decided in London. Even Edinburgh has little influence. I doubt men in Parliament in London even know we exist, here in the Outer Isles. Oft times I wonder if Edinburgh knows it.'

'And you suppose that this Stuart creature will change that?'

'No, sir, I don't suppose it for a moment, but I cannot entirely condemn those who hope he will.'

'I am shocked, sir, shocked!' blustered the fat little Minister, glaring around at us all, his face the colour of raw beef and his eyes bulging from their sockets.

'We miss the lads sorely, Reverend MacAulay,' interposed Flora sweetly, 'we hope they will soon think better of their decision and return, but our lasses,' she waved her hand around the kitchen to include us all, 'are a great support to us. I haven't properly introduced you to Betty, have I? Betty Burke.' I bobbed him a curtsey, as a well-trained servant should, but got no acknowledgement from him.

'I employed Betty during my visit to Edinburgh as a lady's

maid,' Flora went on, 'she agreed to travel home with me to help with the spinning, but she's been turning her hand to anything and everything we ask of her. Already she has learned to milk the cow, and here she is, new come in from gathering kelp on the shore with Elsbet and Màiri! I'm sure we're all hungry after such a busy morning's work. Would you care to join us at the table, sir?'

The Minster's fat lips trembled as though he was minded to accept (and who would not? The smell of hot beef-and-barley broth with warm baps would have enticed His Majesty King George himself). But whatever words he found there, he did not utter. Instead he turned and, brushing past me without a glance, marched out of the door, saying only, over his shoulder, 'I trust I shall see you and your sister at the Kirk on the coming Sabbath, Sir, the tides being favourable!'

After this outburst we all sat silent through Angus's muttered grace and Bridie's doling of the broth. Bridie didn't always eat at Milton, but today it seemed Lechie had taken the bairns on a beachcombing excursion of his own, so she stayed with the rest of us.

'So we must go to Kirk on Sunday,' said Flora, with a little grimace. 'You'll come with us, Betty?'

'Yes, Miss, to be sure,' I answered, and said no more.

'You're all very quiet,' she said, looking around the table. 'Was the wind cold on the beach? Did you find much kelp? No Carrageen I suppose?'

'They've two creels of kelp out by the back,' said Bridie. 'I fancy Betty and Màiri did most of the work.'

Bridie had been used to having most of the trouble of getting these young maids to do their work, and she sometimes spoke harshly, especially to Elsbet.

Elsbet scowled now, muttering '*You* didnae come and help us!' under her breath.

Thinking to lighten things, since Angus seemed still to be smarting under the Minister's blame, and Elsbet's humour was sour,

I said, fossicking in my apron pocket, 'See here! I found something amongst the weed. It must once have belonged to a fine lady, do ye not think? 'Tis only a little spoiled.' I laid the silver comb on the scrubbed bare table, to murmurs of wonder and surprise.

Flora reached across and touched it with her finger, 'Oh, 'tis a lovely thing, Betty! Wherever did you find it?'

Whilst I tried to describe just where on the beach I'd been when I found the comb, Angus came out of his brooding, picked it up and examined it, holding it up to the light.

'The design is only a little rubbed, and two of the teeth broke,' he said, 'A treasure indeed, Betty! I'd estimate you could sell it in Stornoway up in Lewis, for thirty or forty shillings. In Glasgow, maybe more.'

'Oh 'tis your dowry!' exclaimed Bridie, clapping her hands excitedly, you'll be like the girl in that song we learned from you, The Lasses from Banyon! She began to sing, 'Me father has forty white shillings, shillings, shillings! Me father has forty white shillings, and the price of a goat and a cow!'

'And me mother has said I can marry, marry, can marry! Me mother has said I can marry, and she'll leave me her bed when she dies!' Flora and I chorused, laughing. Even Màiri warbled the tune deep in her throat. All of us, except Elsbet, who scowled even more furiously.

'That's stupid,' she burst out. '*She* does nae need a dowry! Naebody's going tae marry Betty. She's as plain as… as a *bap*, and as tall as the An Carra Stone by Kildonan!'

Flora had pointed out this stone to me as we drove back from Nunton. The An Carra standing stone, she'd told me, was seventeen feet high.

'But am I allowed to keep it?' I asked, ignoring Elsbet. Her words rubbed me raw, but I was determined not to let her see it. 'If it came from a ship that was wrecked, can anyone who finds it keep it?'

'Probably,' Angus answered, slowly, 'although upon reflection, I believe you should let Lord Clanranald know of it. I'll write on your behalf and notify him. We seldom find anything of value washed up on this shore. More ships are wrecked sailing the Minch to the East of Uist than on this Atlantic coast. It's a matter of the currents, d'you see? Although the ocean to our West is often tempestuous, for much of the year the strong current pushes shipping up beyond Lewis and Harris to the far North.'

'Whereas, between the inner and outer isles, the water we call the Minch is as fickle as can be,' Flora broke in, 'and has the most unaccountable currents! For some reason ships and their cargoes are most often wrecked on the rocks by Eriskay.'

'The Eriskay folk keep what they find and never tell anyone,' stated Elsbet, *'they* never tell the Chieftain! If 'tis bodies, they just bury them. *I* think Betty should go back to the shore and look for the woman's body. You never know, she might not be drowned, even! She might have swum ashore. Then Betty could give the comb back.'

Her angry face told me it was not that she had any wish to restore the comb to its owner, she only wished that I might not have it.

'I'd have seen, if there had been anyone in the water,' I said, thinking of the time I'd rescued John Begg from the waves, 'I'm sure of it. The wind was strong out there, and the waves were lively but not mounting so high.'

'A ship might well be lost out there in a storm,' said Flora, 'but they don't sail close since there are no harbours on this side of the Long Island. We'll never know how 'twas lost.

'It could be,' she said soothingly, 'that the lady merely leaned over the rail of the ship and the wind snatched it from her hair.'

She patted my hand, thinking mebbe I was sorrowful that I might have to give my treasure up, and I'll confess I was, a little. In times past good fortune hadn't often come my way.

Angus stood up, the comb in his hand, 'I'll place it on the mantel above the range for safe keeping,' he said, walking across the kitchen. 'Tonight, I'll pen a word to Lord Clanranald,' he said to me.

He turned to come back to the table, but just then the outer door banged and old Colin the postman stumped in.

'Twa letters fer ye!' he grunted, pushing them into Angus's hands.

Bridie held up the soup ladle, meaning would he eat? The old fella, needing no further encouragement, sat himself down and said something in Gaelic. I'd guess 'twas that he'd to wait anyway in case Angus meant to reply, and meanwhile he'd be pleased to take some broth.

One of the letters was from Lady Clan, announcing that, if the weather should prove fair for the morrow and the tides, as she believed, agreeable, she proposed to drive over and pay a visit to Milton. Furthermore, if her husband continued in much improved spirits, he was minded to accompany her.

The second letter was addressed to Flora, and was, at long last, from her cousin Jane.

'Oh, Betty, this will interest you!' she declared as she quickly scanned it. 'Jane and Ewan are safe back at Largie, but they came by Edinburgh and had such adventures and frights – and had to rescue Aunt Effie and two of her maids, and take them with them to Kintyre!'

I wondered which two? I doubted Jessie would have been considered. Perhaps 'twas best, perhaps she'd gone home to her Mammie.

Chapter 21

Painted Rooms Are Bonny

'That's it, no more beachcombing for today!' cried Flora, clapping her hands. 'It's every hand to the toil! If Lord and Lady Clan are to come here tomorrow we must make ready!'

She set us to work. Bridie hurried to clear the kitchen table to begin the baking, banishing old Colin and his broth onto a stool in the still room out of her way. Màiri and Elsbet were sent to sweep the parlour and take all the hanks of spun wool and lay them away in the press. I was entrusted with the beeswax and rags to polish the dining table, the chairs, and any and all wooden surfaces about the house.

A visit from the Clan Chief's wife, let alone the Chieftain himself, was a rare occurrence, a rare honour I was told, and a rare cause for fret! Like any careful housewife, Flora wanted her home to look its best. Like any careful farmer, Angus wanted his fences to be stout, his sheep and cattle healthful, and his peat stacks, his harvested crops, his goats, his fowl runs and his barns all neat and ready for inspection.

It took us the rest of the day and into the evening. Everything, inside and out had to be attended to, made bright and clean, and apart from Angus, there were only we womenfolk to do it. Wasn't I out in the barn brushing Tibby's coat when the Eastern star rose above the housetop?

'That's enough, Betty,' Angus told me on finding me there. 'You've done your share. Flora can call you to rise early if there's anything else that's needful. Go to your bed now.'

I was glad to do it, and only a little surprised to find neither Elsbet or Màiri asleep in the maids' room. They must both have decided to go home to their grandmother. I wondered, had they better gowns and clean aprons there, that they'd want to be wearing for this special occasion on the morrow?

I was only a little surprised that they both chose to go home, but surprised indeed when there was no sign of them next morning.

'We must have worked them so hard they've slept late!' Flora said, chuckling. 'How cross Elsbet was when I made her go back and dust above all the door lintels. She said Lady Clan would never "look sae high"! And she's probably right, but I couldn't rest easy until everything was perfect.'

Angus had calculated that the causeway would be passable about eleven of the clock, and so we could expect the Chieftain and his lady in time for a light luncheon, after which they might stay two hours or a little more before the tide began its return.

Bridie came early to finish up the tarts and patties and bake a fresh batch of her scones. To be sure, the lightness of Bridie's scones, had he tasted them, could have made the Young Pretender abandon all his thoughts of thrones and conquests, and settle on the Long Island for ever!

I donned my best gown, the one I'd worn only once since coming from Edinburgh, together with my best boots and an apron Bridie found for me, as white and stiff with starch as would be suited to a lady's maid to Queen Caroline of Ansbach herself.

Elsbet and Màiri did not come.

The morning wore on.

'Will I be running to Old Peg's croft and see what's amiss?' I asked Flora, my hands travelling behind me ready to untie my apron strings.

'Mebbe the old woman's taken sick,' said Bridie, nodding agreement. 'Before the Prince came, we'd have sent Calum!' she added, gazing across the yard to where Angus was knocking a last nail into a fence.

'It could be they're waiting by the croft to see the Clanranalds drive by,' said Flora doubtfully, 'the grandmother will want Lord Clanranald to see the state of her roof.'

Bridie nodded and began to say, ' 'Tis needing attention, surely, before winter sets in… although your brother promised…' her voice faded away as we all three saw a black-clad figure approaching. The old woman's spine was bent nearly double, her feet dragging so that she staggered and nearly fell, only her hawthorn staff saving her. As she hurried as best she could, she called out to us in a harsh cawing voice.

'Why it's Peg Macdonald!' gasped Flora, her fingers flying to her cheeks, 'Whatever can have happened?'

Even as she spoke, the old woman tripped on a clump of bog reeds and fell. Angus, having looked up and seen her approach, ran to her and lifted her up in his arms and carried her past us through the kitchen and into the parlour, where he laid her on the settle. We crowded in after him.

'Tha iad air falbh... tha iad.... air... falbh...' the old grandmother gasped, and fell back, her eyes rolling up in her head.

Not having the Gaelic, this to me was just a bubble of sound, but to the other three it meant something.

'*Gone?* Who's gone?' asked Flora., and then, the only likely meaning coming to her, she said, 'Elsbet? Màiri? Gone? Gone *where*, Mistress Macdonald?'

But the old grandmother, exhausted, seemed unable to tell us.

We stood about, helpless. Why Elsbet and Màiri were gone – if they were – and *where*, I couldn't begin to guess, and Flora and Bridie seemed at a loss to equal mine. I could only think of the dirt marks Peg Macdonald's bog-sodden boots were leaving on the fabric of the settle. How would we get it clean before Lord and Lady Clanranald arrived?

Angus, however, fathomed it more speedily. '*Calum*,' he said, his voice grating, exasperated. 'I'm thinking young Elsbet's been fancying she's in love with him this last few months. She's kept sneaking outdoors to try and speak to him whenever your backs have been turned. *He* doesn't care a straw for her, but he's gone to join the Prince. You've all been harsh on her... not that she didn't deserve it, but this is just the kind of daft thing she'd think to do. If I was a wagering man, I'd lay a golden guinea she's run off to try and find him. To find the Prince and his army.'

'Ach, no wonder she was always sae willing of late to milk the cow, fetch the eggs,' breathed Bridie, 'and there was I thinking they were tasks she'd found she could dally over, before we'd find something harder for her to do.'

'But what can we do?' whispered Flora. 'In less than an hour Lord and Lady Clanranald will be here!'

'Fetch a cup of water,' said Angus. 'Let's try if we can revive the grandmother, and perhaps she can tell us at least which way they went.'

I ran to fetch the cup, while they propped the old woman up on cushions. Slowly, after swallowing a draught she seemed to revive a little, and Angus, kneeling beside her, coaxed a few harshly whispered words from her lips.

'It seems they set off at daybreak,' he told us, 'packs on their backs, towards Loch Boisdale. Old Peg thinks a man with a cart load of peat picked them up at the end of the track. Billy MacNeil, it could have been, but she's not sure it was he. Her eyes are grown dim.'

'Billy McNeil's slow in his wits!' said Flora.

'Aye, and daft enough to take those two silly creatures up, and never ask where they were going or why!' added Bridie.

'Would they have any money?' I asked, thinking it unlikely they would get very far without.

Angus consulted their grandmother again, but the poor old soul seemed not to know. It was Flora who turned and stepped into the kitchen, and returned, shaking her head, her face sorrowful.

'Betty, they took your comb.'

'Och, the wicked wee thieves!' cried Bridie. 'That would be Elsbet! She was sae bitter, *you* found it, Betty. She wanted to have it herself, I could tell.'

'And I was fool enough to say it might be worth forty shillings!' said Angus with a groan.

'They can't have gone far,' said Flora, not with Billy MacNeil.

His horse is a broken down old creature. If I went after them on Tibby, I'd maybe catch them up!'

'But that you cannot do, Flora,' said her brother, pulling out a pocket watch from his "Sabbath" waistcoat, 'Lord and Lady Clanranald will be here in no time at all. It would be the height of rudeness for you or I to be away chasing after those two little fiends. You know well that Lady Clan has always thought you foolish to take them in and try to train them.'

'And it may be they'll come to no harm, Flora, *ghràdhach*,' soothed Bridie, seeing tears start in Flora's eyes. 'Most folks know them, and if they go asking the fishermen to take them o'er the water, most likely they'll not do it, guessing they've run off.'

I untied my apron strings. 'I'll go,' I said. 'I can't ride astride a horse, but I was used to drive my brother's old horse, Molly. I think I could manage Tibby in the trap, if you'll allow it?'

I'll not deny it was the thought of catching up with those young wretches, and taking back the silver comb that was at the front of my mind. 'Twas myself found it, and whether I was permitted to keep it or no, I was verra disinclined to let Elsbet have it. Elsbet, I told myself, might go to the devil! She was an ungrateful little beast and a thief besides. Màiri, I'd had better thoughts of, but everyone had warned me she was a weak-minded creature and easily led.

Angus put Tibby into the shafts of the cart, and I climbed aboard and took the reins warily. Although it was true I'd many a time taken Molly's reins from Pat, as we ambled back and forth down that long road to Carrickfergus harbour, Molly was such a quiet old creature, and knew every inch of the way so well, to be sure there was no need for me to be doing anything at all. 'Twas hardly needful to pull on the reins, even when some other carter with a resty animal made a sudden swerve, or a dog ran barking into the road. Molly had seen it all, and if she'd any thoughts in her head they were of the watering spots along the highway, and the bundle of hay up on the cart behind her which would be hers at journey's end.

Tibby, Flora's dapple grey pony on the other hand, was a mite younger and a deal more lively. When I flicked the reins she set off down the track at a smart trot, with myself hanging to the edge of the seat with my one hand for dear life. Ach, I thought, she's after thinking we're going to Nunton! How will I get her to take the contrary road? Angus had told me to turn right at the end of the lane and take the track to the south and east. Loch Boisdale, where I had never been since my first arrival on the fishing boat, was four miles or so in that direction. As we got to the end of the lane to Milton, I gave Tibby warning by pulling on the right hand rein. She slowed, and her ears twitched, as if this puzzled her and she would like to have askt me was it certain I was? But then she made the turn, and we began to roll over the moorland track between the peat bogs and the lochans, the track rising slowly as we travelled towards the hills.

Taking a glance behind me as we breasted a low rise, I caught a glimpse of a smart chaise with yellow wheels bowling down the roadway from the north. It was too far off to see the occupants clearly, but I was certain the only folk that might own such a pretty jaunting car must be Lord and Lady Clanranald.

Chapter 22

I wish I Were In Carrickfergus

I'd thought we should be hurrying to catch the girls, but Tibby did not share my opinion, so we went at her pace, which was steady. It seemed to me verra slow. I'd no way to urge her to go faster save I beat the poor creature, and why would I be doing that when she was only doing what best she knew? And onyway I'd nothing to hurry her with but a slap of the reins across her rump. So, to ease my fretting I sang:

> I wish I were in Carrickfergus,
> Only for nights in Ballygrand,
> I would swim the deepest ocean,
> But the sea is wide and I cannot swim over,
> And neither have I the wings to fly,
> I wish I had a handsome boatman,
> To carry me over, my love and I.

I thought to myself, 'tis a nonsense of a song. Why would the girl be wanting a handsome boatman if she already has a lover? I'd to slow the rhythm of it to fit it to the jolting of the wheels, but Tibby's ears flicked to and fro as though she was listening. I used to sing this ditty to Molly when we drove down to that very harbour, and it was my belief that she'd pick up her weary hooves the better for it. Pat did not agree, he'd just laugh and say it was myself enjoyed the singing and the jaunting. The horse had no choice in the matter!

As we travelled on towards Loch Boisdale I was all the while working up my anger against those girls. How could they treat Miss Flora so, that had done so much for them? How could they leave their old Grandmother all alone, with no one to care for her? And myself, I should be at Milton, helping to serve the fine repast Flora and Bridie had prepared, and mebbe, when the meal was done, Flora would be opening the spinet, and I'd have been asked to sing for the laird and his lady. *And* hadn't those two wretches stolen my one treasure?

'It's not that I've a conceit of myself,' I told Tibby's ears, 'but my poor face can never be my fortune, 'tis my voice is such luck as I have.' Tibby's ears flicked faster, and it was my belief she agreed with me. 'If a man has a fiddle,' I went on, 'why wouldn't he be playing it? And if a young woman has a voice to sing with, surely that's what she should do?'

Lady Clanranald had liked my singing, and at Flora's ceilidh too, hadn't they all praised me? A dream had been growing in my mind that if it was true that the silver comb was worth a deal of monies, I might buy myself new gowns and slippers, and a fine embroidered shawl, and set myself up, singing in the houses of the gentry. I could be getting myself known for it all over, folk would be asking me to sing at weddings and ceilidhs and all manner of revels. 'Wouldn't that be just grand?' I askt Tibby, as the road began to drop down towards the harbour at Loch Boisdale. Tibby trotted faster, as if she knew we were getting to our stopping place.

I urged her on, right down onto the quayside. We hadn't passed Billy MacNeil or onyone of his description on the way. So I was thinking they'd reached journey's end, and if the luck stayed with me, this was where I'd find the two runaways. There were fishing boats anchored out in the bay, the tide being a fair way out still, and men working at the nets aboard them. To my bewilderment, however, the only person standing on the quay itself was Shona, Lady Clanranald's crotchety maid! She turned to face me as the cart approached, and I saw that she'd a bundle clasped in her hands, and she was weeping, it seemed, with fury.

'Shona! What in the world would you be doing here?'

'They...' she pointed out across the bay, although I couldn't tell from her wavering finger whether she meant the net menders, who seemed from time to time to glance in our direction, or a ship that I now saw was sailing out of the harbour into the sea loch, '*they wouldnae take me!* They've taken those two *straipachs*, and they wouldnae' tak me!'

I knotted the reigns and climbed down from the cart. '*Who wouldn't take you where*, Shona?'

'I'd the monies!' she shouted, stamping her feet and shaking her fist like a bairn in a fret. 'Those two cannae pay them!'

'But where are you going, Shona? Does Lady Clanranald know?'

'I'll tak my oath she doesnae!' said a man's voice from below us, and I looked down and saw Rhuri Macdonald, the big fisherman I danced with at Flora's ceilidh, coming up the stone steps from the shore. 'She's trying tae run away and join the Prince!'

'And that I will, I will!' Shona shouted, and then broke into a stream of Gaelic.

Rhuri shook his head and sighed. 'Although what she thinks the Prince needs auld biddy like her for, trailing in the wake of his army, I cannae imagine,' he said to me.

'I'd be washing his clothes! Cooking his meat!' Shona shouted, stamping her feet again. 'Those Frenchmen could haf taken me, but they took those two daft *straipachs* instead! *They'll* be nae use to my Bonnie Prince!'

I looked a question at Rhuri Macdonald. He pulled a face.

'*Straipachs* iss...' he frowned and looked uncomfortable. His soft island speech then became more marked. 'Iss... young women that iss no better than they ought to be,' he explained. 'The English word iss mebbe, *strumpet*? I'm guessing it's those two young maids of Miss Flora's you're come about?'

'That I have, but is it so, what Shona says? They're gone with some French sailors? That ship moving out towards the mouth of the loch?'

'She iss a three-masted frigate, out of Bordeaux,' said Rhuri, shading his eyes to follow her progress. 'The *Clementine*. She came in on the early morning tide. Something had fouled her rudder, was what I understood them to say. Two of the sailors rowed ashore.'

'You speak French, Rhuri?'

'Nae, he doesnae!' snapped Shona, who was giving us both the foulest of looks. 'They two spoke English, after their own fashion. They left the men aboard tae dive under her and clear whatever was fouling her, and the twa o' them came ashore tae get whisky and supplies.'

'And 'twas supplies they got,' stated Rhuri with a grim smile. 'Twa daft lassies, wi not the least idea in their heids what those sailors iss intending tae do with them! I'm sorry, Mistress,' he said to me, 'If I'd been ashore at the time I'd have stopped them, or tried to. I wass out attending tae my own boat. By the time I saw they wass rowing out to the ship with those men, it wass too late tae stop them. Miss Flora will be sore angry at me.'

'But where are they going?' I asked, ignoring his sighs, 'Back to Bordeaux? What brought them into these waters?'

Rhuri shrugged, 'Spying, most likely, for the French. Testing how well the west coast of the mainland iss guarded. They've nae interest in these islands, I doubt. I couldnae see she wass armed. Just reconnaissance, I'm thinking. Mebbe thinking tae bring a battalion o' fighting men to join the Prince at a later date. I'd guess she'll go back south and then to France to report.'

'Nae, she willnae!' Shona interrupted, 'they tellt me she's bound for Skye, and then out by Harris and into the Northern seas by Shetland. I askt them tae tak me to Skye. 'Tis only a wee way 'cross the water to tae the mainland frae there.' Her voice rose higher and higher, until she could probably be heard in the crofts along the shore.

'Shona, the Prince issn't on Skye, *or* staying in Scotland!' Rhuri hissed, exasperated. 'They say he's set forth from Edinburgh the noo, making for England. If the weather holds up, he'll tak Carlisle. That's a town just to the south of the border, and then they'll march south, on towards London! Wass ye planning tae walk four hundred miles tae join him? 'Tis October nearly ended already, and winter'll be coming on!'

Shona said nothing to this, just glowered.

All the while we were talking (and having our ears scarified by

Shona), I was noticing that a man from one of the larger boats moored amongst the fishing fleet was watching us. Now he shinned over the stern of his craft into a row boat and came sculling towards us. As he grew closer I knew who he was.

He brought the row boat in as close to the harbour wall as the low tide allowed, tied the painter to an iron ring in the rock and scrambled up to join us.

'Good day, John Begg,' I greeted him, '*here* you are, and there was I was thinking you were gone over to the mainland!'

He grinned at me, in no way mortified. 'Those plans were changed at the last minute, lassie,' he said, 'so here I am returned. Am I right in thinking you're wishful to follow the *Clementine* and catch up with her? Someone's gone aboard her that shouldn't have done?'

'Can ye catch her? *Can* ye?' demanded Shona, darting at him before I'd a chance to go seeking after my tongue. 'I'm wanting tae be over in Skye, and this missy-missy is wanting to bring back twa servant lassies that's run off frae their mistress.'

I was noticing she did not mention that she too had run off from her mistress.

Rhuri Macdonald stared up at the sky with its hastening clouds and hissed through his teeth. 'It *might* be done,' he said to me, slowly, gazing out toward the mouth of the wide sea loch and the eastern horizon where the *Clementine* was growing smaller, 'she's wallowing in the troughs, not making much way, and she's not out of the loch yet. They ran up topsail too soon tae my mind. You might catch her but I wouldnae advise it. You'd have tae be gey fast about it, the weather's nae going tae last. The wind's rising. They'd hae done better tae have stayed anchored in the shelter o' the loch thiss night.'

'Ladies, be my guest!' said John Begg, sweeping us a mocking bow. I noticed then that he wasn't wearing his uniform as a militia man, but the rough trousers and jersey favoured by fishermen. 'It's best I take ye, my boat's a cutter.'

'A cutter?' It meant nought to me.

'Fast and light,' he declared, 'she truly cuts through the water, doesnae limp along like a fishing boat.' He grinned at Rhuri, 'Not tae say your old bathtub doesnae do the job she's built for, but I'm no out tae catch sprats!'

'A cutter, iss that so?' said Rhuri, thoughtfully. It seemed he was not a man to rise to any bait John Begg might cast before him.

'The best there is, she leaps through the waves like a dolphin!' John Begg was boasting now.

'Then what are ye waiting fae, man?' demanded Shona, 'Let's be awa!'

I didn't know what to think or do. Miss Flora and her brother were expecting me to return, either with Elsbet and Màiri, or, if I had failed to catch up with them, alone, but as quickly as possible in view of the grand visit from the Chieftain and his wife. Would they expect me to take to the waves to bring those two foolish maidens back? I bethought me, too, of Tibby and the pony trap, waiting patiently on the quayside.

'Dinae fash yerself, Mistress,' said Rhuri, laying a kindly hand on my shoulder, 'I can send Dougie tae Miss Flora wi' a note tae say what's happened. He'll ride the pony and come again for yourself and the trap.'

Dougie, it seemed, was his son, a boy of twelve years just outgrowing his strength, all legs and arms, who had now appeared at his side, eager and excited to be to be trusted with this errand.

'Verra well,' I agreed, doubtfully, making to step down to the shore and John Begg's row boat. Into my head came the words once more, "I wish I were in Carrickfergus", and how I did then wish it! My life had oft times been hard, times I'd been hungry and wretched, but it had always been clear to me what I must do. Since my choices had been so few, there'd been precious few to make. Here I'd a choice. Go or stay. Go after those silly colleens through the mounting waves, or stay safe on land? *Ach, Miss Flora,* I thought, *I wish I knew if this is what you'd do!*

Chapter 23

The Tall Lofty Ship

John Begg's certainty persuaded me, he seemed so cocksure that we could catch the *Clementine* if we hurried. Even so, we'd a delay as Shona found she'd left her bundle on the quay and had to go back for it. (Wasn't I guessing all along she was a bird of ill omen?) All the while the *Clementine* was drawing further and further out towards the Minch. I looked back as we boarded the cutter, which nestled in amongst a huddle of fishing boats. (Almost you could say the soldier had hidden her there.) Rhuri Macdonald, his son, and Tibby the pony, stood side by side on the quay, watching our departure. 'Twas probably my fancy that they looked uneasy, all three.

John Begg told us, as the cutter sliced through the waves just as he'd boasted it would, that this was a new type of boat, of the kind now most favoured by His Majesty's Customs' men.

'But I thought *you* were… a Highland Militia man?' I gulped, for the churning of the waters was already affecting me, although as yet we were nowhere near the open sea. Flora had insisted that we'd been remarkably lucky to have a calm crossing when we came from Kintyre that time. Then, I'd only half believed her.

'I'm a man o'pairts!' he replied, and moved to attend to the sails.

I noticed then he'd another man aboard, a small wizened fella in tar cloth britches, barefoot but verra nimble on his feet, who looked somehow the more undoubted sailor. I couldn't tell you why this should be so, but my feeling soon proved me right. From the very moment we set out, this unknown man was arguing with John Begg, gazing ahead and pointing at the *Clementine*, which seemed to be veering first towards one side of the long mouth of the sea loch and then to the other.

'Is she alright?' I queried of Shona as we crouched in the bow, thinking she perhaps knew more of the habits of ships than I did. 'Should she not be setting a straighter course?'

'How can she with the wind coming in great gusts from the northeast like it is!' she snapped, but she too sounded anxious. Perhaps, I was hoping, 'tis just her stomach, for this leaping through the waves was certainly causing uneasiness to mine.

John Begg now came forward to speak to us, shouting above the noise of the wind, 'I'm sorry, but Bruce, the wee mannie that's with me, says the wind's risen up too strong of a sudden! We might catch her, but if we do we'd never board her, the way it's gusting out here. You see how she's swinging about, tilting in the water, this way and that? He's fearful her rudder may have failed completely. He believes we must give it up.'

Even as he was saying this the "wee mannie", Bruce, gave an anguished yell, and shouted something in Gaelic. Perhaps he was trying to warn the ship ahead, but what with the racket of the wind and the crashing and hissing of the waves, together with the distance between our boat and the frigate, for sure they never could have heard him. And if they had, 'twould not have saved them. Almost at once the *Clementine* must have caught the full force of a sudden great blast of wind tearing across the eastern slopes of Ben Kenneth, the tall hill to the north of the loch. She seemed to stagger in the water and then slowly keel over until one of her three masts snapped in twain, her huge sails billowed sideways and pulled her over into the sea with a great rending and tearing of masts and spars. We could see anxious figures hurling themselves across her decks, tugging frantically at the ropes to lower the heavy sails, whilst some below decks must have begun to slam the hatches and the shutters to the gun ports, but 'twas too late. Slowly the weight of her falling sails and rigging pulled the *Clementine* over onto her side where she lay, water rising over her deck, so that she began to sink before our appalled sight. Meanwhile, the height of the waves was increasing, and our boat, her long bowsprit still slicing bravely through them, was beginning to drench us with billows of flying spray.

John Begg swore. Shona flung herself into the bottom of the

boat, wailing and keening. Bruce began stowing our sails, so that we were no longer driven by the wind, and became like a cockle shell, bouncing over the churning wave crests. When I struggled to stand and look back to see how far we might be from the harbour, I saw that the whole fishing fleet was following us, being rowed by teams of men at great speed, out of the shelter of the harbour towards the sinking ship.

John Begg placed his hand on my shoulder. 'Bear up, lassie,' he shouted in my ear, 'those that are not drowned, they'll pluck from the water. Bruce and I will row closer and see if we can save any, but the Loch Boisdale fishing fleet are the masters here.'

'Did you do this?' I demanded, wrenching myself away from him, my whole body shaking with the shock. 'Did you scupper the *Clementine*? Because it's a spy you are, are you not? A spy for the House of Hanover and the King's Parliament in London? All this pretending to be a common soldier! She was a French ship. Mebbe she was here to bring monies for the Jacobite cause! Or mebbe to pick up young men that want to serve this young Prince, and ferry them to the mainland. Mayhap the rudder was faulty because you made it so! And now those two poor girls are likely dead and gone!'

John Begg's ruddy complexion was never one that could turn white with anger, but his eyes grew narrow and his mouth became a puckered seam.

'*I* didnae scupper her, you silly chit! Those fools should never have sailed! Not until they were sure of their repairs, had them tried and tested. It's true I've been following her manoeuvres up and down the coast and around the islands, but my masters in Edinburgh wanted her *caught and impounded*, not sunk to the bottom of the sea! Nevertheless, despite your daft suspicions, you may rely on Bruce and myself to do what we can, *and* get you safe back to land!'

With this he turned his back and stepped away without meeting my eye. He took an oar from beneath the bench and Bruce took the other. I sat down with a thump, all the fight gone out of me, and covered my face with my hands. At the listing ship, now quite close to us, I couldn't bear to look.

Shona, however, since no one took any notice of her keening and wailing in the bottom of the boat, now rose up and crouched in the bow, watching, her crabbed face alight with cruel glee.

'There's men in the water!' she cawed, 'clinging on tae pieces o' the mast! I cannae see those lassies, forbye they're drownded! You'll haf tae gae back and tell Miss Flora Macdonald,' she told me. 'She'll likely be glad tae haf bin spared the expense o' burying those *Straipachs*!'

John Begg and Bruce were rowing hard. Thinking to close my ears to Shona's gloating, and not being willing to watch folk drown, I let my eyes rest on them as they strained at the oars. Slowly, though 'twas hard to believe we were making any way through the swelling waves, the cutter began to draw closer and closer to the sinking ship.

But no matter how hard they rowed, these two could not out row the fishermen of Loch Boisdale. Already several of the fishing boats had overtaken us. Eight men rowed each boat. A man with an oar or a spar stood in each prow, feet braced but leaning out over the waters so that a drowning man might grab the oar and be hauled into the boat. John Begg might despise these humble fishing boats as "bathtubs", but every man amongst them knew how to urge his boat up the steep walls of the mounting waves and send the craft skimming over the crests to aid the injured and dying. I saw Rhuri Macdonald haul three men from the deep by the belts of their britches, and dump them down into the well of his boat. He stood, his feet firmly planted in the bow, whilst the other men rowed, each and every stroke perfectly matched. Rhuri looked as calm and able as ever I had seen him, whether dancing at the ceilidh or standing on the quay shading his eyes to watch the rising wind, and warn of worsening weather. Now, he must have spied John Begg in the cutter and hailed him.

'There's twa over to yer starboard side!' he shouted, cupping his hands to his mouth, and almost immediately a man's head bobbed up close to me. Without weighing the thought, I reached my hand into the water and made a grab at his coat. The burden of him, for he was a big fella and his clothes were already sodden, nearly pulled me over into the sea. John Begg stumbled forward and took the man's arm, and between us we hauled him, gasping and spouting water, into the stern. Straightway, another man on the other side of the boat, was clinging to Bruce's oar and in danger of capsizing us. 'Tis probable that was indeed his intention, for when John Begg and Bruce had him over into the cutter and laid on the boards, he lay a few moments, gasping and swearing, his face purple with fury. Then he began to rage in what I supposed was the French language. When John Begg answered him harshly in the same tongue, he scrambled to his feet and snatched a knife from his belt. Dripping both blood and water (for he had suffered a great graze to his forehead) he launched himself at John Begg, seemingly intent on cutting his throat. The soldier held him off with difficulty as the boat began rocking wildly from side to side. Bruce tried to scramble to his feet but the oar which lay across his knees tangled his legs so that he was thrown on his back. In that moment, I, fool of a lass, hurled myself across the boat to clutch at the French attacker's coat tails.

I don't recall much of what happened next, only that a sharp pain took away my breath and then my senses. Later they told me the Frenchman had spun round and plunged the knife into my neck, the blade slipping down under my collarbone and deep into my shoulder.

'How he missed your heart, lassie,' I shall never know,' John Begg told me later, many months later. 'It can only have been the pitching of the boat that spoiled his aim.'

For the rest of that day, I must have lain insensible in the boat, a pile of rope for a pillow beneath my head, and with part of John Begg's shirt torn and pressed and bound against my shoulder to stem the bleeding.

At moments I must have swum into wakefulness, for I recall that other bodies were hauled from the sea and laid beside me, some mebbe living, others not. Once, I opened my eyes and turned my head to look who lay beside me, and saw that it was Elsbet. Her eyes were open but she saw nothing. She'd a great wound gouged into her skull, washed clean by the sea. If she still had the silver comb about her, I'd no strength to search for it. I remember wondering if Màiri, too, was drowned? Other bodies were heaved into the boat. On Elsbet's body I could see no blood, no bleeding. I recalled my brother, Danny, saying of a young man killed in a shebeen brawl, that once the heart stops beating the blood no longer flows. So I knew for certain she was dead.

I recall, too, thinking sorrowfully that although Elsbet had irritated the life out of me, I would never have wished her this terrible end. And Màiri. What might have been her treasure, that voice that bubbled deep in her throat, was it gone? And mebbe mine was too. As my mind drifted away into a place of darkness, and I knew no more, I grieved for Elsbet and Màiri, and for myself. Was I also to die, and never sing again?

Chapter 24

Let Me Go, Let Me Tarry

Dunstaffnage Castle: that's where I found my wits agin. Perhaps, like many a poor prisoner before me, 'twas the first question I asked of my gaoler, 'Where is this place?'

'Dunstaffnage,' she replied, 'they brought thee here with the rest o' the Frenchies.' She'd a strange accent, strange to me, anyway. Not Scottish. English mebbe?

'Why… am I here?' I asked.

I sensed rather than saw the woman shrug. 'They brought all the living ones here, and tha wast with them. We didn't expect thee to live, but tha did, and now I'm thinking they'll hang thee. So much for my hard work, keeping thee alive all this while! Is tha French? Tha doesn't sound it.'

'I'm not French. I wasn't with… those people,' I said, struggling to get my mind to start its work, like an old mill wheel that was stuck in silt. Her words about "them hanging me" I heard, but they seemed meaningless. 'I was with John Begg. We were… trying… to rescue people from the French ship that sank.'

'Tha can tell it to the Sheriff's court!' the woman said. I wasn't sure she was listening. She went away, locking a heavy oak door behind her.

I was lying on a bed of straw, and covered with a rough blanket. My only clothing was a shift. I was reasonably clean, so far as I could tell. My body felt light, weak, and when I raised my hand before my eyes it appeared fleshless. I thought I could almost see the bones within. My shoulder felt stiff and sore. I must have lain here many days. Weeks even?

I turned my head towards the light, and saw that I was in a small stone built room. A cell, bare of everything but my makeshift bed. I was quite alone, although there was another pile of straw in the far corner. As though I had once had company. The room had no windows, only an arrow slit through which light gleamed. I turned the word over in my mind, *Dunstaffnage*... it meant nought to me. The woman, the gaoler, for I had no doubt that was what she was, had said it was a castle. I was imprisoned here. Why? How? My stuttering millwheel of a mind turned up no answer from the muddy depths, so I closed my eyes and sank back down into the silt.

When next I woke, the light had changed, dimmed with the sinking sun which yet tinged the rough grey edges of the arrow slit with a faint golden hue. I had woken because the woman was back. A plump, bustling little woman she was, with a smooth closed face which gave little of her thoughts away. She carried a bowl and a spoon and pushed a wee stool, a *creepie*, before her with her foot. She placed the stool by my makeshift bed, laid the bowl upon it and went back to close the door. She didn't lock it. I thought, she knows I'm too weak to escape. The scent of the bowl's contents made my nostrils twitch and I felt my mouth fill up with spittle. It seemed my stomach was ready to eat.

'Brought thee some broth. I'm thinking tha might swallow it again now? It's bin a while, but tha's here with us again.'

I tried to pull myself up to sit, but my arms were too feeble, my shoulder too stiff and painful. I fell back, and I think I wailed aloud at my defeat.

'It's no bother,' said my captor, placing bowl and spoon back on the creepie and taking several bundles of straw which she pushed behind me so that I was propped up like Miss Evangeline on her many pillows. How was it that I remembered Miss Evangeline so clearly of a sudden? When whatever happenings had brought me to this place *as a prisoner,* I could hardly recall at all?

The woman seated herself and began to spoon broth into my mouth. I swallowed, hungrily.

'Nay, nay, not too much to start off,' she said, 'or tha'll hurl it all back. Tha's just been on a water diet and some powders, and a syrup the doctor gived me for thee – and a dash of whisky bye and bye.' She chuckled at this last, which perhaps the doctor had *not* advised?

'How long have I been here?' I asked. Surely it could not be many days if I'd been fed nothing but that?

'I'd say...' she stopped spooning the broth to consider, spoon suspended, 'Let's see then? I recall they brought tha here at t'end o' November. It took a mortal long time for yon ship to get here from Mull, what with the storms we were having just then.'

'What month are we in now?'

'February, just.'

'February! 'Tis three months or more I've been here?'

'Why, tha's Irish!' the woman said, ignoring the question. My speech had betrayed me, 'However did an *Irish* lass get herself aboard a French ship?'

'I niver was aboard a French ship,' I said. 'It's a mistake someone's made. I don't know what happened. A man stabbed my neck, I remember that... he was a Frenchman, a sailor?'

I tried to make this woman understand between the urgent spoonfuls of broth she seemed so intent on pushing into my mouth. Truth was, I was hard put to explain what I remembered only dimly myself. John Begg had laid me down in the boat. After that I could recall little.

'We were rescuing people... taking them from the sea,' I told her, pushing the spoon away, 'Some of them were dead, drowned. Elsbet was drowned, poor lass.' I felt my cheeks crumple and tears spill from my eyes.

'Aye, they said as there were good few lost,' the woman agreed, unconcerned, 'when t'storm blew up out of nowhere. And of those they brought here, a deal more of 'em died. The rest, those that survived, they took off to Glasgow. That old woman they brought here with thee. She died, just on Hogmanay. They said it was gaol fever, but I keep the place spotless!'

'An old woman?'

'Shona, she said her name was, and she said tha name is Betty.

At least she supposed it was, although she said sometimes ladies call their maids Betty when they can't be fadged to learn the girl's true name.'

'Shona *died?*' Tears were overflowing and streaming down my cheeks now, soaking the neck of my shift. I'd never taken to Shona, nor she to me, and something... she'd done or said something... I couldn't remember what it was, but I knew she'd been no friend to me. Yet I wept for her.

'To be honest with thee,' said my gaoler, laying the bowl aside and settling down for a quiet gossip, 'she mebbe willed it, tha knows? She was for ever crabbing and crying over this young Prince they say is up in Inverness just now with an army. She'd wanted t'be with him and she couldn't. It were like she were in love with him! She said if she couldn't go with him she'd rather be dead. An old woman like that! It weren't decent!'

'I remember,' I said. 'She thought she could serve him, wash his clothes, cook his meals.' Why could I recall Shona so clearly, when so much seemed to have vanished from my memory?

'They'd never have let her near him. I told the daft creature so, and she cried her heart out!'

It seemed my gaoler thought I'd eaten enough, for she laid the spoon away in the bowl on the floor.

'Poor Shona. What is your name?'

'Alice,' she said, and gasped, clapping her hand to her mouth. I understood that she hadn't intended to tell me that, 'but *tha* is to call me Mistress MacKie.'

'Who does this castle belong to, if you please, Mistress MacKie?' I asked, wondering who had imprisoned me. Or why?

'Surely tha should know that!' she exclaimed, clearly astonished that I might not. 'Not that the family are here just now. They're staying with relatives in England, them being on the side of the King. Tha *must* know of him! This German fella that's in London?'

Seemingly she decided that we had gossiped long enough, for she picked up bowl and spoon, rose from the stool and started towards the door.

'If tha'd oblige me, there's a pail over yon.' She nodded towards the corner of the room. I understood she thought I could at least crawl to it to relieve myself and save her some trouble. I nodded weakly.

The light was waning fast as it does in the winter months. I lay and watched it die. Mistress Alice MacKie hadn't left me a candle.

This castle, this prison of mine, must be quite close to the sea. I could hear the waves crashing and breaking against the rocks. I was too weary to weep anymore, but my mind now scurried through such rags and patches of my past life as I could recollect. It was like visiting the rooms of a great house, some lighted, some familiar, others so dark I couldn't say whether I knew them at all. I'd named John Begg to Mistress MacKie, but I couldn't picture his face. Yet I could remember the dead face of Elsbet, lying so still beside me in his boat. I could picture Miss Evangeline Boyd, but where was the face of… Miss Flora Macdonald? Did she know what had happened to me? Did anyone know? Did they sorrow over me, believing me dead?

I recollected snatches of time which must have been spent in this room. I had not, surely, been out of my wits for more than three months? No, although those scenes were hazy, I must have been awake from time to time.

I faintly recalled Shona's voice, lamenting piteously, and had wished she would leave off and let me sleep. Men standing over me, asking questions. Questions I could niver answer. I'd thought in my sickness and confusion that they must be speaking Gaelic, which had perplexed me at the time, because they seemed to stumble over the words and try to help each other out with the aid of a book they had, as though that language was new to them. Yet I had the notion that they were Scots. Now it occurred to me that they must have been trying to question me in French! People here, whoever *they* were, must have supposed me to be French. A French woman, rescued from the *Clementine*. I remembered the *Clementine*. She was the ship that had capsized in that long sea loch. Elsbet and Màiri had gone with the French sailors, thinking they would take them to the mainland, where they'd hoped to find Calum and the Prince. *That Prince agin!* Shona, too, had wanted to find him. I couldn't recall his face or anything about him. Perhaps I had never seen him? Sore of heart, mind and body, confused and bewildered, I must have drifted once more into sleep.

Mistress MacKie must have told those men I was in my senses agin, for when the morning sun rose, there they were, standing between me and the light. Two men, one old, one younger. They were argufying.

'She *must* be French,' the younger one was insisting. 'Everyone aboard that ship was French. I made sure of it!'

'We know the Young Pretender has plenty of Irish *men* in his train,' grunted the older man. 'Some of them have his ear I've been told, having been with him either in Rome or at the French Court. *And* he listens to their opinions too often for the liking of many of the Jacobite Clan Chieftains. One of them, O'Sullivan, decides his battle plans. I've heard it's a bone of contention with them!'

'Then perhaps she was the mistress, or more likely since she's no beauty, the servant of one of them, and he passed her on to one of the French Officers,' insisted the younger man. 'but *I* think she's French.

'Bon-jaw madam-mwa-sell. Com-ont alley voo?'

I sighed, 'I'm Irish, Sir,' I said. It seemed best to confess it, or this fool would go on straining his jaw.

'Aha, aha! I knew it!' gloated the older fella, pleased to be in the right. 'Well, missy, what were you doing on that French ship, hey?'

'I niver was on the ship. 'Twas part of the rescue party I was. Wi' a man called John Begg.'

'John Begg!' the older fella exclaimed.

'This is the man you mentioned before?' asked the younger one.

'Highland Militia… or so they say,' said his companion. 'Listen,

Duncan, I need to talk to her. This is important. Step away out of the light, will you? I need to be able to see her face while she answers me.'

The man called Duncan moved, unwillingly I thought, over to the arrow squint, and leaned agin the wall. Sullen. He'd been so sure I was French, and it didn't suit his notions of himself to be found at fault. Now I could see the old fella clear. He'd a full white wig over a bald pate, a short red nose and a good few purple veins staining his cheeks. He wore a suit of superfine such as I'd seen on gentlemen in Edinburgh. Otherwise there seemed nothing remarkable about him. He perched himself on Mistress MacKie's creepie, which she'd left behind.

'Now then, my lass, where, when, and how did you meet with this John Begg?'

That seemed far too complicated a question for my poor befuddled mind. Where and how *had* I met him?

'I wouldn't know, sir,' I said. 'Oft times and places, mebbe?'

Chapter 25

Then He Did That Girl Betray

I niver learned his name, this old fella. The young one was Duncan, though that could have been his first name or his last. Anyways, I stored it in my mind for the future (if I was to have a future. Mistress MacKie's words about them mebbe hanging me had stayed in my head). The old one went on asking me about John Begg.

'He told you he was a Militia man? Where were you when he told you this?'

'In Edinburgh,' I ventured. Edinburgh was a long way from here, or so I was hoping. I'd no real notion where this Dunstaffnage castle might be. I'd no notion either, what this man wanted from me. So how could I decide which of his questions I should answer, even supposing I *could* answer them? Did I owe ony loyalty to John Begg? He had seemed to befriend me, to wish to help me, yet here I was in a prison cell.

'Edinburgh?' the old fella appeared surprised. 'What was he doing in Edinburgh? What were you doing there, for that matter?'

'I worked as a maid. First I came from Ireland, caring for a sick woman, and then I got work as a lady's maid, sir.'

'I see. And while you were working as a maid you met John Begg… or at least a fellow who styled himself so?'

'Indeed, sir,' I replied, not sure whether he meant that John Begg was not his real name. Or what he was meaning at all.

'And what was John Begg doing?'

'He was… a soldier as I said, sir, a Militiaman at the castle.' Duncan, still brooding by the wall, made a small grunt of surprise.

'Edinburgh castle, it was,' I added, for I was sure I'd heard that there were a great many castles in Scotland, and for all I knew John Begg might have been in any one of them.

'And what did he say to you there?'

I shrugged and then wished I hadn't, for the scars to my neck and shoulder, though they seemed healed, still pained me grievously. 'Nothing of note, sir, not that I recall. He told me the name of one of the hills there. Arthur's Seat, he said 'twas, and he laughed at me.'

'Laughed at you!'

'He called me a wee Irish giantess.'

This made the old fella chuckle, though it wasn't a sound I cared for.

Then the young one, Duncan, chimed in, 'Surely this is of no account, sir? What he said to her in Edinburgh? It's what she was doing with him on South Uist that we need to know. What was his involvement with that shipwreck?'

'*I* need to know if we're talking about the same man!' snapped the old fella. 'It's my belief there might be more than one laddie calling himself John Begg. Otherwise he seems to have the knack of being in two places at once! What say you, lassie?'

'I don't know any more about him,' I replied, grateful for this turn in the talk. I might owe John Begg no loyalty, but the longer I could put off ony mention of Miss Flora Macdonald, the better I thought it would be. 'I saw only the one man. First in Edinburgh and then... then when he took me in his boat to try to rescue two young maidservants that had foolishly gone with the French sailors.'

'It was definitely the same man?'

'Truly, it was, sir.'

The old fella threw up his hands, seemingly defeated. I was tired to my bones, and I could feel my eyes filling up with tears, so weary as I was. I allowed my head to droop in the hope that he'd not see them.

'Och, I doubt we'll get anything useful out of her, she's just a drab of a maid servant!' the young one said. 'I suppose, whatever she was doing or trying to do, this fellow Begg wanted rid of her. Didn't want her hanging around his neck! When she was stabbed, whether it was by one of the sailors from the *Clementine* or not, she could be nothing but a burden to him, so he threw her in with the other captives, and she ended up here.'

They both fell silent. My strength, such as it was, was fast draining away. Tears of weariness and mortification slid down my cheeks. What this Duncan said cut to my heart, yet it seemed all too likely. Injured, perhaps fatally, I would indeed have been nothing but a burden to John Begg. Someone, somehow, had rounded up the living and the wounded from the *Clementine*, and perhaps placed us all aboard another ship. I now recalled some misty and nightmarish memory of being hoisted onto the deck of a much larger boat than the cutter. Had John Begg betrayed me? I began to realise that he must have done.

'I believe we should leave her be for now,' said the old fella, evidently sizing up my tearful, defeated state. 'On the whole, I agree with you, Duncan, in that I doubt this creature has much that is useful for us. You know, I don't care to get rough wi' 'em, unless I really think they're holding something back? It could be Mistress MacKie will get more from her. Sometimes that works better with these women of the lower classes. What we're to do with her, I don't know. She'll have to be kept here for now.'

He hauled himself up from the creepie, and they departed. I listened for the key being turned in the door, but they left it unlocked. I could run, I thought, but where? How? And in my shift only? Truth was, I hadn't the strength hardly to stagger across to Mistress MacKie's pail to relieve myself, let alone try to escape from an unknown fortress perched high above an unknown shore.

Mistress MacKie brought me porridge, apologising crossly that if 'twas dry and burnt from standing too long on the hob, it was because she'd had to wait whilst "them two gentlemen" as she termed them, questioned me.

'I'd brought thee a gown to wear too,' she said, tossing this across the foot of my straw bed. ' 'T'ain't decent for a lass to be in company with gentlemen as tha is. I would have brought it sooner, but they wouldn't wait while it was fetched.'

I understood then that rough as her speech seemed, this was just her manner, she'd no real malice towards me. But no real liking either.

'Thank you, Mistress,' I managed to say, swiping the tears from my face with the back of my hand. 'I'm thinking my own gown was spoiled?'

'Spoiled! 'Twas in rags! And soaked through with blood! When we cut it from thee I threw it in t'fire.'

'It was my best,' I said, sorrowfully, 'for Sunday wearing. My Mistress gave it me.'

'Aye, and likely she'll stop it out tha wages, supposing she'll ever get t'tak thee back at all!' said Mistress Alice MacKie. She stayed only to observe that I had made use of the pail she had provided, leaving me with 'Put yon gown on, lass, and mak thaself half-decent!'

I was afraid to ask what had happened to my boots.

I managed, despite the weakness in my arms and legs, to stand and pull on the gown. It was of an old-fashioned style with full skirts which might once have been kilted up to show an embroidered petticoat beneath. The bodice fit me reasonably well, and the whole hung almost to the floor, so 'twas of a length for decency. The sleeves indeed were on the long side, falling well below my wrists. The fabric was what they call a "brocade", and had once been of fine quality, but was now sadly worn, with many pulled threads from the nap hanging loose. I could ask Mistress MacKie for a needle and thread to turn the sleeves up. Since she was so keen to make me decent, I thought I might try asking her too, for a pair of shoes or slippers to wear. The wooden boards of the floor felt rough and splintery to my bare feet.

I stumbled over to the arrow slit and viewed the world from my prison. I was high above the ground here, four floors up, mebbe? A poor serving wench rather than a princess in this tower, I thought ruefully. A morning of dull grey skies greeted me. Grey skies and clear colourless water. Water so smooth today, the waves were breaking on the sands, gentle as a sigh. I wondered, until I remembered the loud crashing waves of the previous night, if it was indeed the sea or some great inland loch? It was still early, and I now saw a fleet of fishing boats coming in on the tide, followed by the gulls, diving and squawking for their share of the catch. Craning my neck, I could see a small group of white painted crofts huddled in the curve of the bay. Out to sea, on the horizon, crouched in the mist, I thought I could make out the humped back shape of a group of islands.

I thought, find out where you are, where this castle is situated. Is it on the mainland, or on one of the inner islands? Last night Mistress MacKie had mentioned Mull. That was the name of one of the islands of the nearer Hebrides. Miss Flora and I had slept a night there on our journey from Kintyre. But I recalled that Mistress MacKie had said it had taken a long while for the ship to come here *from* Mull. So perhaps that had been a place to take shelter from the storms she'd spoken of, along the way? This must surely be the mainland?

How am I to get away from this place, I was wondering? For getaway I vowed I would, and go back to Miss Flora Macdonald and her brother. If they will take me in agin. Tears started in my eyes, thinking how I'd failed to rescue Elsbet and Màiri. But the dear Lord knows I tried. Rhuri Macdonald would speak for me, surely? I'll manage it somehow. When I had my strength agin I promised myself I'd sing for my boat passage, for my bed and my food at every village, at every wayside inn and harbour until I got there. Until I got to Milton, to the place where I'd once been happy.

But even as I was telling myself these valiant intentions, weary helpless tears were tracking their way down my cheeks once more.

'I mun eat a deal of burnt porridge!' I said aloud, although there was no one to hear me, 'to have strength to run from this place and make my way back to the Long Isle.'

I leaned against the stone embrasure, looking out over the water, and rubbing the smooth pile of my borrowed gown between my fingers, I began to sing softly, a Scottish song, though I'd heard it, and sung it betimes, in Ireland. The lassie singing the words is seemingly determined she'll not be cast down by the loss of a faithless lover. John Begg had niver been my lover, yet somehow he'd betrayed me. It was a song well suited to my mood.

> Sae, I'll put on my gown of green, as a forsaken token,
> That will let the young lads know, the bonds of love are broken.
> Mony a horse has slipt and fell,
> And risen agin right early,
> And mony a lass has lost her lad,
> And found another right fairly

My voice was weak and quavering after these long weeks of sickness, but I swore I would find it agin. I was indeed forsaken, but I would not give in to despair. Those two men, Duncan and the old fella, had said I must be kept here the while, but they hadn't spoken of hanging me. They hoped Mistress MacKie might discover more from me, but what was there to find?

Chapter 26

Oh, Can Ye Sew Cushions? Oh, Can Ye Sew Sheets?

'Mistress MacKie?' I begged, when she came that evening with more broth and morning-baked bread to go with it, 'if I'm to be kept here I'd be glad to have some work to do? A few years back, before I went for a maid, I was working as a spinster in Belfast. I can spin flax or wool or lint. If I'd a chair to sit on and a spinning wheel, or a distaff, I could mebbe be of service to ye? For sure, I'm not used to being idle.'

Mistress MacKie nearly dropped the bowl, she was so taken aback. 'Mercy!' she said, '*himself* never said ought about setting thee to work!' She was evidently shocked that I should even think of it.

I flapped the over long sleeves of the gown at her, and wheedled, 'And if ye'd find me a needle and thread I could sew these up if you please, Mistress? *Please?*'

She was doubtful, verra doubtful, but when she returned for my empty bowl (from this time forward she left me to feed myself) she brought a blunt darning needle already threaded with a length of coarse thread, which was all she said she had to hand. 'I'll not give thee scissors,' she said darkly, 'for fear of what tha might do with 'em!'

I wondered what she thought I might do with them. Kill her? Or kill myself?

Over the next days the two men did not come agin, and I continued to beg her for some occupation. Gazing out the arrow slit told me little about the place where I was that I hadn't already fathomed. Sitting on the low creepie for any length of time caused my back and my injured shoulder to ache. Going over and over it in my thoughts, (although I was beginning, slowly, to recall more of what had befallen me since the day of the ship wreck) gave me little comfort.

However, my pleading, together with my suggestions for

employment, evidently softened Mistress MacKie's suspicions of me to some degree, and one morning she announced that I could help her to hem some sheets. 'To cut and handle t'cloth is work that needs two,' she announced, 'though struggling to bring two chairs up four flights of stairs is a mite more than I'd bargained for.'

She explained to me then that the kitchen, where it seemed she had her chief domain in this part of the castle, was indeed four storeys below. I thought this might be useful knowledge and it also explained some of her resentment of me. Being my gaoler, having to bring food to me and carry down the slop bucket each day was an imposition on top of whatever other duties she was expected to perform. I'd wager the men who were holding me captive had niver given this a thought. Perhaps, like Mistress Afton in the house in Canongate (I was recollecting *her* now), I could win over Mistress MacKie with my willingness to work at whatever tasks she set me?

So began my work at Dunstaffnage. Mistress MacKie brought, by stages, two chairs, the linen and a *huswife* of needles and pins, which she kept very much to herself, together with the scissors which were attached to the chatelaine at her waist by a chain.

We laid the roll of linen out on the floor and folded it back until she was satisfied that we had two sheets of equal size. Then, still not trusting me with the scissors, she knelt painfully upon the boards and cut along the fold (complaining the while of splinters to her knees). This done, she allowed me to take one sheet to turn in and pin and tack the hems. And wasn't she watching me every minute to see that I did it as she thought it should be done? She must have been satisfied, for I was permitted to begin a careful hemming stitch, and after a while she bethought her of other duties and went away, leaving me to it.

So I sat in my prison cell and sang. The song I chose was one I'd heard Bridie sing in the kitchen at Milton. 'Oh can ye sew cushions, Oh can ye sew sheets, and can ye sing ballooloo, when the bairn greets?' 'Tis a sad, sweet little lullaby such as a hard pressed mother might sing to a fractious bairn, but it suited the task and my mood. Like a sorrowful bairn I was in sore need of some comfort.

When the sheets were finished (and evidently my stitchery had passed her test) she set me to sew pillow cases. Now and agin, winded from climbing the four flights of stairs, she would seat herself on the second chair to catch her breath, and ask me about myself. My strength being now improved, I was recalling more and more of my history and the disaster that had overtaken me. So I was able and willing to tell her of my early life and how I had come to be in Scotland. 'I was working as a maid to a farmer and his sister on the island they call the "long island",' I finally admitted.

'Their names?' she demanded, and I knew this was the kind of thing she was expected to report to "the two gentlemen", my captors.

'Oh, Macdonald,' I replied, as though 'twas of no account, 'but then they all were on that island, the whole population of them! Or if they weren't known by Macdonald, they'd some nickname or such.'

She shook her head over this, and I didn't think I had given too much away. Surely everyone here on the mainland would know how common the name Macdonald was in Uist?

In return I managed to learn that she was, as she told me, proudly, a Yorkshire woman from a town called Whitby. There, she admitted crossly, she had been 'fool enough to marry a sailor lad from Arbroath. And then he's drownded, leaving me without a penny, and I'm stranded in *this* benighted land!' she grumbled. 'Nothing for it but to offer my services as a cook and housekeeper to the gentry, which is not what I was accustomed to, but needs must!'

'And so you came to work for... the family that owns this castle?' I tried to keep ony special meaning from my voice. I'd learned from the things I'd overheard Angus and Flora discussing during those evenings in the parlour at Milton (myself working quietly at the spinning wheel), a good notion of which of the clans

184

supported Prince Charles Edward's claim, and which did not. Clearly, the Chieftain who owned this castle did not.

Mistress MacKie replied that "the family" owned a number of strongholds throughout Scotland. This great fortification was only one of several, and there were more modern living quarters across the courtyard, which she told me were only a few years built. These were mainly used in the present times by someone who was styled, "the Captain". This, she explained was not a sea captain but a person appointed by... she nearly let out the name, but hastily changed it to "the family".

'They built the new house on the west range... it must be twenty years ago,' she told me. 'A deal more comfortable and up to date than this draughty old part. If I'd my way I'd be in the new house all the time, and never set foot in this crazy old wing! What with the wind whistling through them arrow slits, and the broken floorboards down below, tha hast to mind tha doesn't put tha foot right through! Give me modern convenience every time!'

I did not press her for more, but asked instead about Shona. How had she died and where had they buried her?

'That one! I'm sure I did my best,' she protested, 'but she did nothing but moan and complain and start up crying over this Prince that's fighting battles all over and upsetting the apple cart... and then of a sudden she took sick with the bloody flux and died on me!'

'I'm sorry for that, Mistress,' I said, although whether I was sorry for Shona or Mistress MacKie, I couldn't say. 'Where did they bury her? Would you be knowing?'

She looked taken aback, or mebbe a trifle guilty at me. 'As to that... well, I'm not sure *where* they would bury her. There's an old chapel in the grounds, where they bury such of the family that die here, and there's an area set aside for the servants. I suppose they might have buried her there.'

'I should like to have seen her grave,' I said, hoping to keep her talking rather than sincerely wishful to see the place where Shona lay, although if I ever got myself back to the Long Island, Lady Clanranald might want to hear.

At this, Mistress MacKie bridled. 'I cannot think *why* tha should. She'd never a good word to say about thee! A Belfast drab, is what she called thee.'

'Yes,' I sighed, 'she'd no good opinion of me. *I'd* no opinion for or agin this Bonnie Prince Charlie, having hardly heard his name before I first came to Scotland, so she thought me a poor silly creature.'

'She told yon gentlemen tha was a spy! Although it seemed to me, that *if* tha was nowt, as she was so definite tha wast, who would employ thee as a spy?'

I shook my head sadly, 'I'm not a spy. Shona can't have believed that.'

'Happen she wanted to have the gentlemen think *tha* was the villain of the piece that caused that ship to sink, and so go easy on her, and let her go!' said Mistress MacKie.

I did not ask my gaoler any more just then, but she seemed more amiable towards me, and even trusted me with a tiny pair of scissors when I offered to embroider the finished pillow slips. Embroidery is not such a grand skill with me, but I'd nothing better to do than take my time over it, and set my stitches as I pleased. Most times now she didn't lock the door when she left. I wondered if she was giving me the chance to escape, but she hadn't provided me with shoes, only some thick woollen stockings. A man's by my guess, they were too large even for my great feet.

Once I'd been a barefoot child about the streets of Belfast, but those days were past and gone. My feet were too tender now. A glance from my arrow slit had shown recent days of rain, and I knew I couldn't get far without a pair of boots, even if I could find a way out of this castle. I reasoned however, that there was nothing to prevent me exploring within if I knew Mistress MacKie (by the rising scent of cooking) to be busy below.

Immediately outside my cell I found a landing, and a flight of wooden stairs descending. Off to my right hand was a corridor which seemed to turn quickly away so that I couldn't guess where it led. I took the stairs quietly (for this the woollen stockings were a blessing) down to the next landing, where I found that the next flight of stairs was fashioned from stone. Doors to the right and left of this landing were locked, there was nowhere to go but on down to where I could hear Mistress MacKie clashing pots in the kitchen. Then, slightly to my surprise, I heard her speaking to someone. There was an answering voice, though whether male or female I couldn't be sure. I scampered back to my cell. For some reason I'd believed that she and I were alone in this part of the castle, but it seemed that in this I was mistaken.

It had not until now come into my mind to wonder what had become of the "Frenchies" she had spoken of when I first came back to my senses. I had thought, in so far as I'd thought at all, that these must be French sailors rescued from the *Clementine* and brought here, together with Shona and myself, as prisoners. Were any of them, like me, still held captive somewhere in this drear fortress? If so, 'twas no wonder Mistress MacKie had need of kitchen help.

However, when she brought my evening bread and broth she seemed dour and silent, as though her thoughts were on anything but me. I didn't tease her with questions. I'd a fear on me that the "two gentlemen" must have returned, so I held my tongue. I'd determined to explore that corridor to see where that led.

It was some days before I found an opportunity to do so, as Mistress MacKie kept me busy with sewing and mending until after 'twas full dark. However, the nights were lightening as the new year moved ahead, and one evening I found the chance to slip from my cell and tiptoe down the corridor. It led to a door, which I supposed would be locked, but not at all. Beyond it, a rush of cold April air told me that I was out on the ramparts, looking down on to the castle's wide inner court. I took a deep breath and stepped out. Now I saw that this fortress of Dunstaffnage was vast, encircled by huge and forbidding outer walls. The great arched gateways were barred by massive wooden doors. 'Twas an early April evening and the light was fleeing over the misty islands and seas to the west. I could see a horse tethered by the east wall, and candle light spilling from the windows of what must be, from Mistress MacKie's description, "the new house" where "the Captain" had his quarters, its roof and many chimneys rising high above the curtain wall.

So, from this time forward, since Mistress MacKie niver now locked the door to my cell, I went walking on the battlements in the evening air whenever I pleased.

Then, one soft evening, the light still lingering, I took my usual walk, only to find all changed below. Now there were several horses tethered by the wall, and many rooms in the "new house" were lit. As I watched, a servant lad ran across the greensward, his arms full of logs, and disappeared up some steps into the house. Important visitors, unannounced although not entirely unexpected, I was guessing. Small wonder Mistress MacKie had seemed distracted these last days. Two grooms came out and led the horses away to the stables. Lanterns had been lit and hung at intervals below the battlements to cast light into the great court below. No one, I thought, would be glancing up to see me walking above, provided I didn't linger in those pools of light. I made my way along, stopping now and then to stare across the court from a new angle, but no matter how far I went I could not see into the lighted windows of the new house. More servants emerged and hurried hither and yon on a multitude of errands. None stopped to look upwards. I leaned against the crenulations and thought of John Begg chaffing me as I gazed out from the castle walls over the rooftops of Edinburgh all those months ago. *Why* had he abandoned me? Why had I ended up a prisoner here? *(A small voice whispered that this must always happen to women and girls when soldiers go off to fight battles. We women are nothing but a nuisance and must be discarded – and I had no claim, not even that of friendship, on John Begg.)* Then, what must Miss Flora have thought when I failed to return to Milton? Did she know what had befallen Elsbet and Màiri? Answers, alas, had I none.

Lost in my melancholy thoughts, but becoming aware of the cold striking through the thin fabric of my shabby borrowed gown, I began to walk back towards my prison cell. Now I'd found that I could walk free on the battlements, I vowed I would do so, not just in the evening air but in the warmth of the day. Without thinking on't, I must have passed through a pool of lantern light and was approaching the door that led back inside. I was paying no attention to the folk scurrying below, when I heard a strangled yell. Turning in the doorway, I looked down and saw a youth in the middle of the court, staring up, his mouth hanging open. He was pointing. Another, older, fella joined him, and then a woman carrying a basket of loaves. They were staring at the spot where I stood, and what was there to see but myself?

' 'Tis her, oh, 'tis *her*, in her gown of green!' warbled the woman with the loaves. 'Is she smiling, Davie? Did you see her smile?'

Chapter 27

My Gown Of Green

Back in my prison cell I threw myself onto my bed of straw. I was cold right enough from my outdoor traipsing, but what had just happened there made me shiver more from uneasiness than the cold. Those people had been *frightened* by the sight of me. *'Tis her, in her gown of green!* the woman had exclaimed, and then *Was she smiling, Davie? Did you see her smile?* What in the wide world could this be all about? What was it about *my* appearance that could have a sturdy halfling of a laddie yelling in fear? No doubt word had gone around that they were housing a Jacobite spy, although I was sure I had more than half convinced them that I was no sich thing. The whole business was beyond my understanding.

I heard heavy footsteps then on the turn of the wooden stair, and panting breath, and knew that Mistress MacKie herself was approaching. Since she rarely visited me agin in the evening once she'd brought my supper, it was strange. I bethought me that she should not see how distressed I was, so I scrambled up from the straw and seated myself on my chair, taking up the pillowslip I had been embroidering (of late she had provided me with a stout candle, not easily knocked over to fire the straw) and made as if I was just now setting a final stitch.

'Ah! Leave off *that*, lass!' she panted, exhausted from her climb, 'they wants thee in the new house. I've brought tha boots.'

So my escapade on the ramparts must have been reported. Parts of me were filled with fear and my heart pounded against my ribs, and then again a small part of my mind was wondering, would I be satisfied at last? Would I discover how and why I had been brought here? And why my appearance just now in my green gown should cause such uproar?

Even, in the midst of these tumbling thoughts, I found myself pleased to be given my boots agin. The very boots I'd laced on that autumn day at Milton. My best, in preparation for the visit of the Clan Chieftain and his lady. 'She'll need them for church attendance and walking out,' I remembered Miss Flora Macdonald telling the disdainful old woman in the hand-me down clothes shop in Edinburgh.

They would not fit over the woollen stockings, so I thrust my bare feet inside them, tied the laces and followed Mistress MacKie from the room.

We clambered down the full four flights of stairs, and she unlocked a door with set of keys she had at her waist, and led me out through an archway into the great court. No one now was there, although a pair of hounds, chained by the wall, barked and whined at the sight of us.

'Pay no attention to 'em, they'll not get at thee!' muttered my gaoler, although I sensed she was reassuring herself as much as me. Strange, I thought, that she seemed just as anxious about what was to come as I was. Mebbe she'd taken me in some small amount of liking, after all these months we'd spent together?

'Twas fully dark without, no moon, but the new house blazed with lighted sconces. Within, we found ourselves in a hallway with a high ceiling and a stairway disappearing up into shadows. A number of Militia men stood about, wearing a uniform I wasn't acquainted with, swords and pistols at their sides. They stared through Mistress MacKie and myself as though we were invisible, but before either of us could open her mouth to speak, a door opened and the young fella, Duncan, gestured that we should follow him.

'Here they are,' he told the old one, who was seated at a table within, 'here *she* is.'

We crossed the room and stood before him. A branch of candles stood on the table, but much of the rest of the large room was lost in the gloom of night. I could not help but recall the time Miss Flora Macdonald and I had stood before Colonel Dalgleish in Edinburgh castle. Then, I had stood to one side, a maidservant, happy to be disregarded. This time, Mistress MacKie pushed me forward.

'Well, Davie,' said the old fella, turning to the youth who stood to one side, beyond the candles' bright circle of light, 'Is *this* your ghost?'

'I... I dinae ken, sir,' the boy stammered, and the flickering candle flame revealed a dark flush spreading up over his plump cheeks. 'Ah mind *it... she...* could be. I thought... I *thought* she was the ghost, right enough!'

'I see,' said the old fella, 'and what were you doing, young woman, wandering the battlements and frightening these superstitious servants of ours to death?'

He gazed sternly at me over steepled fingers. Before I could attempt an answer, to which naturally I had none, he fixed his gaze on Mistress MacKie, 'and what possessed *you*, Mistress, to dress her in green and let her wander about the place as she pleases?'

To my surprise, and probably to his, Mistress MacKie had got over whatever fright this summons had originally caused her, and answered straightway, 'Why, for the Good Lord's sake! Is *that* what ails them? They're nothing but a pack of fools, sir! I dressed her to make her decent. You can see the lass is as tall as a maypole. It was the only gown I could lay my hands on that wad come down further than her knees! And if she walks on the battlements, what of it? That door has no key to it, and it leads nowhere. She sits all the day sewing. What harm can it do for her to stretch her cramped limbs of an evening?'

This *Sir*, whoever he was (I was niver to learn his name) regarded me thoughtfully, his fingertips pressed together before him, his head on one side, his eyes bright as a robin's. 'Are ye claiming to be *unaware*, lassie, that this castle of Dunstaffnage is said to be haunted by the ghost of a maiden dressed in green? That she walks the battlements and the corridors, and when she smiles it is said to presage victory for... for the Clan? And when she frowns, *as I see ye are now*, it presages misfortune or defeat?'

'No, sir, I mean, yes, sir!' I stammered. 'To be sure, I niver heard o' such a thing! And if I seem to frown, sir, 'tis only that I'm in a puzzle over this.' I forced myself to smile, since his tale seemed to require it.

'And ye're sure ye didn't tell her of it, Mistress?' he demanded of Mistress MacKie.

'I did not! Why would I? It's a lot of foolishness! *I've* stopped here these five year, and never seen any ghosts or bogles. It's nothing but foolishness and sinful superstition!' my gaoler retorted.

I winced, thinking this would earn her, if not me, a reprimand, but it seemed the old fella had other things on his mind.

'Well, Davie,' he said to the lad who stood beside him twisting his hands, 'it seems this lass is not our ghost, but ye have now seen her smile with your own eyes, so ye may go and tell the other servants so. There is nothing to fear in any case. Now that His Royal Highness Duke William is interesting himself in the, err… current affair, I'm sure all will go well for us. No matter whether our lassie in green smiles or frowns on our enterprise!'

Davie removed himself from the room by a rear door, his feet scuffing up the fine carpets as he went.

'And so,' the old fella went on, 'we have kept this young woman locked up for all these weeks, and discovered nothing useful from her?'

Since this seemed to be addressed to Mistress MacKie, I said nothing. 'She sews neatly, sir,' she said. 'She insists to me that she must ha been sent here by mistake. All that the other woman, Shona, said about her is nought but a parcel o' nonsense. She's no spy in *my* humble opinion.'

'Ye'd agree with that?' he asked me. 'The other woman, this Shona Macdonald, told a packet of lies about ye?'

'Sir, I can't know what was said whilst I lay sick,' I answered. 'Or why Shona would tell lies about me as it seems she did. I'd only the slightest acquaintance with her. I can only think 'twas that she wanted you to believe I was the guilty one so ye'd let *her* go free.'

'There may be a morsel of truth in that, sir,' Duncan, standing by the door, now spoke. 'That Shona creature was desperate we should release her. Despite what she told *us*, in Mistress MacKie's hearing, she made no secret of the fact that she wanted to follow the Stuart Pretender. We assumed the pair of them were in it together, but Mistress MacKie tells me this young woman, now she's recovered, seems to have precious little knowledge of Charles Stuart *or* his followers *or* his cause. *Seems* just to be caught up in something she doesn't understand. That doesn't, however, I believe, excuse her going about with John Begg, who must, at the very least, be playing a double game, and she must know it!'

'Are you saying *I'm* lying?' demanded Mistress MacKie, her bosom swelling and her eyes glaring, evidently taking offence at this *seems*. 'I'm not so easy taken in by young wenches! When I helped my father run the inn at Whitby, I'd many a young lass under me, and I know all their conniving ways! This one's nobbut a lower servant like they were. Why would this man John Begg tell her anything at all? Even if she shared his bed?'

I had begun to feel easy, thinking they could no longer suspected me of being a Jacobite spy, but of course it was no such thing. I *might* be an unfortunate caught up in something I didn't understand, but they hadn't forgotten that I had freely admitted to knowing John Begg. And, though I niver knew it afore, it seems to be what soldiers will do when they've to interrogate some poor body. They let their prisoner think all is well, and then trap them with soothing words.

'Well, lassie,' the old fella now said, his tongue as sweet as honey, 'I suppose we must decide what to do with ye. Have ye remembered, I wonder, just a *leettle* more about the circumstances that brought ye here?'

I'd that feeling of a door closing, and myself on the wrong side of it with no key. I suppose my face told its story. What had I already said when they came before to my cell, with myself then hardly knowing what I did say?

'Mebbe… a little,' I stammered, since I could see the man would not take no for my answer. 'But I cannot think of anything you'd mebbe want to know!'

'Then tell me what ye do know, and I'll decide,' he said.

Ach, but then my thoughts were like a whirlwind in my head! *If I told them... but surely they'd already know... and I might say something that would betray... but then hadn't the man betrayed me?*

'I know so little, sir,' I wheedled, 'I met a man calling himself John Begg in Edinburgh, as I believe I told you. Then I saw him agin... in Uist. He was swimming by the shore, and he was in difficulties with an injured shoulder, so I went to his aid and...' I stopped speaking, sensing that they were mystified by this. Duncan had moved closer, and now stood at my shoulder. Mistress MacKie had stepped back, out of the circle of candlelight, and stood, her hands twisting, clasping and unclasping, as though she thought me a fool to say anything, and was washing them of this business and of me.

'You went to his aid? Go on. What else?'

'Sir, he told me he was going to the mainland.'

I decided not to mention the letter and his request that I should report to him any *"happenings"* in his absence. Since I had never done so, what of it?

'And then? Did he leave for the mainland?'

'I don't know, sir. I don't know what he did.'

'So, when did you meet up with him again, *as we know you did?*' interrupted the man, Duncan, angrily. He was standing so close at my shoulder that I found myself shrinking away.

' 'Twas the day the ship sank.'

'This we know. What was he doing? What were you doing?' Barking these words, he leaned forward and slapped the table with the flat of his hand.

These questions, I recalled, these two must have already asked me as I lay in my cell, but could I now remember what I had said then? 'I was sent, sir, by my Mistress, to try to catch up with two young maids who'd run off. I drove the pony cart down to the harbour at Loch Boisdale. I was thinking it would be easy. I'd no knowledge, do ye see, of the French ship having come there? I thought the fishermen there would niver take those girls to the mainland and I'd easy catch up with them…'

'Why did you suppose that the fishermen wouldn't take these runaways?' asked the nameless one.

'Because they knew my… employer.' I realised her name was on the tip of my tongue, and halted. 'They had respect for the family, and they knew the girls too, that they were a pair of foolish creatures.'

'But you discovered these foolish maidens had managed to inveigle their way aboard the French vessel?'

'They had, sir, and I didn't know what to do, for the ship was sailing then, just.'

'So what *did* you do?'

'That was when I met John Begg agin, sir.' No help that I could see for me to deny it. 'He had a boat there. He called it a cutter, he said 'twas speedier than a fishing boat, and he offered to take me out, to see could we catch the frigate.'

A sound of derision came from Duncan. 'How did the man suppose he could catch a frigate, *a frigate,* that had already sailed?'

'To be sure, he thought he could,' I said, turning my head to answer Duncan. 'The wind was rising and he said… no, one of the fishermen said… that they, the French sailors, had run up too much topsail.'

A silence prevailed.

'Then someone, I disremember who 'twas, said the rudder must have come adrift agin, and she, the *Clementine,* couldn't steer a straight course.'

'And whoever *they* were, they were right,' said the old fella, 'she capsized. *We* have reason to believe there was gold and silver coin and a consignment of armaments on board, *as John Begg no doubt told you.* Gifts, it seems, from the French king to this tiresome Stuart fellow. The authorities in Edinburgh castle trusted this John Begg to disable the ship and retrieve them. Seemingly he had disabled, or caused someone else to disable the *Clementine,* but the crew put into Loch Boisdale and made repairs. Or supposed they had. Presumably John Begg had not had chance to retrieve the gold and the armaments before they did so. It must have been a bad shock to him to see her sail. Little wonder he went after her, although why he took you with him I cannot fathom.'

I shrugged my shoulders. 'He niver told me about the gold or the guns, sir. I thought 'twas just a good turn he was doing – to see could we get those lasses back safe?' Mebbe my voice had a whining note in it. I must have sounded like a tinker girl that's been caught with her hand in a rich fella's pocket at the horse fair.

'What nonsense!' snapped Duncan, 'and I don't believe for a moment that you're telling us the truth about this. I don't know what your relationship with this man John Begg is...' he moved nearer, seized my upper arm in a fierce grip and shook me, 'and it doesn't interest me! But you won't pull the wool over *my* eyes, you stupid hoor!'

His pinch hurt and I yelped. Then, with his other fist he swung back and punched me, hard, on the side of my head.

My head reeled, my eardrum felt like 'twas split, my legs staggered and my eyes blurred with tears. 'That's nothing, to what will happen if you don't tell us *everything* you know! Now!'

No one had ever hit me so hard in my whole life, not even my Da. Sure, he was handy with his belt, but most times he was drunk, and half his lashes caught only the empty air.

'Whoa, now, Duncan!' exclaimed the old fella, mildly. 'Go easy with those fists of yours. If you knock her senseless she can't tell us anything,' and then, to me, cajoling, 'Come on now, lassie. You must have had *some* idea what this man John Begg was doing... what his plans were...' his voice faded away as I felt my legs fold beneath me and I sank to the ground. I wasn't senseless, but I could no more have risen to my feet at that moment than taken wing and flown up to the rafters. I sensed that Duncan was looking down at me, scowling, stepping from foot to foot, mebbe considering would he kick me where I lay, when the door at the back of the shadowy room opened and the lad, Davie, came blundering back in.

'The messenger's here, sir!' he gasped as his boots came into my line of sight. He was near to tripping over the laces, seemingly having pulled them on agin in haste. 'The redcoats are massing above Inverness! Ready to give battle! Duke William is there! We mun ride and join him!'

Chapter 28

The Winter It Is Past

Three days having gone by since my captors had departed, I found myself wandering along the cliff beyond the castle. The sound of the waves beating on the shore below me seemed to match the throbbing of my bruised face, still swollen and aching from Duncan's blow. The track wound inland towards the ancient Chapel, almost hidden amongst trees. A short flight of rough-hewn steps rose up to the arched doorway. Somewhere hereabouts Mistress Mackie thought they might have buried Shona, but not inside that place, surely? No, it was more like they would have dug a rough grave for her beneath the trees, thrown her into a common pit even, since many of the French sailors had died here too. The ground was soft and miry with fallen leaves beneath my boots, the winter having been a wet one. I wandered on until I found a place on the edge of the wood where someone had dug. The ground was disturbed and I could see where a dozen sods had been re-laid. Whether this was where Shona lay, I'd no way of knowing, but it seemed likely. I couldn't recall much of the prayers for the dead, only a few of the words the priest at St Bridget's had said over my mother, so I spoke those aloud. Then I wandered on, not knowing what else I should do.

The trees, I noted, were slowly unfurling into leaf, it being April now, and the winds blowing southerly. I trod the path until I stood beneath the tallest of them, and looked up, gazing at the pale blue of the sky and the tenderness of new green buds. A robin sang on a high branch. I might have sung too, *"the winter it is past and the spring is come at last, and the small birds are singing in the trees,"* but both my jaw and my heart ached too much for singing, or even rejoicing in the mildness of the spring day.

Nothing had been said, these last days, by Mistress MacKie or any other, but it appeared I was no longer a prisoner. I was free to go where I chose. But where could I go? And how? Very few of the Clans folk remained at Dunstaffnage. The men, all but the very old, were marching through the Great Glen towards the town of Inverness, to this battle they expected would put paid, once and for all, to the pretentions of Charles Edward Stuart. Had it happened yet or no? We, back at the castle, had no way of knowing. Mistress MacKie merely shrugged when I asked her. Such foolish carryings on, she told me, would never happen in Yorkshire, where what she called "these argumentations" were more sensibly managed. We'd hear soon enough, she thought. Messengers would surely hasten back with the news. All those left behind seemed certain that the victory would go to "those that's on King George's side," meaning the owners of this castle.

The women who oft times worked here, cooks and maidservants, lived and worked on the crofts down in the bay. There was no need for them to be at the castle whilst the men were gone, and this was the time for the planting of seed potatoes. For now, Mistress MacKie told me, all that was needful over in the New House she could do herself. She did *not* tell me in so many words that I could take myself off, escape, go free, just so long as I did it whilst her back was turned. She seemed to think that once victory over the Young Pretender was assured, "the gentlemen", as she named them, would have little further interest in me and what I might have known about the ship laden with French gold that John Begg was supposed to have stolen. Never the less, it would be wise, she hinted, to be gone when they returned.

But how could I go? I'd no money and no means of leaving that place. I'd asked her, how far was it to Glasgow, or some other town where I might find a ship to take me to the islands… or even, all else failing, to Belfast? She told me the town of Oban was close by, and mebbe there were boats there. She added that 'twas 'only a step away, mebbe a mile or two'. When I askt where did she think boats there would be bound, she shrugged. As she must have known well enough, I'd no money and with my bruised jaw I was in no state to try if singing would earn enough for my passage. The traditional way by which a penniless young woman pays for what she wants, with her body, she must have assumed I would try. But, foolish as I knew it to be, I still had my pride, and was unwilling to risk that, even for a passage to the Long Island.

You'll be understanding that my spirits at this time had sunk verra low. From this headland on that fair day, the inner isles of the Hebrides were easily seen, and even a vague shape that might be the Long Island, a more solid patch of mist on the horizon. So near it seemed, and yet my heart swelled with sorrow. I'd no boat, and as one of the songs I'd loved best says, "neither had I wings to fly".

As I emerged from my wake beneath the trees, however, and glanced idly out to sea, I saw that a heavily laden merchantman was tacking to the west round the bulk of Skye, making way to pass over the north of Scotland. She displayed the flag of St George with the Scottish saltire overlaid, and would be carrying supplies, I was guessing, mebbe from Glasgow, for his Royal Highness, the Duke of Cumberland, who was believed to be assembling an army in Aberdeen. Whence, even now, the men of Dunstaffnage were marching overland to join him. Another sizeable ship, a brig, seemed to be following close behind her, but as I watched, she swung her bow towards the mainland, dipped and curtsied across the churning waters of the merchantman's wake, and slipped smooth and quiet into the bay below the castle. A tiny figure on the deck dropped anchor, and a boat was lowered into the water. A man tossed a rope ladder over the rail and clambered down it. A smaller figure, a child, seemed to hesitate on the deck and the man in the boat held up his arms, encouraging the boy. Even at this distance I could sense the child's fright, but slowly, one rung at a time, at the man's coaxing, he scrambled down. Who in the world was coming ashore here? I wandered to the cliff edge to watch. If they're bringing dispatches to the castle from the Duke, they're surely too late?

'Twas something about the manner of his rowing that informed me. At this distance I couldn't make out his features nor judge his height, but the last time I'd seen John Begg he'd been rowing, straining at the oars. Now here he was, I was sure of a sudden, rowing toward the tiny harbour at Dunstaffnage! The young boy sat opposite him in the bow, his hands clutching the sides of the boat as though he'd little faith that his father would bring them safe ashore.

'You're wise not to trust him, laddie,' I muttered from my lofty headland outlook, 'beware he does not toss you into some other boat, bound who knows where, as he did with me.'

Anger mixed with curiosity filled my breast. That John Begg, hireling soldier, might have a wife and bairns had not seemed likely, but why should he not? His manner to me had been a bandying of words, a mixture of joking and impudence, such as most men will use to a young woman as has no husband to frown him away. But he'd never plied me with pinches or squeezes, for which I'd been grateful. Certainly he'd seemed to treat me with a kind of respect I hadn't had from others. Flora's step-papa for one. But then worse, he'd betrayed me to the inhabitants of this place, to be subjected to imprisonment and blows. Why?

'He shall answer me!' I determined, setting my feet on the downward path, clutching at my jaw as I ran, for the jolting of my steps throbbed through it like fire.

I ran as fast as I dared down the steep curving pathway, skirting tree roots and fallen masonry, afraid that by the time I reached the shore he would somehow be gone, but when I reached the rock strewn beach he'd pulled the boat up onto the shingle and was lifting a pack out onto the ground. The young boy stood some distance from the boat, his face averted as though he had been brought here under protest. None the less, he was coiling a rope neatly.

'Hoy man!' My voice sounded to my own ears like the cawing of an angry corbie. I could hardly open my mouth to force out the words on account of my bruised jaw. What a strange creature I must have appeared, with my shabby over-long green gown gathered about my knees, boots without laces, and half my face a mass of purple bruises. I hurtled towards him like a lunatic escaped from Glennagalt!

He jerked upright, cursing, and letting the pack fall to the ground. 'What in Hell's name!' he grunted, and his hand went to his coat pocket and closed over something bulky there. A pistol. Then he squinted closer at me, his face cracked open into laughter and amazement, and he dropped the pistol back into its place. 'Why, 'tis Miss Elizabeth Burke!' he exclaimed, 'is it really you? Surely it cannae be, but it is!' The man seemed delighted. How could this be?

'It's good to see you, Betty, and a fine and useful thing too!' he went on, disregarding my mouth which must have fallen open like a fish stranded by the outgoing tide. 'I've been at my wit's end what tae do about the bairn,' he added, nodding towards the rope coiling child. 'You're the very one can help me!'

My fury wavered, and the words I'd intended hovered uncertain on my bruised lips, but only for a moment.

'Don't be giving me your sweet talk!' I broke in on him, all the anger I'd been holding in these last weeks now summonsed up agin, '*Why* did you have me sent here, a prisoner? Was it because of the gold on that ship? The *Clementine*?'

He gawked at me then as though I was speaking Erse. 'I got these bruises because I couldn't say what ye did with it!'

'Och, *that* gold!' he replied, shrugging and spreading his hands. 'Lassie, there was nae any. Or not by the time she came into Loch Boisdale. Did someone tell you there was? Nae gold, nae guns. If there ever were any that damned French buccaneer had landed it ashore somewhere. Or stolen it fae himself before ever he left Brittany. There's been no end o' rumours that the French King, the Spanish king, *the Pope in Rome himself even*, have sent gold and armaments for Charlie, or are *going* tae send them, but we have nae found any sign o' any – yet.'

'That man, Duncan, that was here,' I thrust an arm towards the castle, 'believes you stole it!'

'*Duncan?* He was here? He's the one hit ye?' He'd noticed my bruises and moved closer to examine them, clicking his tongue in what seemed to be sympathy. Could I believe that? 'Wait while I catch sight o' him in the thick o' battle!' he exclaimed. 'A dirk tae his ribs, and nae questions asked, even though we're on the same side!' Smarting with resentment as I was, I couldn't tell whether this was his notion of a joke or not.

'He believes I'd helped you steal what was on that ship, and that then you'd abandoned me, put me with the French prisoners and sent me to this place!' My voice was a croak, but growing louder now, despite my sore jaw.

John Begg stared at me in blank amazement. 'Betty, *I* never sent you anywhere but back to the farm at Milton! Yon woman, Shona, said she'd ride with you in the pony cart. She'd take care of you, she said, with the wound you had to your neck!'

I felt as though the hard packed sands fell away beneath my feet, 'You're saying 'twas *Shona*, betrayed me? I narrowed my eyes, looking into his to see was he lying? I saw nothing but that his astonishment seemed real.

Suddenly I found myself believing him. Hadn't Shona been desperate to reach the mainland, no matter how? One of the other boats in the bay must have been commandeered by the Militia. Perhaps it was already there awaiting such an outcome, (I might believe *some* of John Begg's story, but I still thought he'd scuppered the *Clementine*), to gather up the wounded and take them as prisoners to Dunstaffnage. Perhaps I had been laid on the quayside alongside with the rest of the wounded, and Shona, *silly creature that she was*, had told those taking them aboard that *we* were from the *Clementine* too! How she'd supposed she could then escape to follow her Prince once the mainland was reached, the Lord God only knew. And of course she hadn't been as canny as she'd thought. Having told our captors we were from the French ship, no way would Duncan and the nameless one be in any hurry to turn her free, no matter what she said. Little wonder her angry complaints and laments had penetrated my fevered dreams all through those lost weeks.

The young boy had all this while been coiling and uncoiling the rope, his back to us, gazing out to where the brig rode at anchor in the bay under a stiffening breeze and a clouding sky. Now I realised he'd turned, and was staring at me through a tangle of ill-cut hair. His shirt and coat were torn and filthy and must have been inherited from a much older lad. His britches came only just below his knees, patched, and ragged. His feet were bare, and caked now with sand and grit. It passed through my mind, *surely you could have found something better for your son?* (for John Begg was always neat and serviceable, whatever he was doing). Then the boy raised his eyes and began to stumble over the stones towards me, and I felt a lightning shock pass through my body. The raggedy child was no son of John Begg's. This child was no one's son!

Chapter 29

Bring Me a Boat That Will Carry Two

'Our little Jacobite traitor,' said the Militiaman, with a bark of laughter at my astonishment. 'Jimmy, formally Jessie! I had to bring her along wi' me or she was bound for transportation to the West Indies! But come, we'll not stay here where every eye in this wee place will be on us! Let us walk up under the castle walls, out of the view of those women digging their crofts, and then you can tell me how it comes that you ended up here, Betty? I assure you 'twas no doing of mine!'

Since he was right that we had best not stand about on the shingle where the crofters (and Mistress MacKie, were she so minded) could wonder at us, I did not stay to argue. Jessie and I trudged after him up the beach to the lee of the steep headland on which the castle of Dunstaffnage stands.

'I niver! I'm no… what ye said I was!' said Jessie, defiant and on the edge of tears, as we settled ourselves on a stony outcrop below the battlements. 'I only telt 'em what Morag said tae say! And give 'em any wee notes like she said tae do.'

'Right under our noses,' said John Begg, grinning, and slapping his knee with his "heeland bonnet" as though he could still hardly believe it. 'Colonel Dalgleish was beside himself when he found out! *His* house a nest of spies! Small trades people wi' Jacobite sympathies, the fishwife, the baker's laddie. Calling at that house in Canongate and passing notes and messages back and forth about who the big sympathisers were, which households would be happy to house the Prince and his supporters when they came. Who was collecting money for the Cause, and verra likely how much! O' course they were the small fry, these folk who knocked at kitchen doors, delivering the fish and the morning baps. They, poor fools, most likely did it for the chance of a few coins rather than "the Cause", just as Jessie here did. Behind them were those wealthy

Edinburgh merchants who want to see Bonnie Charlie black the eye of Parliament in London! Men o' the same mind, but of different religious persuasions, who couldnae easily meet in public. Or be seen wi' their heids taegether over a dram. The High Command up at the castle couldnae make oot what was going on, why the Prince's army could march into Edinburgh sae confident of their welcome! But they did, and only then did we discovered how that was and why!'

'I... remember,' I said, searching my memories of my time in Canongate. 'The baker's laddie would never look me in the eye if 'twas myself answered the door. I thought he was a mite slow in his wits.'

I also recalled that Miss Flora had wondered about the tradespeople, but if she'd mentioned it to her cousin, in the fuss and flurry over his betrothal he must never looked into it.

'Aye, Jonty Nicol's no a lad wi' much wit aboot him. Tae find *you* there when he'd been told tae give the note and the money tae naebody but wee Jessie... and now he'll likely be transported tae Barbados tae cut the sugar cane.'

Jessie now began to sob in earnest, feeling guilty no doubt at the trouble she'd so unwittingly fallen into.

'How did they fix on Jessie?' I wanted to know. 'Who would think to use a child for such work?'

' 'Twas Morag telt me tae, if she was nae by!' cried Jessie, indignant perhaps that I'd called her a child. 'Old Nessa, the fish wifie, asked *her* wad she do it fae a few pennies, and Morag was agreeable. She wanted tae have some siller fae a new collar fae her Sunday goon. Gowrie found out aboot the notes, and he...'

I saw clearly then how it had happened. Morag, the girl "frae the orphans' place", longing for a "wee bit" lace to trim her best gown, and Jessie, twelve years old, and desperate to help her poor Mammie with all those wee brothers and sisters at home... in their place to be sure, might not I have seized on this way to earn a few bawbies? Take the note from Jonty, pass it on to Old Nessa next time she called, in return for a penny slipped into the pocket of my apron... mebbe some of them had not even known who the Prince was? Or why his supporters should need to use this "backdoor" means of passing information?

'And though Nessa'll no admit it,' interrupted John Begg, 'and Colonel Dalgleish cannae prove it, though he's got her in a cell up at the castle on dry crusts and water, I'd say Nessa Jordan was the one who killed Gowrie! Ye'll recall the knife the Colonel showed tae Miss Macdonald that day at the castle? 'Twould be a fine knife for either the gutting o' a fish or the killing o' a man!'

I recalled the big, raw-boned fishwife although I'd only seen her once. She was by no measure a young woman, but determined and armed with that knife, and with Thomas Gowrie near senseless with drink as I knew he'd been, she could surely have done it.

'But if this Nessa *did* kill him, why that night? She cannot have known about the attack on Jessie and myself?'

'Och, I'd say just waiting her chance to catch him when he was fair sottered, drunk that is,' said John Begg, easily. 'Nessa knew what had happened to Morag. It seems she was gey fond of Morag, and if she knew he'd discovered how the messages were being passed, he was a danger to her too. But I doubt she'll ever admit it even though she'll be sent tae Barbados in chains... if she isnae hanged.'

'What we *don't* know, and will never know, is why Gowrie didn't report tae the high-ups what he'd discovered. Mebbe he thought to trace it to the big fellas, the merchants with the siller and gold, who'd set this business up. Mebbe he wanted tae present the Colonel with the names of all those involved. Chances are, we won't find out, especially if this battle at Inverness should go against us.'

We sat, all three, mute as monuments, pondering on that.

'The people here are for the King in London,' I said, jerking my head towards the castle high above us.

'They are, and so am I,' said John Begg, but then he sighed, 'though not wi' any great zeal. I chose tae sign my pledge and take the King's shilling wi' the Highland Militia when I came home frae the Low Countries, and I'll stick tae my oath. Although I have tae admit King George is no the man tae inspire me! They say when Charlie got within a hundred miles o' London town the King was ready tae bolt fae Hanover, and leave the throne standing empty! His son though, William, he that he's made Duke o' Cumberland, he's no quitter. An efficient fighting machine, is the young Duke. Mebbe too efficient. It'll gae hard for those who've supported Charlie if he wins.'

At this, Jessie burst into noisy sobs. 'I'll be hanged, an' I'll niver see my Mammie agin!' she wailed.

'You've had the luck so far not tae be, Jessie,' said John Begg, severely. 'It turned the Colonel queasy tae think of a bairn like yourself being sae easy led astray. So I rescued ye, and then what'll I dae wi' ye? I'd ma orders tae leave fae Inverness. However, I've a grand idea at last. I'll be leaving now, and gae to fight this battle – if it's nae over before I get there – but oot there in the bay rides the *Eenhoorn*. Eenhoorn, that's a unicorn, her Master's a Dutchman,' he added for my benefit, 'and I'll row ye both oot tae her and tell him tae take ye tae Loch Boisdale if he can, and leave ye there. How's that?'

'Sure, 'tis good of ye,' I said, hardly daring to believe my luck had turned.

'I'm an *negotiator*, Betty,' he said, and when I'd looked at him in puzzlement, niver having heard of such a word, he'd laughed and added, 'A man who solves problems! I see what needs tae be done, and I find a way tae do it! To me, this whole rebellion is a foolish carry-on, and I cannae gae along wi' it. However, there's plenty good men who have, and when 'tis all over, as I believe it soon will be, Scotland will have need of them. If I can save them I will. Sometimes, ye ken, in times of war and rebellion, there are compromises to be made. Men may be sworn enemies, or have loyalties they cannae break, but might still be willing tae talk wi' one another. Try is there another way tae break a deadlock, d'ye see? And mony a man, woman or bairn may have been caught up in something they niver asked for, and be in need o' rescue.'

I hardly took in his words, thinking only that I was going back to Uist. It was what I'd been dreaming of, these last weeks and days, but now I was worrying. Could I just walk back into the farm kitchen at Milton (with Jessie at my heels) and expect Miss Flora Macdonald and her brother to give me a welcome? When I'd failed to rescue Elsbet and Màiri as I'd promised to do? When I'd been gone for long months with no reason given?

'To be sure, that would be grand,' I said with a sigh, 'but they'll have had no word of me all this time. They may not want me. Elsbet was dead, was she not? I don't know what became of her sister.'

John Begg shrugged. 'I've nae idea, Betty. Verra likely we didnae find all the bodies from that ship. Some mebbe washed up later, on the shore. Yon Frenchie did, after Bruce hit him wi' an oar.'

'And Shona died of gaol fever. What will I be telling Lady Clanranald?' But 'twas clear John Begg wasn't inclined for any more talk, and urged us down to the shore and into the rowing boat.

'The wind's coming up,' he said as he plied the oars, 'and Captain van de Molen will want tae be awa. Too many foreign ships in these waters of late. He was delivering truckles o' cheese for Glasgow when I found him, but he's already been boarded twice, and questioned. 'Tis seventy odd years since we'd any disagreement with the Dutch, but anyone wi' a foreign name is suspect just now. However, you two'll be safe enough out there in the islands. If the Hanoverians win, that'll be an end to it. If Bonnie Charlie wins, he'll make straight for London to claim the throne for his father. I can guarantee the islands will never see hide nor hair o' him agin.'

Jessie, sitting beside me whimpered softly, 'I dinae want to be on this island! They've dirt floors, Miss Morrison telt us so! They'll mak me sleep on the dirt agin!'

I laid my hand on her arm, puzzled. 'Why are you thinking

you'd have to do that?'

'I had tae, in the Tollbooth when they came and took me in charge!' she said. 'Sleep on the dirty straw, and my claes is all spoiled. I was stinkin' after that!'

'True enough,' agreed John Begg, 'They hadnae changed the straw in that place fae years, and they dinae provide a privy. All I could find for her were these things I got in an alley behind the Custom House in Greenock. Still, it looked better, to have her as a boy. I said she was my nephew, a son tae my sister that's deid, and naebody's questioned it. You'll do fine if ye gae wi' Betty, lassie! 'Tis the best I can dae for ye!'

'You cut off her hair?'

'I did, wi' my dirk, I'd nae scissors. It'll grow, while you're ruralising on yon island!'

Now, after all I'd been through, I was having fearful doubts about the kind of welcome we'd likely receive on Uist. But I saw there was no going back, and no use to fret aloud over it. The Dutch brig, the *Eenhoorn*, was above us already, it's rope ladder dangling down over our heads.

'Up you go, the pair o' ye!' said John Begg. 'I'll come aboard and tell the Captain who ye are and where he's to tak ye.'

I pushed Jessie, who was as reluctant as she had been when they arrived, up the ladder before me, telling her I'd catch her if she fell. I doubt I could have done so, for I'd to hold my heavy skirts bunched in the one hand. The wind was rising, as John Begg had told us, and the ship was already beginning to roll. The deck, when we reached it, pitched beneath our feet. Hazy, fever-wracked memories of the rough passage we must have had crossing to Mull, and then on to Dunstaffnage, came back to me, but there was nothing I could do. If we were to be caught in a storm, I must bear it.

John Begg spoke to the Captain, a stout fella with a grand moustache on him, and handed him money, perhaps for our passage, perhaps also for the boat, which he soon rowed away in.

'Dinae get yerself kilt, Uncle Johnnie!' Jessie leaned over ship's rail and shouted after him.

I suppose I should have thanked him agin. I'd held sich black thoughts of him, all those weeks I'd been a prisoner in the castle. 'Twas hard to let them go, to grasp that he was not the one to blame for my troubles. That he had tried to do his best for me, never guessing at Shona's treachery. Now he was off to the battlefield and I might never see him agin. And I found myself sad and sorry.

Chapter 30

Blow Bonny Breeze

We'd a stormy night crossing the Minch on the strong easterly breeze, and my stomach let me know about it, though the next day dawned fair, with the Long Island already in distant view. Jessie had proved to be the better sailor. I'd lain half the night trying not to heave up the portion of cheese, salt herring, and ship's biscuit one of the sailors had brought for us. Jessie, however, had slept soundly in her hammock, snuffling peacefully, just as she had when we'd shared a bed in Canongate. Now she was up betimes and ranging about in the poky cabin Captain van de Molen had given over to our use.

'Betty,' she said in a small voice, after she'd stared out of the porthole awhile, 'will we find Miss Flora Macdonald on this island where we're going?'

'I'm hoping so,' I replied from beneath the blanket. I didn't yet want to share with her my fear that Miss Flora might not be best pleased to see us.

'I'm wishing I'd some decent claes tae wear,' Jessie continued, 'I didnae mind it, being dressed for a laddie, when I was wi' John, but I dinae want Miss Flora tae see me like this!'

'I'm sure she'll understand,' I mumbled, although I was sure of no sich thing, 'but we'll have to find her first. The farm at Milton is on the western side of the island, and I fancy this ship will put in on the east. We'll likely have a long walk ahead of us.'

'And me wi' nae shoes tae my feet,' mourned Jessie. For myself, I thought that might be the least of our troubles.

Captain van de Molen put us down on Eriskay. Almost for sure, I thought, this must be the same bay where the Prince had landed nine months before. Beyond the white sands, above the shoreline, I could see a black house with the smoke rising from the centre of its turf-thatched roof. It could it be the very same where *he* had stayed with that relative, another Angus Macdonald, of Flora and her brother. The crew of the *Eenhoorn* let the ship drift as close in as they dared to a shallow sandy spit without she ran aground. Then we had to plunge in and wade, John Begg having taken the boat. I recalled Miss Flora's brother saying the Prince and his supporters had had to do so too. Jessie stumbled and fell into the waves before we reached dry land, which had the advantage that she was a deal cleaner than she had been when she emerged. She wailed and wept for a good while, as we sat together on a rocky outcrop and watched the *Eenhoorn* hoist sail and disappear over the southern horizon.

'Ach, whisht now, Jessie!' I said, after a time. 'We're safe enough here, and it's not so cold in this spot, out of the wind.'

No one seemed to be looking out from old Angus's black house, nor, I thought, could we be spied here from the other crofts beyond the ridge. 'Be thankful those poor patched things John Begg found for ye are so thin that you'll soon be dry agin.' I kept wringing at the hem of my green grown, which though 'twas old and worn in places was of a heavy, dense cloth that held the sea water.

'That's a queer goon you're wearing!' Jessie said, looking me up and down, and perhaps noticing for the first time what I had on. 'Where did ye get it, Betty? It looks tae me like what they say ladies wore in bygone days!'

'I fancy it is,' I replied, trying to smooth out my crumpled brocade skirts. 'The housekeeper at the castle, Mistress MacKie, gave it to me. She said 'twas all she could find that was long enough for one of my great height. It caused a deal of trouble too!' Despite all that had gone before and indeed, after, I smiled at the memory. 'It seems that Castle is haunted by the ghost of a young woman in a green gown, and when they caught sight of me one evening, I affrighted the servants there something terrible!'

'They thought *you* were a ghost, Betty?' Jessie burst into giggles.

'Can you believe that? They did!' I said, beginning to laugh with her. I told her about my walks on the battlements and the terror on the faces of the servants crossing the castle ward when they'd spied me up there... and about being sent for by "the Captain" and paraded before the lad, Davie... and being ordered to smile for him, because if the ghost frowned it meant things would go badly for them all.

'Perhaps it will go badly for them if they had to *make* you smile?' said Jessie. 'You said they're for the King in London, those that live in that castle, but *I* want Bonnie Prince Charlie tae win!'

'But if he does, what will happen to your friend John? He's Highland Militia man, and they're backing the King in London.'

Jessie shrugged. 'Och, he'll be all right. He said tae me, he'd gae tae America if things went agin him! He's a sonsie lad!'

'How did it happen that he rescued you, Jessie?'

Forgetting about the misery of her wet clothes, Jessie sat up and launched into her tale. The Militiamen had come to Canongate and arrested her in the middle of eating her midday broth! She'd tried to kick and scream, she said, but one of the soldiers had thrown her over his shoulder and carried her all the way to the Tollbooth and tossed her into a cell together with Old Nessa and Jonty Nicol, and several others whose names she didn't know. 'It was a horrible, foul stinkin' place. Betty, you've ne'er seen or smelt the like!'

For some days, she couldn't recall how many, they had remained locked up there, fed on nothing but stale crusts and water. Then they were summonsed to stand before the court, and two soldiers with swords came to escort them thence. Jessie seemed to have little idea, even now, what this appearance in court would have meant for her.

'I cannae say,' she said shaking her head, when I questioned her on this part of the tale, 'what was there, or what happened to Nessa and Jonty. I never saw, for as we was walking doon the passage way, John Begg was there, standing in a corner by a great door that was half opened, and as we walked past him, he put his finger tae his lips, seized a hold o' me and put me behind him, behind the door. And he said, verra quiet tae me, 'dinae make a squeak!' and I didnae, and when they were all gone by we hurried awa, and he bid me hide in an old hoose by the Haymarket. There was an old woman there, and she gave me broth and a bap wi' dripping tae eat, and the next day we went in a drayman's cart tae Glasgae.'

'You didn't know John Begg before. Were you not afraid to go with him?'

'Nae, for I didnae want tae go tae the court,' Jessie confided, 'I heard Nessa whisperin' tae the others that we might be hanged, or we might be sent on a ship far across the ocean! So I was glad tae go with him. He told me, he knew *you*, Betty, *and* Miss Flora Macdonald, and he said he thought you twa wouldnae want me to be hanged. So I reasoned 'twas best tae go wi' him.'

She sat silent for a while, hugging her damp knees. 'I was mad at him though, when he said we should get off the ship and he would ask that Wifie – you said her name, Mistress MacKie was it? – that's the housekeeper in that castle, would she gi' me a place? I didnae want to work there, I wanted tae go and see the battle!'

'They would niver have allowed it, Jessie,' I said. 'For sure, they don't allow women and girls onto a battlefield.'

'I could hae stood on top o' some wee brae and watched! I wanted tae see Charlie charging on his white horse, wi' his great sword, and cutting doon them Redcoats!'

'One of those redcoats is John Begg,' I reminded her.

'Nae, not John, he's tae canny! But now I'll never get tae see Bonnie Charlie.'

I made no reply to that, and we spread ourselves out like two seals on a rocky promontory, only now and then raising our heads to look around, letting the tender spring breeze dry the clothes on our backs.

'It's fair long walk to Milton from here,' I said after a while. 'When the tide is out we'll be able to walk across to South Uist, I'm thinking. A good part of the way between the islands will be on sand, so it'll not be too hard on your feet.'

She made no reply, and I realised she had fallen asleep, curled on her side with her thumb in her mouth like the bairn she still was. Though I doubted *I* could fall asleep on this comfortless couch, I must indeed have done so, for when I woke the sun was high in the sky, and a voice, filled with the soft speech of the islands, was speaking my name.

'Betty Burke? Iss it yourself?' It was Lechie Mor, Bridie's man, driving Tibby, the cart loaded with peat.

Evening was drawing on when we arrived at the track leading to Milton. The sun was sinking in the western heavens trimming the edges of the pale grey clouds with scallops of salmon, rose, and gold. The farmhouse squatted amongst the spring flowers that embroidered the machair, still glowing warm in the last of the sun, while behind us the eastern bens were sinking into the shadows. One lazy plume of smoke curled from the parlour chimney. Lechie dropped us, having still to deliver the peat he'd fetched from Eriskay before he brought Tibby back to her stable. We began to walk up the lane, myself marvelling at the glory of the sunset, Jessie muttering about the pain of the stones beneath her bare feet, just as I recalled Elsbet and Màiri used to do. As we drew closer I saw a figure cross the barnyard, pail in hand, and then pause, having caught sight of two figures approaching. It was Angus Macdonald, about his evening tasks. Cattle stood close to the fence, lowing softly, waiting to be milked. It was still early in the year, they'd not been taken up to the shieling in the hills yet.

'Who's there?' Angus called.

Myself alone, I suppose he might have known me from my tall stature despite my strange clothes, but the "boy" at my side he'd never seen.

Before I could find my voice to call out who we were, another figure emerged from the kitchen door, shading her eyes to look at us. Then she set up a high warbling yell, and came running and stumbling over the rough ground towards us.

'Màiri! Oh, Màiri, I thought you were drowned!' I found myself hugging her, tears pouring down my cheeks.

'Ah th-ya-wa-dr-ta!' she said, patting at my arms and chest as though she doubted I was a solid being.

Two more figures appeared in the kitchen door, drawn by Màiri's wild shouts. Here came Flora, with Bridie at her heels, carrying bundles of tweed, which they dropped to the ground before they both came running to greet me.

What cries of gladness! They gave me to understand that they'd thought me drowned at the shipwreck, my body niver found – and now here I was, safe and sound! What jumbled words of joy and thankfulness on all our parts! Even Angus patted my shoulder and said 'Fàilté! Fàilté, Betty!' which I supposed spoke of a real Highland welcome, more suited to the occasion than the English word. I was glowing with happiness. Here was my home, I had always felt it so, and here were my dear friends to greet me.

'And *this* is Jessie,' I said, once the first cries of concern (for my bruises) and astonishment at my tale had died away. 'You remember Jessie from Canongate, Miss Flora? And John Begg?'

After a moment of thought, Flora nodded, 'Sergeant Begg, I remember him, yes and Jessie too,' but I realised from their blank faces that the others had no notion who I was talking about. None of them had ever met John Begg. Only Flora, and Captain Macdonald, Flora's step-father, besides myself, had ever set eyes on him.

'No, you won't know him, most of ye niver met with him,' I said, flustered, 'but he was the Highland Militia man that was rescuing folk from the *Clementine,* that day at Loch Boisdale... 'tis a long tale, but then agin in Edinburgh, in these latter days, he was able to rescue Jessie, and then because...' I stopped. Indeed this tale was too difficult to tell.

'He brought me oot from the Tollbooth. That's a terrible place!' chimed in Jessie, 'and he said I had tae be a laddie until we could get awa safe!'

'So we're hoping you can find her a gown to wear?' I put in, 'so she can go back to being a lassie agin?'

Before any of them could answer, we heard a shout from the track, and Lechie came driving Tibby towards us at a furious pace.

' 'Tis done!' he cried, his voice harsh with shock as the cart jolted to a stop. Then he broke into Gaelic. Around us, I saw all their faces fall. Plainly the news was bad.

'The battle is done?' demanded Angus. 'And the Clans have lost?'

'*All, everyone o' them lost*, they're saying,' Lechie's voice hardly rose above a whisper. 'Nigh on twa thousand men. The Duke Cumberland's Recoats have slaughtered them all on Culloden Field!'

'The Prince?' Flora asked.

'No, not he,' said Lechie. 'They're saying his friends took him away when they saw how badly it was going.'

'Poor soul,' said Flora. 'what will he do now?'

'Make for Aberdeen if he's mite of sense,' said Angus, grimly, 'and find a ship that'll take him back to his father in Rome!'

Chapter 31

It's Home I'd Like To Be

I had loved Milton from the first time I set foot in that farmhouse. Its kitchen, its parlour, its barnyards and its dairy. I took pleasure in them all. I been expecting that Jessie would love it too, foolishly as it turned out. Jessie had lived all her twelve years amidst the smoke and dirt of Edinburgh. She had never seen the machair, and seemed to care nothing for its bright carpet of flowers. Cows and goats terrified her. Even the chickens, clucking and darting under her feet when she was sent to feed them, made her squeal with fright. As for poor Màiri, Jessie couldn't abide her.

'She's a dafty!' she complained. 'I cannae understand a word she's saying, and I'm scared tae sleep in the same room. I'm afeared she'll murder me in ma bed!'

'Ach, don't talk so foolish,' I chided her, 'Màiri won't hurt ye! She was born with a hare lip is all, and can't speak so grand. Onyway, I'm sleeping in the same room with the two of youse, so if she starts up to murder ye, I'll save ye!'

'She's a dafty,' Jessie repeated.

'Not so daft! She's doing fine with the spinning, and leading the waulking with her singing. I'm yet to see you do those things!'

When we'd arrived so unexpectedly, the waulking of the woven tweed was almost finished for that year, but Lechie had produced one last length, a lovely piece, shaded with the blues and greens of the sea and lochans, and the pinks and purples of the machair and the moors. We laid it outdoors on a table made from smoothed planks of wood. Then Flora, Jessie and Lechie to one side, and Bridie, Màiri and myself on the other, clutched at the damp cloth and pulled in time to Màiri's warbled singing, to stretch it back to its full length and breadth after its soaking and rinsing had taken the loose dyes and tightened the weave.

'Miss Flora says she'll save a length or two this year and we're to make ourselves cloaks with hoods 'gainst next winter,' I told Jessie afterwards. 'Won't that be grand? New cloaks of our very own that'll keep off the rain?'

'I dinae want tae be here 'til winter!' Jessie moaned. 'I wish John Begg would come an' take me back tae Edinburgh!'

'I niver thought how I'd be missing Elsbet, but I am!' I confessed to Bridie one wet afternoon, as we sat in the kitchen hemming up two old gowns of Flora's for Màiri and Jessie to wear. Old Peg Macdonald, Màiri's grandmother had passed away during the winter, and Màiri, orphaned, now lived permanently at Milton.

'To be sure Elsbet was a lazy creature and forever giving me the cheek o' the devil, but at least she'd a cheery way with her. Jessie does nothing but grieve to be back in Edinburgh.'

I wished John Begg would come too, if only to know that he was still alive and could tell us more about that terrible battle on Culloden field. Angus received frequent letters from Lord Clanranald and from a friend on the mainland, over which he most times shook his head grimly, and told us only that the slaughter had been dreadful. Flora and I drove up to Nunton twice over the next few weeks, once to deliver a length of tweed, and once that we might entertain two elderly cousins of Lord Clanranald's with my singing and Flora's skill at the keyboard. My bruised cheek was mending, and if I had not the full strength of my voice with the soreness of my jaw, no one at Nunton was unkind enough to mention it.

'We must continue to live life as normal!' Lady Clan cried, trying to appear bright and cheerful for her visitors, although she was wearing her blacks for a cousin, a young man known to have died in that disastrous charge at Culloden. I'd been wondering, should I say something about Shona, but Flora said no, Lady Clan knew she was dead from a letter she'd had from another relative on the mainland, there was no need. Every family, gentry or not, seemed to be affected in some way. Poor Shona, I thought, she lies dead and buried and no one here really cares what became of her. That was the way of the world, was it not? Lady Clanranald wore black for a relative she'd most likely niver met. Shona, her servant, a woman she must have spoken to daily, was forgotten already.

Flora, on both these visits, went and sat for a time with Lord Clanranald, who remained, frail and tremulous, hunched in a bath chair in his library away from the visitors. What conversations they had, I wasn't party to, but Flora came away with sorrowful looks, quite unlike her usual cheerful manner.

'It's so cruel,' was what she said, as we bowled home from Benbecula across the sands after the second visit. 'It's as well you should know, Betty. I doubt we shall ever see our farm lads again, even if they survived the fighting. So many were slain, but it seems that was not enough for Duke William. That dreadful man has ordered reprisals! All who escaped death on the battlefield are to be rounded up and taken prisoner. I don't doubt they'll be lucky if the worst that befalls them is transportation. Parties of English Redcoats are scouring the glens, catching up with wounded men attempting to return to their homes, and putting them to the sword. Crofts, houses, castles even, have been set ablaze, and their inhabitants slaughtered.'

'And the Prince? Did he find a ship to carry him off safe?' Princes, I thought, sourly, seem always to have loyal friends to spirit them away in their time of trouble.

'No one seems to know for certain,' Flora replied. 'The ports of Aberdeen and Inverness were, and remain, blockaded by the English navy. Some say he must have escaped from the east coast by a fishing boat, but others insist he and a small party of friends are in hiding somewhere along the length of the Great Glen. They're saying some of the Chieftains tried to raise a second army. As many as three thousand men, including Clanranald's son, waited for the Prince to join them at a place called Ruthven, but he sent word that as the money and armaments hadn't come from France, it was hopeless to continue and they should disperse.'

'That was verra harsh on them, surely?'

'He'd lost faith I think,' she sighed. 'Angus said from the beginning that his campaign was ill thought-out and would end in catastrophe, but then the Jacobites seemed to gather support. Money was supposedly on its way from King Louis. They were winning battles! Folk boasted that the English Redcoats could not withstand the Highland Charge.' She sighed again. 'Even Angus, and you know how gloomy he is, began to think there was a chance they might win. But it seems the Prince was poorly served by some of his advisors.'

'Someone told me he'd an Irish fella, O'Sullivan, to plan the battles,' I said, shuddering as I recalled Nameless one at Dunstaffnage.

'That may be so,' said Flora, 'Lord Clanranald says he should have listened to Lord George Murray, who knew the terrain better than any Irishman could have done. The choice to make a stand on Drummossie Muir, hard by Culloden, could not, he says, have been more unfortunate. It was too boggy at that season, the ground too uneven and crisscrossed with ditches, for an effective charge. Besides the Duke had brought a huge battalion of artillery. The Clansmen were cut down where they stood... Och, Betty, I shouldn't be criticising the Prince's Irish friend, and lowering your spirits as well as my own by telling you all this!'

As she spoke, Tibby left the sandy causeway and began to trot across the heath past dozens of tiny lochans. A cloud of midges, the first of the season, descended on us fluttering against our necks and faces.

'Whoa! Let me down, Miss Flora,' I gasped, 'Let me strip some branches of bog myrtle to ward them off!'

'These are not the biters, Betty!' Flora called after me, as I pulled frantically at the wands of yellowy blossoms. 'It's too early for them. Still,' she spluttered as they swarmed into her open mouth, 'fetch me a branch to fend them off!'

When we arrived back at the farm it was to find Jessie wielding a broom over the kitchen flagstones around the feet of Angus Macdonald, who sat staring into space, a letter drooping from his hand. Since I'd rebuked Jessie for her scornful treatment of Màiri, the child had been at pains to show us how hard she worked, what a useful little creature she was – provided the work was indoors – and took her nowhere near the cows, the hens, or, worst of all to her mind, the goats.

When we entered, she nodded towards Angus, and hissed behind her hand, 'Miss Flora, I askt him, verra polite, please will he move, but he does nae hear me.'

At this, Angus looked up, and saw that his sister was present. 'Bad news, Flory,' he said, 'two pieces of news and both of them bad.'

Flora moved towards him, 'Bad news? But… we've just come from Nunton and Lord Clanranald has heard little that was new since last week.'

'A letter from our cousins in Kintyre,' he said, indicating the sheet he held in his hand, 'who have heard it from James Dalgliesh.'

Thinking it were best, knowing what I did from John Begg of her childish devotion to the Jacobite cause, I made to shoo Jessie out of the room. Before I could close the door however, Angus continued, and I couldn't help but hear, so she heard him too.

'Firstly,' we heard him say, 'King George and the Government in London have placed a bounty of thirty thousand pounds on Charles Stuart's head.'

At this Flora gasped, 'Thirty thousand pounds! Och, he'll be betrayed for sure!'

'Probably, but worse still,' said Angus, grating out the words, '*much* worse I fear, the Prince is here.'

'*Here?*' Flora's cry of surprise and shock reached us in the hallway beyond the kitchen, even as I pulled the door to. 'Och, he cannot, *we* cannot…'

In the gloom of the passage, Jessie's eyes were shining. 'Bonnie

Prince Charlie is here! Will we see him?' she demanded, 'will we see the Prince? He's really coming here?'

'Ach, I hope not,' I said, 'It's too dangerous.'

'Why?' Jessie's eyes were wide. 'Why is it dangerous, Betty?'

'Because the English will send a company of their own soldiers to catch him. They'll be searching for him everywhere. *We* could all be arrested, taken up suspected of harbouring him – that's if someone does not turn him in straightway for the reward.'

'Thirty thousand poonds is a gae lot?' the bairn asked me, her eyes wide.

'That it is,' I said, 'to be sure you could be buying a grand house and land, and living like a queen all your days, Jessie, if ye'd thirty thousand pounds.'

'But naebody wad be speaking tae me, wad they?' she said, thoughtfully. 'They'd guess what I'd done tae get it.' Then she stood silent for a moment, seemingly thinking on't. '*I'd* nae do it,' she said, 'but likely there's some hereabouts that would. 'Tis a great shame tae be thinking on all that siller gaeing tae waste.'

I was about to voice my complete agreement with that, but warn her not to repeat what we'd heard, when we were startled from our wits by a series of loud thumps at the kitchen door. Which was followed by the sound of something slithering to the ground without.

Jessie squeaked with alarm, 'Och, it cannae be the Prince come already can it, Betty?'

I did not reply but went to open it a crack, half expecting the billy goat had escaped and was ramming at the door with his horns, hoping to force his way in. I knew he'd lately destroyed a fence after that fashion. What I found was a bundle of rags laid across the threshold. Then the rags stirred and I saw there was a man inside them.

'Gilbert?' I said, 'Is it yourself?'

The old man raised his head and gazed at me with hollowed cheeks and bloodshot eyes. 'Aye,' he sighed, ' 'tis just myself come hame. Finn and young Calum are gone tae their rest wi' the Lord God above. The Redcoats caught up wi' us by Glen Garry. I fell in tae a ditch and played I wass deid a' ready, so they didnae run me through.'

Chapter 32

I Will Build Thee A Bower

Soon after Gilbert's return, Captain Hugh Macdonald, step-father to Angus and Flora, arrived on horseback one morning at the head of a small troop of local Militia. Unusually, he brought the men inside to bear witness to what he had to say, and summonsed the whole household to attend him in the parlour.

There, he swept his one eye over us all. For the first time in my acquaintance with him the eye did not twinkle. He was wearing "the kilt", the first time also I had ever seen him in this garment, and quite a respectable red coat with a snowy stock at his throat. He'd discarded his old woollen bonnet for one with a proud badge and a feather. Even his sea boots, I noticed, had been given a lick o' the blacking.

'We live in difficult times,' he gravely informed us, 'and ye'll hear rumours and counter rumours, so 'tis best I'm frank wi' ye all. The Government in London is sending both army and naval troops to search the islands. *These islands.* Three thousand men! The word is out that Charles Edward Stuart is hiding somewhere either on Benbecula or South Uist. Anyone thought to be aiding or sheltering him will be arrested, taken prisoner, and put to death by hanging. I and my men will be patrolling throughout the Long Island. I would prefer…' again he swept our faces with his one eye, his expression severe and fixed… 'not to have to take anyone from *this* household in charge. However, do not suppose that I would not do so! I cannae disobey my orders. Take heed, all of ye, this is a solemn warning.'

So much, I thought grimly, for John Begg's guarantee that whether he won or lost the battle, the islands would never see Prince Charles Edward agin!

Then the Captain changed his tune, dismissed the men to the yard, and sat down in the kitchen with a clay pipe and a glass of whisky, as easy as ever, asking Angus when he planned to take the cattle to the shieling up at Alisary, and Flora, did she have a length of tweed put by for her mother?

Then away he went, taking with him his troopers, two geese, a dozen eggs, a side of bacon and a length of the best tweed, leaving us not knowing what to expect. Or whether we'd onything to fear from the approach of these English soldiers and sailors, now expected on these shores at any moment.

'Three thousand troops, Papa said. Do you believe we're in danger?' Flora asked her brother as we sat eating our dinner.

'Not if we leave well alone,' he replied, 'keep our own counsel and don't try to do anything foolish. Father has spoken for us, and his word seems good with the Authorities. It's known that he never pledged his support to the Jacobites despite their entreaties. We need only to continue in our usual habits, and we won't be a cause for suspicion. There's plenty of work, as always, about the farm at this season. Gilbert and I must see to the sheep shearing as best we can. Two men from Askernish have promised to come and give a hand, so I hope they'll not give me backword now. Then I'm thinking to send Gilbert away, up onto Ben Sheaval with the cattle. It's best he's not on view if these English Redcoats do come here – and best the cattle are not on view either, or they could be requisitioned. I doubt Gilbert would be recognised as one among many who fought at Culloden, but if by ill-chance one of these militiamen *was* there and *did* recognise him, it might go badly for him.'

And to be sure, as he had said, there was indeed plenty to do in the days that followed. Jessie and Màiri, I was comforted to see, had come to some sort of understanding whereby Jessie plied mop, broom and duster about the house, and Màiri sat at the spinning wheel, which she now managed creditably, or fed the fowls or churned butter in the dairy.

'I still say she's a dafty,' said Jessie to me, her eyes sliding sideways to judge was I still angry with her, 'but there's mebbe nae harm in her.'

'There's a relief!' I said to Bridie later, 'I was afeard I'd done wrong to burden Miss Flora and yourself with Jessie, but with Elsbet gone, I thought we could use an extra pair o' hands.'

'She's grand little worker,' said Bridie, biting her lip anxiously, 'but I'm wishing she wouldnae keep asking though, whereabouts is the Prince hiding? It's better, surely, that none of us know?' she fretted.

'No fear she'll find it out from me, for I don't know,' I said.

'Lechie knows, but I've said tae him, dinae tell me! I'm thinking Angus must be knowing too. They say he's moving about, staying in this place and that, but never too long for fear they'll catch sight o' him, or someone will sell his whereabouts to the Redcoats to claim the price that's on his poor heid.'

The summer days stretched out on the Long Island. The darkness of night dwindled to almost nought as we passed through the month of May and into June. The airs were mild and the machair was ablaze with flowers of every colour. The milk from the house cow and the goats streamed forth in great abundance, and the hens laid more eggs than our household (and Bridie's) could eat. Yet we never could be easy. Oft times we heard the tramp of marching feet, a lone drum beating, and shouts of command as a company of Militia passed by on the track that came close to Milton. They'd oft times be coming and going from the harbour at Loch Boisdale on the way that led north to Benbecula.

Captain Hugh Macdonald, seemingly more anxious than he was admitting, visited us two or three times a week, accompanied by his own little band of Independent Militia, and sat talking a long while with Angus in the parlour. Always he asked Flora, 'They're nae bothering you, these Redcoats, lassie? Or the maids? If any of those rogues so much as poke their noses in here, you're to send for me, d'ye hear? I've given my word ye've none of ye any notion where the Prince may be, and ye'll not dream of making any contact with him or any of his followers.'

Flora assured him that none of the foreign soldiers had yet come to the farm. 'Though how I'm to send for you, Papa, if they did,' she said, 'I can't tell. Since losing Finn and Calum, we've no one that can be spared. Gilbert is on his own up at the shieling, and Angus has to ride up there every few days to take him supplies of food and drink.'

'Send Betty!' said he, slapping his knee with his bonnet. 'She's a fine strapping lass that could hold her own I'm thinking. Put her in a pair o' Angus's old britches and, tall as she is, who'd question whether she was a man or no? Striding across the moor with a pack on her back and a staff in her hand, would any think she was ought but a shepherd lad? Send her in place of Angus with Gilbert's rations. Your brother has enough tae do hereabouts.'

It was a day of mist and rain, and I was seated in the window of the parlour with a pair o' paddle combs, teasing some of the first of the summer shearing, so I could not help but overhear. At first, as you'll mebbe be understanding, his words cut me to the heart. My appearance had always been a great sorrow to me. I've always been too tall for a lass, my shoulders as broad as any man's, my face as plain as a "bap" as Elsbet had once declared.

Later that night though, lying in my bed, I thought the more on it, and wondered how it would be? Flora and her brother had been good to me, had taken me back into their household after I'd been missing for months, never uttering a word of complaint or blame. Was this something I might do for them to ease their burden in these difficult days? John Begg had dressed Jessie as a boy and no one had questioned it. My hair is by no means my crowning glory, and stuffed inside a heeland bonnet 'twould surely not give me away?

Next morning I went to Flora and said if she could find me a pair of britches, a man's bonnet and a woollen jaiket, I was ready to do it.

'Betty!' she cried, flustered that I'd overheard her step-father's remarks, 'Papa wasn't serious!'

'Mebbe, mebbe, not,' I replied, 'but it's a good notion I'm thinking. I could walk up to the shieling with Gilbert's rations. If I should meet with a troop of Redcoats, I'd let them think that I'm deaf, dumb, and as Jessie would say, "a dafty".'

And so 'twas that I became a man, or rather a youth. Flora, verra doubtful, went to the clothes press and brought forth a pair of knee britches which she told me had belonged to her brother Ranald, who had died young. For moment she seemed to forget why we were there, gazing beyond me to a time of sorrows past.

'It was over on the wee small island of Canna he died, an accident with a fowling piece, terrible sad 'twas,' Bridie told me, when, later, I asked her about Ranald. 'Angus and Flora have missed him sore,' she said, 'and seldom speak of him. A braw laddie he was, bidding to be taller than Angus though he was the younger, and the image of his grandfather, the strong Minister.'

His britches fit me just grand. And, as you'll surely be guessing, Màiri and Jessie fell into fits of laughter at the sight o' me.

'Enough o' that, young Jessie!' I said, 'Ye looked a deal worse than I do in those breeks John Begg found for you!'

'Och, Betty, the shock Gilbert will have when ye come striding up tae him!' she said, doubled up with mirth.

But it wasn't Gilbert who received the shock. I had been only once to the shielings at Alisary when, the previous autumn, we had all gone together to bring the cattle home. It had been a happy outing except for Elsbet's moaning at having to walk "sae far", and I was remembering how, on the homeward journey we'd sung, our voices blending into harmony as we tramped the heather-covered moorland, Milton's chimneys and the deep rolling breakers of the Atlantic growing closer with each of our songs.

Thus, a few days after I was fitted with my male attire, I strode out, a pack of provisions strapped to my back and a shepherd's crook in my hand. 'Twas a mild June day, thin cloud above, grouse cackling in the heather, curlews crying, and somewhere above me, just a black speck against the clouds, a lark sang. I longed to sing too, but I knew I must not, for my voice would give me away for a lassie. I recalled Captain Macdonald speaking of the local men lying in the heather with muskets, and wondered, idly, if there were any hereabouts today? Then I tramped on, thinking no more of it.

I was within sight of Milton's shieling, a rough-built stone bothy roofed with heather and broom and enclosed within a wall where the cattle could be herded together on occasion, when it happened. As I rounded a fallen rock, a man rose up before me, and pointed a pistol at my head.

'Halt, Sirrah!' he drawled, in English, 'Who might you be young fellow, and where are you going?'

At the moment of his speaking the sun inched its way out from the clouds and lit the curls that ringed about his bonnet's brim, causing them to glow like the red-gold halo on a painted angel.

I'd niver seen a portrait of the man. I'd only the words in my head that Miss Evangeline had read out about him, telling how he looked. *Surely this couldnae be…?* Here, standing before me, a long smudge of peat dirt to his cheek, mud on his fancy buckled shoes, a rent in the pocket of his coat of blue superfine, was Charles Edward Lois Philip Casimir Sylvester Stuart, the man they called Bonnie Prince Charlie. And it seemed he had it in mind to shoot me.

Chapter 33

I Will Give My Love An Apple

I gave him an apple. Well, what would ye have done? I'd several in my pocket which Bridie had given me to eat along the way. Shrivelled they were, so late since the picking, but still sweet. And a man who takes an apple he's not expecting in his one hand is confused enough to think twice about firing the pistol he has in the other. Meanwhile I was asking myself, was I to play the eejit here, or no?

'Provisions,' I said, making my voice as deep as I could in the hope he'd take me for a youth with voice as yet unbroken. 'Provisions frae Milton farm fae the wee mannie that guards the cattle. Up at yon shieling?' I gestured over his shoulder to where I could now see Gilbert together with two other men, gazing down from the ridge above.

'Oh, I see,' said this princeling, blinking rapidly. He'd very sparse eyelashes, above large mournful brown eyes. A bonnie lad, as they all insisted, but seeing him close to, his nose and cheeks had the pallor and red veins that betokened ill-health or a fondness for the drink. He suddenly seemed to realise that he was pointing the pistol at me, flushed, and stuck it back in his pocket. From whence, because of the tear, it fell to the ground with a thump. I stooped, picked it up, and handed it back to him with a wee bow. Which the fella seemed to expect. If I hadn't already put a name to him I'd have known him then. Niver been used in his life to pick up onything he'd dropped! I could have shot him as soon as given it to him, but seemingly he niver thought o' that either.

'Well… one supposes,' he drawled, 'that in that case you had better deliver the goods to your man.' He'd an English accent with just a touch of something from a sunnier land.

'Why, thank you *soir*, ' I said, sounding to my own ears like a tinker's hoor that's just taken a penny tip with one hand while stealing the purse off ye with the other. I stepped around him, and continued up the hillside, niver glancing back. He followed me, stumbling over the tussocks and swearing in a language that was mebbe French. It was only when I reached them that I saw that one of the strangers on the hillside was grasping Gilbert by the arm, and that this fella, too, was holding a pistol.

'I stopped this young fellow,' said the Prince in his drawling voice. 'He *says*... he's bringing provisions for the cowherd.'

The man with the pistol at Gilbert's head, bared his teeth and snapped, 'State your name and business, boy!'

A Kerry accent, I'd be knowing it onywhere. I dropped the pack to the ground, pulled off Angus's old bonnet and let my hair fall loose about my shoulders. 'My name is Elizabeth Burke, sir,' I said. Catch these people on the wrong foot and see what they did about it. The look of shock on their faces would have delighted Màiri and Jessie if nought else! Gilbert, who must have been more worried about the pistol than my sudden appearance in britches, burst into wheezy cackles.

' 'Tis the truth she's telling ye!' he gasped to these baffled fellas, 'She's Betty Burke, that is maid tae Miss Flora Macdonald of Milton. Why she's got up as a laddie I have nae a notion.'

'It's easier to avoid the attentions of the Redcoats,' I told them, 'or so I was thinking. And it makes for easy walking o'er rough ground.'

The third fella, who was stirring a sluggish fire of heather stalks and turf with his foot, looked round sharply at this.

'Flora Macdonald!' he exclaimed softly.

'You know this lady, Neil? This young woman's mistress?' enquired the Prince.

'An old acquaintance, your Highness. Sister to Angus of Milton.'

'Ah, he. *Not* one of our admirers.'

'No, your Highness. But Flora...' he frowned, colouring, evidently thinking better of what he had been about to say.

Meanwhile the Kerryman was using the long barrel of his pistol to nose through my pack. 'I'd say she's telling the truth, your Highness, just provisions.'

'Splendid! Something decent to eat dare one hope?'

'Nothing remarkable, your Highness, but it'll serve.'

'They've a good cook at Milton, your Highness. Bridie Mor,' the man, Neil, remarked.

I know who you are, I thought, *you're Neil MacEachen, the one whose name made Miss Flora blush when 'twas spoken at Nunton.*

'Then you must stay and eat with us!' beamed the Prince, 'Miss Burke, I pray you be seated!'

'Your Highness, it would be better not to...' blurted the Kerryman, baring his teeth once more.

'No, no, I insist!' said this eager princeling. 'The lady has walked a long way, 'tis only polite to offer her some refreshment, Felix.'

And then what'll ye do with me? I wanted to ask, but did not. It was slowly coming to me that whilst this shieling might be high on a hill, I was deep in the sloughy bog lands. Could these men, *would* these men, ever let me go, and still living? Slowly, I settled myself down on the grass. They'd pistols. I'd seen no muskets. How far will the bullet of a pistol travel? Could I run far enough and fast enough before Felix, the Kerryman fired? That I doubted.

The Prince folded himself down onto the turf beside me. Once he was safely seated, Neil MacEachen passed him the brandy bottle and a glass. It was probable, I thought, that even as a child he had niver sat on the bare ground. His nursemaid would have stopped him for fear he'd ruin his silk pantaloons. These many weeks traipsing about the bens and glens of Scotland must have opened his eyes.

'So, Miss Betty,' he said, smiling, seemingly wanting to have me at my ease (before his henchman shot me) 'how long have they had you wearing men's apparel?'

'Only now, just, sir,' I replied, amazed to hear my own voice speaking so calm to a Prince of the blood. 'The English Redcoats are everywhere, and my Mistress was worrited that they'd use me insolently.'

'I fear she's entirely right,' said he, with a sigh, 'They tell me many of these men have been plucked from the stews of London and other big cities. They have taken the King's shilling, but they hate me and they hate this place, and care for none.'

'Your Highness, with respect,' the Kerryman interrupted (which did not seem very respectful to me) 'by her speech this young woman has herself been plucked from the stews of Belfast, and is undoubtedly well able to take care of herself. The wearing of men's apparel is probably just a dare, and her mistress knows nothing of it. There is no need for you to take pains over her.'

'Ah, Felix!' said the Prince, 'you quite mistake me. I am delighted to take pains over Miss Betty. Her daring has given me an idea. I admire tall women, and she is a veritable Juno!

'Unusual in this place where most of the population seem to be uncommonly small,' he added. He glanced at Gilbert, who stood at a distance, not daring to leave or stay too close. Gilbert was indeed a small fella, and was trying, I was guessing, to make himself even smaller in the presence of these chancy beings.

'Neil,' the Prince continued, 'I sense that you know this young woman's mistress, Miss Macdonald, reasonably well? Tell me about her.'

'We were friends as children, and are distantly related,' Neil MacEachen said, looking up from the fire he was still trying to coax into life, 'but her family do not keep the Old Faith as mine did, and as I do.'

'Never the less, this young woman is well respected in the locality?' The Prince gestured that the man he called Felix should pass him another glass and into this he poured a small quantity of brandy, which he gave to me, and then filled his own to the brim. 'Not a lady's drink,' he said with a bow of the head, 'but a little will revive you after your long walk to get here,' and then he went on, addressing Neil MacEachen, 'Clanranald's present wife is a Presbyterian, is she not? Yet you have heard from several people that she has some sympathy for my current plight. And, two Protestant ladies in a strongly Catholic community, are they not therefore likely to be on friendly terms?'

'Undoubtedly, your Highness,' said Neil, shortly. 'Flora is, I believe, a great favourite with them all at Nunton. With the Chieftain as well as his lady.'

'As I hoped,' said the Prince. 'And this Miss Macdonald is also, if I am not mistaken, step-daughter to the obdurate Captain Macdonald who has spurned us in the past, but yet might be open to persuasion? Who has a wife living elsewhere?'

'On Skye,' said MacEachen.

'As I thought. And Miss Flora must visit her mother from time to time? It seems odd that she should prefer to live with her brother.'

I sipped at the brandy, which was pleasant enough on the tongue but burned in my throat. It was hard to credit, I was sitting on the ground next to a Royal Prince. What would Miss Evangeline think of me now? What would Shona have given to meet with this man? Her life. As indeed she had. I took another sip.

Neil said, 'Flora keeps house for her brother, your Highness, and has a great deal of freedom here as well as being always welcome at Nunton. Once he marries she will probably go and spend more time with her mother.'

'He intends to marry?' The two henchmen looked at one another and shrugged their shoulders, unsure.

'Yes, sir,' I said, emboldened I suppose, by the brandy, 'and if 'twere not for yourself being on the Long Island, he might have done so already. Miss Penelope Macdonald, his betrothed, is living in North Uist. Since the Redcoats arrived you should know, all the passing places, the causeways between one part of the Long Island and another are guarded. Folk are being stopped trying to cross to Benbecula, and then again to the North Island. So it is difficult for him even to visit her. He says we are under military occupation.' I knew this, as Angus had come home two days ago, disgusted because a troop of Redcoats had stopped him as he tried, at low tide, to ride over the sands from South Uist to Benbecula, not with any intention of going on to the North Isle, but merely to see another farmer about a strayed heifer.

'Yes, everyone tells me about these gangs of Redcoats,' the Prince sighed, seeming to fall into dejection in an instant. '*We* cannot go to Benbecula to confer with people there who might be persuaded to help… and when I speak of boats they tell me the tides and currents are wrong, and in any case British Naval frigates are patrolling every inch of this coast line. Even the fishermen are afraid to launch their boats for fear of being shot at with cannons. I begin to believe I shall live and die an old man on this wretched isle.'

'If we could just get you across to Skye, your Highness…' said Felix.

'Here comes O'Neill,' said Neil MacEachen, 'perhaps he'll have news.'

'Is it likely?' growled the Kerryman, 'He went to one of the crofts by the shore to see would they sell him some fish. All he thinks of is food, and I doubt they'd know anything.'

Something in the way he spoke of him told me he didn't like this fella O'Neill, who now appeared around the curve of the hillside above where we sat. When two Irishmen take each other in dislike, it's not a grand idea to stay around.

'May it please you, sir?' I asked of the Prince, 'they'll be missing me at Milton, and I wouldn't want them to come looking for me. May I go now?'

From the scowl on his face, Felix was agin letting me go, but the Prince was pouring himself another brandy to drown his sorrows in. Neil MacEachen however, stretched out a hand to draw me to my feet.

'I'll walk down with you, lassie, he said, 'I've a mind to speak a word with Flora if she should be on her own without her brother glowering at me over her shoulder.'

'Do sho, Neil,' said the Prince, his voice now becoming a little slurred. 'Shee if she might be per… suaded to pay her mother a visit… an' take… me along.'

I nodded to Gilbert as we left, hoping he'd understand that more provisions would be sent to him as soon as I could arrange it? Perhaps this Neil MacEachen would bring some back? It seemed to me that Milton was now being required to provision not one fella but five of them.

Chapter 34

Will Ye Go, Lassie, Go?

Leaving that place with Neil MacEachen, I found my legs were trembling, the shock of it all catching up with me now it was over. I pulled Ranald's jaiket tight around me despite the airs being warm. Could it be true that I'd been an hour on a lonesome hillside talking with Bonnie Prince Charlie?

'You'll not speak of this, telling where you found us,' said Neil MacEachen, plodding at my side and mebbe sensing my confusion, 'not to *anyone*. You understand that?' This man had been a schoolmaster. It was natural to him to check if his pupils understood him.

'To be sure, I won't,' I replied. ' 'Tis a secret safe with me.'

For if I did speak of it, I felt certain the Kerryman would seek me out and shoot me with ne'er a moment's thought.

'Not that'll we'll be staying too long at the shieling,' he went on. 'we'll go back to the place where we were before, if the weather lasts. We came away because the rains were terrible, *and* we nearly were caught by a troop of Redcoats. Men from some town in the Midlands of England by their speech. How *they* ever found their way into that glen I cannot think. It's a wild place, there are no roads. No one, *no one*, knew we were there! We had to hide in the trees on the side of the glen for hours to be sure they were gone.' He fell silent, seeming to mull on this.

'I suppose it could be that nobody betrayed us, it *could* just be that they were lost,' he decided. 'At least we've been sleeping dry in the bothies at Alisary, but we daren't stay. Keep moving, that's the secret!'

I made no answer to that. It seemed to me that he was just giving tongue to his thoughts. I was thinking then that these men had no real notion *what* to do. 'Twas no wonder to me that the Prince had become despondent. A Prince cannot be used to hiding from his enemies under trees in the rain, or sleeping on the damp floor of a cattle shed.

'Why *did* His Highness come here, sir?' I asked, seizing my chance. Once, I'd have been afraid to question "my betters", but I'd been through so much these last months at the hands of others who *thought* themselves my betters. In ony case I was pretty sure this Neil fella had no pistol about him. I didn't care for him, but I wasn't afeared of him. As I would have been of the Kerryman if *he* had chosen to escort me back to Milton. This one had fallen silent, but I'd the boldness to break it.

'Sir, they were telling me Inverness is near to the east coast of Scotland. Was there truly no way, when the battle was lost, that the Prince could leave safe from there?'

He said nothing for twenty more paces, sighed, and then said, 'Probably we *could* have found a fishing boat... but to begin with... well, we couldn't believe it was the end, that we'd lost everything. It didn't seem possible. We'd been doing so well. Perth, Prestonpans, Falkirk, Inverness! We marched into Edinburgh to cheering in the streets. True, the expedition into England was a mistake. We'd truly thought the Catholic lords in the North would support us, but they wouldn't budge. Even after... Culloden... some of the Clan Chiefs were willing to stand and fight again, but not without money for boots and weapons, not without artillery. Three thousand men were waiting at Ruthven, but... the money never came. His Royal Highness always held fast to the belief that King Louis *had* kept his promise of gold and weapons.' He heaved another mighty sigh, 'But if so, and what became of it, who can tell? There was rumour and counter rumour. Maybe you heard some of them at Milton?'

I nodded, anxious about where this might be leading, but he went on, 'When we met with Lord George Murray and his men at Ruthven Barracks there was still no sign of it. The Prince was in despair, believing it stolen either by the English navy or else by pirates. He told them all to go home and forget about him. However, there was no confirmation of any of these rumours, and you may be sure the Navy would have boasted of it if they had it. His Highness began to hope that the gold must still be *somewhere*, either on a ship at sea, or it had been landed on the coast and hidden.

'Soon after we left Ruthven, when we heard of a French ship that was sailing up the west coast, through the islands, he began to believe it was the one, come at last. Then we were told *that* ship had sunk. Then *no*, the ship *hadn't* sunk, but had put into Loch Moydart, and the gold taken ashore and buried, they told us, somewhere close by. We spent weeks trying to trace the truth or otherwise of *that* story. Then we heard, no, the ship was still on its way, held back by stormy weather in the English channel. We waited on the mainland as long as we dared to try and intercept it, but the Duke of Cumberland's men were snapping at our heels. So we set sail, as we thought, for Skye, but by ill-luck, a storm drove us south, back here to the Long Island. I never thought we'd end up here! Even so, at first I believed it could be providential. Folk here told us of a French ship that had put into Loch Boisdale, but had foundered. You must have heard about that at Milton?' I nodded, wondering why he was telling me all this. Mebbe he just wanted someone to hear the tale of their misfortunes anew?

'The wreck of this ship, the *Clementine*, seems to have been common knowledge throughout the Long Isle,' he went on, 'They *say* though, that no arms or treasure were found aboard when the local fishermen salvaged her. One of our notions was to pay some of the fisher lads to dive down and search the seabed, but we've been assured that was done when they brought up the dead, and nothing of value was found.'

My heart was racing now, my rememberings of that terrible day running through my head. I was so close to saying, 'But John Begg searched the *Clementine* before ever she came into Loch Boisdale, and found nothing!' I managed to bite my tongue, hard.

It was just as well I did, for now we were nearly at Milton, and who was the first person we met up with, just coming out of the front door? John Begg!

'Betty! Glad am I to see you!' he exclaimed, ignoring Neil MacEachen, and clapping me on the shoulder. 'I mun rush awa', but you'll be able to comfort her.'

'Who? What has happened?' I must have sounded as bewildered as I felt.

'Wee Jessie. I'm awa' tae the mainland… on business, but I had tae call here and tell her. Her Mammie's deid. Puir woman, she fell under a drayman's cart wi' twa o' the younger weans in her arms, three weeks back. One o' her neighbours that has nae any bairns of her own has taken the other twa. The oldest one, Jeanie, Mistress Afton has taken fae the kitchen at the Canongate hoose. Mistress Dalgliesh is back home agin by the bye, so if you're tired o' this rural life… and wearing the breeks! I daresay they'd find you a place?'

I started to exclaim, to thank him for taking the trouble to come and tell Jessie himself, but he clapped me on the shoulder once more and said he must go. And went. A thousand questions raced through my mind and onto my tongue, but he was away, striding down the lane to where I now saw he'd tethered a horse beneath the rowan tree.

I turned to speak to Neil, thinking what should I say? Surely I should attempt to explain who John Begg was, *although in truth I'd no idea who he was!* But Neil too was gone. All I saw was his heel just disappearing around the corner of the byre.

I found Jessie in the kitchen, seated on a stool, greeting her heart out. Màiri was attempting to pat her hair and shoulders, full of sympathy, but was being roughly pushed away. Jessie would accept no comfort from a dafty. Bridie, up to her elbows in flour for the bread, was shaking her head over them.

'A man came, Betty, a soldier I'm thinking,' she told me, 'but what company he might be wi' I couldnae say, tae tell her some bad news. He said his name was John Begg and that you and *this one*,' she nodded towards Jessie, 'know him well.'

'I met him as I came in,' I said, pulling off Angus's bonnet once more. 'I wouldn't say I know him well, but there was a good turn he did for me, finding a way to get me back here from the mainland. He did a sight more for Jessie, bringing her out of that prison in Edinburgh. It's right sorry I am, Jessie, about your Mammie.'

'He said my sister Jeanie's gone tae Canongate!' she wailed, kicking at the leg of the table and causing a small storm of flour dust to escape from Bridie's bowl.

'Jessie, he was doing his best for her!' I said, holding hard to my patience, 'Otherwise she would have had to go to the orphans' place, wouldn't she?' I tried to explain, above her howls, about the kindly neighbour being willing to take the two younger ones, but I should have saved my breath, as they say here, "tae cool ma porritch".

'I dinae *want* Jeanie tae have ma place at Canongate!' she sobbed. ' 'Twas *my* place. If I was tae gae back tae Edinburgh… they'll no want me now!'

Bridie's eyes and mine met across the table. We shook our heads and tried not to smile. Yet she was probably right, as I realised when she told us (between sobs) that John Begg had also said that Colonel Dalgliesh had not, after all, married Miss Ann Elliott, and so the house at Canongate went on, as it always had, with just Mistress Afton, Miss Morrison, and now wee Jeanie as the maid of all work.

'Did he say *why* the Colonel didn't marry Miss Ann?' I asked, thinking to distract her and put a stop to her bellowing.

'Be… because *she*, Miss Ann, liked the Prince tae well!' Jessie hiccupped, 'and he wouldnae change his al-al… '

'Allegiance?'

'Aye. He wouldnae. So they pairted.' At this sad tale of thwarted love, Màiri too, began to sob.

'He's caused a deal o' trouble, this Prince,' said Bridie, slapping the dough onto the table top, and causing a dust storm of her own, 'and I could use some help wi' the evening meal, in place o' all this crooning and greeting!'

'Indeed he has,' I answered, ignoring Jessie's scowl, 'let me but go and find my skirts agin, and I'll come and help. Stop your uproar, the pair o' ye, and start in to shell the peas!'

'Twas from the window of the maid's room, as I slithered out of Ranald's britches and into my work gown, that I saw Neil MacEachen agin. To be sure, since I was changing my clothes, I stood well back, so they niver knew I was watching. Flora was standing stock still in the barnyard, a china bowl filled with eggs cradled in her arms. Neil stood before her, his arms out, hands gesticulating. Slowly, she was shaking her head. Pleading with her he was now, laying a hand on her shoulder. Pleading with her? 'Twas impossible for me to hear what was being said. (At Milton in those days, even the maids' room had glass to the window). Never the less, a cold feeling settled in my stomach. I couldn't be telling you why. I'd no notion what he was asking of her, and it didn't appear to me that she was receiving his words with any sign of eagerness. Yet suddenly I was afraid. Afraid of what he wanted of her, afraid that it had something to do with the Prince. There had once been a childish friendship between these two, Flora and Neil, though as they grew older it had come to nought. Religion and now politics must have widened to a broad flowing stream between them. Surely he would not use the claims of their "auld acquaintance" to persuade her into something that might bring danger not only herself, but to all of us?

They niver saw me, so earnest was their talk, and neither did they see coming from the byre just then, brother Angus. He paused. He'd seen them too, and by his face he liked Neil's presence no better than I did. He turned and walked away without drawing their attention to himself, without looking back.

Chapter 35

The Water Is Wide, I Cannot Get By

Old Colin, the postman, was first with the news. We were all in the kitchen except Flora. Bridie was stirring the broth, Màiri was wielding the hot smoothing iron over some bedsheets. I was darning a pillow case. Jessie sat at the other end of the table, polishing the best silver spoons, a task she seemed to believe only she could do to satisfaction. Angus had just stepped into the doorway from the yard and was pulling off his boots.

'Ye cannae gae up tae Nunton wi' oot a passs now,' old Colin announced, slapping down two letters on the table.

'A pass? What kind of pass?' Angus picked them up, and delved in his waistcoat for his pocket knife. 'Who told you this, Colin?'

The old fella scratched his poll, and then broke into a stream of Gaelic.

Angus listened patiently, his brow darkening. 'And who is issuing these passes?' he demanded, and then repeated himself in Gaelic.

Colin answered at some length, and I picked out the words Captain, Hugh, and Macdonald although there were other names as well.

'I see,' said Angus. 'Father has been tasked with issuing passes to anyone who wishes to cross between the islands. It's no longer enough that there are soldiers guarding the causeways?'

This provoked another stream of Gaelic, just as Flora entered, her arm full of flowers.

'Not go to Nunton? Or anywhere in the Islands? Or to the mainland?' she demanded, shocked, 'unless we have a signed pass to say we may travel? That's barbarous!'

'One of these is from Father,' her brother said, indicating the post, 'I recognise his hand. No doubt we'll learn more from him.'

He slit open the seal and read. 'Colin has the right of it,' he said.

'Father says it's now well known to the Authorities that the Prince and his companions are here, hiding in the hills. They're convinced that they'll seek to escape any day now, either by travelling up to the North Island and thence to Lewis, or by sea to the south or east in the hope that they'll be picked up by a foreign ship.'

'Surely not a French ship?' said Flora. 'Rhodri Macdonald was here two days back if you recall, bringing that creel of salt cod, you ordered, and he said there are English naval vessels fairly crowding one another in the Minch. They'd have no hope of escape that way.'

'So one might suppose, Flora,' said her brother, his mouth a grim line, 'but the fact is, England is not at war with France. *Not yet*, although if the French King is seen to be interfering, that could change soon enough. There are other foreign ships besides. Norwegians, Spaniards, traders from the Low Countries, any of whom might be persuaded, for a fee… At night, with her lights doused and her flags lowered, who is to know where a ship is from, or whither she's bound? The Prince has contacts in Rotterdam, in Oslo, and in Antwerp they say. The ship need not be bound for France.

'In some ways,' he said, slowly, as though the thought was new to him, 'it might be a relief to the English if he *could* be quietly spirited away. Though this Captain Fergusson Father speaks about has vowed to capture him, what would they then do with him? He *is* a Prince of the Royal Blood, a close relative of King George himself. *Can* they behead him as they did his great grandfather? I doubt His Majesty would countenance it, and in any case if they did so, that *would* start a war with France. No, much better if he could be quietly removed from these isles, though *how* it could be done, I don't know.'

There was silence in the kitchen, although I heard Jessie mutter something. I think 'twas the name of John Begg. Perhaps, I thought. Wasn't that likely indeed? For what else had he come here now? For sure 'twas not just for kindness, to break the sad news to Jessie that her Mammie was dead. I recalled what he'd told me on the beach below Dunstaffnage castle. Though he had sworn an oath of allegiance to King George, he'd said he was willing to... talk with those who held contrary allegiances. He was employed to solve problems, to bring men together who might for whatever reason, feel unable or unwilling. To *negotiate*. Sure, that was the fancy word he'd used.

I'd been sore angry with him at the time, thinking he'd betrayed me, and then surprised out of my anger when he'd convinced me he had not. And by his offer to help me return to Uist. I'd not given this word, negotiate, any more thought. Now I wondered. Was he here to see if he could get the Prince away? What Angus said rang true. Prince Charles Edward *as a prisoner* would be an embarrassment to King George and the Government in London. Yet the Duke of Cumberland had given his orders. The Scottish rebellion must be, and would be crushed. Harsh punishments were being meted out to the Clans on the mainland, and soon it would surely happen here? These were the thoughts that sent the mouse feet scurrying down my spine.

However, the next days passed without incident. Captain Macdonald had sent a bundle of passes in case Angus or Flora wished to travel to Benbecula or the North Isle, but they never stirred from Milton. Only I did that.

Once agin I donned Ranald's britches and walked up to Alisary with provisions for Gilbert (generous provisions in case he still had visitors, but I found him alone). We sat together awhile and ate from the store in my pack, but I didn't stay long. Gilbert was discomforted, firstly to be speaking English, secondly to be in the company of a lassie dressed as a man, and thirdly, most probably, that we might at any moment be visited by a platoon of Redcoats. Indeed, from the heights, we saw a small detachment of them marching along the track towards Benbecula.

Before I left he took me to see two fine calves that had lately been born, and which I understood I was to be sure and tell Angus about. When I turned to go he said, 'Whisht, lassie! Will ye be taking care! Stay off the tracks as much as ye can. If they ssee ye, dinae run, mak oot you're a shepherd looking fae a lost ewe! And tell Miss Flora,' he called after me, 'the cheeses iss coming on fine!' One of his tasks during his lonely vigil there was to milk the goats and set the milk to make cheese.

'That I will!' I told him, but on the return journey I saw no one, although I disturbed a deal of birds. Curlews and snipe exploded into the air as I strode lightly over the heather. Sure, and don't the men with their britches have the best of it? In my skirts I'd have been forever catching them on bushes and briars, but in my breeks I could bound along and even leap o'or the small streams and patches of bog.

But that day, back at Milton, I found a disagreement in progress. Flora and her brother seldom argued, but I found them in the barnyard with strong words flying between them. Flora, it seemed, had received a letter from Lady Clanranald, and was wishful to ride to Nunton that day while the tide was low, and sleep the night there. She'd Tibby ready saddled and was intent on starting out. Angus, it was clear, wished her not to. Seeing me approach she turned to me and said, 'Betty, Lady Clan wants me to go up to Nunton urgently, but I'll ride Tibby and go on my own rather than take the gig.'

'If you *must* go today, for which, as I say, I see no good reason,' growled Angus, 'I believe you should take Betty. Father has made it clear to these Sassenach soldiery that you are his daughter, and a young lady of breeding. They're under orders to treat you with respect! Will they still believe they should do so if they see you riding astride like a hoyden? With not even your maidservant to attend you?'

To my astonishment, though perhaps not to his, Flora closed her mouth firmly, put her foot in the stirrup and swung herself up onto Tibby's back. Without another word or a glance behind her, she urged the pony out of the yard at a fast trot.

Angus snorted and shrugged his shoulders. 'Flora can be very wilful at times,' he remarked, 'I wish she would have taken you with her, Betty. I'll admit I didn't see a reason for her to keep employing you, once she arrived back from Edinburgh, but in these perilous times she should have someone with her!'

'For propriety,' I murmured, recalling Mistress Buchanan and her like.

'For safety!' he replied, 'armed with a riding crop I'd think you could see off any ruffian who tried to stop you!'

I gave him Gilbert's message about the calves, but he seemed not to be listening, frowning as he watched Flora and Tibby disappearing up the track.

I didn't risk spoiling his good opinion of me by questioning him on Flora's reasons for this sudden decision. Instead I took myself indoors, certain that Bridie would be able to tell me what this hasty summons was all about, but found her nearly as mystified as myself.

' 'Twas a letter she had, from Lady Clanranald,' she told me, setting a batch of scones on the griddle, 'it set her all on edge. Nothing would do but she must ride up to Nunton before the tide turned. Angus told her, *I* told her, wait for Betty to get back and then you can drive up together in the comfort of the gig, but would she? She would not!'

'Perhaps Lord Clanranald is taken ill?' I pondered. 'He's not been well at all, I'm hearing?'

'Never a wee bit! Lechie says the old man is oot his bed again, and giving orders right and left! Planning a strategy, how will they get the Prince and his companions safe off the island!'

'Ach, how might they do that at all? Does Lechie know?' I knew it probably wasn't fair to ask her, but Màiri and Jessie were outside, out of earshot, having been set to sweep out the weaving shed.

Bridie gave me a long look, and pursed her lips. 'I daresn't ask,' she finally said. 'Och, I'm that fearful Lechie will get himself drawn in. 'Tis hard, ye understand? When the Chief and his lady ask the men of the Clan tae do something, they mun dae it.' She sighed, wiping her floury hands on her apron.

I sighed too, recognising the truth of this. 'I hope they'll not ask too much of Miss Flora,' I said.

'Why? What could they ask of *her*?' Bridie demanded, startled.

'I wouldn't be knowing,' I answered, 'but that Neil MacEachen fella was asking her something, *begging* would she do something. I saw them together in the barnyard the last time I came back from Alisary. Angus saw them too.'

'Och, Neil's in love with her, has been since they were both wee bairns,' said Bridie.

'Will she marry him, d'ye think?'

'Och, no,' said Bridie, 'Isn't he a Catholic?'

It was on this word, "Catholic" that three figures erupted into the kitchen. I'd been aware of the rattle of cartwheels outside, but had dimly supposed it was Angus backing the spurned pony cart into the barn. Now I saw 'twas no such thing. The Reverend John MacAulay strode forward, frowning, perhaps at *that* word, his wide-awake hat in his hand. With him were two people I'd niver seen before. One was a thin man with a long sad face, neatly but not smartly dressed in black, and a young woman in teal silk and a charming chip-straw bonnet.

Chapter 36

Oh, Won't You Marry Me?

'Good day to ye!' barked the Minister, addressing Bridie and myself, 'where's Milton? And his sister?'

Bridie was so taken aback at the sight of these three that she was speechless, so it fell to me to answer with a quick bob (forgetting I had on my britches), 'Sir, Mr Macdonald is busy in the barnyard, and Miss Flora has ridden out.' I niver could get used to Angus being referred to as "Milton" the name of his farmstead, but I'd learned it was the custom here, where there were so many with the same clan name.

'Then I'll go and find him!' decided the Minister, striding out agin.

'I told you! I told you it was Flora, Uncle! We saw her in the distance, riding as though the evil one was clutching at Tibby's tail!' said the young woman, pulling off the bonnet and revealing a middling pretty face and a charming smile to go with it.

I wanted to say, 'and who might you be, Miss?' but I think I'd guessed anyway. Bridie knew her straightway.

'Och, Miss Penelope! Angus niver said onything about you coming tae visit us!'

'That's because he didn't, he *doesn't* know!' she chuckled. 'My Uncle has to go to Lewis on a matter of urgent business – my brother is already over there – and he didn't like to leave me all alone at home in these difficult times! He's only one pass for Lewis so he couldn't take me with him, could you Uncle?'

Her uncle, who seemed to be a man of sorrows, merely looked resigned to his niece's merry chattering. By now her eyes had grown accustomed to the dark kitchen and they widened as she realised that I wasn't a youth, as she must have at first supposed, but a young woman dressed in man's attire. I felt a hot tide of shame surge up my throat.

'I'll go and change,' I murmured to Bridie, and dodged quickly out of the room.

By the time I returned, having scrambled hastily into gown and apron, I found Bridie had marshalled the visitors into the parlour and was offering a dish of tea, promising 'the scones will be ready by the bye.'

'Do tell me your name?' the fair one demanded when I carried through the tray of the best china and began to set it out on the table. Uncle, looking uncomfortable, frowned and cleared his throat.

'My name is Betty Burke, Miss,' I told her.

'And you're Flora's maid? She brought you back from Edinburgh and is very pleased to have you? Yes, even in North Uist we hear most of the news you know!'

Uncle cleared his throat again, 'This is most unfortunate, Penny, Flora being from home,' he pronounced. 'If, as Bridie Mor tells us, she intends to stay at Nunton overnight, it places me in a pickle. I want to get back before the evening tide and go over to Lewis tomorrow, but it's hardly proper to leave you here with Angus and the maidservants. Can't like it. MacAulay won't like it. Daresay Angus won't like it.'

'Och, fiddle!' said Miss Penelope Macdonald. 'Why, in these terrible times are we fretting about my reputation? I'm promised to Angus, after all, and I shall have Bridie and Betty to take care of me.'

'Can't like it,' sighed her uncle. 'I don't believe Bridie Mor sleeps in. I don't know this Betty, and why was she dressed in men's clothing just now? It's not at all what your poor father would have wished, not at all, Penelope.'

'Phish!' said Miss Penelope, taking a sip of her tea, and raising her fine grey eyes as Angus and the Reverend MacAulay entered the room. 'Then why don't we get married straightaway?' She gazed around at our astonished faces, and said, 'Here am I, having put off my blacks for my poor brother, and put on a gown that I believe suits me well. Angus is here, smelling not too much of the cow byre. *You're* here, Uncle, to give me away, and Mr MacAulay is here to read the marriage service over us. I wish Flora could be here, but otherwise, what could be better?'

They say when 'tis completely silent ye can hear a pin drop to the floor, and to be sure had one done so, ye'd have heard it for certain that day in the parlour at Milton, even allowing for the Persian carpet.

'Well, am I not right?' demanded Miss Penelope.

I knew, having heard folks say, that to marry in Scotland it's enough for the couple to declare themselves wed in the presence of witnesses, but I niver imagined that a bride might propose it so boldly. The mouth of the Reverend MacAulay opened and closed like that great fish in the Bible, the whale that swallowed Jonah. Miss Penelope's uncle, however, seemed less taken aback than the rest of us.

'Well, I suppose that would be a solution,' he said, producing a pocket watch from his coat as though planning to encourage them to be speedy about it. 'What say you, Angus? It would save us all a deal of tumult and expense.'

Angus swallowed hard, adjusted his cuffs, bowed to his intended, and said, smiling, 'Why, certainly, if Penny wishes it.' He held out his hand to draw her up and to his side.

'But... we are not in church, sir! stammered the Minister. 'We cannot be said to be fully in God's holy presence.'

'Does that matter greatly?' asked Angus, 'since you are here to read the form at least? It will be a Marriage by Declaration, true, but we can come to church at a later date to receive God's blessing.'

By now, having sensed that something of interest was going forward indoors, Màiri and Jessie had abandoned the weaving shed and were peering around the doorjamb, with Bridie, bearing a dish of scones aloft, looking in over their heads.

Caching my eye, Bridie mouthed, 'The feast? What'll I do fae a feast? I cannae serve scones, just!'

So they were wed, and she didn't have to. The bride's uncle had thoughtfully brought a ham (though he cannot have expected it to be put to such immediate use). This I carved with more haste than skill. A second batch of scones were served still hot from the griddle pan. We'd soda bread and bannocks, butter fresh churned by Màiri that morning, a fish pie, and Flora's gooseberry jam. In the store cupboard too, Bridie discovered a fruit cake she and Flora had been saving against some future visit from the Chieftain and his wife. From the parlour cabinet Angus brought forth a flagon of Madeira, and glasses to drink it from.

Jessie, perhaps thinking it still too plain an affair, went and picked a bunch of flowers from Flora's garden, to stand in a bowl on the parlour table. One red rose she laid carefully atop the cake, saying she had seen it done 'in the windae o' a wee baker's shop in Edinburgh.'

I nearly said, 'Would that be the baker Jonty Nichol fetched the baps from?' but thought it best to leave it be. If Jessie ever thought of her fellow connivers in Canongate, and what had befallen them, she'd niver spoken of it. In the midst of a joyful occasion, 'twould have been unkind to remind her.

Ach, and haven't I nearly forgotten to mention, that just as Angus and Penelope began to speak their vows, in walked Captain Hugh Macdonald with three of his troop of Militia? And with them, to my astonishment, John Begg!

'What goes forward here?' John Begg hissed in my ear.

'A wedding, to which *you* have not been invited.'

'Involving a shotgun? I'd never ha' thought it o' Angus!' he said.

'Take a scrub brush to your mind! I'll tell ye later,' I replied. That, however, I didn't need to do. Captain Macdonald was as surprised as anyone to find his sober sides step-son marrying in haste. He held his peace whilst the Reverend read the service over the couple, and was first to then demand a toast and an explanation.

Explanations done, Flora's absence excused, and many toasts to the happy couple pledged, one of the Militia took a penny whistle from his pocket and struck up a tune.

'The first dance tae the happy pair!' someone called, and Angus and Penelope joined hands in a stately reel. In later years people have told me 'tis called a "strathspey", but I don't believe it was ever called so in the islands. Others began to join in. Captain Hugh seized Bridie by the waist, one of the Militia giving his hand, no doubt out of kindness, to Màiri, to her great delight, and all at once I found myself swung onto the floor by John Begg.

It was the dance Rhuri MacDonald had tried to teach me, and I found I recalled most of the steps, but 'twas of no account whether I did or no, since John Begg was the most terrible dancer that ever trod a measure! In attempting to avoid stepping on my feet I'd think he stepped on everyone else's, and each time we turned in the dance he hit someone a great buffet with his shoulder.

'I'm thinking we should sit this one out!' he gasped after a while. 'Anyway, I want to talk to you.' We retreated to the window seat, next to the grandfather clock. 'I understand ye've met the Prince,' he said, keeping his voice low, masked by its steady ticking, 'what did ye think of him?'

'I think someone should *negotiate* him,' I replied, 'if I've remembered that fine word of yours aright? He's living rough in the hills with these companions of his, but 'tis surely not what he's used to, poor fella. His clothes are torn and dirty, he drinks too much brandy I'm thinking, and from the way he was scratching his head I'd be mortal certain he has the lice.

'*Someone* should find a way,' I said, 'to get him off Uist.'

'Aye, that's the devil of it. You may be sure *I'm* doing what I can to that end, Betty. I know from Captain Macdonald that several attempts have already been made, but they've foundered on the weather and folks' natural reluctance to put themselves in danger. Mind you, they could be rid of him, *and* earn themselves thirty thousand pounds from the authorities in London, but they're a stubborn people hereabouts!'

'So, they are,' I agreed, 'but as wee Jessie pointed out to me, if someone *did* betray him for the money, everyone here would soon know it, and no one would ever speak to them agin.' I gave him a hard look, 'If you're hoping to wheedle from me where I saw him, don't try it. They're all gone from that place anyhow.'

'I know,' he said, 'I most probably know where they are just now, but it's of little use tae me. Felix O'Sullivan will not agree tae deal wi' me.'

'That's the Kerryman? He threatened to shoot me.'

'You're fortunate he didn't. He's as sore as a lion wi' a thorn in its paw because they all think 'twas his bad counsel lost them Culloden. The lie of the battlefield did them nae favours. And they didn't have the artillery, though that wasn't O'Sullivan's fault. Blame that on King Louis.'

'You were there? You were in time for the battle?' I'd had hardly anything but a glimpse of him since we parted at Dunstaffnage.

'No, it was all over long before I arrived. Less than half an hour it took, a terrible bloody mess it was, and I'm tasked wi' trying tae save who and what *can* be saved. It's no going tae be easy!'

I wanted to ask him who had so tasked him, who his masters were, but I knew he wouldn't tell me.

'By the bye, the bride's uncle?' he nodded to where Penelope's uncle sat with the Reverend MacAulay frowning at the dancers. 'They say he's going over to Lewis to see a sea captain he knows, who sails regularly between Stornoway and Orkney. According to Captain Macdonald he hopes this man might take the Prince and his companions to Kirkwall. Yet he doesn't look tae me to be a man that wad support the Jacobite cause?'

'I niver met him 'til today,' I said. 'I'd doubt he'd be a Jacobite, but ye niver know. He's just married his niece to a man that supports the House of Hanover. It may be clan loyalty, do ye not think? Since I came here, I'm learning how strong that is. He may have little time for Lord Clanranald, his chieftain, but he'll do as he bids?'

'True enough,' agreed John Begg. 'Let us hope he's successful, and,' he added with a heartfelt sigh, 'that the Prince finds a Norwegian vessel lying waiting in Kirkwall harbour.'

'Will the Prince agree to sail to Norway?'

'He's no choice, if that's what offers. I'm hearing there are some wild alternative plans being spoken of, in case this doesn't come off. Not just by the Prince's companions either. People here are beginning to feel trapped, harassed by the English. Trading between the islands and mainland is almost at a standstill. Food and goods are beginning to be in short supply for those who don't have a larder ready stocked by Bridie Mor! Be very careful, Betty. I wouldn't like to see *you* swept up in some dangerous plot.'

'You'll not, if I can help it!' I replied, rising to my feet. Bridie had been signalling these last few minutes that I should come and sing with her to give the dancers a break. It felt strange and wrong to me, to even think of singing without Flora to accompany us. John Begg stayed a few minutes, listening as we sang "The Three Lovely Lasses", with Màiri warbling the third refrain, and the only Gaelic song I'd mastered, the "Love Lilt" which they say had its birth in Eriskay, but is surely sung all over the islands? The guests called politely for more, although I thought our voices sounded thin without Flora's spinet. Evidently John Begg must have thought so too. After a while he kissed the bride and went away.

Chapter 37

Love's A Jewel When First 'Tis New

Flora rode home next day through heavy summer rain to find she'd a new sister-in-law. She was, naturally, surprised, but if she was angry or upset to have missed the wedding she hid it well. As soon as she'd shed her wet cloak she kissed Penelope, hugged her brother, and told them both how delighted she was.

Almost the first thing she said to *me* however was 'Betty, exactly how tall are you?' This question flustered me, as I hadn't any clear idea myself and couldn't imagine why anyone would want to know. Seemingly someone had askt her about me, and now nothing would do but she must stand me against a wall and make a mark for the top of my head. Then she measured the distance between the mark and the floor with a measuring rod borrowed from Angus.

'*Hmm*, you're an inch above Angus but not so tall as they say his Royal Highness is,' she said. Seeing my puzzled expression, she flushed slightly, and seeming to realise some explanation was necessary, went on, 'Lady Clan has her step-daughter, Margaret, with her just now. She's a tall young woman too. I don't think you met her the times we've been at Nunton? She's been staying with her mother's relatives in Ayrshire. Margaret is the daughter of one of Lord Clanranald's former wives, I think the second one, though I'm not too sure of that. Our Chieftain has had four wives. This girl is eighteen and embarking on sewing her trousseau, although I understand she is yet to be betrothed! I wished I'd taken you with me, Betty. You could have helped her more than I ever could with the laying out and cutting of the fabric.'

Flora had always been open with me, had shared such information as she thought I needed to know, although not, as was right, those things that were none of a maidservant's business. Now I felt uneasy. Here she was sharing things I didn't need to know.

Why? The girl sewing her trousseau I might niver set eyes on. Time enough to tell me about her if I was about to meet her.

Why had it been necessary for Flora to rush off yesterday at Lady Clan's command? The step-daughter was not even betrothed yet. Why the hurry? And why was my attendance on her so firmly refused? If it was advice on the sewing that was wanted, that was something I might usefully have done. I didn't ask Flora any of these questions, since it was not my place, but I'd an uncomfortable feeling that she wasn't being quite straight with me, which was something I had niver expected from Flora.

I was feeling anxious and uneasy in the coming days, wondering what was happening about the Prince (John Begg's remarks had stayed with me) and I suspected Flora, for some reason she couldn't tell us, might be just as uncomfortable. It wasn't in her nature to be secretive, or to disappear when there was work to be done, yet over the next few days and weeks she became almost invisible.

Once, looking for the shears to cut up some old bed sheets for polishing rags, I found her sitting at the dining table in the parlour, composing a letter. As soon as she saw me in the doorway, her left hand stretched out to cover what she was writing.

In the past she'd always worked in the kitchen with Bridie, and had seemed to love to cook and make jams and pickles at which she excelled, for the store cupboard. Now she absented herself from the kitchen completely, and when Bridie said something about missing her light hand with the pastry, she replied, 'Och, I'm just holding back to let Penny have her domain. Angus's bride must be mistress of Milton now!'

That was true of course, and I thought how unselfish it was of Flora to let Penelope to take command of her new home. Penny had seemed a little subdued for a day or two after the excitement of her spur-of-the-moment wedding. Perhaps the requirements of the marriage bed had been a little shock to her? It seemed her papa was dead and her mama remarried and away on the mainland, so that was why she was in the care of her uncle.

Mistress Penelope soon rallied however, and showed herself for a competent housewife, lively, humorous and kind-hearted – and in love with her Angus! She was good with us servants too. Bridie and myself she treated with respect, asking our advice, but still doing exactly what she felt was right. Màiri and Jessie she handled firmly but kindly, and with understanding for their youth and natural ignorance.

In some things at least, Jessie was not so ignorant as Penelope may have supposed. 'She'll be getting a bairn now,' she grumbled to me, 'you see if she doesnae! I dinae want tae be a nursemaid tae her bairns. I went tae Canongate tae get awa frae Mammie's bairns. Allus greeting an' puking an' shitting bairns are!'

'You were a bairn once!' I told her as we made beds together one late summer morning, just as I recalled we'd done, over a year ago now, at the Canongate house.

'Aye, but I dinae remember,' the child replied, 'and I'm no aboot tae offer tae be a nursemaid! Let Màiri do it. I've a fancy tae be a lady's maid like Miss Morrison.'

'Not like me?' I teased, 'I'm lady's maid to Miss Flora.

'You're no a *real* lady's maid, Betty!' she said, 'you're jest an… ordinary maid o' work! No pride tae ye at all!'

Pretending to be downcast, I lowered my eyes as if in shame, and then burst out laughing, 'No, you're right, Jessie, I've no pride at all!'

I'll admit from then on I was seeing wee Jessie in a new light. Thinking on't, it struck me how wrong I'd been to think of her as put upon, overworked and exploited in Mistress Dalgliesh's household. That certainly hadn't been how Jessie had seen herself. Far from resenting the work she had to do, at twelve years old she'd become, in her own eyes at least, queen of the household, free to roam every room, carry every message, answer the door to every caller. She must have felt still more important when she inherited Morag's role in passing on those secret notes and pocketing the coins that came with them. Of Gowrie alone she'd been fearful, and perhaps Nessa Jordan had offered to remove that fear on her behalf? No wonder then, that Jessie still sighed for Canongate.

Even here at Milton, I was now realising, she'd created her own "position" in the household, insisting on inside work because farm work was "no what she was used tae". She had first bullied, and then tolerated Màiri, once she'd established which tasks she could appropriate for herself, and which could be left to "the dafty". Though Jessie was at least two years the younger, she ordered Màiri about as though she was the superior servant! (and Màiri had accepted this, so used had she been to following Elsbet's orders). Little wonder Jessie had no ambition to be a nursemaid, tied, as she might have put it, to "a passel o' bairns!"

The next few weeks were a strange time. Everything seemed different from how it had been. I spent more time in the kitchen with Mistress Penelope and Bridie, and saw less and less of Miss Flora Macdonald. Twice, I'd donned my britches and walked over the moors and up into the hills to take provisions to Gilbert. I saw no sign, those times, of Bonnie Prince Charlie and his friends.

Flora made one more trip to Nunton on horseback on her own, but spent most of her time in the parlour, apparently on the reading and composition of letters. Old Colin, who must have been given a pass that covered him for any number of journeys, rode back and forth, presumably to Nunton, at least once a day and sometimes oftener. Sometimes the letters were for Angus from Lord Clanranald, but more often they were for Flora, in Lady Clan's beautiful flowing script.

Captain Hugh Macdonald came several times, announcing he was come to see his children and enjoy the company of his new daughter-in-law, but on each of these visits he spent more time talking privately with Flora than he did with Angus and Penelope. Once, when he was at the front door on the point of leaving, I could not help hearing him say, as he pulled on his bonnet and turned to go, 'Think on't, Flora. If you leave it too much longer the thunderstorms of August could be upon us.'

'Och, he's trying tae persuade her tae go over tae Skye to see her mother,' said Bridie. 'I'm surprised she's no suggested it herself, seeing that Mistress Penelope is settling in sae well.'

However, for several more days Flora gave no hint of planning a sea crossing. She said nothing of it to me, and I wondered, if and when she did, would she want me along? I was curious to see Skye, having heard many folk here on Uist speak of it. It was, they told me, though barely forty miles off, very different from the Long Island, being rugged and mountainous, a land of deep glens and soaring rocky peaks. I was curious, too, to meet Marion Macdonald, she who as a young widow had been "carried off" by that twinkling brigand, Hugh Macdonald, leaving her three children behind in the care of their grandmother.

Then, one cloudy, breezy summer afternoon, Flora came and found me working at the spinning wheel.

'Betty,' said she, 'how many days is it since you went up to Alisary, to the shieling?'

'Three,' I replied promptly, 'I was thinking I ought to go agin on the morrow if I can be spared.'

'*I* was wondering about going later on this afternoon,' she said. 'The long days are still with us, and the light lasts well into the evening. I'd like to go, I enjoy a good walk, and Gilbert has always been a favourite with me, but with these platoons of soldiery roaming everywhere, I wouldn't care to go alone. Would it suit you to come with me, Betty?'

That was my Flora! Ony other mistress would say to her maid, 'I'm away to the shieling, put on your things and fetch that pack of provisions, you're coming with me.' Only Flora would ask would it suit me! (I try to remember it now that I'm a mistress to maids myself, but that was then far in the future).

'Will I wear the breeks?' was all I asked of her. She smiled and said, 'Yes, perhaps it would be best, a woman accompanied by her manservant, rather than a maid, in case we should meet any Redcoats.'

We set out in the late afternoon, rather late to my way of thinking, since we would miss the hour at which the household ate supper. I thought little of it however, supposing Flora would have asked Penelope or Bridie to put something by. It was a remarkably warm, still evening, the breeze having died away. The Atlantic swell was falling in soft wavelets upon the sands below the farmhouse as we set out inland. So unusually warm it was, I would have gone in my shirt sleeves (or rather Ranald's shirt sleeves) but Flora insisted on us taking a pair of cloaks. I puzzled over this, niver having seen these garments before anywhere about the farmhouse. They were the kind of short cloaks such as young country girls wear in Ireland, the fabric full-skirted at the waist and gathered into a yoke on the shoulders. The hood is fashioned as much to frame a pretty colleen's face as to keep off the rain. Flora wore hers, although she must have been over warm in it. Mine, I carried folded on my arm, since in my opinion it would look outlandish on the young man I was supposed to be.

'I thought it would keep the midges away,' Flora explained, and these certainly were bothersome with no wind to prevent them massing about our heads and necks. When I plucked wands of bog myrtle, she was glad enough to have one.

We set out in silence across the deserted moorland, Flora stopping every few yards to free her long skirts from the woody stalks of the heather.

'I see now why you've been so obliging about wearing Ranald's trews, Betty!' she said after a time. 'They're much the best thing for this kind of excursion, and I wish I had a pair. Men are so much more rational in their dress than we are,' she added. 'Perhaps we should have a national decree that all Scots, both male and female, should take to wearing the kilt!'

We walked on, Flora chatting of this and that. Of how delighted she was that Angus and Penelope were so happy; how pleased and relieved we all must be that Jessie and Màiri were getting so much better now... how much she looked forward to seeing the new born calves at the shieling, they were so charming, the babies on their tottery legs… I sensed quite soon that she was anxious, excited even, not about the calves, oh no, but about something else, something she hadn't decided whether to tell me about before we got there. Something – or some*one*, who was waiting for us up at Alisary. Every few yards of the way I looked back over my shoulder to see were we followed?

I said nothing, asked her nothing. I knew why we'd come, had guessed who we'd find waiting at the shieling. To no one but John Begg had I spoken about my encounter with Bonnie Prince Charlie and his companions, but I knew they would all be there. And I wished more than anything that they would not.

Chapter 38

Will Ye Gang O'er the Lea Rigg?

They were there. Flickering light glowed from within one of the bothies, not the one that Gilbert used as his sleeping quarters. I could hear the faint hum of men's voices within. No one had stopped us as we approached, which seemed to me verra careless. Surely someone should have bounced out from behind a rock and levelled a pistol at us? We could be a stealthy advance guard of Redcoats for all these fools knew.

It was Gilbert who saw us come o'er the rise and ambled towards us. He'd been milking one of the goats that had lost her kid, and was carrying the wooden croggie of milk.

'Mistress Flora!' he hissed although what there was to keep silent about, I couldn't tell ye. 'They told me they'd be needing this,' he nodded towards the lighted bothy. 'They're making a grand surprise for ye!'

It wasn't such a grand surprise as it might have been, because they seemed quite unaware that the bothy leaked light from all four of its walls. These bothies had no windows, being built up of rough stones and thatched with heather, but although whoever built them had done so with great skill, choosing the stones according to their size and shape so that they fitted close, to be sure it would have been impossible to close every small chink. Grass and bunches of heather had been plugged into the biggest gaps to keep out wind and rain, but in the half light of a Highland gloaming, the flickering of candle flames could be seen glinting through.

Someone must have been on the watch however, for as we drew close, the rough canvas curtain that served as a door was thrust aside and Neil MacEachen looked out.

'Flora?' he called softly.

'Here I am, Neil,' she replied.

He noticed me then, and said, 'You shouldn't have brought her. Didn't the letter say come alone?'

'Och, don't be silly!' she replied, approaching the doorway, ready to step into the room. 'Do you expect me to tramp the countryside unattended? I trust Betty entirely. You all know that. She never told a soul about meeting you here. The Prince himself told Papa about it. Now *don't* keep us standing here to be eaten alive by these midges!'

So we entered, and saw not one but several surprises! A table had been set up in the middle of the space (these bothies have only the one room). It consisted of a number of planks of uneven lengths and was propped up on whisky barrels. In the middle of this table, a "centrepiece" of ten or twelve candles stood anchored in their grease, all of them ablaze. Fired clay bowls were set around, and there were more barrels and rough-hewn stools for seating.

His Royal Highness was enthroned on the only chair, and on a bench along one wall sat Felix O'Sullivan, Alasdair Macdonald of Boisdale, Captain Hugh Macdonald of Armadale… and John Begg.

'My dear Miss Macdonald,' drawled the Prince, 'I cannot *begin* to say how delighted I am to make your acquaintance at last!' He did not rise, but held out a languid hand as though he expected her to kiss it.

Sure, and aren't I pleased to report that Flora ignored this, instead bobbing a small curtsey and placing the croggie of goats' milk on the table?

'I believe this is needed for the meal, your Highness?' she asked, smiling in a friendly fashion, 'I'd no notion 'till just now that I was being invited to dinner! How splendidly your people have set everything ready. I wonder who is your cook? Should I take it to him?'

'Con O'Neill is outside,' the Prince replied, 'where he has built a small cooking range. I cannot bear to have the smoke and fumes of cooking indoors. This place has not even a hole in the roof to let them escape.' He waved a hand towards a gap in the back wall. 'Someone relieve us of this… milk.'

'It was John Begg who rose and took the croggie. As he passed by me, he grimaced and winked his eye. So, I thought, you must have got your wish to speak to O'Sullivan!

The meal to which we'd been bidden consisted of brown trout from one of the lochans, fried in butter. Flora and the Prince were each given one of the plumpest. Flora remarked that she hoped Gilbert had provided the butter.

'Your herdsman fellow? Why yes, I would imagine so,' said the Prince, vaguely, as though he had niver set eyes on Gilbert, and had niver given a moment's thought to where the butter might have come from.

John Begg and I, seated together at the furthest end of the table, were given the trout with the least flesh yet the full complement of bones, and only bent-tined forks to pick at them with. I sat stiff, staring at my bowl, not daring to catch his eye in case we should both fall into a fit of laughter at the sight of these poor shrivelled creatures. A flagon of brandy and stone jars of wine were passed around the table to fill our clay drinking cups. The brandy made only one circuit before it came to rest with the Prince and went no further. As the evening progressed, his Highness's speech grew more and more slurred. Flora, seated at his right hand, next to Hugh Macdonald, edged closer to her Papa as the evening wore on.

After we had all spent some time fighting with our fish bones and listening to an exchange of pleasantries between the Prince, his close friends, and Alasdair of Boisdale, all sides expressing the wish that a successful solution could be found to the Prince's present difficulties, Flora's step-father cleared his throat to command everyone's attention. Now we were to hear what this was all about. John Begg, silent at my side, rolled his shoulders and straightened his spine, eager no doubt to hear what was to come.

'I have spoken to my daughter, your Highness, about how she might be helpful in the present circumstances,' said the Brigand.

'She is doubtful, naturally enough. The plan seems to her… impractical, but she is willing to listen.'

Flora nodded her agreement, and we all waited for the Prince to swallow more brandy before he replied.

'But it's such a charming plan!' he said, 'I'm sure it will work. Sure of it! As soon as I met your splendid maid, Miss Flora, it flashed into my brain! Everyone here must know you have an exceptionally tall young woman as your personal attendant? Betty, is she called?'

'Indeed, your Highness,' said Flora, pursing her mouth and looking grave.

'Quite a delightful picture she presents you know, striding over the hills in her pantaloons!' the Prince went on, 'And it occurred to me, what if I were to shed *my* pantaloons and don *her* skirts? Would people not mistake me for her? Providing, of course, I was at some distance?'

'It would have to be at a distance, sir,' said Flora carefully. 'Your Highness is several inches the taller, your shoulders are broader than Betty's, and your faces are not at all alike. My father has spoken of this, and the ladies at Nunton would be happy – *are* happy – to sew some suitable clothing for you. Indeed, they have already made hooded cloaks for you as samples. I've brought two of them for you to try.'

'Oh, do let me try them at once! I do so love dressing up, ever since I was a child!' cried the Prince.

Since I had placed the two cloaks on the end of the bench close to me, I saw that it fell to me to take them to His Highness, which I did, and didn't the fool of a fella promptly swing one of them around his shoulders, swiping Alasdair's trout supper off his plate onto the floor?

Prince Charles Edward didn't even notice, busy settling the cloak and turning his head this way and that within the hood. 'How do I look?' he demanded.

'Much prettier than the maid, Sire,' growled O'Sullivan.

Bad cess on all Kerrymen, I thought, though I suppose it was true, if ye didn't look too close at the purple veins starting on the Prince's cheeks.

'So, we're agreed,' said this merry prince, 'Miss Flora is to obtain a pass to visit her poor sick mother on the island of Skye, and I'm to accompany her disguised as Miss Betty. When we get there, the Chieftain and his lady wife, cousins of Clanranald's, Boisdale tells me, will conceal me until a suitable ship docks in Portree harbour. How soon can we leave?'

He seemed not to notice the in drawing of breath around the table, none more sharply drawn than Flora's.

'Papa!' she cried, 'nothing was said to me of *this* plan! You told me Penelope's uncle was arranging a ship to take his Highness from Stornoway up to Orkney? I thought my task was just to cross with him to Lewis!'

'Yes, well…' the Brigand cleared his throat agin, embarrassed, as well he should be! 'Unfortunately, my dear, the ship he had in mind had already sailed, and the owner had sailed with her, so the scheme failed.'

'As will this one! I won't do it, Papa!'

I'd niver seen Miss Flora Macdonald lose her temper before, but we were all seeing it now. ''Tis ridiculous! Where will you find a boat to take us to Skye with the whole of the English navy scouring the Minch? A hop across to Stornoway to a ship known to be ready laden and ready to leave was one thing, but this!'

'There's nae a problem, my lass,' he'd the check to pat her shoulder, 'Boisdale here can arrange all that. He's had a wee word with Rhuri, and he can raise a boat and men to row it.'

'Och, dear faithful Rhuri,' she said sadly. 'I suppose he would do it for me if he thought it was what I wanted.'

'But it *is* what you want, Flora!' her Papa insisted. 'We're fully agreed, are we not, that the Long Island can do no more for the Prince? He's trapped here, with a regiment of Redcoats scouring the place from end to end, and no decent harbours where a ship of any size can dock. This *fiend*, Captain Fergusson, is blocking Loch Boisdale with this penal ship while he waits to lay hands on his Royal Highness. Skye is much better placed with Portree, Armadale, and Dunvegan, and if those harbours should fail, it's only a hop and a skip across to the mainland, and down to Moydart, a harbour the French vessels already know. Besides, though the people of Uist are loyal to a man, woman and child, food stocks are running low and trade has all but ceased. You *know* this is so, my dear!'

Around the table, heads were nodding. Either they all thought it a grand idea, or more like they'd none of them any that were better!

Flora had her head in her hands. 'It's too hazardous, Papa! I am not afraid for myself, but I won't put our honest fishermen in danger. And how will it look if I return to Milton without Betty? Am I to say she fell over board?'

'No, no! Betty will remain at Milton. If she's asked why she's there, she can say she became unwell at the last minute, and so disembarked. I'll write a covering letter to your mother meanwhile, offering the supposed Betty's services as a spinster for the time you are there. Marion will be delighted to have someone to spin for her!'

'Papa, that is nonsense, and you know it! His Highness cannot spin!'

'Er, alash, no!' slurred the Prince, draining the last of the brandy flagon and signalling to Neil MacEachen for more.

'But your dear Mama won't know it until you get there, and then she'll be so honoured to meet…'

'But aren't I to take the Prince to Macdonald of Slèat and Lady Margaret?'

John Begg and I looked at one another. 'Isn't this a terrible thing they're suggesting?' I whispered.

'Worse than terrible,' he whispered back. 'Will they notice if we slip awa?'

I couldn't bear to hear any more of this dangerous foolery, so not caring whether they did or no, I slipped out after him.

Chapter 39

Wild Mountain Thyme

Several hours had passed since we arrived at the Alisary shieling, and the gloaming was teetering towards night, or as dark as the July nights in Uist ever are. The moon had not yet risen and the clouds had thickened, although there was no sign of rain. After the glare o' the candles inside the bothy it took a few moments for my eyes to adjust. Without stopping to discuss anything at all, John Begg and I walked across the sheltered dip in the hillside in which the shieling stood, and sat ourselves down on a large flat stone that lay half buried in the earth. Next to it grew thick clumps of mountain thyme, and I plucked some to rub between my fingers The scent of it was soothing to an uneasy mind.

'What were ye hoping for?' I asked after a while.

'Not *this,* that's for certain!' he replied. 'This flight to Skye is madness! Will Flora do it?'

'I'm afeared they've made it difficult for her to refuse. They're all for it, and they've roped in Rhuri Macdonald of Boisdale. You remember him? The fisherman who saved so many when the *Clementine* capsized?'

'I remember him. To be sure he's a grand fella, as you Irish folk would say.'

'How *do* you refuse a Royal Prince?'

'Verra difficult, lassie.'

We sat in silence awhile longer, myself surprised to realise that we'd become friends, comrades even. How had that come about?

'You're the man that solves problems, you told me so,' I said, after a while. 'Can ye no think of anything, anything at all?'

'I've bethought me of a number o' things,' he replied. 'My best hope was that the Prince would agree tae give himself up, and I could have him taken to the mainland. He'd be a captive o' course, held in some loyalist stronghold. Stirling most likely. Dunstaffnage mebbe, just as you were, Princess Betty! But with his own cook and serving men, and all the comforts of home. A better bed than a pile o' straw. They'd haul him off tae London after a while and tak their time pondering what tae do with him. Likely he'd grow old before they decided, and then they'd let him go.'

'But he'll not agree?'

'I could nae hold his attention. 'Tis divided between Felix O'Sullivan, Con O'Neill and the brandy bottle.'

'And *they* would not agree?'

John Begg chuckled, 'I'd might hae got the brandy bottle tae agree, but not the others! I can understand it. First they're hearing what became o' some young fella, he was a Mackenzie mebbe, though I'm not too sure, that was run through on sight by a party o' Redcoat soldiers who mistook him for the Prince. Folk say he did look the spitting image o' His Highness, poor laddie.'

'Then there's Cumberland, and the cruel orders he's giving for the suppression o' the clans. And Captain John Fergusson. That's a man that's filled tae the brim wi' hatred. If *he* gets his hands on Bonnie Charlie, he'll have him in chains and it's straight to the Tower o' London as fast as yon frigate he's commandeered can make way! There's a fella called Caroline Scott too, Caroline after the Queen, seemingly, that's said to be scouring the glens for the Prince, and slaughtering the inhabitants, both high born and low. If Fergusson does nae catch the Prince, that one'll be slaughtering the islanders here next.'

'Slaughtering men who've done nothing? Who niver fought at Culloden?'

'Aye, and women and bairns too, I'm hearing,' he grunted. 'These men are *Scots*, Betty, can ye believe that? Frae Edinburgh or Aberdeen! Yet they've a hatred fae the Highlanders and are only tae glad tae carry oot Butcher Cumberland's orders. Wad the Irish ever turn on one another as cruelly as this?'

I shrugged, 'They might. Protestant agin Catholic, mebbe.' I could see that happening. 'Irish agin the English for sure.'

We sat a while longer, and I began to feel sleepy, my head drooping till it touched his shoulder and I'd to jerk it away quick.

'So this escape to Skye with Flora is the only way?' I askt him.

He grunted. 'Unless I can think o' a miracle, and I'm short on miracles just noo! That, and my employers are impatient. There are other wars in other lands, Betty. Other obstinate people needing to have their heads banged together! Needing to be made to compromise and make the best o' things by John Begg! Did ye hear o' the war o' the Austrian Succession?'

In the deep gloaming, with a few stars beginning to be seen above us, winking between the clouds, it was difficult to read one another's faces, but I think he didn't expect to see bright understanding on mine.

He sighed, and I felt agin that little prickle of annoyance I'd felt at him in times past. 'No reason why you should,' he went on, as though I'd spoken or he'd read my thoughts, 'but it's one o' the reasons, I believe, that the Prince never got that money from the King o' France. King Louis wad hae liked tae invade England sure enough, but not sae that Charlie or his old Dad could sit upon the throne! Then this trouble blew up in Austria, and not just in Austria, ye mind! The Emperor Charles ruled a mighty realm, wi' lands in Hungary, in Italy, and in the Balkan countries. He'd lands that bordered on France too, in the Low Countries. He died of a sudden, leaving only his daughter to succeed him, *which* many o' the local princelings wanted tae dispute. His title was the Holy Roman Emperor, and their argument is, a woman cannae be that! The Prussians saw their chance whilst they were quarrelling over it, and invaded Silesia. Ye'll never hae heard o' Silesia?'

'I niver did,' I said firmly, pinching at my strands of thyme. 'Why would I have heard of these faraway places? It's troubles enough I've had in my own life.' The sweet smell of the thyme floated in the air all about us.

'Aye, fair enough, lassie. Anyway, King Louis was… distracted, shall I say? His advisors at Court were ne'er tae impressed wi'

Charlie. They mebbe counselled, "wait and see." I've been told he put those courtiers' backs up. Too high an opinion of himself when he was nae more than a stray puppy dog, hanging around the great French Court!'

'So the King niver sent the money?'

'I doubt he did. Or if he did, it was stolen. If it was still on its way, and *if* that ship was the *Clementine*, that Captain and his rascally officers must have decided to divide the spoils, and who's tae know for sure? He's deid, lassie, and cannae tell us.'

With the scent of the thyme and the stars shimmering in the haze above me in the half-dark, I suppose my head was weary with thinking on't, and when next I knew, it was laid on John Begg's shoulder, and his arm about me to hold me in my place.

'Wake up now, lassie,' he said, softly, 'the party's broken up. They're coming awa.'

I sat up with a start and blinked, both mortified to have fallen asleep in John Begg's arms, and afraid Miss Flora Macdonald would have missed me, and be angry.

Light spilled from the bothy. Neil MacEachen was holding back the curtain, and Flora and her step-father were just issuing forth. Flora was pulling on one of the cloaks we'd brought with us which I now knew to have been made by the ladies at Nunton. Seemingly the Prince had kept the other. I stood up in haste, rubbing my eyes, and stumbled across the clearing.

'Ah, there you are, Betty,' said my Mistress. 'I thought Neil or Con had perhaps commandeered you to wash the dishes!'

I couldn't but be honest with her, 'No, Miss. I was learning of history and geography with Sergeant Begg. It was very educational. I know about the war over Silesia now.'

She accepted this with a sweet smile, although I could see that old rogue, her Papa, was near to choking himself with laughter and disbelieving.

'I'll walk you both hame tae Milton,' said he, 'I can see Miss Betty's head is floating above her shoulders. So full it is o' facts aboot the Austro-Hungarian empire, she'd be leading ye both into one of the lochans!'

As we began to walk away Gilbert appeared, a shadowy figure in the half light, and Flora hailed him, 'Thank you for the milk, Gilbert!' she called out to him, 'Our honoured guest is to drink it for a night cap. It will help him sleep.'

'Aye, well laced wi' brandy it might!' muttered her step-father, too low for the faithful herdsman to hear.

Little was said as he escorted us back across the moor. The clouds were thickening and obscuring the new risen moon. We'd to take care not to walk into the bog or trip on tufts of heather. Flora seemed distracted and silent. Captain Macdonald kept glancing at her sideways, and several times grunted as though he would have spoken, but mebbe bit his tongue.

It was only as we were entered the barnyard at Milton that he addressed me, 'Sergeant Begg had nae good ideas for solving the Prince's dilemma, Betty? He told me they sent him to see what could be done last year. First tae warn Charlie off, which did nae succeed, and then, since the misfortune of Culloden, tae get him out o' Scotland... if he could.'

'No, Sir, he said the Prince and his companions didn't care to listen to any of his suggestions.'

'A bunch of fools, those laddies! I'm meaning those compatriots of yours, Betty, O'Sullivan and O'Neill. They still think the French money may come, and if they go over to Skye they'd be on hand to receive it. Living in the land of dreams they are, those two! Even Neil MacEachen has more sense! His Highness, I suspect, had given up hope of ever seeing that gold some months back.'

'I'd best come in,' he went on, opening the kitchen door to shoo us inside. 'I've a letter to write to your mother, Flora. Whether you decide to go or not, 'tis best you have it by you.'

He seated himself at the kitchen table.

Flora laid a hand on my arm. 'You go to your bed, Betty, I'll find whatever Papa needs.'

I was loath to go, Flora looked so weary and troubled, but it was a matter between the two of them, and what I thought, I must not say. For what can the opinion of an ignorant Irish maidservant count? John Begg had made me feel sich a foolish creature, with his talk of wars in lands I'd niver even heard of. In after times I've wondered if I should have said something. Would they have minded me? Would it have made any difference? In my heart I know it would not. As I closed the door behind me, Flora was handing her step-father paper and ink from the kitchen dresser, and he sat in thought, chewing the tip of the shaft of a goose feather quill.

Chapter 40

Tomorrow Is The Day When We Maun Ride Away

After that strange night meeting at the shieling, in the next days nothing was said (or to my knowledge, seemingly done) to aid the Prince's departure. We'd few days of fine weather and the last of the hay to get in. Angus called on some of the Askernish crofters to help, which call they answered willingly enough, although 'twas only the men came, and we womenfolk had to walk behind the men as they mowed and toss the hay with pitchforks. Sweet was the scent of that cut grass with all the flowers and herbs that were a part of it. And how proudly we looked on the tall stooks we made to let them dry in the sun and the wind.

Jessie, no need for me to tell ye, disliked this work. 'If ye do your share, as we all must lest the rains spoil it,' I told her, 'I'll teach ye darning and hemming.' Seeing her puzzlement at this, I told her, 'You'll be needing those skills if you're aiming to be a lady's maid. If your lady tears the flounce on her gown, if she's holes worn in her stockings, then 'twould be your job to mend them. I'll show ye how to do it so neatly it can scarce be seen.'

That spell of sunny weather lasted just long enough, aided by the stiff breezes from the ocean, for Milton's hay crop to be dried and carried to the barns.

Then we'd three days of rain and mist and nothing could be done outside. I'd only to look out across the shorn expanse of the machair at the rain driving in over the sands, to imagine how agitated the Prince and his companions would be feeling. I pictured them sheltering in an abandoned bothy or under an overhanging rock, cursing the wet. Flora had worked as hard as any of us at the haymaking, and had given no sign of what her decision had been, would she leave us for Skye? Compelled to stay indoors agin, she settled once more to letter writing, leaving Penelope and Bridie to work together in the kitchen. This year's batch of gooseberry preserves would be by Mistress Penelope's hand. Angus rode up to the shieling on his tall bay horse, Ossian. I was glad not to go, not knowing if the Prince's party were still there or no. If they were, he made no mention of it on his return. He did, however, tell me that my time of tramping the bens and moorland in his brother's britches was at an end.

'Rhuri Macdonald has spared me his young son, Dougal,' he said. 'Rhuri has no need of him for the fishing just now. Dougie will stay up at the shieling with Gilbert and he's a lad of great energy, so he'll come down to collect the foodstuffs whenever they need them.'

Perhaps those words should have told me. Rhuri Macdonald of Loch Boisdale was a fisherman, a man, as I'd been told, who owned his own boat. Why would he not be needing his son for the fishing? Sure, it could only be because he was to do something other than fish? Something for which he didn't wish to have Dougie a part of?

The next day dawned a day of sunbursts and showers. Flora came to me in the middle of the morning and found me hemming a new gown. To be sure 'twas an old gown, refurbished. I'd taken the best o' the green brocade from the one that had caused such a commotion when I was a prisoner at Dunstaffnage. I'd refashioned it, with a new bodice taken from a piece of green figured cloth Bridie had discovered for me, put away in a chest. Of course it was Mistress Penelope's permission we'd had to ask, could I use it? She was the Mistress of Milton now. She gave it readily enough, but must have mentioned it to Flora, because on seeing it spread across my lap she said,

'That looks very fine, Betty. If it's finished you'll be needing to wear it tomorrow. We're bidden to Nunton, and I want you to drive with me, and maybe bring Tibby home alone if I go over to Skye to my mother's.'

A cold stone settled in my stomach. 'You're to go over to Skye, Miss Flora? On your own? You'll not let me come with ye?'

She smiled and shook her head, 'They tell me there will be space for myself and only *one* personal maid, Betty. The world knows I've only the one.' A maid cannot argue with her mistress, can she?

'It's a sailing ship?' I asked.

'No, as you'll recall from that time we came from Kintyre, Betty, we've a grand tradition of rowing here amongst the isles? Rhuri Macdonald is organising a team to row one of the long boats. Six of the best men. And two passengers only. By their efforts we'll be in Skye by morning. I'll see the other passenger safe to the home of Lord Alexander Macdonald of Slèat. He's the chieftain there, superior within Clan Macdonald, even to our own Chieftain, Clanranald. Then I'll walk or ride to my mother at Armadale. I wish I *could* have you with me, Betty. I've written to her about you, and I know she'd be overjoyed to meet you. She's written often how pleased she was to hear I'd my own maid since Edinburgh, as a young lady should! She blames Papa for the hoyden I've become, encouraging me since I was small to be as wild and independent as my brothers!'

The morrow showed much the same weather as before. Sunshine, short bursting rain showers, though the breeze had slackened, and by noon the rain was gone. We set out late in the afternoon, waiting on the tide. Angus, Penelope, and the maids gathered in the barnyard to see us off. Angus had private words for his sister, no doubt telling her to take care, and not to agree to anything foolish or put herself at risk. But, I was thinking, how could she not? Flora hugged everyone, and assured them she would return as soon as she had spent a few weeks with her mother.

'I'll see you all before the autumn storms set in!' she said, and then she hopped up into the pony cart and took the reins. I was already in the seat beside her, with her pack containing her night things and such clothes as she might need in the next days, stowed behind.

'We'll be in Nunton before dark,' she told me, 'and then we'll see what the morrow brings!'

We were well on our way across the moor, the track starting to slope gently down to the crossing, the tide well out as we'd expected, when Flora suddenly gave an exclamation of dismay. 'Goodness, Betty, I've forgotten the pass!' she exclaimed. 'It's on the mantel in the kitchen. Papa left it for me. I forgot to pick it up.'

'Must we go back, Miss?'

'No, no, we'd miss the tide. Surely, if I explain they'll let us by? I've Papa's letter for my mother in my reticule, and that should be enough.' She straightened her shoulders and set her lips. 'These English Redcoats must all know who I am, that my father is a Captain in the local Militia, loyal to the crown. I hope I am not *proud*, Betty, but I do believe I'm entitled to some respect from these people!'

But she was wrong about that. A big lout of a soldier stood in our way as soon as the cart reached the Benbecula shore.

'Halt! Where's yer pass, Missy?'

Honest and straightforward as she always was, Flora did not attempt to plead ignorance or pretend to search her reticule. 'I'm sorry, Sir,' she said, 'I'm afraid I've forgotten it. We're driving up to Nunton to spend the night with Lady Clanranald.'

'Can't go through without a pass. You'd best turn back.'

'But then we'll miss the tide!'

'Too bad, Missy. Can't let yer through without a pass.'

'But my father is Captain Hugh Macdonald — you must know him, Highland Militia? He does regular patrols hereabouts?'

'Never 'eard of im, Missy,' said this jack-a-dandy, 'Can't let yer go through. It'd be more than my life's worth.'

And so, to cut a tedious tale short, this eejit imprisoned us in the part-ruined bothy that he and his slack-jawed comrade were using as a guardhouse! (and on cold nights as a privy, by the smell). By the time they hustled us inside I was about ready to crack them both over the head with a peat spade I found propped in a corner.

Flora seemed to find amusement in it, at least at first. Once night drew in and we'd nowhere to lay our heads, and only a rough wooden bench to sit on agin the damp stones of the wall, she wasn't so well pleased. We couldn't even talk about the journey to Skye in case the soldiers listened at the door. It was to be hoped that they knew no more than what she had said to them, that we had intended to visit with Lady Clanranald and stay the night. I longed to try to persuade her agin the Prince's wild plan, but knew it was probably too late. Flora had made up her mind to go through with it.

'I hope they're taking care of Tibby,' she said after a hour or so had gone by. '*We're* evidently not going to be offered anything to eat, but then 'tis likely they've little but crusts and rough beer for themselves. I daresay none of our crofters will sell them anything.'

Being so tall as I am, if I stood on tiptoe I could just see out through a knot hole high in the door.

'I can see Tibby, Miss,' I told her. 'They've taken her from the shafts and tied her to a post with a rope through her halter, but she can crop at the grass.'

'I'm glad of that,' she replied, 'so, to keep our spirits up and keep those brutes from their sleep, what will we sing, Betty?'

So we sang. Oh how we sang, at the tops of our voices! We sang "I Know Where I'm Going", we sang "The Three Lovely Lasses", we sang "Band O' Shearers", and "Gown of Green". We sang the lovely little lullaby Bridie had taught me, "Can ye Sew Cushions", and sang it loud enough to wake a babe rather than soothe it to sleep! Flora at last taught me *all* the Gaelic words to the "Eriskay Love Lilt". If those brutish English soldiers got a wink of sleep 'twas no fault of ours!

However, towards morning, just when the cold was creeping up through the soles of our boots something terrible, Captain Hugh and his platoon came riding up to the guard house (or cold and dirty bothy as it surely was) all of them full of good cheer and, I thought, not a little whisky. Can ye imagine his surprise at finding his daughter imprisoned there!

'Flora! Did I not give ye a pass? I did? Ye forgot it? Well, there's careless.'

To the soldiers, 'My daughter, yes, sirs, and I see the foolish girl's had an uncomfortable night of it. Oh, her own fault, her own fault entirely. I'm not laying blame on you, lads, not at all, you were just obeying orders.'

'And Lady Clanranald'll be wondering where ye are, Flora! You'd best get along, and be in time for breakfast there at Nunton. Here, I'll give you a bunch o' passes for the return journey.' He winked as he said it, knowing full well that Flora would most likely not return for some time to come.

So we were bustled on our way, though Tibby the pony, who had done better than we had, in that the soldiers had given her a bucket of water and a bundle of hay, was disinclined to bustle.

'I wish you didn't have to go, Miss,' I could not stop myself saying, as we drove down to Nunton, the wide half-moon bay with its stedding of small fields spread before us like a patchwork bedspread, 'I wish John Begg could have found some other way for the Prince to leave.'

'John Begg? Sergeant Begg? Did he think he might find another way?' Flora looked at me curiously, 'I know you talked with him up at the shieling, but you said he was telling about the wars they're having in Europe? He never mentioned over supper any other ways he might find. Had someone asked him to try? What did he say to you?'

I sighed deep, 'He said he was hoping for some miracle, but he was fresh out o' miracles. I don't know who tasked him with trying. Your cousin, Colonel Dalgliesh perhaps? Or mebbe a General, or someone like that? John Begg said to me that he *negotiates*. He said that people on the losing side in any war or disagreement are not necessarily fools. They mebbe chose that side for a good reason, and whoever won the battle may still hold them in high esteem, and want them to work with them to…' I ran out of words to explain.

'I see,' said Flora, 'at least I think I do. The losers must be helped to make the best of things, to work with the winners to make things right again, or as right as they can be once a peace is declared?'

'I think so.'

'An interesting man, then, this Sergeant Begg, not just an ordinary soldier as I'd supposed. *You* seem to have got to know him quite well, Betty?'

She gave me a long look, as though she was expecting to hear more about my friendship with the man, but we were approaching Nunton, and I found the excuse to jump down and open the gates.

Chapter 41

Pull Your Oar Bravely

Our not coming the previous day had thrown Lady Clanranald into a frenzy. Were we coming at all? Had Angus forbidden his sister to come? Had Flora herself decided she wouldn't help the Prince after all? Why hadn't Flora sent a message? What was she, Lady Clan, to say to the Prince if and when he arrived? We found her prostrate on her sofa. Her new maid, Ailsa, Shona's replacement, a plump young woman promoted from the sewing room, was sponging her mistress's brow with vinegar water, clumsily dripping a good deal of it onto the pillows the while.

'So, here you're at last!' accused the step-daughter, Margaret, as soon as Flora entered the room, 'Step-Mama has been out of her mind with worry, and poor Papa has taken to his bed!'

'I'm sorry to have caused you such anxiety,' soothed Flora, not apparently a whit put out by Miss Margaret's unfriendly greeting, 'but we were *arrested!* Arrested at the causeway! I forgot to bring a pass, and some mooncalf of a Redcoat would not let us come on, although I told them who I was, and that we were coming to you. So we were imprisoned in a very dirty ruin of a bothy until about four o'clock when Papa arrived at the head of his troop and set us free. We haven't had a so much as a drop or a crumb, so we'd be most grateful for a bite to eat?'

'Oh, you poor child!' cried Lady Clan propping herself up on her sofa, 'send Betty to the kitchen for something… whatever they have.' She flopped down on her damp pillows again. 'Come nearer, Flora dear, and hear all that we've been planning and doing!'

I took that as my dismissal, naturally. Since I was to be left behind, there was no need for me to know what they were planning and doing. Indeed, I thought it better if I did not. I was thinking that I would have to travel back to Milton this evening, and did not relish the thought of being stopped and questioned about where my mistress was.

I found my way to the kitchens, where there looked to be nobody at all. The excitement had seemingly destroyed all the routine of that household. Whilst I was wondering what I should do about Flora's breakfast, Ailsa, the new lady's maid, was sent to join me. It appeared she too was not to be told too much.

'Iss you the lass that was with Shona in Dunstaffnage?' she asked me as I helped myself to a basket of floury baps and began to slice and butter them. 'Wass you with her when she died?'

I told her that I was, must have been, as we were locked up together, but due to the terrible fever I had at that time, I couldn't tell her anything about Shona's death.

'Och, that must hae been a terrible thing,' she said, round-eyed. 'Shona was my auntie, just.'

I hadn't thought much of Shona of late, though now and agin she drifted into my mind, and I smiled at Ailsa, pleased to know that *someone*, her "niece just" missed her.

'I'm right sorry,' I said, 'I wish I could tell you more, but the fever carried her off... I tried to find the place where they buried her, but no one could tell me for sure.'

'So you never saw had she that broach pin on her? Were they after burying her with it?'

I looked into Ailsa's round blue eyes, and it wasn't grief I saw there. I shook my head. 'I don't know, Ailsa. I niver saw any broach pin. Perhaps they did.'

'Och, isn't that a shame,' said Ailsa, 'she'd promised me that broach pin when she died.'

So it wasn't sorrow she felt for her aunt, but disappointment for that pin she'd coveted. I'd hardly thought on it 'til now, but I recalled the silver comb I'd found, and lost when Elsbet stole it, and 'twas lost agin, when the *Clementine* sank. Did I still grieve for it? No, 'twas glad enough I was, I told myself, to have my health.

I put the baps, a cup and a jug of chocolate on a tray and sent Ailsa up to the parlour with them. I found I didn't want to see her, or any of them, not even Flora, more than I had to.

I spent the day in the kitchen, helping (or mebbe hindering) the cook. We sent cold meat cuts up for luncheon, and then made up a grand picnic basket with bread, meat, smoked fish, fruit cake and beer. And brandy.

'A picnic?' I asked the cook. 'In the rain?'

The day was much as the two that had gone before, with glinting sun followed by sharp spurting showers.

'That iss my orders,' she replied. 'They're all going tae ride oot tae some bay tae the east o' the isle. 'Tiss a cracked notion tae my mind, but those indeed are my lady's orders. "And mak twice ass much as you usually do, Jinny," she says tae me, "for we're to meet with some others." Will you go with Miss Flora Macdonald?'

'If she wants me to. I'd rather stay,' I said. Jinny the cook gave me a strange look, 'Och, and I thought you were Miss Flora's devoted slave?' she said, 'The Irish girl iss her devoted slave,' that's what all of them are saying. Even when you wass thrown into prison on the mainland, you came back.'

So that was what they thought of me? A slave, a fool to herself? I blinked back tears of anger.

'Miss Flora is the best and kindest of mistresses,' I said, 'but I don't care for what they're asking her to do just now.'

Niver the less, when the time came I went with them. They took Lady Clanranald's landaulet, a heavy open carriage which did not fare well on Benbecula's rough tracks, and so was seldom used. Although it could seat four, with Lady Clan, her step-daughter and her maid (but not her own young daughters) together with the picnic hamper and a great cloak bag, there was in truth no room for a fourth. So Flora and I followed behind with Tibby and the pony cart. Two men servants followed on foot. Lord Clanranald was said to be "not too strong, the poor dear man", and there was niver any question of his joining this expedition.

We travelled almost to the causeway that led to North Uist, the nearest ever I was to that island, and then turned inland on an even rougher track which would eventually take us to the rocky coast to the east. The rain had blown through as it had the previous day, and the airs were dry now, but with the wind gusting strongly from the west. All around us were the little lochs and lochans surrounded by thick clumps of reed mace and yellow flag irises. The going on the track was soft and muddy after the recent rains, and, as I would have thought anyone could have guessed, soon the landaulet sank up to its axle in the mud. Even though 'twas drawn by two horses, it could not be pulled free. So down came Lady Clan, her niece, her maid, the hamper and all the bags, and then down came I, so that the cloak bag could be safely stowed in the gig. Flora drove and the rest of us followed after on foot. The old coachman stayed with his horses, and the two younger menservants were tasked with carrying the rugs and the picnic hamper.

It was a long way we walked, or so it seemed. A walk ye've niver taken before always seems the longer, I've found. Lady Clanranald and her step-daughter were soon complaining of the wet stealing into their shoes. Ailsa and I, having stout boots, were better served.

After a time we could see the sea butting up agin the rocks. The east coast of the Long Island doesn't have such fine sandy beaches as that below Milton.

'*This* is Roshinish?' Miss Margaret demanded as we grew closer, 'But there's nothing here!' To be sure, she was almost right. There were one or two crofts somewhat inland from the shore, and by the water's edge a bothy. Another tumbled-down bothy! Hadn't I, I grumbled to myself, seen more than enough of those?

We walked as close as we could to the shore, stopping atop a low grassy headland, and found there an inlet cutting back through the rock, and in it, a long narrow boat, the kind I'd learned the islanders call a berlinn. 'Twas hidden from view until we were almost on top of it. In this long boat were rough bench seats, a folded foresail and a pile of long slender oars.

'This is the place,' said Flora, looking down from her perch. 'This must be the berlinn. Rhuri and his men will be somewhere about. They'll appear when our passenger arrives.'

The men servants laid down their burdens and Ailsa, who had been carrying one of the rugs, helped to spread them on the grass. *The damp will be creeping through those soon enough!* I thought to myself, *and 'tis not just wet shoes the ladies will be complaining of!*

Lady Clan, however, being used to island life and island weather, spread her skirts and seated herself on the lid of the picnic hamper. Miss Margaret plumped herself down on the cloak bag, and looked around as though she expected someone to object. 'So, the clothes will be a little creased,' she said, pettishly, 'but no one would expect a waiting woman's dress to look as though it was bought in Paris!'

'Of course not, Meg dear,' replied her step-mother, gazing around. 'I wonder how long we shall have to wait?' This last she addressed to Flora, who remained seated in the gig, and could thus see the furthest. We servants stood around, stepping uneasily from foot to foot, crushing, and sending up the scents of grass and thyme and camomile, wondering what we were here for? No picnic could be served whilst Lady Clanranald sat on the hamper!

After a few minutes had gone by, Flora, having gazed all around at the empty rocks and the gorse and heather of the moorland, turned her eyes towards the sea, and gave a little gasp.

'What, Flora, dear?'

'Wherries!' Flora whispered, 'Naval transports, they're quite close. Oh, surely they cannot be coming here! Oh, don't stand up to look, Lady Clan! I can see soldiers aboard, and if they see you they'll launch the boats! Sit down, everyone!'

By everyone she meant us. We servants flopped down and lowered our heads. The two Macdonald ladies clutched their shawls around themselves and bent at the waist, seemingly ready to leap up and flee. Flora herself ducked down onto the floor of the pony cart.

'I think they've not seen us,' she said, looking out through the stathes, 'or if they have they think us an innocent picnic party.'

'How many wherries? Are they slowing?' asked Lady Clan, 'should we creep away and hide?'

Flora did not answer for a moment, then she said, 'Five of them, I think that's the last. Sailing south, all with troops aboard. Probably that new regiment Papa says General Campbell is sending down from Skye. They're passing so close they must be making for Loch Boisdale. I just hope they don't spot our visitors walking down from Reuval. They'll be very visible, a group of young men coming down the track.'

They must have been hidden by a dip in the hillside as the transports passed, for no hue and cry was raised, although the Prince and his followers soon appeared, and began the descent towards us. Then, even as we waited for them to reach us, a young boy came running along the headland from the south.

'Fergusson! Fergusson!' he gasped.

'What, where! Oh, dear Lord, we are ruined!' cried Lady Clanranald, staggering to her feet and tipping the hamper on its side.

'Half... a... mile... off, Mistress,' the boy spluttered, 'wi' a troop o' Redcoats, coming this way!'

Having heard this, Rhuri Macdonald now appeared from within the bothy where he must have been waiting all along, together with his five rowers.

'Your Ladyship, if Captain Fergusson iss still half a mile off, we can still do it,' he said, 'but we mustn't waste another moment. Here iss our passenger (the Prince was now only ten yards off) and we'll away.'

However, they could not go straightway, because of course it was now time for the Prince to don his disguise. Prince and cloak bag were hurried behind a rock, O'Neill and O'Sullivan in attendance.

Then he emerged. Ach, what a terrible sight that creature was! Or perhaps 'twas just myself that found him so? Was this how *I* looked? Was this how people saw *me*? A great shambling gawk of a niddy-noddy-who-knows-what? He flicked his skirts about, cavorting like an eejit at the fair. I felt my cheeks flame with shame, and tears start in my eyes. I buried my face in Tibby's mane, not wanting to see this... *clown*, this *gobshite*, who was stealing my Mistress and my name.

Flora's face was a blank, no way to guess what she thought! All Lady Clan said however was, 'That hood to his cloak, it's too loose. He needs a cap to cover his hair and to prevent it slipping off. Here, Betty, let him have your lace cap. I'll soon send you another.'

I put my hands to my head. It was the lace cap Miss Evangeline had given me. Not for ten gold coins would I have parted with it, but there was no time to plead. A servant must obey her betters, alas.

The rowers scrambled down into the boat and pushed her out onto the water. The wherries were now too far off to see them. Flora jumped down from the gig and handed me the reins. His Royal Highness Prince Charles Edward, the picnic hamper and the rugs were hastily bundled aboard.

A brief argument had broken out between Con O'Neill and Neil MacEachen, but Flora, now standing in the bow of the boat with her hands on her hips, and looking as fierce as I had ever seen her, called out, 'No, Captain O'Neill you cannot come! It must be Neil. He has the Gaelic to speak with the local people when we get to Skye, and if we need him, he can take an oar!'

O'Neill looked to the Prince expecting him to overrule Flora, and when he did not, flung away like a sulky child.

Rhuri Macdonald's men were pulling on the oars, and the boat moved smoothly out onto the waters of the Minch. We saw the sail raised and she gathered speed. Speed, bonny boat.

The Nunton serving men had already gathered up a forgotten rug and the empty cloak bag. Lady Clanranald and her daughter were climbing into the gig, taking it for granted I'd drive them back to Nunton.

I did not immediately mount, having noted a handkerchief blowing agin a gorse bush. I went to take it, thinking 'twas best nothing at all was left behind for this Captain Fergusson to discover. As I plucked it from the thorns a low voice spoke from amongst the rocks and gorse.

'Dinae be upset, Betty. That man just looks like the fool he is. He'll never be taken for a grand lass like you.'

So John Begg had been here all the while, watching and listening.

'He's gone from us at last,' I whispered back, 'I'm just praying they'll get away and free! But only for Miss Flora's sake.'

Chapter 42

I Never Did Intend Tae Gae To A Foreign Land

The Prince was gone, flown away, our bird of rare plumage. The whole of the Long Island, from Bernaray isle in the north to Vatersay beyond the southern tip, heaved a sigh of relief. It was as though every man woman and wean had been holding their breath. It soon proved, alas, that we should have held it longer, but then we did not know it. Days went by, with plenty o' rain and wind. If that boat had sunk, or its crew and passengers had been captured, we heard nothing of it.

At Milton all was as before, except that Mistress Penelope gave the orders. Angus said to me, when I arrived home at last and told him how it had gone, that I was welcome to stay on with them until, as they all hoped, Flora returned. I set my mind to spinning, and teaching Jessie to sew and hem.

' 'Tis nae fair!' she grumbled over her stitching, 'you got tae see him! I didnae, and I liked him better than ye!'

'Very true,' I told her, 'but this life is often unfair I'm finding. I've a kerchief, Jessie, that I *think* was his. Would you like it for a keepsake?'

It was the handkerchief I'd found hanging on the gorse bush at Roshinish. I'd stuffed into my pocket as we hurried from that place and thought no more of it. Days later I found it there, a crumpled ball, pulled it out and looked it over. It was of a very fine lawn cotton, hemmed with tiny stitches, almost too small to see, and in one corner a design had been embroidered, initials, **CR,** and a wee crown. Whether it really was his, I'd no proof, but I thought it would please Jessie to have it.

She was delighted with it and took it away, washed it, and even permitted Màiri to iron it for her.

'Do ye think,' she said to me, one afternoon as the rain lashed agin the glass, 'that John Begg will ever come and tak me back tae

Edinburgh? If I'm tae be a lady's maid, I'll need tae go there, I'm thinking.'

'I think he must be gone to the mainland, Jessie. Perhaps even to some far off place called Vienna. He told me he might go there.'

I'd not seen him or heard any word of him since the Prince's departure. Thinking on't, I hadn't even *seen* him then, only heard his voice speaking from amongst the rocks and bushes. I suppose I sighed aloud, for Jessie gave me a sharp look, 'You liked him the best did ye not? Better than the Prince, ye liked him!'

'He called me a grand lass. The Prince niver called me that!'

'Then you shall marry him, and I'll marry the Prince, when he comes back tae claim his kerchief!' giggled wee Jessie.

But whilst we were laughing over our stitchery as the rains blew in off the Atlantic, storm clouds of a different kind were gathering over the Long Island.

Old Colin had not ridden to Milton with the post so frequently since Flora left. We'd had no word from Lady Clanranald. No lace cap had been sent to replace the one I'd so unwillingly given up. However, one wet morning the old postman rode into the barnyard, not with a letter from Skye, from Armadale as we all hoped, but with a piece of news. The news was for Angus, though we all crowded round to hear it.

'They're saying that Captain O'Neill iss captured!' the old man blurted in a mixture of English and Gaelic, 'And yer man, Fergusson, went to arrest Alasdair Macdonald o' Boisdale that is the Chieftain's own brother! It seems they believe he helped the Prince wi' money and supplies. But they couldnae because he was from hame, so they searched his house and treated his poor lady verra disrespectfully!'

The next day Angus did receive a letter. This one was from his step-father and was brought by a trooper. When he read it, Angus's face was grim.

'Reprisals,' he said. 'Someone's talked. The oarsmen returned from Skye and someone was fool enough to feed them whisky.

Rhuri Macdonald is arrested and the Prince's flight with Flora is known.'

'They've arrested her? Oh, poor Flora, we should never have let her do it!' cried Penelope.

'*I* should have forbidden it,' groaned Angus. 'I didn't like it, but I let them talk me into it. Father, and Con O'Neill, whom I'd met one time when I went over to Antrim to buy cattle. They insisted there was no risk to her... and Lady Clan was so distressed by the Prince's sad plight... She's always been so good to Flora. How could Flora deny her?'

The trooper, who until now had stood to attention saying nothing, now said, 'Sir, she's to be questioned by General Campbell himself. Campbell's a fair man, I've served under him.'

Angus thought about that, 'Yes, and he's a relative of ours in some degree through our Kintyre connections. I'll write to him, get Father to write, since most of this is *his* fault! Lord Clanranald will write, I know, and Slèat, and Cousin James, and Penny's uncle...'

We were all thrown into a terrible state at this news. Bridie and Màiri wept, and I could hardly breathe for the worry weighing like a stone on my chest. Jessie, still half believing Miss Morrison's spite, had always been less fond of Flora, but she made herself useful, scrubbing and cleaning as though that might drive out the household's fears.

Towards evening, after we'd all eaten, Angus and Penelope walked out to take the airs by the shore as they sometimes did together, the nights still being light. Angus was grieving over what he saw as his bad judgement in allowing his sister to risk her life for the Prince. I watched them away, Penny holding his arm, and talking to him soft, trying to comfort him.

Within the farmhouse all was quiet, a sadness lay over us all. I lit a lamp, turning the flame high, and sat at the kitchen table to try could I furnish a new cap from some scraps of cotton and lace we'd discovered at the bottom of the chest. Màiri went out with a pail of peelings for the hens. Jessie was washing the dishes, Bridie's apron hitched up under her armpits. Bridie was long gone. Her youngest bairn, Archie, had the croup from all the wet weather we'd been having. The grandfather clock ticked loud in the parlour.

When I heard men's voices without, I thought it was Captain Hugh Macdonald, come to talk with Angus.

The two Redcoat soldiers burst into the kitchen and shouted at me to 'Stand up, girl!' One of them levelled a pistol at my head.

'Betty Burke? You're under arrest, accused of giving articles of women's clothing to the so called Young Pretender, and thus aiding his escape!' He'd an English accent. I wouldn't know from what place.

'I niver did sich a thing!' I cried, (although here I was fashioning a new cap... but how could they know of the other one?)

'She's the one, alright,' said his companion with the pistol. 'Only girl tall enough on this God forsaken isle to lend her toggeries to that charlatan!'

I cried out agin in protest, but they seized hold of me, and began to bind my arms to my sides with rope. 'No! No!' I gasped, my mind racing. Angus and Penelope were no distance away across the stedding. If I screamed loud enough...?

Jessie had turned away from the sink when they entered, her mouth fallen open in shock. Now she rushed forward, the carving knife in her hand, screaming like a wee banshee, 'Leave her! Leave her ye nasty bampots!' she yelled.

The one with the pistol shot her dead. *Deid*, she would have said. Oh, Jessie! I stood and watched the scarlet stain spread across Bridie's apron bib, and the light die away in that poor child's eyes.

Now I must not scream. As they bundled me out of the kitchen I dared not even glance across the barnyard in case Màiri was there. In case Angus and his wife were returning. These eejits would shoot onyone who got in their way.

'Where are ye taking me?' I whispered, 'Who wants me?'

'Captain Fergusson,' replied one. 'Our orders are to deliver you to the *Furnace* in Loch Boisdale harbour. Get walking!'

'And don't waste time talking!' snapped the other, the one jabbing at my spine with his pistol. 'The *Furnace* is the ship on which he's collecting all you filthy rebels. It's well named, a burning fiery furnace. You'll not burn there, though you'll likely hang!'

We set off down the track that led to Loch Boisdale.

'Do we know she *is* a lass?,' said the fella with the gun after a while, coming up close behind me and tearing away the shoulder of my gown, 'we should *examine* her! I reckon we should be sure she's female, and not the Prince himself after all!'

He dragged my gown down to bare my breasts. I squirmed away from him, but I knew 'twas useless. They would rape me and then shoot me. If I tried to run, clumsy with my arms lashed to my sides, they'd just shoot me, saying I'd tried to escape. My thoughts were running about inside my skull like a mouse in an empty meal bin. What would I do? I'd best run. They would shoot me anyway, but if I dived into the heather they might miss, though that wasn't likely.

'Halt!' a shout came from the track ahead and the ground began to shudder with oncoming hoof beats. A shot rang out, the bullet whistled close. One of my captors cried out, dropping his pistol, which bounced into a water-filled ditch. The shoulder of his coat flowered a darker red in the gloaming.

'Hand that woman to me!' commanded the man atop the horse.

'We're taking her to Captain Fergusson. Orders!

'Counter orders! Fergusson wants her immediately, and it's four miles to Loch Boisdale. Seemingly *you* weren't intending to get there in any hurry!' He frowned at my nakedness, and I wriggled to try to hitch up my torn bodice without the use of my hands. 'Come here, girl, I'll take you up.' He reached down, took my elbow, and hauled me up onto his saddle-bow, clamping his left arm tight around my waist. 'Help your comrade, you fool!' he instructed the uninjured soldier. Then he wheeled the horse and galloped away.

'I'll stop in a wee while and untie ye,' said John Begg after we had gone some way. 'Ye'll be more comfortable.'

'They killed Jessie!' I said, a sob wrenched from me. '*You're* not taking me to Fergusson?'

'Poor wee bairn,' he replied, hissing through his teeth, '*This* would never hae happened if the Prince and his cronies had listened tae me! Another week, ten days. I'd found a way tae get him off clear, wi' none o' this crazy galumphing aboot dressed as a lassie. Did ye not see the look on Miss Flora's face? She *knew* it was a disaster, but then 'twas too late to draw back.'

The wind was rising, blowing through the grass and the heather, making a high whistling sound. After a while we swerved off the track, and finding a rock with a thorn tree beside it, he pulled his horse up and dismounted, lifting me down and untying the rope.

I hitched up my torn gown as best I could. He unwrapped his plaid from around his shoulders, and settled it around mine, making me decent.

'Is that the worst they did, or did they... hurt ye?'

'No, but I'm sure that was their intent. You came just in time... to... save me,' I began to weep in earnest. 'But not poor Jessie! She was only speaking of you, this afternoon. Wishing ye'd come and take her to Edinburgh agin. She'd a grand notion to be a lady's maid!' I sobbed.

He pulled me closer and I wept on his chest.

'Angus and Penelope were walking by the shore when those Redcoats came,' I sobbed, 'and Màiri was only across the barnyard, feeding the hens. I ought to go back, John, to tell them what happened!'

'Hush lassie, that ye cannae do,' he said, with a sigh. 'Fergusson believes the Prince must have been wearing your clothes. Disguised as Miss Macdonald's tall Irish maid! It makes good sense to him. He doesn't know of Lady Clanranald's part in it. He's issued a warrant for your arrest.'

'So what must I do?'

'Come wi' me to Vienna!' I gawked at him amazed, and he laughed, 'The *Eenhoorn* is waiting in that wee bay off Eriskay. *Finally*

I got the message tae Captain van der Molen, and tonight I heard he's there, just, since noon. Trading twenty barrels o' Schiedam gin for twenty o' herring, if anybody asks! Which suits him well enough. The Dutch are mightily fond o' herring. He tells me they fish for it themselves but they're always glad o' more. *This* was *my* scheme tae tak the Prince safe awa, but he and his friends were too impatient, tired o' living in caves and dreary huts. The Prince was too weary o' the midges and the lice... and the brandy was running oot.' He sighed, 'The *Eenhoorn* would hae taken him in comfort to Rotterdam, or to Antwerp, if he'd a fancy for it, but it was not tae be.'

We remounted his horse, myself riding behind this time, my arms of necessity, around his waist. The wind rose higher as clouds raced over the island, whistling and shrieking across the moor. The track being faint, we rode at a steady pace, south toward the causeway.

'Now this sea captain is bound for Vienna instead?' I said, keeping my voice low, for although the land around us seemed deserted and the wind was loud, I was fearful to raise my voice.

'Not Vienna, lass. Vienna is far frae the sea, on the river Danube. But the rivers there are wide and navigable, and flow out to the North sea. We'll get there, by one means or another.'

'We? What would *I* do in Vienna?' I had to shout now, the wind had become boisterous.

'Well now, lassie... I'm in need of a... Wad ye consider...?' The wind blew half his words away and I heard only snatches of what he said, 'new orders... a lodging house in Vienna where... diplomats, men of affairs... who cannae meet in public... My orders... a "select establishment" a home awa frae home for... English Duchesses, French Marquises, politicians... men frae every country ye can think of... deals o' one kind or another... someone... laundry, order the dinners... keep the maids in order.'

The moaning of the wind made listening too difficult, and my head was too full of whirling fears and sorrows to understand what he was saying. *Duchesses and Marquises*, what could *they* ever have to do with me? With Jessie dead on the kitchen floor at Milton, and Flora thrown into some filthy dungeon?

We jogged on through noisy gusts for a while without speaking, and presently I saw the isles of Eriskay and Barra ahead, dark shapes in the darker waves,. The tide had crept o'er the causeway.

'Damnation!' said John, 'I've misjudged it. The tide's just turned. We mun wait here a wee while.'

He helped me down from the horse's back and we settled ourselves in a grassy hollow where the wind's shrieking was dulled. What I should wait for, I'd no notion.

'Flora,' I said, now I could make myself heard, 'I want to go to her! I *must* go, she should have her maid with her! This Captain van der Molen, would he take me to Skye?'

'He would not,' said John Begg. 'It's trouble enough he has brewing for him for coming this close! He plans tae sail north to Orkney tae pick up some seal skins, staying clear o' the isles.'

'But Flora!'

'Nae Lass! Flora chose her ain road. Ye didnae ask her tae go! And I doubt she'll suffer tae much for it. A young lady o' the gentry class is Miss Flora Macdonald. Misled through her sense of honour and justice tae help a desperate man! And she's *mony* a one that'll speak up for her! Alexander Macdonald of Slèat, the high Chieftain, the Chief of the Macleod's, that old rogue of a step-father of hers, Hugh Macdonald o' Armadale! He set this up, yet no wisp of suspicion has touched *him*. And the ladies too, Lady Margaret Macdonald, Slèat's wife, Lady Clanranald, for they haven't yet fathomed that 'twas *she* provided the Prince's garments. General Campbell himself – *he* won't want tae send sich a charming and refined young lady to the gallows, particularly as I'm told they're kin!'

'But she'll think I've deserted her! She rescued me from starving on the streets. I should be with her!'

John Begg sighed, 'It cannae be, Betty. Understand that *you're* the one in desperate danger, not Flora! Don't hope Lady Clan is going to confess that she and the women at Nunton sewed the Prince's clothes, just to save *your* neck from the noose. She might, but more likely she won't. Not for an Irish serving maid, no matter how often or how sweetly you sang in her drawing room!'

'I suppose not.'

'Fergusson's a brute. He thinks he has proof on you. If you try to tell him otherwise, he'll call you a liar. He's rounding up all the so-called rebels he can lay hands on. He'll ship them to Glasgow and then to London, where they'll swing.'

'Ach, Rhuri,' I sighed.

'Not Rhuri,' John ground out.

'How so? Have they let him go?'

'No, I lent him my pistol.'

I looked at him for a long moment. 'You… mean he shot himself. John, *why?*'

'"Twas the best I could do for him, lassie, truly it was. These damned English Redcoats went to arrest him, and when he resisted they threw him from the harbour wall and broke his legs on the rocks. Even if he didn't hang, he'd never walk again. He told me he'd sent Dougie, his young son, to Angus before he left. He knew full well the danger he was putting himself in, by agreeing tae take the Prince to Skye.'

'He did it for Flora. He loved her,' I said sadly, thinking of that grave and charming fisherman who'd tried to teach me to dance.

'Indeed, but even had she loved him in return, in these Clan lands a marriage has to be approved by the Chieftains. They were too unequal. Clanranald and Slèat would never have agreed.'

We sat awhile, sorrowful and silent, gazing out over the causeway, now lost beneath the waves.

'Here he comes,' said John. 'D'ye see? Van der Molen said he'd send a boat. I'll turn the horse loose. Lechie Mor promised he'd collect him later. I'll leave the harness under yon rock.'

Screwing up my eyes, I could just make out a black dot skirting around the edge of Eriskay, moving steadily towards us through the silvered wavelets. The wind and the waves were dying down now that the clouds had blown through. They were coming closer, two men in a row boat.

John Begg took my hand and we scrambled down to the shingle.

' 'Tis make up yer mind time, lassie,' said he, laying his hands on my shoulders and peering into my eyes in the half light, 'Are we to marry, or are we not?'

'Marry! You niver said anything about marrying!'

'I did so! Och, that'll teach me! Never propose tae a lassie on horseback in a howling wind.'

'You said... about this lodging house in Vienna, and you needed someone to... send to the laundry and keep the maids in order. I thought 'twas *work* I was being offered! I niver heard you say would I *marry* you?'

'Then will you? Och, Betty I'm no hand at this! There was a girl by the Waters' o' Leith, years back. I'd a mind tae marry Peggy, but when I came home frae the Low Countries she'd married another, and I determined never tae wed. But when I saw you that time on the battlements o' Edinburgh castle, I thought, she's the one could change my mind! A lass o' spirit, and now they've fed you at Milton on butter and cream, and put the roses back in your cheeks, a fine handsome girl!'

I stared at him a long minute. 'But if I agree, how can we, *when* could we? In this town, you speak of, Vienna?'

'Och no, we're in Scotland yet! We can *declare* ourselves handfasted tae Captain van der Molen and a couple o' his crew. I'll write some lines tae put our names to, and we'll both sign. Van der Molen will be happy tae add his name. He's good man. Will that suit ye? 'Twas good enough for Angus and his Penelope.'

The rowing boat was drawing near, oars splashing softly, the rowlocks creaking.

'And I forgot tae say,' said John Begg, 'they're mighty fond o' music in Vienna. You'll have plenty o' chances to sing to our guests.'

A man hailed us in a strange harsh accent.

'Coom!' he called, 'Cap'n sayin' coom! Tide is recht! Ve sail!'

In a torn gown, wrapped in a borrowed plaid that smelled of sheep shit and gorse flowers, I took John's hand and stepped aboard to go and be wed. Stepping from the old life to the new. Leaving the Long Isle and the people I had so loved, perhaps for ever.

The Tower of London,
May 19th 1747

My dear Betty,

I hope this letter will reach you in faraway Vienna. You will see from the address above how I am placed! Dear Betty, I owe your my deepest apologies for the pain and distress my actions must have caused to you and to others. I believed I was acting only for good by removing the Prince from Uist, but alas, I did not fully understand what the consequences would be if our "plot" was discovered. Angus visited me whilst I was held at Dunstaffnage, and acquainted me with the shocking fates of Rhuri and Jessie. I have wept many tears for them. And yourself forced to flee for your life! Oh, it is very dreadful, and, I fear, in a great part my fault. So many dear friends in the Long Island and in Skye have been imprisoned as a result of my actions, and many have suffered more severely than I. I recall how you described your time of imprisonment at Dunstaffnage – I was more fortunate there, and was treated with great courtesy by General Campbell's relatives, as indeed I have been throughout my incarceration. Shortly now, they say I shall be released into the "custody" of the keeper of this place and his lady, and may go out and about in London with an escort. Although I acted so nervously, many people, I now discover, shared my sympathy for Charles Stuart, and are eager to make my acquaintance. Even when I was held aboard that ship in Leith harbour, women from the best Edinburgh families bribed their way on board in order to say they had met me! The celebrated Miss Flora Macdonald! What a strange world we live in. Mistress Ann Dalgliesh was one of them. It seems she has married Cousin James despite their previous falling out, and turned off the servants except wee Jeanie, Jessie's sister, who, she informed me, promises well.

I have also heard that John Begg and yourself are wed, and have a baby daughter, Flora Elizabeth! How I should love to see her! I never knew what to believe of John Begg, but you two seemed to strike up an understanding. I recall how you sat out with him that night at the shieling. He was exasperated that the Prince and his friends would not entertain his proposals for escape, although with hindsight I see that his notions were better. I hope you are both very happy. They say you run a "very select" lodging house, and I wish you every success. For myself, I begin to have hope that a general pardon will be granted and that all of us who tried to serve Prince Charles Edward Stuart will be set free.

Oh, Betty, how often have I wished to have you by me, that we might while away the weary hours by singing together! Do you recall that night we spent imprisoned in the bothy by the Benbecula causeway? How we sang all night long until Papa came and set us free?

Perhaps, one day, we shall meet again, I hope so.

Your friend,

Flora Macdonald

The songs

Each Chapter is headed by a line taken from a traditional folk song which was current at the time and which Betty, who prides herself on her singing, would know. The full lyrics can be found on the internet.

Chap. 1 The Black Velvet Band (trad. Northern Ireland)
Chap. 2. The Old House (trad. Irish)
Chap. 3. Mormond Braes (trad. Scottish)
Chap. 4. Blow the Candle Out (trad. English)
Chap. 5. The Shady Woods of Truagh (trad. N. Ireland)
Chap. 6. Down in the Valley (trad. Origin unknown)
Chap. 7. Farewell *Manchester* (a Jacobite Song, adapted from an earlier one)
Chap. 8. The Laird of the Dainty Do By (trad. Scottish)
Chap. 9. Blow the Wind Southerly (trad. Northumbria but widely known)
Chap. 10. The Green Grass (trad. British)
Chap. 11. Whiskey in the Jar (trad. Irish)
Chap. 12. 'Twas at the Ceilidh I Met Her (from original the Gaelic, the Lewis Wedding Song)
Chap. 13 Waley, Waley (trad. British)
Chap. 14. Soldier, Soldier (trad. British)
Chap. 15. Matty Groves (trad. British)
Chap. 16. The Belle of Belfast City (trad. Skipping Song, N. Irish)
Chap. 17. I Sent a Letter (trad. Children's song, British)
Chap. 18. Early One Morning (trad. English)
Chap. 19. 'Twas Pleasant and Delightful One Midsummer Morn (trad. English)
Chap. 20. I Know Where I'm Going (trad. Scottish)
Chap. 21. Let Me Go, Let Me Tarry (trad. English)
Chap. 22. I Wish I Were in Carrickfergus (trad. Northern Irish)

Chap. 23 The Tall Lofty Ship (trad. British)

Chap. 24. Let Me Go, Let Me Tarry (trad. British)

Chap. 25. Green Sidey (trad. Yorkshire, England)

Chap. 26. Oh, Can ye Sew Cushions (trad. Scottish lullaby)

Chap. 27. Mormond Braes (trad. Scottish)

Chap. 28. The Curragh of Kildare (trad. Irish)

Chap. 29. Waley, Waley (trad. British)

Chap. 30. Home, Boys, Home (trad. Irish)

Chap. 31. Blow the Wind Southerly (as before)

Chap. 32. Braes of Balquidder (trad. Scottish)

Chap. 33. I Gave my Love an Apple (riddle song, British)

Chap. 34. Wild Mountain Thyme (Scottish)

Chap. 35. Waley, Waley (as before)

Chap. 36. Soldier, Soldier (as before)

Chap. 37. Waley, Waley (as before)

Chap. 38. The Lea Rigg (trad Scottish, not the Burns version)

Chap. 39. Wild Mountain Thyme (as before)

Chap. 40. The Bonnie Lass o' Fyvie (trad. Scottish)

Chap. 41. Starka Varna (trad. rowing song from Shetland)

Chap. 42. The Bonnie Lass o' Fyvie (as before)

Printed in Poland
by Amazon Fulfillment
Poland Sp. z o.o., Wrocław